THE TRIDENT SERIES II

BRAVO TEAM

BEAR

Book 2

Jaime Lewis

This is a work of fiction. Names, characters, businesses, events, and incidents are the products of the author's imagination. Any resemblance to actual persons, living or dead, or actual events is purely coincidental.

The Trident Series II – BRAVO Team
BEAR
Copyright © 2023 by Jaime Lewis

All rights reserved. No part of this book may be reproduced or transmitted in any form or by any means without written permission from the author.

ISBN: 978-1-952734-32-8

Table of Contents

Prologue	1
Chapter 1	5
Chapter 2	13
Chapter 3	20
Chapter 4	29
Chapter 5	43
Chapter 6	61
Chapter 7	80
Chapter 8	96
Chapter 9	101
Chapter 10	113
Chapter 11	129
Chapter 12	150
Chapter 13	179
Chapter 14	185
Chapter 15	189
Chapter 16	209
Chapter 17	221
Chapter 18	228
Chapter 19	242
Chapter 20	244
Chapter 21	249
Chapter 22	252
Chapter 23	258
Chapter 24	264
Chapter 25	269
Chapter 26	275
Chapter 27	280
Chapter 28	283

PROLOGUE

Twelve years ago

"Are you sure about this?" Jocelyn asked Bear, gazing into his grey eyes as they stood on the private dock overlooking the calm waters of the Chesapeake Bay.

It was a beautiful late May afternoon. The sky was cloudless, leaving the sun to saturate the land and sea below it with its warm rays. A mild breeze blew in off the water, sending a few strands of her light brown hair into her face.

He smiled, brushing the wayward strands off her face before cupping her cheeks with his large hands.

"I've never been more sure about anything in my life. In fact, I think you stole my heart that day in kindergarten when Danny O'Toole took my *Ho Ho,* and you felt bad and shared your *Twinkie* with me."

She giggled, giving him that infectious, radiant smile of hers. Her smile alone could light up the darkest of rooms. It was one of the many qualities he loved about her—the happiness she brought to life helped balance him.

She gently placed her dainty hands on his chest, and Bear immediately felt the warmth that her touch emitted beneath his service dress uniform.

Spotting the worry in her eyes, he pulled her close. Marriage was a monumental event in their lives, and he needed to ensure she wasn't getting cold feet. God, he hoped she wasn't.

"How about you? Are you having second thoughts?"

With a slight shake of her head, she gave him a small smile. "I'm just nervous that our parents will find out." She nibbled her bottom lip. "Well, more so my parents than yours."

Her concern was valid, considering Jocelyn's parents, Paulina and Edward, weren't big fans of the Walker family. His family was filled with military members, whereas her parents were committed pacifists. They don't believe in war or violence to settle a dispute. Bear agreed that peace talks were always the first course of action when a dispute arose. However, some people don't see words as peace negotiators and only seek violence and destruction to settle their problems. Unfortunately, that sometimes leads to war to protect the innocent.

Drawing her in closer, his arms locked around her waist, he said, "We talked about this. We'll accomplish what we both set out for in the next two years. If everything goes smoothly, I should finish BUD/s right around the time you complete your master's. Once I find out what team I'll be assigned to and we get settled, I promise I'll give you the wedding you deserve."

"Bear, I've told you before. I don't need a big fancy wedding. All I want is you. That's why I'm standing here right now. I love you and want to spend the rest of my life with you."

I love you. Those three words were music to his ears and a phrase he would never tire of. Jocelyn was his world.

"I love you, too. You already know my entire family loves you and will welcome you with open arms."

"Your family is amazing. They have always made me feel like a part of the family, especially your sweet mom. She's someone who I look up to and admire. And let's not forget how awesome it will be to have siblings." She scrunched her little pixie nose up in an adorable way. "Well, sort of. They'll be my brothers and sister-in-law, but still."

Bear understood what she was saying. Being an only child, Jocelyn never got to experience a sibling bond as he had with his brothers and sister. But just like his mom and dad, his brothers Justin, Ethan, Zach, and his sister Clover, all adored Jocelyn.

He just wished he and Jocelyn didn't have to sneak around. Nobody even knew they had started dating two years ago. They had considered telling his family, but they feared it would get back to her parents. With everything they were about to embark on, they decided it could cause undue emotional stress, and it was best to keep their nuptials under wraps until they were settled.

Light footsteps fell against the wood planks, making Bear glance over Jocelyn's shoulder. Seeing the marriage officiant and his wife approach them, Bear turned his gaze to the woman who owned his heart and soul. A smile spread across his face as he looked deep into her dark brown eyes that were sparkling with happiness.

"Tell me, Ms. Thompson, are you ready to become Mrs. Walker?"

The smile on Jocelyn's face couldn't get any bigger, hearing her soon-to-be last name roll off Bear's tongue.

Meeting in kindergarten, when she and her parents moved to the small Tennessee town, she and Bear had been best friends for most of their lives. Because she was shy, making friends was challenging. She blamed her timidness on the fact that her parents didn't have much of a social life. Therefore it rubbed off on her. She had only been in the school for a little over a week when a boy from her class bullied her on the playground because she wore big, clunky glasses. He had approached her as she stood under the monkey bars. The wickedness his smirk exuded should've warned her that he wasn't stopping by for a friendly chat. Just when he reached for her glasses to rip them off her face, another boy swooped in out of nowhere like a savior, putting himself between her and the bully. He pushed the taunting bully away, growling at him to leave her alone. When her tormentor realized the boy standing up for her wasn't messing around, he took off toward his two friends, who had been watching the spectacle from afar. After it was evident that the bully wouldn't be an issue, her knight in shining armor turned around to face her. It was then that she was able to recognize him as the boy from her class who sat at her table.

That was the day she met Tripp "Bear" Walker, and ever since that day, the two of them had been inseparable. As they grew older and started high school, she had always wondered what it would be like to be his girlfriend. However, neither of them went down that path because they didn't want to ruin their friendship should things end badly. That's not to say there were times when she felt jealous of the girls that Bear dated. But she never expressed her feelings because that wouldn't have been fair. However, despite having girlfriends, he never stopped being her best friend. He always found time to spend with her and keep their friendship intact. That alone made her respect for him grow even more.

She, on the other hand, never ventured into the dating pool. Her focus was studying and getting accepted into Texas A&M University in hopes of becoming a hydrologist. She wanted to be a part of a team helping to bring clean drinking water to underdeveloped nations.

Peering up into his gorgeous eyes, she saw something different than she hadn't in the past—love. She knew without a doubt that she was making the best decision of her life. She was marrying the man she admired and loved—her best friend and soulmate.

A big smile spread across her face. "I want nothing more than to become your wife and stand by your side for the rest of our lives."

CHAPTER ONE

Present Day

"Lana, are you serious?" Jocelyn asked in astonishment as she walked through the East Wing of the White House with Lana Evans, the First Lady of the United States.

"I'm dead serious. You're perfect for the job, Jocelyn. You've got all the qualifications to lead this project."

"Wow..." Jocelyn uttered, following Lana into her office and sitting on the sofa.

Lana studied Jocelyn's reaction. "Is that a good wow or a bad wow?"

"Oh! It's a good wow. Definitely good." Jocelyn assured her as she shook her head, still in shock that Lana tapped her to head up the very first clean water project for her Global Clean Water initiative. "I don't know what to say."

Having completed numerous water projects worldwide, leading an assignment of this magnitude would catapult her career if she succeeded. It was the type of assignment that she had studied her ass off in college. It was her chance to show the world what she could do. The thought of being under the watchful eyes of many world leaders was nerve-wracking—but it was also exciting. She knew she would have her work cut out for her, but she was ready for it.

"Tell me you'll say yes," Lana pleaded, going as far as giving Jocelyn puppy dog eyes.

"Of course, my answer is yes. I'd be stupid to turn down an opportunity like this. I'm just in awe that you chose me over several more qualified applicants."

"I chose you because you have strengths that the other applicants lacked."

Jocelyn squinted her eyes as she tilted her head. "Like what?"

Lana smiled. "Compassion, understanding, and patience. You have a natural way of connecting to people others could only dream of. And the village first on the list that you'll be working in certainly needs someone with those qualities. You were built for this job, Joce. Plus, your brilliant."

Hearing Lana's compliment helped elevate Jocelyn's confidence. Not that she didn't have the confidence in herself to tackle a project with that much significance. It just verified that everything she's done career-wise up to this point had been worth it.

"Thank you, Lana. I'm truly grateful and touched by your confidence in me."

Lana was beaming. "No thanks needed, Joce. You're ready for this. You've earned this, and you're going to do great."

Now that she had secured the job, Jocelyn was curious about where Lana and her team had decided to place the water wells. The last time Jocelyn had researched it, there were forty-one countries throughout the world that had inadequate drinking water.

"Have you decided on all the locations yet?"

"We've selected the first location. It was a rather easy decision because most of the logistical groundwork has already been laid."

"Really?"

Lana nodded. "The village has been on the radar of several non-profit organizations over the last year or two, but the permits were yanked at the last minute for some unknown reason. Anyhow, the drilling company I've contracted is the same company one of the prior organizations was going to use. Hence, they already have the area's layout and where the well should go. They just need your guidance and expertise regarding the water flow and whatever else it is that you do."

Well, that did make things a little easier. But she was curious why the permits had been retracted. She could understand if it happened once, but for it to happen several times seemed to be a little alarming.

"Where exactly is this village?"

Lana bit her lip, hesitating, but after a few seconds, she finally answered.

"The village is called Massendai and is in Chad. About a thirty-minute drive northwest of Lake Chad."

"Chad?" Jocelyn repeated. She didn't know much about the country, but what she did know didn't make her feel warm and fuzzy. While Chad wasn't the most dangerous country in Africa, it was still pretty high on the list. Even the State Department had labeled it as a country not to travel to. She tried to conceal her worry but wasn't doing a good job.

"Jocelyn, I can see the concern you have. I know that Chad doesn't have a good reputation regarding safety, but I want to assure you that you'll have around-the-clock protection."

Now that was something new. Her previous projects had offered security, but it was mediocre at best and wasn't twenty-four hours. It made her curious if the security was so tight because the U.S. government was sponsoring the project.

"What type of security are we talking about?"

"I don't know exactly. Rick is handling your security detail. When I told him I would offer you the position, he was adamant that I let him handle that part."

Hearing that Rick was handling her security detail lessened her concern a little. Being the President of the United States had to have some benefits.

"Knowing that Rick is overseeing the security particulars does make me feel a little better."

"Are you sure? I mean, I'll understand if you want to reconsider or think—"

"No!" Jocelyn cut Lana off, knowing what she was offering, but Jocelyn wouldn't back out. "I'm good, Lana. You don't need to worry about me."

Lana reached across the table, placing her hand on Jocelyn's.

"I can't help but worry. I've known you since you were just a little girl. Gosh, I worry about all you kids."

"I appreciate that, but seriously, everything will work out. And if all the small details are already ironed out like you say they are, then it should only take a few weeks to complete the project. Before you know it, I'll be on a plane back here."

Lana sighed and leaned back in her chair. "If you say so. But Rick and I would like to have you over for dinner before you leave. Promise that you'll accept?"

"I'd like that." Jocelyn wasn't about to give up a home-cooked meal. Plus, it would be nice to share a meal with familiar faces.

"Excellent. Let me talk to him this evening, and I'll let you know what day and time."

"Sounds good."

Lana gave Jocelyn a side-eye. "You know, maybe when you return, I can convince you to consider my Chief of Staff position."

"We'll see," Jocelyn replied with a grin, knowing Lana was serious.

"Hey, I have to try." Lana snickered, holding up her hands in defense. Her laughter soon died down, and her tone became serious as she changed the subject. "Not to bring up a sore subject, but how's your head?"

Jocelyn's smile faded, and she gave her shoulder a slight shrug.

"It's okay. I still get headaches now and then. But the doctors told me I'll likely have those for the unforeseeable future."

"Well, you did take a nasty hit to the side of your head. I'm just glad that with everything that happened with Clover, the paramedics could get to you in time."

"Me too," Jocelyn whispered, recalling the harrowing event a little over a month ago.

She didn't remember much, but what she could was frightening and not because there was a deranged lunatic after Clover. The lunatic part had taken a backseat in her mind. What bothered her was her reaction to seeing her ex-husband. She hadn't seen Bear in over ten years since he was assigned to his team and left for his first deployment. He had been handsome back then, but damn, had the military and maturity done him good over the years.

At least when she first walked into the room and saw him for the first time, she wasn't the only one who looked like a deer caught in the headlights when their eyes met. From his stunned, jaw-dropping, and wide-eyed expression, he hadn't been briefed that she was joining them for the weekend.

However, before they could speak, all hell broke loose at the President's country retreat of Camp David. It wasn't until Jocelyn was teetering between consciousness and unconsciousness that they uttered a word to one other.

She still had no idea what the now-deceased ex-Vice President of the United States had whacked her in the head with. All she could remember was sitting in the bedroom when the power went out, plunging the entire cottage into darkness. Not wanting to wake Clover, she sought out one of the secret service agents stationed outside the cottage to see if they knew what had happened.

She had been near the front door when a shadow figure appeared next to her, and before she had time to react, the person clocked her upside the head with a blunt object. The next thing she remembered was someone touching her head. She had mumbled something, but she honestly couldn't recall the words. For all she knew, she had just moaned in pain.

But it had been Bear's deep soothing voice that had her blinking her eyes open. She was met by a scowl on his face and two other large men looming over her. One of the guys was poking at her head while the other was calling for the paramedics.

When the paramedics arrived, everyone moved out of the way, including Bear, but he had stayed near her head and kept his hand on her shoulder the whole time as if knowing she needed that comfort. Her head throbbed so much, and the pain was torture. But through it all, she remembered him whispering to her that she'd be okay and that he'd be right there with her. She would've laughed at his statement if she hadn't been in so much pain and slowly succumbed to the darkness moving in.

"And what about Tripp Walker?" Lana asked, pulling Jocelyn back to the conversation. She snapped her head in Lana's direction, meeting her gaze.

"What about him?"

"Well, for starters, I heard and saw how he was by your side most of the time you were in the hospital."

Jocelyn had heard the same thing from Aaron, her nurse. It seemed that Bear's visits to her room always coincided with when she was sleeping. It made her wonder if he had done that intentionally to avoid having to talk to her. However, he had kept his promise and was there with her. So, she had to give him that. But she still found his behavior odd, considering the last communication she had with him had been in the form of divorce papers ten years ago. Who knew? Maybe it was for the best that she was sleeping because she honestly had no idea what she would've even said to him, not after he had broken her heart.

She looked at Lana, who appeared to be trying to conceal her smile, but she wasn't doing a very good job.

"What happened between you two anyway?" Lana asked.

"What do you mean?" Jocelyn countered, wondering if Lana knew about her and Bear's past. She had been out of touch with everyone for a long time. It made her wonder if Bear ever told anyone about their relationship.

"You two were inseparable growing up, and it stayed that way even when you went to college and he attended the Naval Academy. Where one of you was, the other was nearby. I remember Tripp's mom saying that the two of you seemed much closer."

Jocelyn swallowed hard, having difficulty since her mouth suddenly felt dry.

"She said that?"

"She did. It was the Christmas before you completed your master's, and he graduated from the Academy. She said there was something different about the two of you. She couldn't put her finger on it, but she mentioned the two of you appeared more connected than you did in the past."

That news didn't surprise Jocelyn. If anyone suspected anything, it would have been Jenelle. However, Jocelyn wasn't about to head down memory lane. Shaking her head, she gave Lana a somber look.

"It doesn't matter. Bear and I haven't spoken in years."

"I beg to differ. You didn't see the broken man we saw in that hospital. The one who questioned the doctors about every test they wanted to run on you or how he'd sit by your side for hours and watch over you while you slept."

"That sounds creepy," Jocelyn joked, trying to lighten the mood and deflect the painful topic.

"Oh, believe me. The day Rick and I were there, it wasn't creepy at all. I witnessed a man watching over a woman he cared deeply about."

"Okay, now you're being delusional. There is nothing between Bear and me. Yes, he was my best friend. But you know how it goes as you get older. Some people tend to grow apart."

"Yes, they do. And speaking of the Walkers, are you attending their belated July 4th celebration and anniversary party?"

The mention of that blasted party made Jocelyn cringe. She had been putting off her RSVP but knew she needed to decide. Since Jenelle and Ray Walker's anniversary party and Annual Fourth of July celebration got postponed because of the Clover debacle, they decided to host a party celebrating both. Even though Jocelyn was leaning towards declining the invitation, she hadn't entirely decided yet.

Initially, she wanted to say no when Clover first texted about the party. But a nagging voice inside her head told her to consider it. When she didn't give an instant answer, Clover must've told her mom and given her Jocelyn's number because a few days later, she received a call from Jenelle Walker. If anyone knew Jenelle, they knew there was no such thing as saying no to her.

"I haven't decided yet."

"Jenelle cornered you, didn't she?" Lana questioned. The corner of her lips twitched upward in a slight smirk, knowing how persuasive Jenelle Walker could be.

Jocelyn grinned. "It's hard to say no to Jenelle."

"Yes, it is. And I miss her terribly. She and I used to be so close. I mean, we still talk now and then, but I miss our morning meetups for coffee downtown at the café and our bi-weekly lunches. With Rick being President and my duties as the First Lady, we don't return to Tennessee enough."

"I can relate. There are times when I find myself missing it too."

"When was the last time you visited?"

"When my parents were packing up to move."

"Wow! That was like ten years ago."

Yep. Ten years and two months since she stepped foot in the little town she had once called home. It was a town full of wonderful people and unforgettable memories.

If someone were to ask her where home was now, she'd shrug her shoulders and tell them wherever the water led her. She loved her job. Being a hydrologist allowed her to travel all over the world. She could've taken many avenues with her career—most were safer and less dangerous. Once she had completed her master's, she was approached by federal agencies, several state agencies, and even private consulting and engineering firms with job offers. A few had been very generous offers. Some would probably call her an idiot for declining a six-figure salary and substantial benefits package fresh out of college. But when she suffered a health setback and a broken heart just weeks after receiving her degree, her future wasn't about how much money she made or a great benefits package.

After months of healing, physically and mentally, she was determined to make the most of her life, helping others in need. So, for the last nine years, she has lived an incredible and rewarding life traveling the world and bringing fresh, clean drinking water to underdeveloped communities.

Jocelyn looked at Lana. "Yeah. It's certainly been a while. I don't know. Maybe getting back there and seeing what has changed would be nice."

Or maybe I'm making a big mistake, she thought to herself.

CHAPTER TWO

Bear picked up a cherry tomato off the serving platter in front of him and popped it into his mouth. He closed his eyes as soon as he bit down on the ripe fruit, savoring that gush of juice as the burst of sweetness hit his tastebuds.

His mom gave him a wry grin as she hustled around the kitchen, ensuring all the food was prepared for the party.

"You keep eating those, and there won't be any left for the guests."

He gave her a boyish smile. "Sorry. You know I love these things."

"I know. And that's why I got this." She walked over to the huge, industrialized refrigerator, opened it, and pulled out another container of cherry tomatoes.

Bear chuckled. "See, you were prepared."

He was sitting at the large island in his parent's kitchen, keeping his mom company as she did her thing, preparing for the onslaught of friends and family arriving for their belated Annual Fourth of July backyard barbeque and his parent's anniversary party.

He tried to get her to let him help, but she was adamant she had everything under control. Anybody who knew his mom understood if she said she had everything handled to stay out of her way.

"So, how many people are you and dad expecting today?"

"Not including our family or your teammates, I would say about fifty or so."

The Walker backyard barbeques were always a hit. But this year was extra special. It had been a while since the whole family was home for the annual gathering. Since he and his three brothers were all Special Forces operators, and his sister Clover was a Marine, it was challenging to have everyone home simultaneously.

"Speaking of guests. Did your sister tell you who accepted our invitation?"

"No. She didn't mention anything to me."

Seeing the small jubilant smile playing on his mom's lips and the twinkle in her eye, he figured this mystery guest had to be of some significance, or else she wouldn't have mentioned it.

"Jocelyn!" She squealed, bouncing on her toes and clapping her hands.

It was a damn good thing Bear knew how to compose himself and deliver a poker face, or else he might have given away the secret he had been harboring from his family for the last twelve years because the name that his mom just dropped delivered a shocking blow to him. He was lucky he didn't fall off the stool. Or worse, choke on the tomato he was about to put in his mouth.

Since Jocelyn re-emerged into his life recently, he couldn't stop wondering if it was fate's way of giving him a second chance.

Trying to curb his enthusiasm and not give himself away, he acted calmly.

"Really?"

"Your sister told me that when she texted Jocelyn about the party, she thought Jocelyn would decline the invite. So, she gave me Jocelyn's number, and I called her."

Bear chuckled. "Let me guess. She couldn't say no to you."

"Of course not. Especially when I told her your father was looking forward to seeing her. You know how much your dad loved having her around. I can't tell you how badly it tore him up seeing your sister and Jocelyn in the hospital."

Bear couldn't help the smile tugging his lips as he reminisced about the good old days. That was a time when life seemed so simple and uncomplicated. It was a time when he thought his future was planned out. Boy, had that backfired on him.

His mom walked over to the island and stood directly across from him. Bear was all too familiar with the serious look she was giving him.

"I promised your father I wouldn't meddle in your business, but it's been driving me nuts. What in the world happened between you and Jocelyn? I mean, you two used to spend every free minute you could together. I know you visited her in Texas a few times, and she was going to Annapolis to see you. I was even starting to think that...."

She stopped short, biting her lip, but Bear finished her sentence for her.

"Starting to think what? That Joce and I were a couple?"

Nodding, she sighed. "I just thought the two of you would one day see what everyone else saw."

"What exactly did everyone see?" He was curious to hear what others thought.

She dropped the dish rag on the counter and looked him in the eye. "Love."

Bear felt his entire body still. *Love.* That one powerful and meaningful word sent an imaginary arrow right through the center of his heart. That one word was why he never got involved in a serious relationship. There was only one woman he could ever love—Jocelyn.

For the past ten years, he'd been punishing himself for throwing away the most precious thing he had in his life. A life with Jocelyn would've made him complete. She was the only woman who could truly make him happy.

Men in his profession would kill to find a woman like her—someone who understood the undertakings and sacrifice to be in a committed relationship with a special forces operator.

"Tripp?"

Hearing his mom call his name, he snapped his head up. "Sorry," he apologized, giving his head a slight shake.

His mom smiled softly. "Want to talk about what's bothering you?"

"What makes you think something's wrong?"

"Oh, please! Sometimes, I think you and your four siblings forget that I raised you. Just because you, your brothers, and your sister are all grown up doesn't mean you can hide your emotions from me. It's a mother's intuition to know when something's bothering one of her children."

Bear wasn't about to delve into his and Jocelyn's past with his mom on the day everyone was celebrating her and his dad's anniversary.

"Mom, Joce, and I have spent many years apart, especially after we started our careers."

He kept it simple, but he could see the wheels turning in her head and that she wanted to say more, but instead, she nodded as if she understood. Before she turned away and returned to prepping, she looked him in the eye. "Hopefully, the two of you can find some time to catch up today."

"Mom..." Bear lowly growled out, and Jenelle chuckled, throwing her hands up defensively.

"I'm just saying things happen for a reason, and while it still upsets me with what happened to your sister, it did bring Jocelyn back into our lives, and..."

"Here we go," Bear mumbled under his breath, bracing for what his mom would say.

"You're not dating anyone, and neither is she. Maybe the universe is aligned."

"Jesus, mom. How do you know she isn't seeing anyone?"

She scoffed at him. "The only man I saw sitting by her side was you. When I wasn't with your sister, I was checking in on Jocelyn. The nurses told me nobody except us visited her in the hospital." She shook her head in disgust as she chopped up a few celery sticks. "Even her damn so-called parents didn't have the decency to come and check on their own daughter. How awful is that?"

Pretty shitty, Bear thought to himself. But it didn't surprise him. Her parents were assholes. They were why he and Jocelyn had to sneak around in the first place.

"Didn't they move to Costa Rica or somewhere in Central America?"

"I think so. I heard from our neighbors, Delores and Stan, that they joined one of those missionary organizations that travel all over South and Central America."

Bear snorted. "They definitely weren't fond of our family."

"No, they were not. And it didn't help when your father set up that obstacle course for you and your brothers right next to their yard."

Bear snickered, remembering how pissed off Jocelyn's dad would get when he and his brothers would use the obstacle course late at night. He had even called the cops on them one night. Jocelyn was so embarrassed the next day when she found out what her dad had done. Bear and his family never held her parent's actions against her because she was nothing like them.

Jenelle looked at her watch. "Oh, geesh! Where did the time go?"

Bear heard the front door open, followed by his sister's loud, husky laughter. A few seconds later, Clover and Joker stepped into the kitchen hand-in-hand.

Jenelle smiled. "How are my favorite daughter and favorite future son-in-law?"

Bear nearly choked on his drink. *Son-in-law?* Had he missed something? Surely, Joker would've given him the courtesy of telling him that he would propose to Clover.

"Mom..." Clover sighed, making it evident that she was ruffled by their mom's rush for her to walk down the aisle.

Joker draped his arm over Clover's shoulder and kissed the top of her head. He was grinning as he looked at Jenelle. "I promise I won't make you wait too long, Mrs. Walker."

Jenelle's smile widened. She looked pleased hearing Joker's vow.

Bear was happy with the news as well. His sister and Joker deserved nothing but happiness after what they went through.

Clover moved closer to the island and stole a carrot stick off the vegetable platter, garnering a side-eyed look from Jenelle.

"Between you two, all the vegetables will be gone before anybody gets here."

Clover laughed while taking the open seat next to Bear.

"So, did mom tell you who's coming today?" She asked him while munching on another carrot stick.

"If you're referring to Jocelyn, yes, she told me a few minutes ago," Bear tried to play it cool, even though he was both nervous and excited to see Joce.

Clover smiled. "I'm excited. It will be nice to catch up with her."

"Mmhmm," Bear agreed, concealing his own excitement.

"She and I didn't get much time to talk before…you know," she said, as her words trailed off. However, Bear knew she was referring to the shit show at Camp David a little over a month ago, resulting in Clover and Jocelyn being severely injured. It was probably the most terrifying day of his life. And that was saying a lot, considering the degree of missions he's been a part of in his career.

He hadn't seen Jocelyn in over ten years, and when she walked into the sitting room at the President's home at Camp David, it felt like the world had stopped spinning. One innocent look from her had ignited a spark deep inside him, causing his heart to skip a beat.

Just because he never saw her didn't mean he wasn't thinking about her. In fact, there wasn't a day that Jocelyn hadn't crossed his mind. Whether something he saw or heard reminded him of her or he just thought about her. He never told anyone, but he still carried his wedding ring and a picture of Jocelyn with him wherever he went.

He never expected their reunion to play out the way it had. Finding her lying on the floor semi-conscious, with blood pooling around her head, wasn't how he imagined they would reconnect.

He had made a stupid boneheaded mistake when he walked away from the woman of his dreams. But he had been paying for that blunder for ten long years. There were many days he wanted to beg for her forgiveness. There had been once he had built up the courage to call her, but all he got was a recording saying that her number had been disconnected. He even wrote her a letter, which was returned with a notice stating that the addressee no longer lived at the residence. He knew people and could've found where she was, but he thought that she had moved on.

It wasn't until she was in the hospital recovering that he learned she was living in Washington, D.C., which wasn't far from him.

He did have to agree with his mom. He was pretty sure that she wasn't seeing anyone. That even crossed his mind while he sat by her bedside, watching her sleep. Spending time with her made him realize it wasn't too late, and he wanted to fight for her. He wanted to fight for them. He just hadn't expected to walk into her hospital room the next day to find an empty bed and learn that she had been discharged earlier that morning. He had all intentions of tracking her down, but before he could start scouring the nation's capital, the team was placed on notice, and a few days later, they were officially called up for a mission. They had just returned last week, and Bear had already decided that after this weekend, he would take a few days and travel to D.C. But now it looks like that won't be necessary as Jocelyn was coming to him.

Bear wrapped his arm around Clover's shoulder and pulled her in for a side hug.

"I think that we all are excited to see Joce," he told her, drawing a small smile from her as she laid her head on his shoulder.

CHAPTER THREE

Standing from his perch high above the backyard, Bear looked over the masses of people enjoying themselves as the music played and kids swam and splashed around in the pool. His mom wasn't joking when she said she was expecting fifty *or so* people. He didn't take a head count, but he knew his mom had rented two hundred chairs, almost all occupied.

He leaned his hip against the deck railing and twisted the cap off the beer bottle before taking a swig.

He was half listening to his dad and his brother Ethan arguing over who had the better seasoning for the hamburgers—his dad's savory mixture of Old Bay Seasoning, Worcestershire sauce, or Ethan's sweet mixture of spices.

Despite all the fun around him, Bear was on edge as he awaited Jocelyn's arrival. The party had started over an hour ago, and he was beginning to think that she may not show.

He glanced at his watch again, realizing it had only been seven minutes since he last checked.

"Do you have a hot date or something?" Joker asked, catching Bear off guard.

"Why do you ask that?"

"Because you've been glued to your watch for the past forty-five minutes."

Knowing he'd been caught, Bear grinned. There was no use fibbing about it.

"Just keeping an eye on the time. I thought Jocelyn would've been here by now."

Joker became serious. "You don't think something happened, do you?"

"I honestly don't know. It's possible that she may have changed her mind about coming."

"I hope that isn't the case. Since your mom told Clover that Jocelyn was coming, that's all Clover's been talking about. From how Clover speaks of her, I can tell that Jocelyn means a lot to her."

Bear smiled. "Jocelyn was like an older sister to Clover. You have to remember Clover was outnumbered by us boys. Growing up, Jocelyn practically lived with us. Her parents were assholes; from my perspective, they haven't changed. Did Clover tell you what they said when the hospital called to notify them about her injury?" Joker shook his head. "According to Jocelyn's nurse, once they found out that she was expected to make a full recovery, they didn't see the need to drop what they were doing just to come and sit by her side."

Joker looked disgusted. "You're kidding? That's fucked up."

"The first time Jocelyn came over to our house, I think my parents fell in love with her, especially my dad, since Clover hadn't been born yet, so he was in heaven having a little girl around."

"I remember your dad, and Justin were talking about her one day at the hospital. I just didn't realize she was that close with you guys."

Oh, she was close, alright. Bear thought to himself.

Suddenly, Clover bounded out of the back door, nearly tripping over her own feet. "She's here!" She rejoiced, bouncing on the balls of her feet.

Everyone, including his dad, brothers, teammates, and a few neighbors from down the street, turned their attention toward the back door.

Bear's heart was racing. He wasn't sure what to expect, but as the door opened and Jocelyn's radiant smile appeared, his chest tightened, stealing his breath and rendering him speechless.

The heavenly glow of the afternoon sunlight enveloping Jocelyn's frame only accentuated her beautiful smile. She looked like an angel of the sun. His eyes traveled the length of her shapely body—all five foot nine inches of her. She looked classy but stunning in the flowy, patriotic red, white, and blue racerback tank she paired with white linen shorts showcasing her tan, long legs.

"Look who I found outside," Jenelle announced excitedly as she and Jocelyn walked further onto the deck.

"There's my other girl!" Ray called out loudly as he rushed over before anybody else could and plucked Jocelyn from Jenelle's grasp. "Damn, it's good to see you, Joce," Ray told her, giving her another good squeeze, which made her laugh.

"It's good to see you, too," Jocelyn responded.

As Ray released her, she took a step back, removed her sunglasses, and slipped them on her head.

"Hi, everyone!" She waved as her eyes traveled around the deck, connecting with everyone in view.

The second her dark chocolate eyes connected with his, he didn't think twice and offered her a warm smile. To his surprise, her smile grew wider, and the positive energy her smile emanated instantly calmed his raging anxiety.

"How's the head doing, honey?" Ray asked, causing Jocelyn to turn her attention away from Bear.

"It's much better," Jocelyn answered. "I still get headaches now and then, but my doctor said that it's normal with the severity of my injury. The good news is that I was cleared to return to work full-time, meaning I can travel again."

Bear wondered where she traveled to.

"Well, that's great to hear. We've all missed you around here," Ray told her.

"I've been trying to tell her that," Clover teased, giving Jocelyn a little nudge with her elbow before pulling her from Ray's arms and hugging her.

As soon as Clover released her, Justin, Ethan, and Zach surrounded her next. Of course, those three started to fawn all over her, which annoyed Bear.

"About time we see your gorgeous smile around here again," Justin said as he gave her a side hug and a kiss on the cheek.

Ethan approached next, lifting her and twirling her around. "You're looking good, Joce," he gushed, prompting Jocelyn's cheeks to flush.

"He's not lying. You're a walking goddess—gorgeous and brilliant," Zach added to Ethan's comment as he enveloped her in a big hug after Ethan set her down.

Jocelyn laughed, waving off their comments. But the redness creeping on to her face gave away her embarrassment, which Bear found cute.

He was using some serious self-control as he not so patiently stood in his spot as his family peppered her with questions. He understood his family's excitement to see Jocelyn, but watching her hugging and talking with everyone was torture when he hadn't even gotten a chance to say hi.

Finally, after what seemed like an eternity, people started to break away until it was just Bear and Jocelyn left standing on that section of the deck. She turned to look at him, and he smiled as he walked closer to her.

"Hey, you," he greeted her as his eyes locked onto hers.

She offered him a warm smile. "How are you, Bear?"

He swallowed hard as the sound of her seductive voice made his cock instantly hard, and he lost all self-control.

"I'll be a lot better when I get my hug," he told her, wrapping his arm around her waist and pulling her close. Hearing the light gasp slip from her lips made him grin before he kissed her cheek, letting his lips linger against her smooth skin.

He felt her body tremble slightly, and when he finally pulled away, he noticed her dark brown eyes were filled with so many emotions. He could see the struggle in her trying to decide if she should stay or run.

Please don't run, he thought to himself.

For a few seconds, they silently stared into each other's eyes. Then with a deep breath, a small smile began to play on her lips.

"That was the best hug I've gotten all day," she told him, her smile growing more prominent.

Considering their history, he wasn't sure what her reaction to him would be. But seeing her beautiful smile again, and knowing he put that smile on her face, made his heart beat faster.

The last thing Jocelyn expected when she arrived at the Walker's barbecue was to find herself getting lost in Bear's arms. But, holy hell, one look into his stormy grey eyes had ignited a slow burn deep inside her, and before she knew it, she wanted to snuggle closer to his warm, muscular body. But panic started to set in when the fog clouding her brain began to recede, and she felt her body tremble.

Her nerves had been at an all-time high when she pulled her car into the Walker's driveway. When she hit the downtown area, about ten minutes from the Walker's house, she called Jenelle. Jenelle said she would meet her out front, which Jocelyn was grateful for because being with Jenelle would make her feel less awkward than walking into the party alone.

When she arrived, Jenelle practically pulled her out of the car and hugged her. Her warm welcome had literally brought tears to Jocelyn's eyes.

The seven-hour drive from Washington, D.C., had given Jocelyn much time to think. She had decided that she and Bear should come clean about their past. It wasn't fair to his family or her and Bear to have to carry around the weight of their secret any longer.

She knew that revealing the truth would most likely cause some hurt feelings, but it was the right thing to do, especially if she wanted to salvage any relationship with Bear's family, which she hoped for because she missed them terribly.

She had to admit that she had started to overthink a few times and almost turned the car around. But now that she was standing there looking slightly up into the eyes of the man she had loved since she was six years old, she was glad she had stayed the course because he seemed just as happy to see her as she was to see him.

"That was the best hug I've gotten all day," she admitted, and he cocked his head to the side, and a cute grin appeared on his lips.

"Is that so?"

She nodded, and before she knew it, she was again pulled into his embrace. But this time, his arms held her tight. She felt his lips near her ear, sending shivers through her body.

"It's really good to see you." He whispered and kissed her cheek again before releasing her.

Feeling a tad bit bashful and turned on, she grinned.

"It's nice to see you too."

Giving her another one of his sexy smiles, he gently tugged on her elbow and started leading her down the stairs.

"How about we get a drink, and if you'd like, I'll introduce you to my teammates. I think Clover's down there with Joker too."

"I'd love that."

"How long are you in town for?" He asked as they walked toward the patio beside the large kidney-shaped pool.

"Just the weekend. I'd love to stay longer and see the town, but work calls. How about you?"

"Same."

As they walked and chatted about things in general, Jocelyn couldn't help but feel like there was a giant elephant in the room that neither one wanted to acknowledge, which drove her crazy.

Just up ahead, she saw Clover sitting at a table surrounded by men and assumed that was where they were heading. But before they got there, Jocelyn decided to break the ice.

She slowed her pace until she was fully stopped, and Bear followed.

"What's wrong?" He asked.

She bit her lip nervously. "Is it just me, or do you find this is a bit awkward?" She asked him as she waved her hand between her and him.

His shoulders relaxed.

"It isn't just you. Since Mom told me earlier today that you were coming, I've been a basket case."

She hated it for both of them, but she did feel a little better knowing she wasn't the only one feeling nervous.

"I had to convince myself numerous times on the way out here not to turn the car around."

"I'm glad you didn't," he told her; the sincerity in his tone told her that he was being honest. He looked away for a moment. But when his eyes met hers again, she knew there was more he wanted to say. "I know there is a lot we need to talk about. Well, mainly I need to, as I have much to explain. But I'd much rather do it someplace more private where it's just you and I. Plus, I feel my family will be smothering you all day."

She nodded her head. "I'd like that. You said that you're here for the weekend, right?"

"Yep."

"How about tomorrow around noon? We can pick up some sandwiches from Sam's Deli downtown and walk down to the park on the river. We should have enough privacy there."

Bear smiled. "That sounds perfect."

"Are you guys coming over, or will you stand there all day whispering to each other?"

When they both turned around, Clover stood there with a big grin.

Bear chuckled. "I guess we better get over there before she makes a scene."

When Jocelyn got to the table, Clover pulled her over to the empty seat next to her and handed her a *Truly*.

"I'm sure you could use this right now."

"How did you know these were my favorite?" But then she shook her head, already knowing the answer. "Never mind. I remember your mom asking me what I liked when she called me."

Clover's cheeks reddened as she winced, showing a bit of remorse.

"Yeah. Sorry about siccing Mom on you. But in my defense, I had a feeling that you would say no."

She wasn't wrong. She had every intention of declining the invitation. She didn't want to get into a discussion leading to questions about her absence, so she decided to change the subject.

"So, tell me, which one of these hotties is Joker?"

Clover's eyes lit up. "Oh! That's right. You haven't met any of the guys yet."

Clover started the introductions, putting her hand on the arm of the man sitting next to her. "This handsome guy is Joker."

Joker smiled and reached his hand out. "It's nice to meet you finally."

Jocelyn shook his hand. "Likewise. Clover talks highly of you." She winked at Clover, who blushed.

"We'll just go around the table," Clover said, pointing to each guy as she introduced him.

"There's Aussie, Playboy, Jay Bird, Snow, Duke, and last but not least, Nails."

Clover leaned over and whispered, "Watch out for Nails. He's a ladies' man. Though, I don't think Bear will let him get close to you." She winked and Jocelyn felt her face redden.

All the guys said hello, and seemed pleasant, although she appreciated Clover's warning about Nails because the playful glint in his eyes told her that he was definitely a player.

She looked across at Bear, who was talking to Duke. As if sensing her gaze, his eyes turned in her direction. Even now, she could feel the power of his eyes as they locked onto her.

Even after enduring heartbreak and everything she had gone through during the first year of being apart from him, she still missed him like crazy. Some people would call her crazy, and maybe she was, but she couldn't help it. Her heart, for some reason, refused to cut the cord that connected them. She had hoped that he would one day realize his mistake and return to her. But after a few years with no communication, she assumed he had moved on, so she also tried to.

Dating hadn't been an easy task for her. She went on a few dates, but nothing materialized. There was never any spark or even really an interest. The few men she had dinner with appeared more interested in themselves and their careers than they were in her.

It was comical, considering SEALs were all about their careers. They lived and breathed it. But with Bear, she knew it would've been different. She learned and understood the aspects of his career, and she accepted them. She had prepared herself to be a military wife. Sure, Bear loved the Navy, but he also made her a part of it. And the times they were able to spend with each other, his focus was always on her, not his career. It was a marriage she had always dreamed of having. Hell, she still wanted it to this day. Her eyes widened in shock at her admission.

I told you to have faith and that things happen for a reason. Just follow your heart. The voice of her subconscious told her.

CHAPTER FOUR

Bear had forgotten how peaceful sitting on the porch swing could be, looking across his family's property, giving him a spectacular view of the mountains in the distance. The evenings were even more stunning when the slanted rays of the falling sun extended their reach into the darkening sky, creating a vibrant medley of shades of orange, pink, and purple across the heavens.

Laughter from the backyard made its way to the front, indicating everyone was having a good time. Overall his day had been outstanding. He always cherished any time he got to spend with his family. But what had made it an even better day was having Jocelyn there, though he wished he would've gotten more time to spend with her. But he couldn't very well hog her the entire day, nor did he want to smother her. The last thing he wanted her to feel was uncomfortable.

He enjoyed seeing her interacting with his team. That was how he had imagined it would have been if he hadn't screwed it up.

The first few years after the divorce, he threw himself into his career. He wanted in every training and operation he could get his hands on. He wanted anything that would keep his mind busy and off the fact that he had given up the most important thing in his life. But even then, it was hard, especially during the downtime. He was constantly reminded of her.

The last two years had been even more of a struggle as he watched his buddies from Alpha Team all meet their significant others and begin settling down with families. He was happy for them. But it also got him thinking about his life after the teams.

He finally decided when the time came, and he resigned his commission and retired, that he wanted to make his home in Virginia Beach. It was where he had spent his entire career and where his friends were. The area had become his home.

So, he started laying some of the groundwork. A few months ago, he had purchased a house. It wasn't a planned purchase. It had been one of those instances where he was in the right place at the right time. After spending an enjoyable afternoon with the guys at Bayside, the local bar, and restaurant they like to hang out at, he had been driving back to his apartment when he passed by a house for sale, and the realtor was hosting an open house. He knew he had to stop when the two-story, snow-white brick home appeared.

When he and Jocelyn were together, she had always talked about wanting a white brick, colonial-style house with black framed windows, shutters, and a big front porch.

When he stepped into the large family home, he knew he wasn't leaving without making an offer. And he did, shocking the agent. There was only one negative about it. Jocelyn wasn't there to enjoy it with him as they had planned.

The sound of someone's flip-flops slapping against the wood decking drew Bear out of his memories. He listened as the slapping sound grew louder. He smiled, knowing it was his sister. She sounded like a Clydesdale the way she walked in those things.

"Hey! There you are!" Clover called out as she came around the side of the house and stopped in front of him. "What are you doing out here?"

"Just taking a minute to enjoy one of my favorite views. Want to join me?" He asked, scooting over to make room for her.

She sat down and nudged her foot against the deck, sending the swing into motion. For a few minutes, they sat there, silently swinging. Clover was never that quiet, and she had sought him out. So, he knew something was on her mind. She would eventually tell him, so he just sat there until she was ready to talk. When she finally spoke, he was shocked that she held out for nearly five minutes.

"It was nice having Jocelyn here today," she said, giving him a small smile.

He laughed. Clover always found a way to slip Jocelyn's name in when the family got together.

"Yeah. It was."

"She looks good."

"Yep. She sure does," he answered, then sipped his beer.

Bear smiled to himself, knowing that she was baiting him. Clover didn't realize it, but she could sometimes be a damn good interrogator, especially when it involved her brothers. She had a knack for getting under their skin and would keep bugging them until they broke under her resolve.

She sighed, and Bear sensed there was another question coming.

"What really happened between you and Jocelyn? Y'all used to be so close. Then it seemed like you were avoiding each other like the plague. And now, today, you both act like best friends again. And don't think I didn't catch that hug—or two you gave her when you guys didn't think anyone was looking. And spare me the bullshit about it being complicated. I'm so tired of hearing that from you."

Well, shit. He just stared at her thinking about how he wanted to answer her question. But the more he thought about it, he wasn't sure how to answer it. He hated keeping his past with Jocelyn a secret. But he also had to think about Jocelyn and what she wanted.

"Bear, you know damn well that when I want to know something, I'll keep digging until I get the answers I want," Clover said when he didn't answer her.

She wasn't lying. Once Clover set out on a mission, she was determined to see it through.

Luckily for him, his phone rang right then, saving him from disappointing his sister because as much as he wanted to open up to her, he couldn't. At least not yet.

He pulled his phone from his pocket and looked at it. His gut clenched when he saw the law firm's name on the screen. He'd been waiting on their call but didn't expect to hear from them on the weekend. His mind flashed back to what led up to this call.

Last week when he returned home from the team's latest mission, he had the urge to tap into his Buchanan's Scotch Special Reserve. After the third glass of smooth, rich-flavored whiskey, he felt pretty good. After some internal deliberations, he decided to pull out a box he kept in his bedroom closet. It was one of the few boxes that had moved with him over the years. It was filled with meaningful items from when he and Jocelyn were together. Everything inside the box was a reminder of how happy they had been, except for one manila letter-size folder that hid the one item that shamed him.

It pained him to be reminded of what he had given up as he sat alone, re-reading old love letters Jocelyn had sent him and looking at pictures from their wedding day. But if that wasn't enough punishment for him, he opened the forbidden folder.

Once he had signed on the dotted line, ending his marriage to the only woman who would ever own his heart, he buried that folder in the bottom of the box, vowing never to open it again. As he painfully flipped through the papers page by page, he noticed an important document was missing—the final divorce decree. He knew he and Jocelyn had signed it, so it had to have been somewhere. He had torn his house apart looking for the document, but it wasn't there.

He couldn't say why, but it bothered him that he couldn't find it. He knew the attorney would have a copy, so he called the office the following day to request one. The lady he spoke to informed him that the attorney who handled his divorce had passed away but that she would pull his case file and get a copy for him, which brought him to where he was now as the phone in his hand continued to ring. Excusing himself from his sister, he walked to the other side of the porch for some privacy.

"Hello?"

"Hi, Mr. Walker?" The woman on the other end inquired.

"Speaking."

"Mr. Walker, this is Glenice Waters from Waters and Bates. I apologize for the long delay in getting back to you. However, it took me a while to locate your file, as my dad was in the process of moving his paper files to electronic when he passed away."

"No worries. And I'm sorry to hear about your dad."

"Thank you." He heard a faint sigh on the other end of the line.

"I'm sorry to call over the weekend, but there seems to be a slight problem, and I wanted to call as soon as possible."

"Problem?" He questioned, wondering how hard it was to make a copy of a document and mail it.

She sighed. And it was one of those sighs that Bear was familiar with. It was when the person was about to tell him something he wouldn't like. How bad could the problem be? Maybe the file was just lost, and they would have to get a new copy from the courts. So, what, that it would take a few extra days or even a couple of weeks. He didn't really consider that a problem.

"Mr. Walker, I'm quite embarrassed to say this, but after reviewing your case file, it appears your papers were never submitted to the court."

Bear shook his head slightly, hoping he had misunderstood the clearly frustrated woman. "I'm sorry. Can you please repeat that? I thought I heard you say that my papers were never submitted. But I know that can't be right."

"I'm afraid you heard me correctly."

"I don't understand. What does that mean?"

Another sigh. *What the fuck is with all the sighing?*

"It means, Mr. Walker, that you and Ms. Thompson are still legally married."

If it were wintertime, people would think he was an ice sculpture as he stood frozen to the spot where he was standing. The only part of his body he felt moving was the accelerated thumping of his heart. He thought it would burst out of his chest if it were to beat any faster. All he could hear was the last part of Ms. Waters' sentence as it kept playing in mind—*still legally married...still legally married...still legally married.*

He tried to make sense of what she had told him, but he couldn't. Was she saying that all this time—ten years of guilt and regrets he was still a married man? That he and Jocelyn were still bound as husband and wife?

"Mr. Walker, are you still there?" Ms. Waters' voice on the other end grabbed his attention, and he pulled himself out of the frigid fog that had blanketed him.

"I'm sorry. I didn't hear a word you just said." He paused, raking his fingers through his hair while taking deep breaths. "I'm still trying to wrap my mind around this."

There was a moment of awkward silence.

"I'm sorry too. I know this information must come as a surprise to you."

He wanted to laugh. *Surprise? Try shock and awe!*

"I do have to say that I'm surprised that neither you nor Ms. Thompson ever caught the mistake over the years."

Bear knew why he never caught it because there was no other woman he wanted to marry. So, there was no need to dig it up. Plus, Jocelyn signed away everything she was entitled to, refusing to take anything from him. Now, seeing that Jocelyn hadn't encountered the error gave him hope that maybe second chances exist and fate brought them together for a reason.

Bear scratched his head.

"How did this happen?"

"Well, looking at the date, your decree papers fell into the time when my father fell ill, and as I said, he was also in the process of converting all his case files to electronic at the time. I'm guessing that is how your paperwork was overlooked. Again, I'm terribly sorry."

He could hear the frustration and embarrassment in her tone. He couldn't fault her for her father's mistake. He also knew that her father was a very independent man, which also fell into his work ethic. He was old school and liked to handle everything himself. He didn't have paralegals that most attorneys nowadays have to help review things.

"It's okay. I guess I need to know what to do to fix this. Do I need to sign new papers?"

Hold on. He thought to himself. Was this something he wanted to fix? That was a question he was going to need to think about before he made any decision.

"I wish it were that easy. Unfortunately, you'll have to start from scratch and refile because of the lapsed time. However, there will be no charge to you, as this was an oversight on the firm."

He didn't give a shit about the cost. What he needed was time. He needed to think through this with a level head and decide how he wanted to approach the situation. First and foremost, he needed to talk to Jocelyn. In the meantime, having the attorney send the paperwork wouldn't hurt. That way, if the situation stayed where both parties had left it or, thought, where they had left it, he'd have it ready. However, if things went his way, the only paperwork he'd be filling out would be adding Jocelyn's name to everything he owned.

Knowing how he wanted to proceed, he relayed the information to the attorney. After a few more minutes of ironing out some details and the attorney wishing him luck, he disconnected the call.

He stood there a few minutes, still processing it all. Things happen for a reason was the mantra his mom always used to tell him and his siblings. He always believed her. All he could hope was that Jocelyn would believe it too.

When he turned around, he met his sister's curious gaze. *Fuck!* He should've known that she hadn't left. He understood her worry. Clover was the best sister. His brothers would agree one hundred percent. She was an excellent listener and would offer sound advice. But for now, he needed to keep this to himself until he could speak with Jocelyn, which he would do today.

"Everything okay?" She asked, standing up and walking over to him.

He hated keeping the truth from her and knew he couldn't lie to her. Running a hand over his shadowed jaw, he looked at her. "Honestly, I don't know." And that wasn't a lie, as he wasn't sure how it would all pan out in the end. All he could do was stay positive and hope for the best.

Bear looked at his sister. "I promise I'll fill you in on what's happening. I just need a little bit of time."

She nodded her head. "Okay. Just remember I'm here if you need someone to talk to."

It looked like he had a new mission to conquer—Operation Win Back Jocelyn.

Just then, everyone started to filter out into the front yard, getting their spots ready for the fireworks.

☙

Jocelyn laughed so hard that she covered her mouth to avoid spraying everyone with her drink. Nails had been telling everyone about a one-night stand with a woman, resulting in him running butt-naked out of her house before the fun even started.

"Wait a minute. She wanted to have sex with you while her two pythons slithered around on the bed with you?" Snow asked, looking a little green.

Nails chuckled. "Yep. She and I were just getting to the good part of the evening when she suddenly hopped off the bed, telling me she had forgotten Monty and Buttercup as she ran out of the bedroom. I thought it was strange, but then I assumed they were her pets and maybe she had left them outside or something."

"I'm guessing Monty and Buttercup were the names of her pet snakes?" Jocelyn asked, trying to hold back her laugh.

"Yeah. Monty is a ball python, and Buttercup is a yellow ball python."

"Fitting names," Jay Bird said with a smirk.

"Do you even like snakes?" Jocelyn asked. She didn't mind them as long as they were behind glass.

"I don't have a problem with them as long as they aren't bothering me."

"So, I'm assuming when your lady friend returned, she had the snakes with her."

"Yep. Monty was draped around her neck, while Buttercup was coiled around her arm."

Jocelyn snickered, imagining what that must've looked like.

"What did you do?"

"I asked her what in the hell she was doing. When she told me that Monty and Buttercup liked to join in the action, that was my cue to leave, and I high-tailed it out of there. I've been with women with crazy fetishes, but I draw the line when it involves animal play." His lip curled up in disgust. "That's just wrong. Plus, I've got my own snake if I want to play with one." The little devil gave her a flirtatious wink, making her blush.

Jocelyn pressed her can against her cheeks, hoping the cold aluminum relieved some of the heat. Nails was definitely a lively character. He had a fun personality and, obviously, enjoyed the ladies' attention. But it wasn't only Nails she enjoyed talking to. All seven of Bear's teammates were equally friendly and surprisingly sociable, considering the stories she'd heard about how Special Forces operatives weren't conversationalists. The more she got to know them, the more her respect grew for them, especially listening to how they all supported one another, whether on missions or at home. It hit a sore spot, reminding her of what she had missed out on in being a part of their small, tight-knit community.

She was happy Clover found her happily ever after with Joker. She wasn't ashamed to admit that she envied Clover and Joker's relationship. Having been happily married at one time, Jocelyn already had a taste of that type of bond, and she missed it terribly. She missed having that special connection with someone. Someone that she could talk to and confide in. That someone was Bear. He made her feel complete and loved despite being hundreds of miles apart.

Accepting Jenelle's invitation was the right decision. Even with things still awkward with Bear, she had a good time and enjoyed seeing old faces and meeting new people.

Having another look around, a few of her old neighbors caught her attention and waved. She politely returned the gesture but continued searching for Bear in the crowd. When she didn't see him, she contemplated going to find him.

Just as she turned back to rejoin the conversation at hand, she spotted Clover walking from around the side of the house. Judging from her knitted eyebrows and troubled facial expression, something was wrong. Once she reached the table, she sat down next to Joker.

"Everything okay, babe?" Joker asked, kissing Clover softly on the lips.

"Something is up with my brother," she replied, shaking her head.

Joker chuckled. "You have four brothers. Which knucklehead are you referring to?"

"Bear. He is acting weird. And I don't know if it's a good or bad thing."

"What do you mean by weird?" Joker asked, looking concerned.

"I just found him sitting alone on the front porch. When I asked him what he was doing, he said he was just thinking about some stuff and enjoying the view. Then he got a phone call, and when he finished with it, he seemed agitated a bit." Clover's eyes slid across the table, and Jocelyn felt her insides twist. "I feel like he's hiding something."

Jocelyn swallowed the knot in her throat, knowing that Clover's statement was directed toward her.

"Is he still out front?" Jocelyn asked. She was willing to pull her big girl pants up and go and talk to him.

Clover's eyes brightened a bit.

"Yeah. But we all need to head out front. The fireworks are going to start soon."

"Once the fireworks are over, I can try talking to him," Jocelyn offered, and the smile tugging Clover's lips told Jocelyn that was the result Clover had been aiming for.

༄

Bear stood on the front porch, still reeling from the news his attorney had dropped on him.

He met Joker's eyes as he climbed the steps with the rest of the team following.

"You okay, man?" Joker asked, raising his eyebrows as if saying, *I know something is up.*

Bear rubbed the back of his neck, feeling a bit anxious. Before he could answer, the front door opened, and his eyes fell on Jocelyn. She was talking to a few of the partygoers. Bear's eyes followed her every movement as she descended the steps and walked out into the yard.

Bear tried to ignore the snickers behind him, but when they didn't stop turned around to find his team looking at him. They all had goofy grins. Well, except for Jay Bird. That man rarely smiled.

"What?" He asked, knowing he sounded lame for trying to cover up the fact he had been caught gawking.

Joker chuckled. "We've been talking to you, but it seems like someone else caught your attention." Joker nodded in Jocelyn's direction.

Bear pressed his lips together. He was clearly not as amused as his friends were.

He turned back to Joker. "Everything is fine. I just have a few things on my mind."

"I know. Clover told me. Well, she told all of us."

Bear rolled his eyes. "Of course she did."

After Clover left him alone on the porch, he had done some thinking. When he and Jocelyn finally got to talk, he was going to suggest that they come clean about their past. He felt awful keeping their secret from his family and teammates.

"When we get home, I need to discuss something with the team," Bear said.

Joker nodded, then leaned in closer. "Does it have to do with Jocelyn?"

Bear stared straight ahead, then with some hesitation, he gave his head a slight nod.

"Yeah. It does."

Joker gave him a sly smirk. "Just from the little time I've spent with her, she seems like an amazing woman."

Bear couldn't stop the smile tugging at the corner of his lips, hearing one of his friends and team members compliment Jocelyn. "She is."

Before Bear could elaborate, the fireworks started as explosions of vibrant colors painted the dark sky.

As much as the fireworks were a delight to watch, Bear couldn't tear his eyes away from the real beauty standing alone, with her head tilted back and her face looking up towards the sky. The huge smile on her face flooded his mind with memories of when they used to watch fireworks together.

It was time to make things right. He glanced over at Joker. He had his arms wrapped around Clover, with his chin resting on top of her head. When Joker met his gaze, Bear pointed toward Jocelyn, and Joker grinned in understanding and winked.

Bear shook his head in amusement as he headed down the steps. He's never been so nervous in his life. Even when conducting high stake missions, knowing he could die, he had never experienced the type of angst he felt now.

You got this. His subconscious told him as if acting as his internal wingman.

☙

Jocelyn's cheeks ached from all the smiling she had done all day. The impressive display of fireworks as they filled the sky with various colors and bright lights was magical. Due to her travel schedule, it had been years since she enjoyed a live Fourth of July fireworks show. Growing up, the Fourth had always been one of her favorite holidays. She loved the patriotic feel of all the red, white, and blue as everyone in the community came together to celebrate America's Independence.

The holiday also held a special memory for her. Thirteen years ago, she stood in the same spot when Bear had gotten down on one knee and proposed to her. It was a beautiful moment that he time perfectly, with the firework's grand finale, and making sure that nobody saw them.

Since their relationship was kept under wraps, she kept her wedding ring in her jewelry box. But Bear had given her a beautiful white gold anklet with two hearts linked together. She could wear it all the time without anyone pointing it out. She looked down at her right ankle, where the anklet still rested. She thought about removing it many times, but she couldn't. It was like her last lifeline to him; removing it would be like putting the final nail in the coffin.

A sudden shift in the air drew Jocelyn from the memories she had locked away. The fine hairs on the back of her neck stood up, and she wasn't sure if it was from the electricity in the air from the fireworks or if there was something else her sixth sense detected.

The anticipation caused a powerful rush of adrenalin to flood her body. The surge of her heartbeat caused her breathing to quicken. It was a phenomenon she had never experienced before, feeling as if something would unfold at any given second.

Suddenly, a large hand landed on her hip at the same exact moment as a brilliant flash of shimmery white light exploded in the sky. Startled, her body stiffened, and before she could move, a strong arm snagged her around the waist, holding her in place.

Just as she was about to put up a fight, a familiar, intoxicating scent hit her nose.

"Easy, Joce," Bear's low, deep soothing voice whispered close to her ear. His warm minty breath tickled her skin, causing goosebumps to spread across her body.

Jocelyn was taken by surprise by Bear's action. However, his touch was an addiction. Once she had it, she craved it. She was flooded with euphoria as she slowly closed her eyes and settled into the familiar warm body pressed against her back.

She was in no rush to untangle herself from Bear's firm hold. However, her mind was reeling with questions while she became reaccustomed to being held his Bear's arms.

Peering over her shoulder, her eyes traveled upward, meeting a pair of light grey eyes, a playful glint shined in them. God, she missed those beautiful eyes. Her belly was soon overtaken by a familiar flutter sensation she hadn't felt in a long time. It was a feeling that she had only ever experienced with Bear.

She offered him a small smile while slowly turning in his arms. His gaze never wavered from her.

"What are you doing?" Her voice shook due to his close proximity.

An amused smirk made its way to his lips. "I'm enjoying the fireworks." His reply came out raspy. Between the sexy smirk and the sound of his voice, it nearly made her knees go weak.

"But you're not watching the fireworks," she countered, as her hands moved, resting on his shoulders. Jesus, she was playing with fire.

He chuckled. "You're right. I'm looking at something even more beautiful."

Jocelyn's eyes widened as her breath caught in her throat, rendering her speechless.

He laughed at her reaction, but his smile turned serious seconds later. "In all honesty, I'm glad you came today."

Pulling back in surprise, she quirked one of her eyebrows.

"You are?"

He looked away for a moment, but she recognized the strained expression on his face. She then remembered Clover's comments about his odd behavior. Seeing how the two of them were currently in each other's arms when they had avoided each other for the last ten years, she had to agree with Clover.

"There's something important I need to talk to you about," he told her. The seriousness in his tone sent a sliver of worry through her.

"Alright," she said nervously, and Bear chuckled.

"Stop looking at me like that," he teased.

"How am I looking at you?"

"Like I'm going to eat you or something."

She scrunched her forehead up. "I can't help it. This is all just very confusing for me."

Pulling her close, she thought he would kiss her, but he moved his head to whisper in her ear. "I know. But I promise that I'll explain everything soon."

Without saying another word, he slowly spun her around, keeping his hands possessively on her hips. As much as she would've liked to enjoy the remainder of the fireworks, it wasn't possible. Her mind was too much of a jumbled mess, trying to understand what was happening.

CHAPTER FIVE

Jocelyn sat on the back porch in one of the rocking chairs, waiting for Bear to finish helping his brothers.

She and he were just about to find a place to talk when Ethan appeared and pulled Bear away to help with clean-up duty. He had given her an apologetic look but told her that he'd come to find her when he was finished.

Since she sat down, she had chewed off all of her fingernails. Unfortunately, when she got nervous, her fingernails suffered. It was a bad habit she had been trying to break for a long time.

Behind her, the backdoor opened, and she looked over her shoulder. She smiled when she saw Ray and Jenelle walking out.

"Oh! Hi, honey. We didn't realize you were out here," Jenelle said as the pair stepped onto the porch, closing the door behind them.

"I was waiting for Bear."

"You were?" Jenelle asked, her eyes widening in surprise. Jenelle glanced sideways at Ray, who smiled, but Jocelyn didn't miss that slight twinkle in his eye.

"Ethan pulled him and the others into clean-up duty out front."

"Better them than me," Ray chuckled as he walked over to the patio loveseat across from Jocelyn and sat down.

"What are you two up to?" Jocelyn asked, admiring the couple she looked up to.

"Well, now that everyone is gone, I'm going to sit my ass down and enjoy an ice-cold beer with my beautiful wife." Ray held out his hand to Jenelle, who shook her head at her husband's antics before joining him and snuggling into his side.

Their show of affection brought a smile to Jocelyn. She loved Ray and Jenelle. They had always been supportive and wonderful to her, even treating her like one of their own children.

"We didn't have a chance to really catch up earlier. How have you been, honey," Ray asked before cracking open his beer and taking a big gulp.

"I've been good. Busy, but holding my own."

"Nothing wrong with staying busy, as long as you take time out for yourself."

"I try to. However, having a demanding travel schedule can sometimes thwart personal time."

"I can understand that. I'm sure you've heard this many times today, but I'm hoping that some of the travel on that demanding schedule includes a few visits here. We've all missed you."

Good lord, here it went again, as that guilty feeling started to manifest itself.

"I'm really sorry. I've missed you guys too. I told Clover earlier that I'll do a better job keeping in touch with you. It also helps that Clover isn't far from me now that she's with Joker in Virginia Beach."

"You know that our door is always open for you. You still have the key to the front door, right?"

Jocelyn nodded. "I do." It was still secured on her key chain.

"Good. I expect you to use it," Jenelle teased, though Jocelyn heard the undertone of a command.

"Yes, ma'am."

Ray smiled, looking happy before he switched gears.

"I spoke with Rick the other day. He said that Lana offered you the job for the new initiative she is steering."

Jocelyn gave him a cheeky grin.

"She did. I still can't believe it myself. I've been involved in several projects, but none compare to this opportunity. I'm excited and honored to work with her on such an important and meaningful project."

"Working with her? Hell, Rick said you were driving it. Where exactly are these projects taking place? From what I understand, several locations were being considered."

"Rick didn't tell you?"

"Nope. He just said that Lana is over the moon that you accepted her offer and that you'll have a full travel schedule for the next year or two."

"Wow! That does sound exciting. So, tell us. Where are you going, and when do you leave?" Jenelle asked, appearing excited. But Jocelyn wondered how long that excitement would last when they heard where she was going.

"I leave for Messandai next week."

Ray drew his eyebrows inward. "I've never heard of it. I'm assuming it's a village and not an actual city."

Jocelyn nodded her head. "It's about an hour's drive northeast of Lake Chad."

Ray's jaw tensed, and his lips tightened. Jocelyn recognized the displeased look. Ray's extensive military background made him aware of the dangers she could potentially face.

"Isn't Chad listed on the State Department's *Do Not Travel To* list because of how dangerous it is?" Jenelle asked, looking between Jocelyn and her husband for validation.

"It is. And believe me. When Lana first told me, I had my concerns, and she even allowed me to back out if I wasn't comfortable. However, since this project will attract attention because it is tied to Lana's initiative, I can tell you that security measures will be in place."

"What kind of security are we talking about?" Ray asked, still looking unsure.

"I don't have that information right now, but Lana assured me I'll have twenty-four protection. Plus, the drilling company has hired a security team for their crew."

"These things can take some time to complete, right?"

"Yes and no. A lot of work goes into finding the right location based on underground water flow. Ground samples also have to be taken, amongst other things. But in this instance, a large portion of the groundwork has already been laid because this village had previously been approved for a well permit. But the permit was revoked at the last minute for some reason."

"So, what does your timetable look like?" Ray inquired.

"As long as we don't encounter any major roadblocks, I'm confident we can complete it in two weeks."

Ray offered her a subtle smile. "I know what you are doing over there is important. And I can't tell you how damn proud of you I am. But I can't help but worry about you. So, the faster you get home, the better I'll be able to sleep."

Jenelle patted Ray's leg before she looked at Jocelyn. "That goes for me too, sweetie. You know we think of you as one of our kids. I already worry about my other five children galavanting around the world, and now it appears I have six."

Jocelyn became teary-eyed as she listened to Ray and Jenelle fuss over her. Her own parents didn't even show a fraction of the love and support that Ray and Jenelle did.

Seeing Jocelyn wiping her eyes, Jenelle started to get emotional, and before long, the two women were hugging each other.

"Promise me that you'll check in with us, even if it's an email," Jenelle requested, and Jocelyn nodded.

"Deal."

Jocelyn held on to Jenelle for a few more seconds, trying to get the most she could out of their embrace. The moment was cut short by approaching voices and heavy footsteps, and Jocelyn knew that the cavalry had arrived.

Jocelyn released Jenelle and tried to erase the evidence of her tears before anybody could see, but she wasn't fast enough, as Bear was the first person to come around the corner. The moment their eyes locked, she knew he saw the tears.

"What's going on? Are you okay?" Bear questioned, his eyes searching for anything that could be wrong.

Jocelyn offered him a small smile. "Everything's fine. Your parents and I were talking, and my emotions got a little carried away."

Bear looked at his mom. She, too, was dabbing her eyes.

"What were you guys talking about that made you both upset?" Bear pressed, crossing his arms over his chest.

"Jocelyn was just telling us about her new job," Jenelle announced.

"You got a new job? I thought you liked working independently." Clover commented.

"I do like the independence of choosing where I go and who I partner with on projects." Jocelyn glanced at Ray, and he gave her a big encouraging smile even though he was still concerned about her upcoming trip. But he now understood how important this job was to her. "But, this was an opportunity I couldn't pass up."

Clearing his throat, Ray answered his son's question.

"You probably don't know this yet, as it was just confirmed last week, but Lana tapped Jocelyn to lead her global clean water initiative."

"Jocelyn! That is so awesome!" Clover exclaimed, and Jocelyn smiled.

A small smile formed on Bear's lips as his grey eyes met hers. "Congratulations, Joce. Does that mean you'll work at the White House with Lana?"

"Some of the time could be spent there for meetings. But mostly, I'll be traveling to the sites where the wells will be dug."

Bear's jaw tightened, and Jocelyn knew he was thinking of all the places that needed clean drinking water.

"Where exactly will you be traveling to?"

"Several places. We've only planned for the first project."

"And where is the first project?" He pressed a bit impatiently, looking between Jocelyn and his parents.

Ray took another drink from his beer before answering.

"The first project is in Chad—a small village northeast of Lake Chad."

It only took a millisecond to know that Bear disapproved, as his expression mirrored his dad's. His lips flattened, and his jaw was clenched so tight she thought he might break his teeth.

"The hell you are!" Bear roared. He not only shocked her with his reaction, but his parents, siblings, and teammates even seemed slightly taken aback.

"Bear..." Ray cautioned his son, but Bear looked ready to challenge his dad.

"What? Are you telling me that you're okay with her going there?"

"No. I'm not thrilled about it."

"Then tell her that she can't go."

"I can't do that," Ray said, appearing agitated.

"Why the hell not?"

"Because I'm a grown-ass woman and can make my own decisions," Jocelyn calmly stated as she turned to face him, meeting his glare.

Until now, she had remained silent while Bear and Ray spoke about her as if she wasn't sitting there. Bear had crossed a line, and she was pissed. He had no right to interfere in her life, let alone tell her what to do.

Standing eye to eye with him, she fired a shot back across the bow at him.

"I don't think you are in a place to decide what is best for me. Just like your job requires you to travel, so does mine."

Narrowing his eyes in frustration, he shook his head.

"Are you seriously comparing our jobs?"

"What if I am," she growled, stepping closer to him. Did he think being a SEAL put him on a pedestal above her? Granted, SEALs worked their asses off to get to where they were. But that didn't mean she hadn't worked her ass off to get to where she was.

"If it makes you understand why I'm going to Chad, yes. I suppose that I'm comparing our jobs. Think about it. We're both in the career field of improving people's lives worldwide. We both had extensive training to get where we are now. But there's one significant element in our jobs that neither of us could do without. Do you want to guess what that is?" She didn't even give him time to respond before she gave him the answer. "A team. We both rely on our teams to get the job done." He gave her an incredulous look, and she quirked her eyebrow. "Don't believe me? Let me give you an example. And this is pure speculation, so I'm not expecting you to confirm it. Let's say you and your team are on a mission, hunting down a bad guy, and one of you gets caught in a position where you now have to rely on one of your other team members to save your ass. Well, guess what? I had to be lowered into a dark hole all because I was the only person on site who was small enough to fit in the narrow space. But the darkness wasn't what bothered me. It was knowing that my equipment could fail at any moment, dropping me to Satan's doorstep. But like yourself, I knew I had a team of people I trusted to ensure that wouldn't happen."

By the time she was finished, she was breathing heavily, but nobody said a word as they all seemed to be taking in her words. Even a few of the guys nodded as if agreeing with her. Clover was beaming and looking like she wanted to give her a fist bump as if declaring girl power. On the other hand, Jocelyn began to feel embarrassed for unloading on Bear. Had he deserved it? Yeah, he did. But expressing herself as she had was very out of character for her. She was usually more reserved.

"That was the hottest thing I've seen," Nails commented, staring at Jocelyn with a goofy grin. His statement drew a few snickers, but his humor fell short with Bear, earning the group's comedian an angry growl.

When Bear returned his stormy grey eyes to her, Jocelyn braced herself for another lecture. As if knowing his son was about to make an ass of himself, Ray intervened before things really got out of hand.

"Jocelyn, I don't think my son was implying that you can't go. You are a grown adult who can clearly make your own decisions. Since we've always considered you a part of our family, we are concerned about your safety. That doesn't mean I'm thrilled about you galivanting off to Chad. And if I'm being honest, I'll admit that it scares the hell out of me knowing you'll be over there. But in the end, it is solely your decision to make. Nobody can stop you."

Before she could reply to Ray, Bear started again. "Jocelyn, do you know the dangers you'll face over there? Chad is an extremely dangerous country. There are curfews in cities across the country because of ongoing violence and civil unrest. There are armed rebels and terrorist organizations that target aid workers like yourself, especially in the areas surrounding Lake Chad. And take my word for it. You don't want to know what happens to the innocent that fall victim to those evil bastards."

Okay, when he put it like that, it made her nervous. And, of course, she was aware of the dangers. But it was her job that she had to see thru to the end. Innocent people depended on her.

"Are there security plans in place? Where are you staying, and for how long?" Clover asked.

Wow! At least someone had some logical questions, she thought to herself.

Avoiding any eye contact with Bear, she answered Clover.

"Yes. I'll have my security detail, and the drilling company we contracted with will also bring their own security team. So, we'll have double the protection when you look at it. And since a majority of the tedious pre-planning has already been completed, the project from start to finish should only take approximately two weeks—give or take a day or two."

"Are you sure about this, Jocelyn?" Jenelle interjected, and Jocelyn knew they were worried, but they didn't know her history or the other places she'd been in the world.

Jocelyn walked over and stood in front of Ray and Jenelle.

"I promise you that this isn't my first rodeo." She could hear a low, rumbled growl behind her and knew Bear was venting his frustrations. But like she told him. It wasn't his decision. It was hers. And she was going.

Both Ray and Jenelle stood up and hugged her. She wanted to cry when Ray whispered that he expected her to check in with him often to let them know that she was okay and that if she found herself in a bind, he expected her to contact him no matter what. She gave them both big hugs and said she'd keep in touch.

Once they released her, Jocelyn stepped back and turned toward the rest of the Walker clan and Bear's teammates, who all appeared upset by the news of her travel destination.

She walked over to Clover and pulled her in for a hug.

"Please be safe," Clover whispered; her concern was evident in her tone.

"Always," Jocelyn responded, giving her an extra squeeze. "I'll call you when I get back, and we can set a date to get together. I've missed my little sis."

"I'd like that," Clover said, appearing teary-eyed.

Pulling away, she turned her attention to Bear. She could be a real bitch and just ignore him, but that wasn't her. Plus, she didn't want to leave with bad blood between them.

She got it. He was unhappy about her decision. But he needed to get over it and understand that this was what she did for a living.

"I know you aren't happy about this, but this is something that I have to do." She could tell he wanted to argue but held back, pressing his lips firmly together. "I promise to be as safe as I can. You heard me tell your mom and dad I'd keep in touch. I can even keep in touch with you."

He still didn't look happy, but he had no other choice. Justin, Ethan, and Zach hugged and told her to be safe. Even though he had pissed her off, she had been hoping she'd get a hug from Bear, but he made no move toward her, so after saying goodbye to the others, she quickly made her exit.

So much for reconciling, she thought to herself as she wiped away a few tears that managed to escape her eyes.

☙

What the fuck just happened? Bear asked himself as he watched Jocelyn turn her back on him and walk away. He was at a complete loss for words.

Jocelyn had just revealed a side of herself that he had never seen. Granted, he knew she was no pushover by no means. But the feistiness he just witnessed as she ripped him a new ass was unexpected but impressive. Though he would never admit it out loud, Nails had been right. Her show of independence and confidence was hot as hell to watch.

He saw the tears in her eyes right before she stormed off the deck, heading toward the front of the house. Raking his fingers through his hair, he looked around at all the stunned faces, except for his brother Zach. He was smirking, shaking his head.

"I'd say you pissed her off," Zach told him.

"Fuck you, Zach!"

"Cool it, both of you!" Ray commanded, getting in between them. He then turned his attention to Bear.

"What in the hell has gotten into you?" His dad asked.

Bear shook his head. "I don't know. Fear maybe." He took a deep breath and swallowed hard. "I'm fucking scared, Dad. You and the rest of us here know the dangers of her going to Chad. We hear about it all the time how the terrorist groups over there are conducting attacks and expanding the scope of their operations. They target people like Joce. And knowing what they subject women to makes me sick. So, yeah. I'm fucking scared to death of her going over there."

Ray's expression softened. "I get it, Bear. I really do. I'm just as scared as you are. But like she said, you can't tell her what she can and cannot do."

"I know that."

"Now, it is quite obvious there is tension between you and Jocelyn. I don't know what happened between you two, but this family is tired of tip-toeing around the subject."

Dammit! This wasn't how he intended the discussion with his family to go. However, it had to happen. They needed to know the truth.

"Let me at least go talk to her before she leaves, and then when I get back, we'll all sit down, and I'll explain everything," he said, addressing everyone.

He took off around the side of the house, hoping to catch her by the time she made it through the inside of the house and out the front door. He reached the front just in time to see her stomp down the steps toward her car.

"Jocelyn!" He called after her, but she completely ignored him, as he expected. He picked up his pace and reached for her upper arm, stopping her.

"Jocelyn, please wait."

She spun around and poked her finger into his chest. She was still fired up, but he also sensed some hurt.

"Why should I?"

"Because we need to talk."

"I think you've said enough."

"Look, I'm sorry. I never meant to insinuate that I'm better than you. And you're right. Our jobs are similar when you put it the way you did. But I'm not sorry for worrying about you. I still think that you should reconsider taking the job."

"It doesn't matter what you think, Bear. You lost that right when you had me served with divorce papers."

Well, damn! Those words were like a slap in the face, but he deserved it.

"Jocelyn, will you please just listen?"

"No! I don't want to hear it. I accepted what you wanted, and I've moved on."

"Moved on? What in the hell does that mean?"

"That's none of your business."

Oh, sweetheart. It's definitely my business, and you are so full of shit.

He gently clutched her chin between his fingers. Her eyes met his gaze, and he had his answer as soon as he looked deep into her brown eyes. The way her pupils dilated was a clear indicator that she wasn't being truthful. He'd make sure to thank his BUD/S Instructor for teaching him that technique.

"If you would please just zip your lips for one second, there's something important I need to tell you."

Her eyes widened, but then she did something that weakened his resolve. She slipped her tongue out and swiped her lips—her kissable lips. God, what he'd do right now to taste her. He couldn't just take a sample.

He wanted to devour her. And he didn't want to admit it, but he was still turned on by how she stood up to him in front of everyone.

His phone ringing was like a bucket of ice water being dumped on him. He considered ignoring the call, but the distinct ring tone indicated it was Derek. Knowing he couldn't miss his commander, he reluctantly released her chin.

"I need to take this. Don't go anywhere," he told her, pulling the phone from his pocket and walking in the opposite direction to take it. He hadn't even taken ten steps when he heard the car door slam, followed by the engine roaring to life. Spinning around as he pressed the phone to his ear, all he saw were the taillights of her car flying down the driveway.

Son of a bitch!

అ

Bear climbed the steps and walked back into the house, shoving his phone back into his pocket. Even though he was irritated and a little hurt that Jocelyn chose not to listen and had not waited for him to take the call, he was feeling a little better now about Jocelyn's little trip to Chad.

It appeared that President Evans was handling Jocelyn's security detail, and he had contacted Derek about sending Bravo team with her. Since Bear and his team had no prior commitments, Derek didn't see anything wrong with it. But he was sure that Jocelyn would see plenty wrong with it.

He would've already been chasing after her if he didn't have his family and teammates waiting for him.

He knew his sister and his mom had her number, so he'd get it from one of them and call her. That was going to be a fun phone call. It would've been much easier if he had discussed the divorce situation with her in person.

Following the deck around to the back, he found everyone sitting there. They were having some sort of discussion, but as soon as they saw him, the talking stopped.

His mom noticed him first and offered a small comforting smile.

"Where's Joce?" She asked, looking concerned.

"Gone. Derek called while I was trying to talk to her, and she left while I was on the phone with him."

"Anything pressing with Derek?" Joker asked, knowing Derek would've only called if it were necessary.

"We're being called up."

"When?"

"We leave Wednesday." He looked toward his mom and dad. "It's not a classified mission."

"What the hell are we doing then?" Nails asked.

"It seems that a certain hydrologist needs a security detail to escort her to Chad." He couldn't stop the small smile tugging on his lips when it dawned on everyone who he was talking about.

"Jocelyn?" His mom asked, and Bear nodded his head.

From what Derek told me, Lana is nervous about Jocelyn's trip as much as we are, and she made Rick promise that he'd find the best detail to escort her."

"So you guys are going to Chad with Jocelyn?" Ray asked, wanting confirmation.

Bear grinned. "Yeah, Dad. All eight of us are going with her."

"Thank fucking God," Ray mumbled, and they all laughed.

"Does Jocelyn know this?" Clover asked, and Bear shook his head.

"Not yet. I asked Rick if it would be okay if I broke that news to her. He said that wasn't a problem." He looked at his mom and Clover. "I'll need to get her number from one of you."

"Of course," they both said.

He looked away for a second, trying to figure out how to start the next conversation he needed to have with the group.

"What's on your mind, son?" His dad asked bluntly before taking a sip of his drink.

Bear sighed, running his hand down his face.

"There's something I must confess to all of you regarding Jocelyn and I."

The smile on his mom's face dropped as if thinking he would deliver bad news. She gestured to the chair across from her.

"We've got all the time in the world. Come sit."

He took the open seat and then looked toward his mom.

"Earlier today, when you asked me about Jocelyn, I wasn't honest with you. And I'm sorry."

"It's okay, honey."

He shook his head. "No, mom. It's not okay. You and Dad raised me to be better than that. One thing I've never done is lie to either one of you. But I've been harboring a lie or a secret. Whatever you want to call it."

"What's this about, son?" Ray asked.

Bear sighed deeply. "Because of my stupidity when I was younger, I may have pushed away the most important person in my life, and I'm not sure I can get her back."

Jenelle gave him a knowing smile. "I'm assuming you're talking about Jocelyn."

He nodded. "This is going to come as a shock to everyone. Joce and I were married."

Gasps and murmured words flooded the patio. He had warned them, but the stunned look on his mom's and dad's faces was one for the record book. Especially his dad, who could hold a poker face like a walk in the park.

"What? When?" His mom stumbled through her questions, looking confused. She glanced at Ray as if asking him if he knew. But his dad shook his head slightly, letting her know this was news to him.

"We didn't tell anyone because we were both entering a stage in our careers and school that we didn't want to be bogged down with planning a wedding. Plus, Jocelyn's parents would've never approved of us being together.

"I didn't even know you two were dating," his mom stated, still appearing shell-shocked.

Bear grinned. "It just kinda happened. She came to Annapolis a few times, and there were a few weekends I could slip over to Texas to see her.

She was my best friend—my soul mate. One weekend while she was visiting, we had a long talk, and we both admitted our feelings and realized we were more than just friends and that we belonged together. We were in love with each other."

"But when did you get married? It must have been after you graduated from the academy," Ray questioned, knowing that Midshipmen weren't allowed to marry before they were commissioned.

"Remember when Jocelyn and I slipped away for about an hour after graduation?" Jenelle nodded. "We met a wedding officiant. It was quick, and then we met everyone for dinner."

"I can't believe this," Jenelle said, covering her mouth. Bear felt horrible for keeping this from his parents, especially his mom, who now had tears in her eyes.

"I don't understand. If you were married, then what in the hell happened between you two?" Ray asked, and Bear knew he must carefully explain the next part. Knowing how protective his dad was of Jocelyn, Bear needed to ensure he didn't give his dad a reason to kick his ass.

Bear met his dad's eyes. "Do you remember that first mission I went on after getting my assignment?"

His dad's facial expression softened, knowing exactly what mission Bear was referring to. When Bear returned home, his head was all messed up. He had gone home for a weekend to escape the reminders of what he had endured both during and post-mission. His dad was the only person he could turn to. Thankfully, his mom had been away on a girls' trip that weekend because she didn't need to witness the state he had been in.

"You were in a pretty bad place. But it was understandable, considering you lost two teammates."

Jenelle looked between Bear and her husband, listening to them. Bear never told his mom about that deployment. He didn't discuss much about his career with his family since most of his missions were classified. However, that wasn't anything new, considering everyone in the family except his mom was part of the Special Forces community.

"I couldn't put Jocelyn through that. I couldn't ask her to sit at home, wondering if I would make it back alive. She didn't need to constantly worry that she would get that dreaded knock on the door and someone in a uniform telling her that her husband had been killed. I couldn't ask her to do that."

"What did you do?" Jenelle asked, wiping a stray tear from her cheek.

"I was a coward, Mom. I did something I'm so ashamed of." He paused for a moment, trying to reign in his emotions. "I filed for divorce."

"And she agreed? The Jocelyn I know would've fought for you two."

"She tried, Mom," Bear confessed, pinching the bridge of his nose. "But I wouldn't give her the opportunity to."

"Tripp, what did you do?"

"She tried to reach out, but I refused to take any of her calls. She was still in school. She still had another month or two to complete her master's degree. I couldn't face her. I felt like a coward. Eventually, she stopped calling. A few days later, I got the papers back in the mail, which were signed. She completely cut all ties with me."

"Well, that definitely explains the awkwardness between you two. And, why we haven't seen her all these years," Ray said. It killed Bear to keep this secret from his parents, especially because of their relationship with Jocelyn.

Bear rubbed the back of his neck. "Yeah. I guess it also helped that her parents moved. She didn't have any reason to come back to Tennessee."

His mom got up and moved to the chair next to him. She took his hand into hers.

"You still love her, don't you?"

"With all my heart," his voice cracked, and he blinked to will away his tears. "I never stopped. She's my other half. And I've been miserable without her."

"Oh, honey!" She pulled him into a hug. He may be thirty-five years old, but there were times when he needed one of his momma's hugs.

When she pulled away, she was crying. He squeezed her hand before looking over at his dad. He had braced himself for a look of disappointment, but all he saw was understanding in his dad's expression.

"That isn't all." Bear continued, and his mom's eyes got very wide.

"Oh, Tripp. Please tell me that you don't have a secret child together. I don't think I can handle that."

Bear barked out a loud laugh and patted his mom's hand.

"I can assure you that there are no spawns of mine out there wandering around."

"Well, then, what else is there?"

"After Jocelyn got hurt during Clover's ordeal, I guess I wanted to torture myself and wallow in self-pity." He explained what he had done, how he couldn't find the final divorce decree, and how he contacted the attorney to get a copy."

"Okay. And did she call you back?"

"Yeah. She called me today," he admitted as his eyes traveled to Clover, who had been silent, listening, just like his brothers and his teammates.

"That was the call you got when I was with you," she stated, and he nodded.

"What did she say?"

Bear pursed his lips. He still couldn't believe it himself.

"According to her, the attorney never filed the signed papers."

Jenelle gasped and covered her mouth. "So, you and Jocelyn are still married?"

Bear nodded his head slowly. "It seems so."

A smile slowly spread across his mom's lips. "That's what you wanted to talk to her about? When your dad and I came out here and found Jocelyn sitting in the chair, she told us that you had something to discuss with her."

"Yeah. I don't think she knows either."

"Hot damn!" His dad shouted in excitement. Bear was surprised to see him grinning. Ray then held up his beer can as if making a toast.

"Well, son, I suggest you use this second chance wisely. I've always said Jocelyn was a part of this family."

Bear shook his head. He didn't know how to approach the situation.

"She's upset with me. I don't even know if she'll take my call."

"Well, then you find a way to make her listen. I always thought you two were a perfect pair."

"I have a real sister-in-law!" Clover shouted, making everyone laugh.

"I know a way to make her listen if she doesn't take your calls," Joker said with a grin.

"Yeah? How?"

"It's a long plane ride to Chad. Plenty of time for you two to talk. And pretty much no escape routes at thirty-five-thousand feet in the air. Unless she can parachute."

"You know what slogan is," Jay Bird commented.

Improvise, adapt, overcome. It was a slogan many soldiers used when things weren't going their way. This was one battle he refused to lose. Jocelyn was his, and he wasn't going to waste the second chance given to him.

CHAPTER SIX

Jocelyn stood with President Evans and Lana on the tarmac at Andrews Air Force Base. They both wanted to come to see her off.

"Ever ride in one of these?" President Evans asked her.

Jocelyn shook her head as she glanced up at the enormous C-17 Globesetter.

"I can't say that I have."

Evans grinned. "You packed headphones or earplugs, right?"

Pointing to the large duffle bag next to her feet, she grinned. "I did. And I have a blanket, pillow, water, snacks, and anything else that you recommended. Oh! And enough paperwork to keep me occupied the entire ride there and back."

He chuckled. "You sound like you're prepared then."

She may have been prepared in terms of items to keep her comfortable and occupied, but she wasn't ready for the long-ass flight. Thankfully, the plane was large and roomy inside. She didn't mind flying as long as she didn't feel cramped. She hadn't realized she had a slight claustrophobic issue until two years ago when she traveled to the Bahamas and had to fly on a small six-seater Cessna. Thankfully the flight from Miami hadn't taken long.

She looked at her watch again. According to the schedule she was given, they were supposed to be wheels up in twenty minutes. But she seriously doubted they'd leave on time, considering the security team that Evans recruited hadn't arrived yet. The security team assigned to the drilling crew, and all the equipment and vehicles were already on board.

Her security detail's tardiness made her wonder how reliable the group was.

She knew that C-17s were large planes and could carry a lot of cargo. Still, she hadn't realized how much one could hold until she watched the crew load in the drilling rig and the equipment that went along with it, a small bobcat, two SUVs, and several pallets of supplies they would distribute to the village on their arrival.

As if sensing her annoyance, Evans spoke. "Don't worry. The team will be here momentarily. They tend to arrive at the last minute."

Jocelyn couldn't help but notice every time Evans spoke about the security team, Lana always gave him a sideways look.

"Ah…there they are now," he pointed out.

Jocelyn turned around and saw several vehicles pulling into the reserved parking area adjacent to the hanger.

Moments later, huge men started filing out the vehicles.

"Who are they?" Jocelyn asked as the eight men approached and shook Evans' hand.

"Jocelyn, I'd like you to meet SEAL Team Two – Alpha Team members."

The lead guy with jet-black hair stepped forward. "I'm Ace, and behind me, from left to right, are Potter, Frost, Irish, Stitch, Dino, Skittles, and Diego."

Jocelyn swallowed hard. Holy shit, those guys looked total badass, even in jeans and t-shirts. But they also reminded her of Bear and his team.

She extended her hand and shook Ace's. "It's nice to meet you." She looked at the others and offered a wave. "You guys too." And they gave her a small smile in return.

She turned back toward Evans. "So, this is the security team?"

Evans chuckled. "No. Ace and his team are just catching a ride to Germany. They'll be getting off when you land there to refuel."

Jocelyn scrunched her eyebrows together, appearing confused. "Where's the security team, then?"

Evans pointed to another group that was approaching from behind her. "Meet Bravo Team."

As Ace and his team moved to the side, it gave her a clear view of the men walking toward her, and Jocelyn felt her jaw drop. Leading the group of familiar-looking men was non-other than her ex-husband. And much to her shock, he didn't look surprised to see her.

Not skipping a beat, she shot a look toward Lana, and from how Lana was nibbling her bottom lip, Jocelyn felt she was the only one left out of the details pertaining to her security detail. *Interesting.*

"Lana, please tell me this is a joke," she whispered loud enough for Lana to hear her.

"Rick planned this, not me. I didn't know he was going to ask them."

"But you knew after the fact! You could've warned me."

"Jocelyn, I honestly didn't know which team would get the job."

Evans looked between Jocelyn and Lana with squinted eyes. "Am I missing something?"

Lana gave a subtle grin while Jocelyn sighed. "It's fine. Things between Bear and I are just complicated. That's all."

"But you're okay with him and his team being your security detail?"

She cocked her head and looked up at him. "I don't really have a choice. Do I?"

On the outside, she made it as if she was joking. However, she was a bundle of nerves on the inside. She had been pissed seven ways to Sunday when she peeled out of the Walker's driveway two weeks ago.

She had ignored his attempts to reach her the past three days. Her actions could be considered childish to some people, but she had a million and one things to do before she left for Chad, and not one of them had anything to do with her ex-husband.

She understood everyone's concern about her travel plans, but dammit, this was what she did for a living. And nobody, especially Bear, had the right to demand that she does not go.

In the message he left her yesterday, he indicated he needed to speak with her, stressing that it was important. She couldn't help but wonder if he knew the whole time. But that couldn't be right because of his reaction when she announced to everyone where she was going.

Crapola! I'm just going to have to bite the bullet. If he's badgered me this much, it must be somewhat important. At least, it better be.

Before Evans could respond to her, the heavy footsteps behind her stopped. When she turned, she couldn't fully read Bear's expression as he approached because of the dark sunglasses covering his grey eyes. But if the slight smirk on his face was any indicator, she thought he found the situation amusing.

"Mr. President, Mrs. Evans," Bear greeted the couple and shook their hands, though Lana pulled him into a hug. He then turned toward Jocelyn and grinned.

"Hello, Jocelyn. It's a pleasure to see you. Has everything been okay since the weekend?"

She raised an eyebrow, wondering where he was going with that question. "I've been fine."

"Huh…I just thought something was wrong since you never called me back."

Oh damn! He did not just call her out in front of everyone. She felt the heat rising in her cheeks, and she wasn't sure if it was from embarrassment or her temper. She cleared her throat.

"It's been a busy few days. You know a trip such as this takes a lot of planning. I didn't have a lot of time for any petty conversations."

His lopsided grin and nod told her he didn't believe one word of the shit that she spewed.

"Actually, I know a lot about planning. Believe it or not, that's a big—well, huge part of my job. Without a good plan, people could get killed."

Her cheeks felt even warmer, and she wished the damn ground would open and swallow her.

Lana began talking as if sensing the tension building between her and Bear.

"Bear, make sure you take good care of our girl."

Our girl? Jocelyn's mouth dropped open, and she didn't miss the snickers from the peanut gallery behind him. It was apparent his team found Lana's statement amusing. Even Bear and Rick were grinning.

What the hell? Had she just entered the Twilight Zone?

After she got over the shock, she looked at Lana.

"Thanks. But I can take care of myself."

Lana chuckled and stepped forward, pulling Jocelyn into a hug.

"You take care of yourself. Keep me updated on the progress. Between you and I, Rick is working out some logistics so I can attend the ribbon cutting."

Jocelyn gasped in surprise and pulled back a smidge to look at Lana.

"Lana, that would be so awesome! If you think we have publicity now on the project, can you imagine if you showed up in person?"

Lana smiled. "I know. But no promises. That area is normally off-limits, but I'm putting up a fight, and Rick's in my corner. So, we'll see."

Lana hugged her one last time, but she whispered in her ear before she released her.

"Take this opportunity to follow your heart."

Jocelyn wondered if Lana knew what she was feeling deep down inside. Before she could question her, Rick stepped forward and hugged her. He then proceeded to give her all the fatherly advice she needed.

"You be safe. Don't wander off alone, and make sure one of the guys is always with you. And lastly, try not to give Bear a hard time as he's just doing his job."

She nodded, assuring Evans she would behave.

"Well, I guess this is it. We'll see you in about two or three weeks, maybe sooner." Rick grinned and winked, indicating he knew Lana had told her about the possible surprise trip.

As she said bye, she took a step backward. She didn't realize someone was standing close behind her, and when she turned around, she slammed right into a brick wall and almost fell onto her ass. The only thing that saved her was her quick reflexes when she grabbed onto the person's arms. And they were strong arms because she could feel the muscles under her fingertips.

"Son of a bitch!" She muttered to herself.

Because of her height, she didn't have to look up far to meet the person's eyes. Bear had removed his sunglasses; the light gray irises were all she needed to see to know who it was.

"Ready?" He asked in that smooth, deep voice that drove her insides crazy and sent a tingle down her spine. She wanted to berate herself for having those sensations. But she couldn't help it. He had that effect on her.

"Yep," she quipped as she released her grip on his arms and took a few steps backward, separating them.

"Alright. Aussie grabbed your two bags and already put them on the plane."

"Oh! He didn't have to do that. I could've handled that."

"No, he didn't have to. But we tend to be nice like that, especially to others who show the same respect back."

She shot him a look. "What is that supposed to mean?" She questioned, on the defensive.

He leaned in close. "It means like having the common courtesy to return someone's phone calls or texts."

She rolled her eyes. "Are we back to that again? Look. I'm sorry, but I'm still a little peeved with how you acted at your parent's house. But you must be thrilled now that you're in charge."

He placed his hand on his hip and stared at her with piercing eyes.

"Did you ever stop and think that maybe I was calling to apologize?"

"Were you?" She countered, staring back at him.

"That's one reason why I called."

"I call bullshit. Just because you and I haven't spoken in ten years doesn't mean I forgot how you do things."

"Do things?"

"You don't do apologies."

"What in the hell are you talking about?" He asked, raising his voice slightly.

"As I said, you're not an apologetic person."

"The hell I'm not."

"Really? Because if you were, you would've already apologized for ripping my heart out."

Bear flinched at her choice of words, and she could tell she had hit a sensitive spot. But he could deal with it because it was the truth, and she had dealt with her share of heartache for years. She didn't want to start this trip out by fighting with him, especially since they would spend a lot of time together. She took a deep breath before she spoke in a calm voice.

"Look. I don't want to fight. I'll do as you say, but only when it comes to my safety, not anything else. I'm not one of your soldiers that you can order around whenever you want. Got it?"

"Got it," he replied.

As she brushed by him and started toward the plane, she saw the rest of the team standing nearby and knew they'd heard everything. *Just fan-fucking-tastic!*

ॐ

Bear was doing everything he could to keep from laughing at Jocelyn's stunned reaction to seeing him and finding out that she was under his protection, although he couldn't quite figure out if she was angrier or shocked by his presence. But when she mentioned him being unapologetic, that struck a nerve. That little dig pissed him off, but what made him even more furious was knowing that she was right.

To an extent, she had a right to be angry. What he did was wrong on many levels, and she was absolutely right. He did owe her an apology. But if she stopped for a minute and would let him talk, maybe she would understand where he'd been emotionally at that time—not that he was using that as an excuse. But at least she would realize his mind's state at the time.

He followed Jocelyn toward the plane, passing by the team, and he wanted to roll his eyes at their amused expressions. He wasn't ignorant. He knew damn well they had overheard.

"What the fuck are you smirking at?" He asked Nails, who looked like he was about to bust a gasket.

Nails being the goofball he was, just shook his head and chuckled. "Y'all sound like two toddlers fighting."

"Yeah. Well, she's a pain in my ass," Bear expressed out of anger. But he soon realized it was himself he was pissed at and was taking his frustrations out on her.

"I wouldn't mind the pain if it looked like her," Nails replied, grinning, as he turned to look at Jocelyn just as she bent over to pick up something she had dropped, giving them both a nice view of her curvy backside she had squeezed into the blue jeans she wore.

A throaty growl erupted from Bear's insides. He loved Nails as a brother, but he was seriously beginning to piss him off. Glaring at Nails, he pointed at him with a stern warning. "Stay the fuck away from her."

Bear stomped up the ramp. He could still hear Nails laughing. *Fucker.* He couldn't wait until Nails found a woman to call his own so he and the others could pull the same shit he had done to them.

Aussie met him near the entrance. "I put Jocelyn's bags in the second cargo area with ours."

"Thanks," he replied with little enthusiasm, and as if knowing Bear wasn't in the mood for any chit-chat, Aussie found his seat.

As Aussie settled in his seat, Nails took the seat one over him. Aussie gave him a quick glance. "What crawled up Bear's ass?"

With a lopsided grin, Nails replied, "That would be the lovely Ms. Jocelyn Thompson."

Aussie's eyes widened. "Oh."

Nails couldn't stop smiling. "Yeah, oh. Glad I brought popcorn because, after the preview I just watched, I'm sure the main attraction is going to be a showstopper. And just think, we have front-row seats," he hooted, making Aussie shake his head.

৯

Bear sat near Joker, secured his seatbelt as the C-17 roared to life, and sped down the runway before lifting into the air.

He couldn't stop glancing toward the front of the plane where Jocelyn had planted herself along the right sidewall. She sat alone, with several seats separating her from the others. She hadn't wasted any time making herself look busy as she sifted through paperwork. She had donned her headphones, tuning everyone and everything out. Bear wondered if she deliberately did it so he would leave her alone.

Alpha team had called dibs along the left sidewall, along with the seven guys from the drilling crew and their four-member security detail. Derek had given him a full report on the drilling company, including the background on the crew members and their security detail.

The crew members all seemed to check out, and he introduced himself to Ralph, the supervisor for the crew.

Ralph was an Army Veteran, 82nd Airborne. He served for twenty-one years until a bad jump resulted in a fractured pelvis and several other bones. Knowing the injury was bad and the fact he was getting up there in age, he opted for a medical discharge. Once he recovered, he started working for the drilling company. He said he had other offers, but he had chosen the current company because of their ties to the community and the philanthropy they spread worldwide like they were doing with this project. Bear was impressed to hear that the company had donated all the project expenses.

During their conversation, Bear had been surprised to learn that the crew's security detail wasn't there for their protection. Their role was to protect the company's assets. Bear had thought that employees were also a company's asset, but he guessed that wasn't the case in this situation. After hearing that, Bear had assured Ralph that if he or his crew needed anything, to ask, and the team would help where they could. After all, there were eight of them. Bear wasn't familiar with the security company, although the present employees didn't throw any red flags.

He looked around the inside of the plane. No matter how many times he'd flown in a C-17, it still amazed him with its vast size and what all could fit inside it. He'd been on flights with a few high-profile government officials, and they had brought along a "Silver Bullet." The Air Force had two "Silver Bullets," as they were nicknamed. Silver Bullets are customized airstream recreational vehicles converted to command centers for government officials to use for both comfort and privacy during long flights overseas.

He closed his eyes and leaned his head back against the sidewall as he mentally made a list of things he wanted to go over with the team before arriving in Chad. He also was aware of his full plate regarding Jocelyn and the balance between business and personal that he needed to navigate. Her safety was the priority over anything else. The rest would fall into place. At least, he hoped.

He wasn't sure how much time had passed when he felt the nudge to his arm waking him from a cat nap. Cracking open one eye, he saw Joker motioning with his head toward the front of the plane. He immediately knew what Joker was telling him as he watched Jocelyn come out of the restroom, rubbing a spot on her jeans with a paper towel.

"Now might be your opportunity before she occupies herself again."

Bear nodded, getting the gist of what Joker was saying. He reached into the bag, sitting by his feet, and pulled out a folder. Joker raised an eyebrow in question.

"My backup," he told him, and Joker nodded in understanding.

As he stood up, Joker slapped him on the back. "Good luck."

I'm gonna need all the luck I can get.

༺❦༻

Jocelyn couldn't believe the predicament she was in. She hadn't noticed her pen had leaked all over her hand and the front of her jeans—mainly centered around her crotch area. She shook her head, mumbling under her breath as she tried to treat the giant ink blob with a wet washcloth she had found in her bag. Not that it was helping any. The soap and water only worsened it, causing the ink spot to grow and spread toward her inner thigh.

Just my freaking luck! Now it looks like I started my period!

Yep! How convenient was it that a red liquid gel pen would spring a leak, staining the crotch of her light blue jeans? Oh! And the color of the pen was called blood red. How fitting was that? If this mishap was any indication of how the rest of the trip was going to be, she better buckle up.

Before the *Code Red* pen incident, she had been undisturbed and content, tucked into her little private corner of the plane. She had purposely chosen the spot at the furthest end of the plane to avoid any run-ins with Bear. At least for a few hours, anyways. She knew they were going to have to talk eventually. And if she were honest, she didn't want to fight with him. She'd rather be on good terms with him since they'd be spending a couple of weeks working together.

She took one more swipe at the expanding ink spot and finally gave up, realizing it was a lost cause.

"Having issues?" The deep voice behind her asked, making her jump. She didn't need to look to know who it was. She spun around so fast she felt dizzy. She quickly sobered and came face-to-face with Bear.

Damn him and his stealthy capabilities.

She thought about searching for a place to escape to, but her choices were slim to none, considering she was approximately thirty-five thousand feet in the air somewhere over the Atlantic Ocean. She met Bear's gaze and knew it was inevitable. She huffed out an annoyed breath. *Just get it over with so we can all move on.*

"May I sit so we can talk? Please," he asked, gesturing to the empty seat next to hers.

She wondered what he would do if she told him no. Thinking of possible scenarios almost made her giggle. She wouldn't do that. At least this time, he asked and even said please. That starkly contrasted with his actions last weekend when he demanded that she cancel her trip.

"I guess I don't really have a choice, seeing there are no viable exits at my disposal."

She heard Bear's deep laugh as she plopped down in her seat. He followed, and she tried to ignore the butterflies in her belly as he slid his large body into the seat next to her, and his muscular thigh brushed against hers. He turned his body towards her, and she caught the scent of his cologne permeating the air she was breathing. It was the same cologne he wore when they were together. It was also one of her weaknesses. When she would visit him, she would always steal his t-shirts and spritz them with cologne so she could have his scent around her.

She closed her eyes and inhaled deeply, allowing the fresh woodsy-based fragrance emitting from him to attack her sense of smell. It was intoxicating, and she couldn't get enough of it. She was spellbound by the aroma, combined with the close proximity of his powerful body engulfing her. She felt her body being pulled toward the enchanting scent as the smell grew stronger.

Hearing what sounded like a deep, low growl close to her ear, her eyes shot open. Once her brain fog lifted, she found herself invading Bear's personal space. If she leaned any further, she'd be in his lap. A wave of embarrassment washed over her, and she quickly pulled herself upright. She covered her face with her hands, feeling the blush warm her cheeks. What in the hell had come over her? How was she supposed to face him after losing her self-control like she had?

Bear's rumble of laughter compelled her to lower the makeshift shield of her hands from her face. She braced herself for the humiliation she was sure that would follow. She still couldn't look him in the eye. Staring straight ahead, she tried apologizing, but her mouth hung open. What was she supposed to say? *'Sorry I almost jumped your bones, but your cologne entranced me.'*

She couldn't just sit there gaping at him like a fish. The first thing she had to do was calm her nerves.

"*It's just Bear.*" She told herself. "*Bear, the man who I grew up with. The man I married—the man who knew all my secrets—well, most of them. I've had many worse embarrassing moments around him than what I did just now. Hell, I've farted in front of him. Though, that was an accident. Still embarrassing. Or, the time we were hiking, and I had to pee, so I found a spot to squat but lost my balance and ended up tumbling down the hill with my pants around my ankles. Again, much worse. Not to mention the number of times I've tripped and fallen in front of him, or the first time I got drunk and he found me in his parent's flowerbed puking.*"

Now that she talked it out with herself, it wasn't as bad as she first thought. Yeah, it was still embarrassing, but not nearly as embarrassing as some of her prior situations.

Taking a deep breath, she turned to face Bear. When their eyes locked, she didn't waste any time saying what she needed to so that she could put the moment behind her.

"I'm so sorry. I have no idea what happened a moment ago," she confessed, hoping he wasn't upset. But, if he was, he could add it to his ongoing list of reasons why he was angry with her.

"Joce, it's okay. I promise," he answered, a small smile playing on his lips.

Jocelyn raised a suspecting eyebrow at his sudden change in temperament.

"Okay, what have you done with the ambitious Bear from earlier?" Not that she wanted that side of Bear to reappear, but she was curious about what had changed so suddenly.

With a heavy sigh, he raked his fingers through his short dirty blonde hair. It was a habit of his when he was stressed or nervous.

She clasped her shaky hands together and placed them in her lap.

"What did you want to talk about?"

"First, thank you," he told her, and she slightly tilted her head.

"Thanking me for what?"

"For giving me this opportunity."

She looked away nervously for a moment before returning her eyes to his gaze. "What can I say? You were persistent."

He slowly nodded his head. "I am. Especially when there's something that I want."

The way he said those words in that deep suave voice of his and licked across his bottom lip almost made her libido explode. She swallowed hard.

"What is it exactly that you want?"

Looking deep into her eyes, he answered with one powerful word that shook her to her core.

"You."

Jocelyn sat frozen in her seat. She stared at Bear, unable to think of anything to say. At first, she thought she may have misheard him, but seeing the intensity and seriousness in his eyes as he stared fixedly at her, she hadn't been mistaken.

"Jocelyn…" he called her name when she didn't respond, and she shook her head, denying his proclamation. She remembered how often she desired to hear that over the last ten years. However, the question she had was, why now? What was so different now than ten years ago, besides the fact they were older and a bit wiser? She was still a hydrologist, and he was still a SEAL.

"Why?" She probed.

For someone so brave and full of courage, she couldn't overlook the vulnerability he expressed in his body language and expression.

He reached out and covered her hands with his large hand. Immediately, the warmth from his simple touch spread through her body. Her insides filled with an electrifying sensation she hadn't felt in years.

Instead of answering her, he handed a file folder to her. She moved her hands to take it but simultaneously gave him a quizzical look as questions filled her eyes with unspoken words.

She watched his Adam's apple bob as he swallowed. The movement looked sexy as hell, but she saw something pass in the shadow of his eyes. His actions mimicked someone who was nervous.

"Go on and open it," he instructed her.

She damned her shaky hands and knew that he saw it too. She took a deep breath and flipped open the folder.

She had to do a double-take when she saw the paper on top. Why in the hell was he showing her their divorce papers? Better yet, why would he bring them with him?

Her head filled with questions upon questions. However, the longer she stared at the document that shattered her world, the more anger overcame her. Was this his idea of a prank? To sit here and tell her he wanted her and then throw their divorce papers in front of her as a reminder that she couldn't have him?

Raising her head, she fixed her watery eyes on him.

"What is this?" She gritted out, visibly upset by his so-called present.

He responded by giving her a look as if she had asked the craziest question.

"It's our divorce paperwork."

She rolled her eyes in annoyance. "I can see that. Why in the hell are you showing it to me? Did you bring it along to remind me? Or wait, was this your idea of a joke to entertain your friends?"

She saw his cheeks cave in. She recognized the look and knew he was mad. *Well, good! Because so am I!* Before she could utter another word, Bear's large hand covered her mouth, silencing her.

She stared wide-eyed at him before narrowing her eyes. She thought about biting his hand.

"Be quiet and flip to the last page," he told her calmly, and again something in his eyes told her to listen to him. *Damn, those eyes!*

She snorted a sigh but did as he requested and flipped to the signature page of the document.

"Okay. Am I supposed to be looking at something?" She asked with an attitude.

"Look at the very bottom."

She looked it over. Her signature was signed in blue ink, and just under it was his scribbled chicken scratch of a signature in black ink. She looked back at him.

"I don't understand what you want me to look at."

"Don't look at what's there. Look at what's missing."

Jesus, if she knew she'd be playing detective, she would've brought along her Sherlock Holmes outfit. She looked it over again for the umpteenth time, and it all looked the same as it did ten years ago. Just as she was about to ask him to point out whatever he wanted her to see, he took her pointer finger and moved it to the very bottom of the page, where a blank signature line was located.

"What don't you see?" He repeated, and she could tell he was doing everything he could to be patient with her. Bear wasn't a very patient man. He never was, even as a kid. That's probably why he makes a good leader because he gets shit done timely.

She looked closely and saw it was the signature line the judge would sign their name on.

"The judge's signature," she answered, looking at him. "I don't understand. These are the original papers I signed and sent back to you."

He twisted his body even more and was now practically caging her in. He took both her hands in his and gently rubbed the tops with the pads of his thumbs. As worked up as she was, his touch was soothing.

"What I'm about to tell you is going to sound crazy, but I see it as a second chance to right my wrongs."

"Bear...."

"Jocelyn, when you returned these papers to me, I gave them to my attorney. Somewhere in the process, he misplaced the file. A few months later, he became ill and passed away." He paused briefly and took a deep breath as if the news had affected him deeply. "I moved around so much early in my career that I didn't know what I had and didn't. I'm very organized and detailed regarding my job because I have seven men who I consider my brothers who rely on me and my decisions. But I'm so unsystematic regarding my personal and home life. Over the last ten years, my belongings were shuffled from one apartment to another until I settled in a house."

He hesitated a moment, and Jocelyn could see the struggle he was battling. Was Bear actually nervous? It took something of great magnitude to get Bear worked up. Unexpectedly, she found herself entwining her fingers with his her touch would help him.

He looked down at their joined hands before raising his head and staring deep into her eyes.

"Jocelyn, when you were injured and were lying in that hospital bed with a head injury, the regret I've carried around for the last ten years amplified. Seeing you at Camp David stirred something deep inside me that I couldn't let go of.

One night I pulled a box out of my closet filled with all our memories. I came across the file with our divorce papers and decided to look through it all to punish myself."

Jocelyn couldn't help it and felt a tear escape her eye. She tried to wipe it away, but he beat her to it and brushed away the wetness.

"The problem was the one document I was specifically looking for was missing—the signed copy from the court. When I couldn't find it anywhere else, I called the attorney's office and spoke with his daughter, who took over the firm."

He squeezed her hands tighter. "That phone call I got the day at my parent's party was the attorney calling me back. It was why I needed to talk to you. Joce, the divorce was never finalized. It was never sent to the courts."

Jocelyn tried hard to hold back her tears as Bear spoke about the past and the time of their divorce. But his last two sentences sent a shockwave through her. Releasing his hands, she covered her mouth and let the words sink in.

"Are you saying..."

He nodded. "We are still husband and wife."

Jocelyn suddenly felt sick. She started sweating, and a wave of nausea washed over her. She bent over and held her stomach.

"I know this is a shock to you. Believe me. I was floored when the attorney told me."

She closed her eyes and shook her head, trying to will away the tears. She suddenly felt a tightness in her chest, as if all the air was being sucked from her body.

As if knowing what she was feeling, Bear rubbed his large hand against her back in soothing strokes.

"Breathe, Joce," he whispered close to her ear as he continued rubbing her back.

She took a big breath. She knew if she released it, she would completely lose it.

Again, he knew her too well. "Just let it out, sweetheart," he said, and she did. She even found herself leaning into him, and he held her as he let her process the shock.

Taking some shallow breaths and wiping away the tears that wouldn't stop falling, she looked up at him.

"That was the call that Clover said you got. It was right before the fireworks started. You found me and—"

"I was by your side," he finished her sentence, taking the words out of her mouth.

"I don't understand. How did neither of us realize?"

"I guess we were both so busy with things going on that we didn't think to check on it."

"So, what happens now?" She asked, not knowing what to do. Hell, she wasn't even sure what to think.

"We have two options." He lifted the original paperwork revealing another set of documents, except those were unsigned. "Option one, we rip this whole folder up, take the opportunity we've been given, and make the most of the rest of our lives together."

"What?"

"I know for you it probably sounds insane, but Joce, I want another shot at what we had."

"So, just because a piece of paper says we're still legally married, you think that after ten years of being a part, we can just pick up where we left off?"

"I'm saying it exactly that way."

She began to lower her head, but he lifted her chin with his fingers. "I know you felt that connection at my parent's house as we watched the fireworks together. The way you relaxed in my arms. The spark in your brown eyes told me there is hope for us."

Jocelyn had to look away because she couldn't look into his eyes, knowing he was right. She had felt the connection between them. There was no denying that the spark was still there. As much as she would love to grab those papers and rip them to shreds, she knew she couldn't make that decision now, not with all the raw emotions surrounding the situation. She needed time to digest all the information.

She wiped away the tears from her eyes before turning to look at him. She closed the folder sitting on her lap.

"What is the other option?" She asked, her voice shaking.

Bear licked his bottom lip. "Option two; if you want to walk away, I'll accept that and sign these documents."

She stared into his eyes. He had so many emotions running through his eyes. She saw sadness and some annoyance, but what touched her deeply was the love she saw. He really did still love her. But again, she couldn't make such a rash decision on the spot.

"I can't give you an answer right now. I need time to think and process everything. I need to make sure I have a clear head when making that decision. And right now, I don't have that."

He covered her hands. "I don't want you to answer right now. When you decide, you know where to find me."

She nodded her head. He leaned over and pressed his warm lips against her cheek, and she closed her eyes, savoring the moment. "I have and will always love you," he whispered in her ear before standing up and walking back to his seat.

Jocelyn sat back in her seat, bringing the folder up and holding it against her chest. She turned her head so her face was against the wall. Only then did she allow more of her tears to fall.

CHAPTER SEVEN

Bear stood next to Jay Bird while waiting for the two vehicles to be unloaded from the plane.

"How'd your talk with Jocelyn go?" Jay Bird asked.

"She knows the truth, and she knows how I feel. The ball is in her court. She said she needed some time to process the information."

For the remainder of the flight, she had stayed tucked into her corner with her nose buried in paperwork or her laptop. He did catch her a few times, stealing a glance in his direction. He had tried to catch a little sleep, but every time he closed his eyes, he saw Jocelyn's eyes filled with tears. It had taken a lot of self-control for him not to go and comfort her.

"Did she say anything to give you a hint of what she's feeling?"

"She said she needed some time to process the information."

"Understandable. What do you think she feels?"

Bear looked away as he thought about Jay Bird's question. He recalled when he spoke with her and her expressions during the discussion. There were moments of sadness, anger, and confusion that crossed her face, but there were also brief moments where hope and understanding filled her dark chocolate eyes. Hearing her tell him that she had waited ten years for him to say to her, and that alone provided him a sense of optimism that there was a possibility they could work things out.

"I think she feels it too. I believe there's still a spark between her and me. But I think she's also scared, which I can't blame her for feeling that way considering the past and how the situation unfolded."

"Then use this time here to give her a little space while she does her job. As an observer, I can tell you both still have feelings for one another. My only advice is don't let the person you love slip away, especially when you're given a second chance. Although, if I were her, I might let you sweat it out first," Jay Bird said with a slight grin, and Bear laughed.

"I deserve it."

Right at that moment, Jocelyn walked up with Duke and Snow. She had covered her eyes with a pair of silver-framed aviator sunglasses.

"What's the plan?" Snow asked.

"As soon as the SUVs are offloaded, we can head out," Bear replied.

"What about the equipment and crew?" Aussie questioned.

"They handle their own transportation. They also normally take care of their lodging, but the village chief arranged with a neighboring village and secured them space to stay. This way, they'll be able to stay close by instead of commuting back and forth."

"What about their equipment? How will it all get transported to the site?" Jay Bird asked.

"Again, the drilling company manages those logistics. They have contracts with equipment transport companies all over the world." Jocelyn pointed to all the equipment and materials sitting on the tarmac. "All of that will be stored in a nearby warehouse tonight, and the transport company will pick it up tomorrow and bring it to the site. Ralph said the crew is staying in the city tonight along with security detail to keep an eye on everything."

"That's smart, especially around here, as things are known to disappear mysteriously," Jay Bird said as he opened the tailgate of one of the SUVs and started loading stuff inside.

Playboy pulled up in the second SUV, and all the others started loading the rest of their equipment in the back.

Bear noticed Jocelyn standing off to the side, looking a little lost. Her two bags and a smaller duffle bag sat at her feet. He walked over to her.

"Is everything okay?" He asked.

She looked up at him, and he wished she weren't wearing those glasses so he could see her eyes.

"That's a loaded question at the moment," she replied, and Bear immediately wanted to kick himself in the ass for his choice of words.

"I'm sorry, Joce. That's not what I was implying." Jesus, could he fuck this up any worse?

"No need for apologies."

Joker walked over. "Hey, Joce. Can I grab your bags and put them in the SUV?"

"Oh! Yes. Thank you."

Joker picked up the two larger bags. Before he walked away, he looked at Bear. "Everything's loaded, so we can head out when you're ready."

Bear nodded. "We'll be over in a minute."

Once Joker was out of earshot, he stepped in front of Jocelyn.

"Joce, look. I know springing that news on you earlier wasn't the best timing as we both have jobs to do here."

"It isn't your fault. Obviously, I had a little time on my hands to think a bit, and if I'm being honest, some blame falls on me. If I had returned your call yesterday when I got my phone back, we wouldn't be in the awkward situation we're in right now. We'd still be facing a decision we need to make." She took a deep breath. "Though, it wouldn't be a front-page news story as we embark on a critical project that leaders worldwide will be watching."

Bear extended his arm and went to cup her cheek but pulled back at the last minute. She wasn't his. Yet. Plus, he promised her time.

"If we're placing blame. I believe the whole situation is my fault. If I hadn't—"

Jocelyn cut him off. "I thought we agreed not to talk about this right now. I need to focus on why I'm here. And you need to focus on your assignment."

He wanted to tell her that she was his assignment, but he understood what she was saying. And he told her to take her time in making her decision, even though it would drive him crazy until she did.

"Well, then, Ms. Thompson. I believe it's time to escort you to your destination."

As he guided her toward the SUVs, she slowed her pace.

"What's wrong?"

She looked between the two SUVs. "Which one am I supposed to ride in?"

"It's your choice."

She turned toward him. "Which one are you riding in?" She asked, and he pointed to the dark blue vehicle upfront.

"Then, I'll ride in that one," she told him, offering him a small smile.

～

Jocelyn thought her brief interaction with Bear went well. They were both civil and orderly. She considered it baby steps.

Having time to think through the situation, she was looking forward to sitting down with him and having an in-depth discussion on what drove him to file for divorce in the first place. After the initial shock had worn off and she had a little time to think, she concluded that she couldn't in good conscience decide until she heard what he had to say. Her body's instinct might be to jump right back into his strong arms, but it was her heart that she needed to protect.

As she approached the SUV, Duke smiled.

"Are you riding with us?"

"I am."

"Well, climb on in and scoot to the middle," he told her, opening the back passenger side door.

Nails was already sitting on the other side as she slid across the leather seat. Once she was settled, Duke got in. As Bear climbed into the driver's seat, Jay Bird took the front passenger seat. As soon as he started the vehicle, the first thing Jocelyn did was reach for the AC controls for the back, putting it on full blast.

The only downfall about living in the village for the next several weeks was that she'd have no air conditioning, and temperatures this time of the year averaged between one hundred and one hundred five degrees Fahrenheit during the day. Some days were even hotter.

While Bear and Jay Bird fiddled with the GPS, Nails leaned toward her.

"What are you wearing?" he asked.

She looked down at her jeans and plain dark green t-shirt.

"What's wrong with what I'm wearing?" She asked, wondering if she may have missed some dress code. Though she researched cultural attire, nothing popped out where she was required to wear specific clothing or accessories as a female.

Nails grinned. "Nothing is wrong with your attire. In fact, you fill out those jeans and t-shirt quite nicely."

"Nails!" Bear reprimanded, causing Duke and Jay Bird to laugh. Jocelyn hid her smile, but she couldn't stop herself from blushing. Thankfully, she had previously met Nails and knew about his friendliness toward the ladies.

"Bear didn't let me finish. I was referring to your perfume or whatever you're wearing."

"Oh! It's probably my lotion. It's called *Cinnamon Donut Swirl*."

"Damn. It smells so good that I could take a bite of you."

Jocelyn swore she heard a low growl come from the front.

Duke shook his head, though, with the small grin on his lips, he obviously was still amused. "Nails. You are going to get your ass kicked."

Grinning like a fool, Nails said, "Nah. Jocelyn knows I'm just playing. Right?" He asked, looking at her for confirmation.

"Sure. Whatever you say."

"So, how far is this village from here?" Duke asked, changing the subject.

"It's about two and a half hours," Bear answered as they pulled out of the parking lot.

Jocelyn looked down at her phone. She had already pulled up the GPS on her app.

"It's two hours and twenty-one minutes, to be exact."

"Is that right?" Bear asked, glancing in the rearview mirror at her. She didn't miss the small smile tugging his lips.

"It is, according to *my* GPS."

"Well, we'll have to see if yours is accurate."

Before settling back in the seat, she pulled her camera from her duffel bag. She had taken up a little bit of photography before she started traveling the world. Once her travels took her to places she'd most likely never return to, she invested in a decent point-and-shoot digital camera to document her adventures.

Even though Jocelyn was tired from the long flight, she wasn't about to doze off. She wanted to take in the beauty of what Chad had to offer.

She learned in her travel journeys that even the most underdeveloped locations offered a sliver of beauty. Whether it was the people or the environment, there was always a form of beauty for her to photograph and document.

So, for the next two hours, she would sit back and enjoy the moment because she planned to hit the ground running once tomorrow rolled around. The sooner they prepped the site area, the sooner they could start drilling. If they could begin the drilling earlier and everything went according to plan, she could potentially be back home earlier than expected.

☙

The drive took longer than expected due to the conditions of the roadway in certain areas they passed through. Of course, the guys ribbed her about her wrong GPS calculation and her making them stop so she could get a picture of herself by Lake Chad. But the trooper that she was, she took it in stride. She even got some cheap shots at Bear about him driving slower than a snail's pace, which the guys found hilarious.

As she suspected, the scenery along the drive didn't disappoint. Chad was broken up into three climate zones. Messandai, the village where they'll be staying, was in the sub-tropical zone, where the country's northern desert transitions to the more tropical region to the south. It was primarily flat, sandy, and rock-strewn land with some mixed vegetation. Since it was the rainy season, the vegetation was greener than the dry season.

In more remote areas where there was no human civilization, she had seen some amazing wildlife native to the land. She had been lucky enough to capture a few pictures. Her favorite was the cheetah resting on top of a large boulder. It was beautiful but such a powerful predator.

The drive was uneventful, but the closer they got to the village, the more she felt on edge. She chalked it up to nerves and stress from the job she was sent there for. But now she also had to contend with her and Bear's situation hanging over her head. During the drive, she caught Bear looking at her in the rearview mirror several times. She tried not to stare back, but it was hard. He looked so in charge and fierce. *Sheesh*...who was she kidding. He looked hot and sexy as hell.

It was so much to take in, and she couldn't afford any distractions. This project was too important, and many people were watching on a world level. She couldn't screw it up because her ex-husband informed her they weren't exes and were still married. *Jesus!* She couldn't make this stuff up.

Duke's voice shook her from her thoughts as they rounded a bend.

"Would you look at that," he stated, looking out his window.

"What is it?" Jocelyn asked, leaning over Duke's lap to get a look.

"It looks like you've got your very own welcoming committee," Bear commented as he maneuvered the vehicle to an area near a large group of people standing.

A smile slowly formed on Jocelyn's lips as she saw what the guys were talking about. Numerous children were standing together waving small American stick flags. One little girl who looked to be about eight or nine held a small sign that read "Welcome," while another child, a boy about ten or eleven, held another sign that read "Thank you."

"That's fucking awesome," Jay Bird commented before he started snapping pictures with his phone.

Once Bear had parked the vehicle, they met up with the team traveling in the other SUV and walked over to the crowd. She noticed as they walked how the team subtly surrounded her on both sides and from behind as if they were forming a human shield. The execution of their movement was so smooth and flawless that it looked rehearsed.

An older, Chadian gray-haired woman wearing a beautiful bold yellow, orange, and green lappa skirt and black shirt standing near the front of the crowd stepped forward. With a big welcoming smile, she extended her hand to Jocelyn.

"You must be Ms. Thompson."

Smiling back, Jocelyn reached out and shook the kind woman's hand. She knew from research that Chadian Arabic and English were primarily spoken in Massendai. But she was surprised at how eloquent and fluent Flora's English was. It was very welcoming, considering Jocelyn didn't know Arabic.

Jocelyn offered Flora a warm smile. "That would be me, and please call me Jocelyn."

"As you wish, Jocelyn. My name is Flora. It is a pleasure to meet you."

"It's nice to meet you as well, Flora." She pointed to Flora's attire. "That is a beautiful outfit you're wearing."

"Oh! Why, thank you. One of the ladies in the village made it."

"Really?"

Flora nodded. "She makes many clothes for people here in the village."

"Well, I just might have to hire her to make one for me."

"I can definitely introduce you to her."

Jocelyn then remembered the eight hulking men standing around her and who many villagers were gawking at.

"Flora, I'd like to introduce some team members to you." She turned to her left. "This is Bear, and next to him is Snow." Then gesturing to her right with her hand. "Over here is Duke and Joker." Then she pointed behind her. "The other four in the back, from left to right, are Nails, Aussie, Jay Bird, and Playboy."

Flora gave them all a warm, welcoming smile. "It is nice to meet you all." She laughed. "And what unique names you have."

"Likewise, ma'am," Bear stated, trying to hide his amusement at Flora's comment about their names.

Flora smiled and then turned toward the crowd of people. "Well, Jocelyn and team, welcome to Massendai."

The little girl and boy holding the signs stepped forward next to Flora. The little girl held a small white flowerpot in her hands with a little pink flower blossoming in the middle.

"Ms. Jocelyn, this is for you."

Jocelyn crouched down next to the children, and the little girl handed her the flower.

Jocelyn smiled as she accepted the beautiful pot and flower. "What's your name, sweetie?"

"Amira."

"Amira. That is a beautiful name. Thank you so much for this pretty flower. That was very sweet of you."

The little girl smiled, and Jocelyn saw she had recently lost two teeth. She was beautiful and soft-spoken. Her light brown skin was flawless. She had gorgeous dark brown almond-shaped eyes framed with thick black eyelashes. Her long black hair was braided with what looked to be small little flowers placed strategically throughout it.

"This is my brother, Maxime," Amira said, pointing at the boy about a foot taller than her. He, too, was a handsome little fellow.

Jocelyn gave the boy a warm smile.

"Hello, Maxime. It's nice to meet you."

The young man returned the smile and shook Jocelyn's hand.

"It's nice to meet you too, Ms. Jocelyn. We are happy that you are here."

A woman behind the children cleared her throat, gaining Jocelyn's attention. When Jocelyn stood up, she locked eyes with the woman. Standing there with her arms crossed and lips pressed together, she looked annoyed. But Jocelyn saw something else in the woman's dark eyes. There was a coldness radiating from them. And it appeared to be aimed at Jocelyn. However, before she could put any more thought into it, Flora introduced the woman, though Jocelyn didn't miss the scowl that Flora threw at the woman.

"Jocelyn, meet Amira and Maxime's mother, Nandi."

Jocelyn said hello, offered the woman a smile, and extended her hand out, but the woman showed no expression and nodded, leading Jocelyn to pull her hand back in. *Awkward*, Jocelyn thought.

"You have beautiful children."

"Thank you," the woman spoke in a low monotone voice.

Flora gave Nandi a stern look, but the woman seemed unfazed by Flora's silent reprimand. Flora then cleared her throat.

"We got lucky when Nandi came to Massendai to stay with her aunt. She studies traditional medicine, which is helpful, considering most villages like ours don't have access to a full-time doctor."

Since learning she would be traveling to Chad, Jocelyn had done an excessive amount of research on the country, and one of the things she remembered reading about was how villages such as Massendai relied on traditional medicine practices due to not having twenty-four-hour access to doctors and pharmaceuticals.

Jocelyn looked at Nandi. "I've read about African traditional medicine. Which specialty do you practice, divination, spiritualism, or herbalism?"

Nandi's eyes widened, surprised by Jocelyn's knowledge of African culture.

"I mainly practice in herbal medicines," she responded in a low, non-enthusiastic tone.

Jocelyn smiled. "That's impressive."

"Yes, it is. As I said, it was a Godsend when she arrived," Flora commented.

Nandi then cleared her throat. "I'm sorry, but my children and I must take our leave."

The little girl looked up at her mother and frowned. "Can't we stay a little longer?"

"No!" Nandi snapped, causing Amira's eyes to fill with tears.

Bear suddenly stepped forward and crouched down, getting on the same eye level as the little girl.

"Hey. You can come to visit us tomorrow or whenever you'd like to. That is if it's okay with your mom." Bear looked up at the mom, who wasn't pleased he had put her on the spot.

Nandi pursed her lips before giving her head a quick nod. "We'll see. Now, come," she sternly ordered, pulling the two sulking children away.

Bear stood up and kept his position next to Jocelyn. On the other hand, Flora stared daggers at Nandi as she walked away from the group. Once Nandi and the kids were out of sight, Flora turned her attention back to Jocelyn and smiled.

"I apologize for Nandi's behavior. She's been under some stress with her aunt's declining health."

"That is understandable," Jocelyn replied. However, Jocelyn felt there was another underlining reason for Nandi's rudeness. Maybe their interaction over the next two weeks would be minimal, and she wouldn't have to deal with her.

Moving on from Nandi's rude behavior, Flora smiled.

"We, the people of Massendai, are thrilled you're here. My husband, Chief Kosso, sends his apologies for not being here to welcome you. However, he had some village business to tend to."

"I'm happy and excited to be here," Jocelyn replied. Helping others would always put a smile on her face.

"When we were told about this project, many people here had doubts that anyone would actually show up."

"Why is that?"

"Because this village has been promised a working well many times over the years, only for our dreams to be crushed."

"Well, I can assure you that by the time I leave here, you and everyone in this village will have close access to clean drinking water."

"Once they see it for themselves, I can assure you that you'll become the newest angel to Massendai."

"I don't know about that," Jocelyn said, slightly embarrassed. She wasn't a fan of having attention on her.

"I promise you, my dear, you'll be appreciated more than you know." Flora smiled and waved her hand. "Come. I'll show you to your living quarters."

Jocelyn kept a lookout as they made their way to another section of the village, making mental notes on certain landmarks to help her remember where places were. Flora pointed out that every family is given a piece of land. The land parcels were of various sizes depending on the number of family members. Most of the housing structures were mud huts.

They made a right turn and traveled down a narrower dirt path bordered on both sides by vegetation. About thirty or forty yards, the path opened to a larger piece of land. In the middle sat a rectangular brick-and-mortar structure. Flora stopped and faced them.

"This is the building you've been given for your stay."

Jocelyn was shocked. She tried her best to hold back her excitement, knowing she'd be housed in an actual solid structure, unlike the small huts that most villagers have on their properties.

She studied the details of the building. There was a door at the far left end and a second door, more toward the middle. Flora opened the middle one, and they all entered. It was one big open room with three rectangular metal tables, several folding chairs leaning against the wall, and a few shelves attached to one wall. Shockingly, it was squeaky clean.

Jocelyn turned toward Flora. "Is this where we're all staying?"

The guys all seemed nice, and of course, she knew Bear, but she wasn't sure about cohabitating with them. That would be a little awkward. However, if that were the plan, she'd deal with it.

Flora seemed to understand what she was asking as she smiled and waved her hand for Jocelyn to follow her. They went back out the door they had come in and followed the concrete walkway to the other door. Flora opened the door, and Jocelyn followed her in. Of course, the others came along as well. It was a similar set-up as the other room, just smaller.

"This can be yours. Unless you'd prefer to stay with the men?" Flora said jokingly, and Jocelyn laughed.

"This will work just fine for me." She looked around the room, trying to figure out what the building was once used for.

"What is this building?" Joker asked as he looked around.

"It used to be where we kept our crops to keep them dry. But over the years, our village grew in population, leading to more farmers, which meant more crops. Needless to say, we outgrew this building. Now it just sits here. Sometimes the kids like to come here and play."

"Where do you store the crops now?" Bear questioned, and Jocelyn was interested in the answer too.

"Three years ago, the village, with the assistance of a government grant, had a newer and bigger structure built near the village's south end. With the new building having easier access, everyone moved their stash there, leaving this building empty."

Jocelyn was surprised they didn't use it for something else. Overall, it was a great building. It was sturdy; she even saw two fire pits built into the wall surrounding the building near the front. Several ideas came to mind on what it could be used for. Maybe once the well was complete, she would present a few ideas to Flora.

"Keep in mind that we share our land with wildlife. And while some creatures may look beautiful and interesting, many are deadly. So be vigilant when walking around, especially when you're in areas where there is a lot of brush. Because of the temperatures here, most animals stay low during the day and come out at night when it's a bit cooler. I do recommend keeping the doors closed to avoid letting any critters in.

The village pretty much goes quiet when the sun goes down. We have no electricity, so if people wander about at night, they use flashlights or lanterns. I didn't know what equipment you'd bring with you, but I put three lanterns in the other room, and there is one in that small cabinet right over there." Flora pointed to the small, rusted metal cabinet under the shelf. Most people go to bed in the early evening because their days start at sun up. Feel free to use either fire pits out front as well."

"Thank you, Flora. Your hospitality is much appreciated," Jocelyn said.

"If you need anything or have any questions, just find me. For now, I'll let you all get settled in. I'm not sure when my husband is expected to return. I know he'll want to come and welcome you himself."

"I'd like that, and I look forward to meeting him when he does return."

Flora turned to leave but spun back around. "Oh. I forgot to mention. I had several buckets of water brought in for your use, along with the purification tablets. Tomorrow just let me know how many you'll need daily, and I'll ensure they're delivered to you."

"Thank you, Flora."

"Have a good evening, Ms. Jocelyn, and company."

Once Flora disappeared down the dirt path, Jocelyn took her time to look more around the room. It felt like she had been handed the keys to a mansion. She had the same metal table the guys had in their room. The folding chair beside it looked so old and rusted that it would crumble when she sat down. She walked over to the small cabinet that Flora pointed out and opened it to find the lantern and a book of matches.

Reaching the cabinet, she pulled the items out and put them on the table. When she looked up, she found the guys looking at her. At first, she was a little taken aback, and she began to fidget under their intense gaze. But then Bear stepped forward with his dazzling grin, instantly putting her at ease.

"What do you say we get the vehicles and unload everything?" He suggested, and Jocelyn nodded. That was a good idea. Plus, it would physically keep her busy, and she could avoid all her thoughts going to Bear and their situation.

"Sounds good. The pathway looks wide enough to drive the vehicles up to the front."

"Alright," Bear sounded off and glanced at Playboy since he had the keys to the second vehicle. "Playboy and I will be back in a few minutes."

Bear's absence left an awkward silence among the rest of them.

"I guess we can be grateful for our accommodations," Jocelyn said as she waved her hand around the room.

"You're not kidding," Aussie stated as he walked around the room, closely inspecting the walls and ceiling. Jocelyn wondered what he was doing, and her curiosity must've shown because Joker looked at her.

"If you're wondering what Aussie's doing, he's looking for bugs."

Jocelyn felt her insides cringe, and she scrunched up her nose. She didn't mind getting dirty or roughing it, but she didn't like creepy crawlers. "Bugs? I hate bugs," she blurted out, and Joker laughed.

"Not those types of bugs. We always look for anything hidden that could be spying on us."

"Oh!" Her forehead wrinkled as she looked back at Joker. "Why would there be anything like that in here?"

Joker smirked but in an arrogant way. "If you've been on missions with us, you'd understand. We always ensure the coast is clear no matter where we are."

"Gotcha," she replied, even though that sort of freaked her out. She definitely didn't want anyone spying on her. The thought of someone watching her through a camera sent a shiver down her spine.

While they waited for Bear and Playboy to get back, she spent the next few minutes talking with the guys. They each told her a little bit about what their main focus was on the team. She figured they all did a little of everything, which they did, but they each specialized in a certain job function. Joker was a sniper, which she already knew from talking with Clover when she visited Camp David. Nails dealt with explosives, which she felt suited his crazy personality. Aussie was a close-quarter combat/breacher. Playboy had the brains for intelligence. Duke was the designated corpsman who took care of patching up the team when needed, which she hoped wasn't often. She wasn't naïve and knew they all probably had some close calls. But what surprised her was when Duke explained that there were times he'd also treat civilians in combat zones when he could. Snow had advanced training in unmanned aerial vehicles, and Jay Bird was one of the best hand-to-hand combat fighters. She wanted to ask them about Bear, but as soon as she opened her mouth, she heard the vehicles pull up, ending their brief "get to know you" session.

The nine of them worked as a team for the next two hours, unloading and getting settled in. It had been an adventure, considering Bear practically demanded that either he or one of the others bunk in her room. He finally settled down and reasoned when Jay Bird reminded him that two of them would always be on night watch, including standing guard at the front of the building, where the only entrance to either room was located.

She prayed Bear wasn't going to be up her ass and overprotective the entire two weeks. Either way, it was definitely going to be an experience she'd never forget.

CHAPTER EIGHT

William Corsica slid out of his bed and stepped into his jeans. He looked at the rumpled sheets half covering the naked woman still sleeping on the other side of the bed. Mieke was one of his regular girls he'd hook up with. She wasn't the best lay, but she was enough to satisfy him until he needed to scratch his itch again.

He walked to the luxury ensuite bathroom and relieved himself before brushing his teeth. He splashed some cold water on his face, then patted the hand towel dry. Before he left the room, he ensured everything was in its rightful place. He had a significant obsessive-compulsive disorder when it came to neatness and organization. It was a disorder he developed later in life. He believed it stemmed from his childhood. His parents and siblings were absolute slobs. Where he was the complete opposite, always having a clean room and putting things back where they belonged. He even went through several housekeepers and staff until he found ones who obeyed his expectations.

He left the bathroom and heard a deep snore from the bed. His lip curled up in disgust as he looked at the pristine white pillow and sheets smeared with Mieke's red lipstick and dark eye makeup. Out of the many women he slept with, Mieke was the only one who knew about his cleanliness. It pissed him off that she'd wear all that shit to bed, knowing he'd be angry when he saw it. He balled his hands into fists as they itched to yank her out of the bed.

One way to punish her was to deprive her of intimacy with him. That would definitely strike a nerve. One of the benefits of being a regular of his was that he'd make sure she was taken care of. That included cash, which was the only reason Mieke kept coming around. She was currently in school and depended on that money to help fund her medical school.

A slow evil grin spread across his face. In the past, he'd typically wake her up, and they would go to breakfast together at the small café just down the street before he'd drive her home. But today, he was going to deviate.

Instead of waking her up, he would have one of his private security guards wake her and escort her out of the house without explanation. She'd understand what she did wrong if she was as smart as he believed her to be. He gave the woman one last glance before he left the bedroom and walked to his office.

His office was on the other side of the one-story, six-bedroom, five-and-a-half-bath home. He had purchased the second home for entertaining privately and for business. The home was built around a central courtyard providing the perfect entertainment set-up. It boasted a large custom swimming pool with a private rock-enclaved jacuzzi.

The home was quite different in scale from his four-bedroom, five-bath private residence in the heart of Johannesburg. His personal residence was a home he took pride in owning, and he never took a woman there. He refused to taint the home that was his sanctuary.

Built-in 1928, the house had been unkept by its previous owners, but something about the old home called to him when he toured it for the first time with his realtor. His lowball offer was accepted, and he had spent over a year and an excessive amount of cash restoring it to its original condition. It was loaded with exquisite wood features and lush Mediterranean gardens surrounding the exterior, featuring numerous koi ponds, fruit trees, and a large vegetable garden that the staff used for fresh produce. It was magnificent. All he needed was to find someone to share the beauty of it with.

He entered his office and was surprised to find his closest friend, who also served as his business attorney sitting in one of the chairs in front of his desk. An early morning visit from Tau typically wasn't a good thing.

Will ran his hand through his thick, dark, shoulder-length hair as he walked around the glass-top desk and collapsed into the sleek leather chair.

"Late night?" Tau gave him a knowing smirk.

Will nodded and then spotted the two tall coffee cups on the desk. He pointed to them and said, "I'm hoping one of those is for me."

"I figured I'd bring you a cup since I'm here bright and early."

"Thanks." He reached across the desk and gripped the cup in his hand. As soon as he removed the lid, he closed his eyes as the steam from the piping hot coffee filled with a butterscotch aroma hit his nostrils. He lifted the cup to his lips and took a slow sip, savoring the sweet taste. He took one more sip before setting the cup down and eyeing Tau.

"Considering you're here at the ass crack of dawn, I'm going to assume this visit is business-related."

Tau gave him a stern look and nodded. "We may have a problem."

Will quirked his eyebrow. "Problem? What kind of problem?"

Tau slid a yellow file folder across the desk.

More than curious, Will flipped open the folder. As soon as his eyes landed on a five-by-seven photograph of the smiling, brunette woman, he felt all the air leave his body. Tearing his eyes from the picture, he glanced up and met Tau's eyes, which were filled with amusement.

"Who is this beautiful creature?" Will asked, captivated by the woman's natural beauty.

"Jocelyn Thompson. She's the one who could prevent you from getting your hands on that land you've been itching to get a hold of in Massendai."

"What does she have to do with the land?"

Will was a businessman who struck it rich by dabbling in minerals throughout Africa. Chad was high on Will's list of target sites for mineral resources, specifically the area north of Lake Chad, as the mining sector and mineral resources were under development and under-explored in that region.

About nine months ago, he received a tip from an associate of his that there were certain minerals in the earth in and around that village. Out of curiosity, Will hired a team for exploration and ground testing. After analyses were performed on the ground sediments, it was proven that the person was correct. The land held deposits of gold, along with something else that would make him richer than he already was. The findings led Will to make an offer for the land for business purposes, only to be turned away by the village chief. He stated that the land wasn't for sale and never would be. Never one to back down from a good deal, Will took matters into his own hands and inserted someone inside the village to pressure the Chief.

"She arrived yesterday in Massendai with a crew."

"A crew? What type of crew?" He asked with his eyebrows bunched together.

"A drilling crew to dig a well for the village."

Will leaned forward, resting his elbows on the desk. He was confused as well as concerned. If that village got access to clean drinking water, he could forget about claiming ownership of the land because everyone and their brother would flock to the village in droves.

"I don't understand. I thought we handled that issue, and the government nixed that project."

Tau nodded his head in acknowledgment.

"The permitting office had pushed it aside until they got significant pressure from the President of the Transitional Military Council's office. Massendai was apparently added to the list of potential well sites intended for the First Lady of the United States' newly created Global Clean Water initiative. Abakar didn't want to ruffle feathers, so he approved their permit without any argument."

Will's nostrils flared as his temper rose, and he angrily slammed his fist down against the desk, making it shake. Abakar worked for the Ministry of Water and oversaw the department for well permits. From the start, Will knew he couldn't depend on Abakar to follow through on the simple task. Something about him at their first meeting told him to go above him and make sure nothing would get in the way of him gaining access to that land. But the weasel assured him Massendai would never get approval to put a well on that land. Now look where it had landed him.

Will tapped his finger against his chin as he carefully read over the details of the proposed project. Yet, he couldn't stop his eyes from traveling to the photo of Ms. Thompson. He couldn't quite put his finger on it, but something about her appearance and impressive background intrigued him. Tau had put together a comprehensive informational sheet on her.

She was definitely a capable woman and well-educated. She had to be, considering she had been tapped by the First Lady of the United States to run a project of this magnitude. He studied her picture in detail, noting her body's curves and radiant smile. She wasn't skinny by any measure. The woman had meat on her bones, especially her hips and ass. Her beauty set aside. She was no match for him. He always got what he wanted. With or without clean drinking water, that land would be his. Who knew, maybe after meeting Ms. Thompson, he could land a two-for-one deal—the land and her.

Will couldn't stop the grin from spreading across his face.

He heard Tau's low groan, and when he looked across the desk, his friend was giving him a pointed look in return.

"What are you groaning about?"

"I know that look."

"What look?" Will asked as he casually leaned back in his chair, still grinning.

"The shit-eating grin that you've got going on."

"I've got a plan in mind. Secure my travel arrangements for later this week to Massendai. I think I want to meet Ms. Thompson in person."

CHAPTER NINE

Jocelyn stood up from the old rickety chair and stretched her arms above her head. She needed to give her eyes a little break. She'd been staring at the computer, reviewing data on the water flow under the proposed drilling site, double-checking that they were planning to drill in the correct spot.

She had woken up around 3:30 am, and as hard as she tried, she couldn't fall back asleep. She had too much on her mind. So, instead of lying in bed waiting for the sun to come up, she cracked open her laptop.

Playboy had peeked into her room around 4:45 am and was surprised to see her awake. She gave him a little wave, and he nodded his head before leaving her to her work. It made her wonder how often they checked on her throughout the night.

Bringing her arms down, she bent over and touched her toes, stretching her legs. Standing up straight, she shook her arms and legs again to get the blood flowing.

She glanced at her watch. It was only a quarter past seven. She knew a few guys were awake because she heard them talking outside the door. She still had forty-five minutes until the drilling crew was expected to arrive.

Today, they were going to the site to examine the land. From the pictures she saw where the well was supposed to go, much of the area was covered in brush. They would have to decide what needs to be cleared before they even thought about drilling. The main priority was ensuring the well was easily accessible and that no vegetation proposed any risk to it once it was functioning.

She reached into her bag and pulled out a clipboard with a pad of paper attached. She grabbed the pen off the table and the file folder that held the site plans and clipped them onto the clipboard.

Before she went to bed last night, she had placed her suitcases and duffel bag on the table. She didn't want to leave anything on the ground just in case any of the critters that Flora talked about found their way inside. She didn't need the Chadian wildlife making a home in her bags.

She unzipped one of the suitcases and pulled out a clean T-shirt. Since they would be working in the brush and most likely getting dirty, she decided to wear the jeans she had worn the day before. She thought, since those were already ruined from the pen incident, why potentially ruin another pair. She quickly changed her clothes and had just sat down on the cot to put her socks and boots on when someone knocked on the door.

"Come in!" She called out as she laced up her boots.

The door cracked open, and Snow popped his head in.

"Hey! I wanted to let you know that the crew just arrived."

"Oh! Perfect. I'm almost ready. Do you mind letting them know I'll be out in a few minutes?"

"No problem."

She quickly laced up the other boot before standing up and rummaging through her suitcase until she found her toiletry bag.

Flora mentioned there were some buckets of water for them to use. She looked around and didn't see any in her room, so she went in search of them. When she opened the door to the outside, she saw Bear, Duke, and Joker all sitting near one of the fire pits with smoke rising from it, and she wondered what they were cooking.

As soon as she made eye contact with Bear, he graced her with his stunning smile before holding up a cup.

"Coffee?"

"I'd love some," she admitted, knowing coffee was necessary for her in the morning. "But first, I need to brush my teeth. Do you know where the water is that Flora said was around here?"

Joker pointed to four white buckets lined up against the wall. She walked over and lifted the lid off one of them. As soon as she saw what was inside, she scrunched her nose up in disgust.

"What is that?" She asked, studying the dark milky-looking water.

"That's the water," Joker replied.

"Eww. Gross. It looks like days-old chocolate milk that sat out in the heat."

Duke gave her a disgusted look. "That's exactly what I said."

"Here," Bear told her and handed her a plastic water bottle filled with crystal clear liquid. "Take this. It's already been purified and boiled. Nails and Playboy cooked up a few bottles last night, so we'd have some this morning until the supply truck arrives later with the drinking water."

She reached for the bottle, and when their fingers brushed against one another's, Jocelyn immediately felt a flutter sensation in the pit of her belly. She looked at Bear and found him staring intently at her. The way his eyes were locked in on her, she knew he also felt something.

Remembering they weren't alone, she broke eye contact with him and cleared her throat. "Thank you," she said before walking over to the side of the building to brush her teeth. She even splashed a little bit of the water on her face hoping to cool her heated cheeks. She needed to get a handle on herself.

Once she finished, she returned to her room to put her toiletry bag back in the suitcase. Before she headed back outside, she slathered on some sunscreen, grabbed her ball cap, and adjusted it on her head, pulling her long hair through the back and making it into a ponytail. As she passed by the table, she picked up the clipboard. When she opened the door, Bear was standing there with her cup of coffee in his hand.

"Don't forget this," he told her, handing the cup to her.

She smiled. "Thanks."

"You still take two sugars and a dash of cream?"

She tilted her head to the side. "You remember?"

The boyish smile on his face was enough to melt her heart. "There's a lot I remember."

So do I, she thought to herself.

Taking the cup from him, she brought it up to her lips and took a sip. It was warm but not hot. However, it didn't taste too bad, and as long as it gave her the caffeine jolt she needed, she'd be good.

"It's perfect. Thanks."

"You're welcome. Do you want anything to eat before you go out?"

"No, thank you. I had a granola bar with one of those small peanut butter cups a little bit ago." Not knowing when the supply truck with the food would arrive, she made sure to put a few things in her bag that wouldn't spoil.

"A few of the guys and I plan to meet the truck around noon. We'll get it unloaded and everything sorted out."

"You're not coming to the site?"

"We're all going to get a lay of the land. But only Jay Bird and Joker are staying."

Jocelyn wasn't sure why she felt a little disappointed that he wasn't staying. But maybe it was for the best. She'd feel more relaxed and able to concentrate better without having him nearby.

"Okay. Well, I'm ready when you guys are."

He grinned, then motioned with his arm for her to go first. "Lead the way, boss."

She looked over her shoulder and gave him a sassy grin, which made him laugh.

୰

As Jocelyn spoke with the crew that had formed a semi-circle around her, Bear couldn't stop himself from inching closer to listen to her. He loved hearing her voice, but he had to admit that what she explained was quite interesting.

At first, he couldn't understand why they had chosen an area heavily covered in the brush when there was a spot about forty yards to the west that was completely bare. But a few minutes later, one of the crew members asked her about it. She explained the data they received concluded that the ground in the brush area was not only better suited for drilling but that the flow of underground water was more prominent under the same area. Bear hadn't realized how complex groundwater flow and water cycles were.

He listened as she went over a tentative timeline for the project. She explained that when it came to drilling wells, she always used the term "tentative" when discussing the timeline because there was always a possibility of issues arising that could throw off the speed of progression. Initially, Derek told them the project could take four to six weeks. Still, Jocelyn anticipated completing it in two weeks because most of the site planning had already been completed before their arrival.

He wasn't educated much on well digs, so hearing how the process works was interesting.

He was also impressed with her public speaking skills. She was clear and precise. It was obvious she had her audience's attention. She was in her element, and Bear could see her passion for what she did. And it didn't just show in her body language or how she pointed out things or used her hands while speaking. It was the excitement and enthusiasm in her voice as she spoke.

Joker, who stood next to him, leaned closer to him. "I thought you were going to help the others unload the truck," he asked, though Bear didn't miss his amused tone.

It was difficult to assign anyone else to watch over her because he wanted to be her sole protector, but he promised to give her space. And he was a man of his word.

"I like watching her," he replied, not taking his eyes off her.

Joker snickered. "Really? Captain Obvious. You've been watching her since we got on the plane."

Bear snorted a laugh and shook his head. "No. I didn't mean it like that." He pointed at Jocelyn. "Look at her. Anybody watching can see and hear her dedication and commitment to her work. She truly loves what she's doing."

It made Bear realize how much he had missed over the years. But he was more than ready to make up for lost time.

He slapped Joker on the shoulder. "Alright. I'm going to head back and help the others. Call if you need anything."

ತ

Jocelyn tied the last yellow cloth strip to a brush cluster. It was literally a thick, heaping pile of dry, dead vegetation. Any vegetation with a yellow strip would let the crew know it had to be removed when they started clearing the land tomorrow.

A ton of vegetation needed to be removed, but she was careful to save as many trees, flowers, or bushes as possible that still appeared to be living plants. Living plants were a scarce asset in the region, not only for humans but for wildlife, especially the African baobab, which was a valued resource for humans in the form of food, water, and health remedies. While she managed to work around most of the larger living plants, unfortunately, some would have to be removed. The issue was the size of their roots and the direction they grew. Over time they could become problematic, causing issues for the well. However, one of the guys on the crew mentioned he'd worked on another dig, and they had run into the same problem. Instead of completely removing them, they transplanted them to an area far enough from the well. She added that to the plans for tomorrow.

Looking at her watch, she was shocked by the time. No wonder she was tired. She'd been at it for six hours in the one-hundred-degree heat and sun.

She only stopped once during the day for lunch when one of the guys brought over some peanut butter and jelly sandwiches and bags of chips for her and the crew.

She had only eaten half her sandwich and didn't even touch her chips, which was probably why her stomach was rumbling.

She saw Joker and Jay Bird standing off the side. She felt bad that they had to stand out there all day. Although, they did sit and talk with her while they ate their sandwiches. Joker, of course, gushed about Clover most of the time, which was fine. Actually, it was better than fine. It was heartening to see a more personal side of him, not the SEAL everyone saw on the exterior.

Jay Bird, on the other hand, wasn't much of a talker. Even when she kept firing off questions to him, most of his replies were one-word answers. She assumed he was one of those people who liked just to sit back and analyze everything around them. And that was fine also.

She will admit that every man on the team was handsome in their own unique way. Although, she was biased toward her grey-eyed ex…err…husband.

Thinking of Bear, she had been relieved when he finally left to help the others with the truck. His presence at the drill site made it hard for her to concentrate. One, he was a huge distraction in his black cargo pants and olive-green t-shirt, especially when he stood there with his arms folded across his chest and his biceps flexed. He looked amazingly sexy in a rugged way. And two, it reminded her that a decision loomed over her.

She walked over to where the two SEALs stood talking. Jay Bird saw her first and gave her a chin lift.

"I'm so sorry you guys had to stand out here all day. It must get boring for you."

Joker offered her a smile. "It's no problem. This is part of what we do."

"I know. But I'm sure babysitting isn't high on your list of duties."

"Believe me. We've had babysitting gigs before, and I promise you, this is nothing compared to those," Jay Bird said. "I'm actually enjoying myself. I've never seen anything like this, and it's interesting."

She wasn't sure if they were being honest or just trying to be nice. Either way, she was very appreciative of their being there.

"You'll probably hear this a lot from me over the next two weeks, but thank you for being here. I'll admit I'm glad I have people around who I'm familiar with and not a strange group of men who I know nothing about."

"It's our pleasure. We should actually be thanking you," Joker told her, and she cocked her head to the side.

"Me? Why?"

"Because there are many worse off places we could be."

Jocelyn pulled her bottom lip between her teeth. There were so many questions she would love to ask them about the places they've been to. But she knew they couldn't talk about it. So, she chose to keep quiet.

"Are you all finished for the day?" Joker asked, eyeing the crew as they gathered their tools and started piling into their vehicles to return to their quarters.

The village they were staying in was about seven or eight miles south. Ralph had told her that their setup inside the building reminded him of his days in the Army when his unit would pack into those large GP tents like sardines.

She looked up at Joker. "Day one is officially complete."

Only twelve more days to go, she thought to herself.

☙

Jocelyn parted ways with Joker and Jay Bird once they arrived back at the building. She opened the door to her room and stepped inside. She was exhausted and hungry. Sluggishly, she walked to the table and set down her clipboard and water bottle. A large white bucket sitting near the table caught her eye. Upon a closer inspection of the bucket, she saw it was filled with clean water. At least it looked clean. There was also a note attached to it. Recognizing the handwriting right away, she knew it was from Bear.

In case you want to clean up.

It was a sweet gesture. And, seeing that she was covered in sweat, and desert filth, of course, she desperately wanted to clean up. But the issue she faced was where?

She scanned the room, searching for ideas, and even considered a few. Until a better idea hit her—outside her door and to the right was a small alcove connected to the building. It already had three walls. All she needed was a sheet or something she could hang to cover the front, and she'd have herself a private little shower stall.

With a plan in mind, she quickly changed into her bathing suit. She threw on her coverup before gathering up everything and going outside to set up her *she shower*.

The area was perfect, and most importantly, it was private. She had already fastened one side of the sheet to the wall and was securing the other side when she sensed a presence behind her. She didn't have to turn around to know who it was because the deep chuckle gave away his identity.

"Hello, Bear," she greeted him, smiling, as she turned and found him standing there with his arms crossed in front of his chest. He appeared amused but also perplexed with her contraption. But damn, he looked sexy.

"What are you doing?" He asked.

"It's my *she shower*."

He arched his eyebrow. "Your what?"

"My *she shower*. You know, like those *she sheds*, women are building nowadays. But instead of a shed, it's my shower."

Jay Bird appeared from around the corner and gave an odd look at the sheet-covered area.

"What are you making there?"

"It's her *she shower*," Bear told him, and Jay Bird chuckled.

"Nice. Like a *she shed*, right?"

"Ha!" Jocelyn pointed at Bear. "See, Jay Bird knows what I'm talking about."

Bear laughingly shook his head at Jay Bird. But suddenly, his amused expression morphed into a scowl. Jocelyn even took a few steps back as his nostrils flared, his eyes narrowed into tiny slits, and his jaw clenched.

"I hope to hell you're not planning on going in there naked," he growled at her.

Did he think she was stupid?

"Of course not," she shot back and pointed to what she was wearing. "I have my bathing suit on."

Bear's penetrating gaze raked over her body, starting at her feet, and slowly traveled upward until their eyes locked with one another's. His eyes became darker, and her knees felt weak as heat filled her traitorous body.

He stepped closer, never breaking eye contact with her. He spoke low and slow.

"I may not be with you at the drill site during the day, but I'll be damned if I let anyone stand here while you shower because I will not allow someone else to see what belongs to me."

Oh hell! Her body was already wound tight. His words and the intensity of them nearly made her explode.

She swallowed hard, only managing a slight head nod.

He quirked one of his brows, and even that small, simple act was sexy as hell.

"Got it," she squeaked out.

"Good," he said, winking as a small smile tugged at his lips. "Now go enjoy your *she shower*."

Unable to utter a word, she slowly turned, pulled back the sheet, and stepped inside. Once the sheet fell, shielding her from the outside world, she placed her hand over her belly, which felt like she had a butterfly farm inside of it.

She knew she was screwed. It was only a matter of time before she caved. *Fuck me...*

ೞ

Bear paced in front of Jocelyn's *she shower*, trying to rein in his desire and act like a gentleman. He couldn't believe how tempted he was to pull back that thin baby blue sheet separating them and join her in there. If they were alone, there was a damn good chance he may have.

The SEALs taught him many skills, but one ability he wished he had right now was reading minds because he would love to know what was going through her head. Even though it had only been a little over twenty-four hours since he broke the news to her about their marriage, he couldn't help but wonder if she was leaning more toward a certain outcome. Was she still in shock? Hell, did she have questions?

He sniffed the air as a sweet floral scent hit his nose. He stopped pacing, closed his eyes, and tried to control himself, knowing the fragrance was from her body wash. In his mind, he pictured her slowly running her green loofa over the curves of her magnificent body as the soapy suds rolled down her silky-smooth wet skin.

He took a deep breath and could feel his heart racing. *Fuck!* There was no way in hell he would be able to function being this wound up.

He needed to get himself under control, or he might need to make use of Jocelyn's *she shower* later to grip something else if he wanted to get through the next few days without embarrassing himself.

❧

Feeling fresh and clean, Jocelyn changed into a pair of loose gray Capri joggers and a light green, long-sleeved sun shirt.

She was planning on having an early dinner with the guys. Bear told her to come out front once she changed. She wasn't sure what they had in mind for food, but she'd find out soon enough.

She slipped her feet into her flip-flops and walked out the door when her computer pinged with an incoming message.

She backed up to the table and used the mouse to click on the messenger tab. A smile slowly formed, seeing the message from Lana. She was checking in to see how things were going.

Jocelyn glanced at her watch. It was a little past four, which meant it was just after eleven in the morning back in D.C.

She quickly typed out her reply, letting Lana know that she and the team were settled in and everything was on schedule. She told her she would send some pictures tomorrow after clearing the land.

Lana responded with a thumbs-up emoji, then asked how things were with the team. Jocelyn saw right through her words. She was fishing for details on her and Bear. She replied, typing out that everyone was behaving and getting along.

She laughed when Lana came back with a smiling emoji.

Before she closed the laptop, she checked the battery. It still had three-quarters of life left. However, she needed to remember to set her solar battery power banks out tomorrow so they could recharge.

As she lifted the laptop to stow it in her bag, a folder slid off the table and landed on the floor, tossing the contents inside all over the ground.

"Crap!" She mumbled, sliding the laptop into the bag and zipping it. She squatted down and started to pick up the papers when she realized which folder it was. Staring her in the face were the papers that Bear had given her on the plane. Was someone trying to send her a message as a reminder that she couldn't hide from the decision she had to make?

Now was definitely not the time for her to think about the situation, not after his blatant show of possession earlier when she went to shower. He had her all twisted up on the inside. She huffed out a frustrated sigh. "No!" She uttered aloud to herself. This huge decision could come with monumental consequences, so she needed to thoroughly think the situation through before committing to a final resolution.

What she could do, though, was use this time with him to rekindle their friendship. After all, it had been ten years, and people do change. Was his favorite meal still a medium rare steak with a loaded baked potato? Did he still like to sleep in his boxers? Would he still surprise her with flowers? Does he still take three sugars in his coffee? God, she could go on with questions. But most importantly, would he still fully love her?

Shaking her head at her crazy thoughts, she quickly gathered all the papers and shoved them into the folder before placing them on her cot.

She needed to collect herself before she went outside to join the guys. She closed her eyes and took a few deep, relaxing breaths. Once she felt a little more grounded, she headed out the door.

CHAPTER TEN

Bear glanced at his watch, wondering if Jocelyn was still planning on joining them for dinner. After she finished her shower, he invited her to eat with them by the fire pits. She told him she would, but that was almost an hour ago. He was beginning to think that she might have changed her mind, but he hoped that wasn't the case because he had been looking forward to spending time with her.

"Dude quit fretting. She'll be here," Nails told Bear.

The last thing he wanted was for his anxiousness to show. He knew Nails was right. But dammit, he was nervous, and usually, he wasn't one to get worked up over things. Even when they were in mission mode and things weren't going according to plan, they had backups to ensure the mission was accomplished. However, his current predicament didn't afford him a backup plan. He only had one shot to convince her to forgive him and that they were meant to be together.

Plus, it wasn't like this was a date. It was just everyone sitting around having dinner and talking. How hard could that be?

Yet, as every minute passed and she still hadn't emerged from her room, he started to worry, wondering if she was okay or had fallen asleep. After all, she had busted her ass out in the heat. He ran his hands through his short dirty blonde hair.

"There she is," Joker said, smiling, and Bear looked up to see Jocelyn walking toward them.

She smiled, looking at Joker. "What, did you think I wouldn't join you guys?"

"Bear thought so," Nails teased, and Bear flipped him the bird.

Jocelyn looked at Bear. "I told you that I would," she told him, grinning.

"I wasn't worried," Bear lied, then motioned toward the empty chair between him and Nails.

Jocelyn walked over and sat down.

"I hope you don't mind, but we all hijacked your *she shower*," Playboy informed her, laughter filling his voice. And the others started laughing along with him.

Jocelyn chuckled. "I don't mind one bit. I built it for all of us to use."

Why in the hell did Playboy have to bring up that damn *she shower*? Now Bear had images of Jocelyn in the shower filling his head.

༄

After a few minutes, Jocelyn felt herself begin to relax. She knew she was fidgeting when she first sat down, but she couldn't help it. She felt intimidated by them, especially knowing they were aware of her and Bear's situation.

She glanced over at Bear, who was kicked back in the chair, appearing relaxed with his feet propped up on the sidewall of the fire pit. He had changed into a pair of jeans and a T-shirt. With his build, he could make anything look good. She couldn't help but peek at his thighs and how the material stretched around his muscles. She was so entranced by Bear's muscles she didn't even hear Playboy ask her a question until her name was spoken loudly.

She snapped her head up and met Playboy's grin.

"What?" She asked, trying to act like she hadn't been caught gawking at Bear.

"I asked if you wanted beef, chicken, or shrimp."

She scrunched her forehead up. "Huh?"

Appearing even more amused, Playboy said, "For dinner, do you want beef, chicken, or shrimp?"

"Where'd you get beef, chicken, and shrimp?"

Playboy held up three *Ramen Noodle* packages: Beef, Chicken, and Shrimp flavor, and Jocelyn felt like an idiot. She loved Ramen. She lived off of it in college because it was so cheap.

"I'll take the shrimp, please."

"Excellent choice."

While she waited for Playboy to boil the water for her Ramen, they asked her what was on the agenda for tomorrow.

"We'll start clearing the land. We marked everything today, so the crew will know what to take out." She glanced up towards the sky. "Forecasters are calling for rain overnight."

"Will that interfere with the work?" Bear asked as he shoved a forkful of noodles in his mouth.

"No, as long as there isn't any lightning. The rain may actually benefit us."

"How so?"

"The ground right now is very dry, making it very hard. Getting enough rain could help soften the soil, making it easier to pull out large pesky roots, especially with some of those big African baobabs. If you don't eliminate the roots, you run the possibility of them becoming an issue with the well over time. I'm hoping we can save as much of the live vegetation with good roots and replant them further away from the well site."

"Why's that?" Aussie asked.

"Because there isn't much vegetation left in the area, and both humans and wildlife depend on those plants and trees to live. Not many people realize it, but much of this area's vegetation is a source of food, water, and health remedies."

Bear rubbed his hand over his whiskered jaw. "I never thought about that."

"Most people don't unless they visit or live in an area where that is the way of life. Plus, remember that woman yesterday, Nandi. She deals in herbal medicine. So, I'm sure she relies on the plants around her to concoct her medicines."

"Speaking of that woman. Those two kids of hers were adorable," Aussie said, and Jocelyn nodded in agreement.

"They sure are. And so friendly, unlike their mother," Bear added, a frown on his face.

"She definitely didn't give off a good vibe. But maybe she was having a bad day. Remember, Flora said that she was under a lot of stress with her aunt's health." Jocelyn said.

"Maybe," Bear said.

"Here you go," Playboy said, handing her a plate of Ramen.

She thanked him, and everyone began to eat and make small talk.

Jocelyn had woofed down her noodles in record time and was almost finished when Nails leaned close to her. She thought he would tell her something, but he sniffed her shoulder instead.

"What are you doing?" She asked him, pulling away a bit.

He appeared apologetic but also had that gleam in his eye that told her he was up to something.

"Sorry. But your lotion is driving me nuts. It's different than the one you wore yesterday. This one has a sweet floral scent, but there's something else mixed with it that I can't figure out."

Jocelyn laughed. "No. It's not the cinnamon one. This one is called Pink Petals and Cake."

He raised his eyebrows. "Huh. Pink Petals and Cake," he repeated, rubbing his hand across his unshaven jaw. After a few seconds, he dropped his hand, and a wicked grin slowly formed on his lips. It reminded her of the shit-eating grin that Grinch gave in *How the Grinch Stole Christmas*.

"If a woman's pink petals smelled that delicious, I'd never be hungry again."

The guys started laughing, though some groaned and shook their heads like they couldn't believe he said that. On the other hand, Jocelyn was speechless and had to plug her eyes back into their sockets.

"That's just…." She couldn't think of the word or words she wanted to say, so Nails decided to finish it for her.

"Sexually satisfying," he stated, sporting a proud smile. "I mean, what more could a man ask for than pink petals and cake? Two of my favorite things."

Jocelyn shook her head and tried to hide her smile, knowing she had walked right into that. She looked at Nails.

"You're such a horndog." Then she pointed at Playboy. "When I first met you guys, I assumed Playboy over there was the philanderer of the group because of his name."

Playboy's eyebrows rose at the mention of his name, and then he shook his head. "Don't compare me to him. Playboy doesn't mean what you think. I don't sleep around."

"Nope, Playboy has his eyes lasered in on his prize," Aussie stated and grinned.

"Gabby's hot as fuck," Nails blurted out, and Playboy shot daggers at him.

"You keep your wandering tentacles away from her."

Nails cupped his ear with his hand like he had trouble hearing. "I'm sorry. Did you say my tentacles or my testicles?"

Jocelyn covered her mouth to keep from laughing out loud, unlike some of the guys who howled in laughter. Duke reached over and slapped Nails in the back of the head. "Behave, asshole."

Nails threw his hands in the air, looking at Playboy, who appeared like he wanted to rip Nails' head off. "Hey! You know that's one rule I have and that I abide by."

"What rule is that?" Jocelyn asked, still unable to keep a straight face.

"I don't poach, especially from my teammates." He looked across the group and met Bear's eyes before turning his eyes back to her. "Because if I did, you and I wouldn't be sitting here now."

Jocelyn's eyes widened just before a low growl emitted from Bear. She had to wonder if Nails really did have a death wish.

"Nails, are you deliberately trying to get your ass kicked?" Joker asked, clearly amused by Nails' childish behavior.

"Nope. I'm just stating the facts and making my *friend* Jocelyn understand the type of guy I am. Just because I enjoy sex doesn't mean I'll screw any woman."

Fearing that Bear was mad at Nails, Jocelyn took a chance and quickly glanced at Bear. He turned at the same time and looked right at her. She offered him a slight smile, and he returned with a wink, letting her know he wasn't upset. Yet, it did make her wonder how much the team knew about their situation. It was something she would ask him when they finally sat down to talk. And she knew they needed to talk, but she just needed to get through a few more days because the next steps in the drilling process were the most critical, and she didn't want any distractions.

Wanting to move the conversation away from her, she looked at Nails. "Nails is an interesting nickname. How'd that come about?"

Again, she heard the snickers and coughs, trying to cover up their laughs, and felt she had just walked into another uncomfortable conversation. However, before Nails could answer, Duke pipped up.

"We've got company."

Jocelyn turned in her chair and saw the two small figures walking toward them. She recognized the two children right away. They were the kids from yesterday.

As they approached, she studied their features. They had several similarities, but the most prominent was their eyes. They both had those beautiful dark brown, wide almond-shaped eyes.

"Hey, kids!" Duke called out in a friendly, welcoming tone. It made Jocelyn wonder if the guys were always this friendly with the public, especially kids when they were deployed.

The kids smiled and waved but also looked a little timid. She'd be a little weary, too, walking up to a group of men who looked like these guys. But she also wondered what the two youngsters were doing wandering around the village close to nightfall by themselves.

Jocelyn smiled. "What are you two doing?"

"Uh…Amira wanted to come to say hi," Maxime said.

The little girl appeared shy as she clutched a brown teddy bear in her arms.

"Hi, Amira. Would you like to come and sit with us?" Jocelyn asked, and the little girl nodded her head.

Jay Bird got up, retrieved two more chairs from inside, and set them between Jocelyn and Bear. Bear then waved over both kids.

"Come on over and have a seat."

Maxime took the seat closest to Bear, and Amira sat beside Jocelyn.

Jocelyn pointed to the teddy bear. "That's a cute bear. Does it have a name?"

"His name is Gus," Amira said softly. Her voice was so angelic. But Jocelyn noticed how profound her English was. If she had to guess, she thought, it might be British.

"You guys showed up just in time," Snow told them, smiling.

"We did?" Maxime asked, looking around.

"Yeah. We were getting ready to make S'mores."

Jocelyn's eyebrows rose, and she looked toward Bear because that was news to her. Bear pointed to the bag on the ground next to his feet. She looked and saw a package of marshmallows sticking out. These guys seemed as if they were prepared for anything.

"What is that?" The curious kid asked.

"Here, I'll show you." Bear opened the graham crackers, marshmallows, and chocolate packages and laid them on a paper plate. He bent over, picked up a stick next to his feet, and then showed the kids how to stick the marshmallow on the stick and hold it over the open fire.

Bear helped Maxime, and Jocelyn assisted Amira. As the kids held their sticks over the fire, Jocelyn glanced at Bear, who instructed Maxime on the perfect color to get the marshmallow. As if sensing her eyes on him, he looked up. His eyes held a slight twinkle to them.

"Ms. Jocelyn. I think my white puffy thing is on fire," Amira exclaimed, bringing Jocelyn back to the task. When she looked at what Amira was referring to, sure enough, she had a flaming marshmallow. Jocelyn pulled it off the fire and blew out the minuscule flame, then showed Amira how to make the graham cracker sandwich by squishing the marshmallow and chocolate between the crackers.

As the kids ate their S'mores, the guys talked with them, and the kids asked them questions.

"How old are you two?" Jay Bird asked the children.

"I'm ten, and Amira is seven," Maxime answered with a mouth full of chocolate and marshmallows. He had it smeared all over his face. Well, they both did. One of the guys had some wipes, and Bear helped wipe most of it off.

"Do you have any other brothers or sisters?" Duke asked.

"No," Maxime answered, lowering his head as if he was upset by not having any other siblings. Jocelyn saw Bear slightly squint his eyes, telling her he had also caught Maxime's sudden upset. On the other hand, Amira appeared unaffected as she munched on her crackers. The little girl seemed to have found a new snack she enjoyed.

"Do you like those crackers, Amira?" Jocelyn asked, and the little girl nodded her head as she continued to nibble on the crackers.

"Do you live in America?" Maxime asked the group, seeming to gain back some of his confidence.

"We do," Bear answered.

"I'd like to go to America."

"What would you like to see in America?"

"NASA!" The boy exclaimed, the excitement beaming in his eyes.

Bear cocked his head, but his expression held a slight grin. "NASA?"

The boy nodded. "I love astrology. Amira and I like to watch the stars at night."

Jocelyn, at that moment, tilted her head back to look up at the sky as it transitioned from day to night. Even with the sun's final rays of the day peeking out as it lowered behind the horizon, some stars were beginning to appear along with the moon.

"Stars are beautiful to watch," Jocelyn said.

"I want to be an astronaut when I grow up. I want to go into space."

"You can be anything you want," Bear encouraged Maxime.

"What do you do?" He asked Bear, and Jocelyn smiled at the surprised reaction on Bear's face. She wondered how he would answer, considering most SEALs don't advertise their status. She wasn't even sure they would admit they worked for the military.

"We protect people."

"Are you protecting Ms. Jocelyn?"

"We are, as well as everyone else in the village, even you and your sister."

The little boy squished his face up. "How are you protecting us?"

"Well, Jocelyn is here to give you water, right?" Maxime nodded. "Well, we also want to make sure that nobody tries to stop that. So, when you look at it, we're also protecting the village to make sure you guys get your water."

Maxime seemed to think about that for a bit. After a few moments, he turned his wide brown eyes on Bear.

"I understand. So, would you and your friends protect us if Amira and I were in danger?"

Jocelyn was caught off guard by Maxime's question. And it appeared so was everyone else, as every set of concerned eyes and ears were directed at Maxime. It was subtle and smooth, but that little boy had everyone's full attention.

It didn't surprise her that Bear took the lead. It was interesting to watch him interact with his team, considering the last time she saw him, he was just a tadpole in the teams.

"Is someone bothering you and your sister?"

He didn't verbally respond. Instead, he shrugged his shoulders.

"Maxime, look at me," Bear ordered in a firm but calm tone so as not to spook the poor kid. Jocelyn watched as the boy slowly raised his head, peering up at Bear.

"If someone is bothering you or your sister, you need to tell someone. Maybe your mom or dad?"

At the mention of his mom and dad, the little boy's eyes suddenly widened in fear, and he began shaking his head. Jocelyn immediately felt a pit in her stomach. The boy was obviously afraid to talk to his mom and dad about whoever might be bothering him or his sister. She wasn't sure what to say or do, so she looked at Bear, hoping he did. Bear's expression was full of concern for the two kids.

Bear placed his hand on Maxime's shoulder in a comforting way.

"Maxime, promise me that if you or your sister need help and we are around, you'll let us know, okay?"

Maxime nodded but again stayed silent. Jocelyn now had many questions that she'd like answers to concerning the kids.

"You have big arms," Amira blurted out as if knowing a change in the conversation was needed. When Jocelyn looked down, the little girl was pointing at Duke, who was wearing a short-sleeved shirt, and had his hands laced behind his head as he leaned back in the chair.

"Their called muscles," Duke replied, smiling, and flexed his arm, making his bicep muscle jump. Amira giggled and then looked at her small arms before looking back at Duke.

"Do you use your muscles to protect people?"

Jocelyn noticed Duke's hesitation, so she jumped in to help him out and said the first thing that came to her mind.

"Or they're used to hold the person they love close to them."

Suddenly, the air around the group stilled. She then realized what she said and who they probably thought she was thinking about when she said it.

She gave her shoulder a slight shrug, trying to act like Bear wasn't even a blip in her head. "What? I've read a lot of romance books."

When her eyes moved to Bear, she swallowed hard. The knowing look in his eyes told her that he knew exactly who was on her mind.

Amira turned her head up toward Jocelyn. "You're pretty. Are you married?"

Jocelyn felt all the blood drain from her face. Of all the questions these kids could ask, they find the one question she's been trying to avoid.

Boy, how the tide quickly turned as she was now the one on the hot seat with eight sets of curious eyes upon her. At least now she had her answer. It was obvious by the understanding look in many of the guys' eyes they knew the gist of the situation.

She gave a tight smile and squirmed a bit in her seat as she debated how to answer what seemed to be the million-dollar question. "Wow...," she uttered under her breath.

She glanced at Bear. He was sitting back in his chair with his leg propped over his other. He appeared much calmer and more collected than she was. He lifted his one eyebrow as if taunting her, but she could see the hopefulness shining in his grey eyes.

She licked her dry lips. *Crapola!* Where was a distraction when she needed one? She took a deep breath.

"At the moment...It appears I am."

Amira grinned. "Can I see a picture of him?"

She didn't miss the fake coughs as some of the guys tried to conceal their laughter. Hell, she'd probably be laughing, too, if she hadn't been the one being interrogated. Looking to her right, she even saw Bear with his hand over his mouth, covering his grin as he watched her squirm.

"Well, I don't have a picture with me, but you can still see him because he is right over there." She pointed at Bear.

Amira's eyes became wide, and she leaned closer to Jocelyn. "Does he use his muscles to hold you?" Amira whispered the question, but her soft voice carried over the still evening air, and Jocelyn felt the heat in her cheeks increase. She knew her face had to be flaming red. *For the love of God!* Could this get any more awkward for her? Hadn't she endured enough embarrassment in one day?

But thinking about Bear's muscles had her making an impromptu trip down memory lane. She loved being surrounded by Bear's strong muscles, especially when they lay in bed after they had made love, and he would pull her flush against his taut body with the rumpled bedsheets tangled around them. Or when he'd use his muscles in the form of pleasurable dominance when he'd secure one arm around her waist, slip his other hand under her long hair, firmly cupping the nape of her neck, as he made love to her mouth. His muscle strength was a form of art she'd be willing to watch or feel anytime.

Someone cleared their throat, and she immediately shut down the images of the two of them fresh in her head.

She lifted her head, glancing at Bear before returning to Amira to answer her question. The desire that shone in Bear's darkened eyes told her he remembered what his muscle power did to her.

She wasn't a liar and had no intention to fib to the sweet, inquisitive girl.

"Yes, Amira. His muscles are full of love."

Thankfully, the guys sensed her awkwardness and steered the conversation to a more appropriate child topic, like cartoons, giving her a chance to calm her anxiety.

ꙮ

About an hour later, Jocelyn looked at the time and saw it was getting late. Amira had climbed into her lap about twenty minutes ago and was having trouble keeping her eyes open, and Maxime was yawning.

She leaned over and whispered to Bear. "We should probably get them home. It's late and dark."

He nodded. "You would think their parents would've been looking for them."

Jocelyn had been thinking the same. She looked at the little girl, who was now sound asleep against her.

"I don't want to wake her up."

"Here, I'll carry her," Bear said, picking up Amira. She stirred a little but settled in Bear's arms, resting her head against his shoulder.

The sight of the little angel in Bear's arms was enough to send her ovaries into overdrive if she still had them.

About ten minutes later, they got the kids back to their home, and Bear laid Amira on the bed she shared with Maxime. She and Bear had been surprised that their parents weren't home.

Jocelyn had taken the time to look at how the family lived and was surprised by the family's property condition. The poverty level in villages like Massendai was high. Many families struggled to put food on the table, so that didn't leave much for extra essentials. But looking around, it seemed Maxime and Amira's family wasn't as bad off as most others. They had suitcases full of clothes, decent cooking equipment, and several high-dollar solar equipment, such as lanterns and fans. Jocelyn swore she saw a tablet sticking out of one of the bags sitting in the corner. Plus, a few pieces of jewelry were sitting in a cup on a table. It certainly made her wonder what else mom and dad were doing for a living to have such nice things when most of the other villagers were barely scraping by.

But another thing she noticed that upset her was that of all the essentials inside, there didn't appear to be much for the kids. There were no toys and hardly any clothing that she could see.

※

Bear got Amira tucked in bed. She was an absolute sweetheart. When he turned around, Maxime was standing there.

"Where are your parents?"

The boy was hesitant to answer, but he finally did.

"My mum is probably with her aunt. She's been sick for a long time, and Mum has been helping her."

"Do you want us to wait with you until she gets back?"

The boy vehemently shook his head. "She goes down there all the time. She doesn't like it when people are here."

Bear was trying his best not to come across as the interrogator he was trained to be, but dammit, he was genuinely concerned about the kids. Some of the comments they made tonight had many scenarios going through his head, and none were good.

He was a trained protector. He'd spent eleven years of his SEAL career traveling all over the world. And in those eleven years, he had seen things he never wished he had, many being women and children who had been victimized.

He and Jocelyn got Maxime tucked in bed next to Amira. Bear thought it was sweet when Jocelyn kissed each child on the forehead. She seemed to be smitten with the youngsters. But he had to admit that he was too.

As the pair exited the property, Jocelyn grabbed his arm, stopping him. He looked at her and could tell she was upset.

"What's wrong?" He asked, stepping closer and letting his hand slide down her arm. He was pleased when she didn't try to move away from his touch.

She glanced back toward the hut where the two kids were nestled in their bed.

"I don't want to leave them there alone. I feel like it's irresponsible of us. I mean, they're only ten and seven years old. Anyone could walk right in there, and..." her voice trailed off, but Bear understood. He didn't like it either. However, he understood that things operated differently in certain parts of the world, like how people parent. It also depended on the culture.

"Joce, it's not just you. I feel the same and believe me. I hate it too. However, we have to respect their culture. Judging from Maxime's lack of concern about his mom not being there tells me they're used to it."

She went to argue, and he stopped her. He wasn't even thinking when he took her hand and squeezed it until she looked down at their joined hands. He thought she might pull away, but she surprised him when she gripped his tighter.

Her body relaxed, and she brushed her hair out of her face before looking back up at him.

"I just don't like it. I can't help it. They are such nice kids. And I also don't like how Maxime always panicked at his parents' mention. It was like he was scared. And what was with him asking if you guys would protect him and his sister?"

As serious as the situation was, Bear couldn't hide his smile because she was cute as hell when she got worked up. He released her hand and grabbed onto her shoulders.

"Joce. Calm down."

She took a deep breath. "Do you think I'm overacting?" She asked him. He released her shoulders and ran his hand through his hair.

"No. You're not overreacting because I'm worried too. Something definitely isn't right. My gut tells me those kids don't live in a stable home." He then grinned. "But damn, they're the cutest kids."

She mimicked his smile and laughed lightly. "Yeah, they are. It's weird, though."

"What is?"

"I just met them, but I feel like I have this connection to them. Not that I would, but it's like I want to pack them up in my suitcase when I leave and take them home with me."

He smiled at her. "You've always loved being around kids. When we were in high school, you always volunteered to help with the kids' games whenever we had festivals in town. You're good with them."

He noticed a flash of sadness in her eyes, but it quickly disappeared.

"Yeah. Those were good times." Seeming slightly uncomfortable, she turned and started walking back toward the path that would take them back to their building.

Bear followed her as they walked through the village. The beam of his flashlight led their path. Neither of them spoke. The only sound was the crunching of pebbles and dirt under their feet.

Bear welcomed the silence—silence was a time when he could let his mind unwind and reflect on things. However, the silence between him and Jocelyn wasn't helping. He wondered what she was thinking about.

"So, this evening's conversation was interesting," he said aloud.

A soft chuckle came from beside him. "Yeah, it sure was. It also gave me the answer to a question I've been wondering about."

"What question is that?"

"Since yesterday, I've been trying to figure out how much your team knew about our history."

He released a sigh. "They haven't known long. In fact, they just found out last weekend."

She whipped her head up.

"Last weekend? At your parent's?"

"Yeah. When I was trying to get you to stay, and my phone rang, it was my commander. He was calling to tell me about this job. With everything going on, I came clean with my family and team about us."

She stopped walking and turned towards him. "You told them everything?"

Shit! He reached back and rubbed the back of his neck nervously.

"Yeah. After you stormed out, Zach and I got into a shouting match that my dad had to step between us. Then my dad demanded to know what was going on between you and me."

Jocelyn was biting her lip. "Were they mad?"

"Mad? No. They were thrilled, though, upset that we had to hide everything from them. But they understood. You know my family could never be mad at you."

She smiled. "I love your family. I couldn't survive knowing they were mad at me."

"I hope you aren't upset with me for telling them. I included the team since they were part of the mission here. And not knowing how things might go between you and me, I felt it was best if they knew the truth."

"I understand."

He wanted her to understand everything. He stepped closer and lightly caressed her cheek with his knuckles. Was he exceeding his boundary? Probably. But he couldn't resist. Not with her staring up into his eyes as her brown eyes shined bright and were filled with affection. Her tongue slipped between her lips and swiped across her bottom lip, leaving a trail of glistening wetness that he'd love to kiss.

As if sensing his thoughts, she coyly lowered her eyes.

"We should probably get back," she said in a low whisper, and she was probably right before he did something stupid, like kiss her.

CHAPTER ELEVEN

"You got about another three feet to the left," Jocelyn shouted over the loud rumble of the machine to Steven, one of the equipment operators. He gave her a thumbs up in return as he steered the excavator, carrying one of the larger trees they were transplanting further from the well site.

She watched closely as Steve maneuvered the bucket until it was above the large hole. Jocelyn took a few steps back so she was out of the way before she gave him the signal to drop it. "Just a little further," she mumbled to herself, and as soon as the bucket was in position over the orange "X" spray painted on the ground, she threw her hand up in the air and yelled to Steve to drop it.

The gears made a grinding sound, and the bucket clanked as it tilted downward slowly, allowing the tree to slide in place. A few crew members grabbed onto the ropes she had tied around the trunk and carefully guided the tree off the bucket and into the hole.

Jocelyn smiled wide when the tree hit the target with a loud thump. Now, she just hoped that the roots would take. She scanned the area and was pleased with the amount of clearing and replanting they had accomplished in just one day. The crew led by Ralph was awesome to work with. Everyone worked hard and were dedicated team members to get whatever task needed to be completed done.

She eyed Kurt and Wayne, two of the crew members, as they strolled toward her. They were twins, almost identical if it weren't for their eyes. Kurt had hazel eyes, whereas Wayne's were blue. In their mid-twenties, both were very good-looking. However, they knew it and liked to flirt. Ralph had given her an advanced warning about them, which was good, so she was prepared.

She smiled in greeting at the two men. "How's it going?" She asked, and they both flashed their dazzling smiles at her.

"It's going well. Though, much better now that we're talking to you, darlin'," Wayne said in his thick southern drawl. His comment and the flirtatious wink made her cheeks warm.

Laughing off Wayne's trifling, she asked, "What's up?"

Kurt cleared his throat. "We know most of the crew are ready to call it a day. However, Wayne and I wanted to know if you'd be okay with us staying a little longer to move more of the live vegetation and get it planted."

Jocelyn looked around, noting that many more plants could be potentially saved if they could get them in the ground today. She was also aware that Kurt and Wayne owned their own landscaping business, so they knew what they were talking about.

She glanced at her watch, seeing that it was only two-thirty. Plenty of daylight was left, but it was hotter than Satan's kitchen. That was the main reason the crew called it quits for the day. Everyone had busted their ass to get all the vegetation cleared so they could be ready to move in the drill rig tomorrow.

She shrugged her shoulders. "Considering there is still three and a half hours of sunlight, I'm good with it. In fact, it'll make me happy to get those plants into the ground so they have a fighting chance. Plus, it'll be less we'll have to do tomorrow. If you need an extra set of hands, I can help."

Both men gave her a big grin. "We never turn down help, especially when the help is as beautiful as you," Wayne said, eyeing her over and letting his eyes linger on her chest.

Jocelyn rolled her eyes. Her first reaction was to cross her arms in front of her chest, but she knew doing that would only push her boobs up further, giving them a better view. She regretted wearing the racer-back tank and sports bra underneath that smooshed her boobs together, creating major cleavage. But in her defense, it was hotter than balls in a pair of skinny jeans. Ignoring their blatant flirting, she grabbed her clipboard off the ground and told the horndog twins to follow her.

She stopped at the excavator and set the clipboard down, using the bucket as a surface to write on. Pulling a blank piece of paper from under her site plans, she drew a diagram of the area, then noted where each large bush or tree should be planted.

Kurt and Wayne flanked her on each side as they stood close, listening to her instructions. Kurt took advantage of his position and pressed his hand against her lower back as he looked over her shoulder. She almost tripped over her words when she felt his fingertips near the top of her ass. Wayne then placed his hand on her shoulder as if they had rehearsed their moves, giving it a gentle squeeze.

She paused and looked between the two, swallowing hard. Their eyes were zeroed in on her, not the plans in front of them. Their tall statures and muscular physique were intimidating, and she felt herself shaking a little from being sandwiched between the two slabs of muscle.

Wayne slid his hand down her arm, covering her hand. His blue eyes never left hers as he lightly ran the pads of his fingertips over her knuckles.

"What do you say after we finish here that the three of us go find a nice quiet place so Kurt and I can get to know you better?"

Jocelyn felt like her eyes would pop out of their sockets hearing Wayne's admission. Slowly she pulled her hand from under Wayne's much larger hand before taking a few steps back. Her movement caused Kurt to drop his hand from her back.

Staring between the two, she shook her head, unable to say a word because she was shocked at their candor. They both seemed like nice guys who obviously liked sharing women, but she wasn't interested and said the first thing that popped into her head.

"I'm married," she blurted out, surprising herself that she actually said the words. But even more surprising was how easy and natural it felt to say. Nonetheless, it seemed to work because she thought she would have to pick up both men's mouths off the ground.

"Oh shit! I swear we didn't kn—" Wayne started to say before being interrupted by a deep voice that emitted power.

"Jocelyn!"

As soon as she heard the familiar voice call out her name, she looked over her shoulder, and her eyes widened as Bear came storming across the wide-open space toward them.

When in the hell did he get here?

She suspected he had seen Kurt and Wayne getting handsy with her.

She spun around so fast that she practically made herself dizzy. But she didn't want to see these guys get their asses kicked.

"If you both know what's good for you, you might want to go and make yourselves busy." She pointed over her shoulder toward Bear, barreling toward them like a bull being taunted with a red cape and looking like he was about to do bodily harm to someone. Or, in this case, two someones. "That's my husband."

Both men were wide-eyed and apologized profusely before taking her suggestion and scurrying away. She took one last deep breath to calm her nerves and turned back towards Bear.

"Hey!" She called out. However, his fierce expression and the death glare he was shooting toward the twin's retreating backs told her he wasn't happy.

જે

Bear was ready to blow his stack. He was beyond pissed at seeing those men with their hands on Jocelyn. When he first arrived at the site with Joker and Duke, curious to see what all the crew had accomplished, he immediately noticed how the twins had taken an interest in Jocelyn. He recognized the flirtatious look and the lust in their eyes. They wanted her, and there was no way in hell he would sit back and watch it all unfold.

Jay Bird, who had been at the site all day with Jocelyn, had initially told Bear that he was overreacting and that the guys were just being friendly. But when the two sandwiched her as if she was the meat between them, and the one guy put his hand on her back, low enough that his fingertips were practically grazing her ass, that was when he lost it.

Whether she agreed with it or not, she was still technically his wife, and he wasn't going to stand around with his thumb up his ass while those cowboy casanovas tried to seduce her.

"Jocelyn!" He yelled, ignoring his teammates' pleas to act civil as his feet carried him quickly across the site. When she looked over her shoulder with wide eyes and met his gaze, he knew she understood what was about to go down.

He watched as Jocelyn quickly turned and said something to the men—probably warning them. Because seconds later, they scampered away in a hurry. It was a good thing they did, or else they might have had a foot up so far up their ass that they'd be polishing their boots when they brushed their teeth.

Jocelyn turned back around when he was within arm's length of her.

"Hey!" She said, smiling, as she stepped in front of him like a blockade, putting her hands on his forearms. He wanted to laugh at her bold move, but damn, the feel of her hands on his skin sent tingles all over his body.

He removed his sunglasses and stared down into her eyes. She was trying to act calm, but he spotted her nervous ticks. Her breathing became more rapid, and her fingernails went straight to her mouth. But he'd give her credit. She didn't back down as she stood her ground and stared back at him.

"What were those guys talking to you about?"

She started to shift nervously on her feet, and her eyes looked anywhere other than his.

"Uhm...They wanted to know if I had a problem with them staying longer to replant the rest of the vegetation we're trying to save."

"I see." He looked over her shoulder as the two guys began working, but he didn't miss the small glances they took at him and Jocelyn. He moved his eyes back to Jocelyn as she started to speak.

"Bear, I—"

"What else did they say, considering the one planted his hand on your ass?"

Her eyes widened, and her cheeks turned two shades of pink. She placed her hands on her hips and squinted her eyes at him.

"His hand wasn't on my ass."

Bear stared deep into her eyes, not backing down, before raising an eyebrow at her. She looked away, sighing heavily. Dropping her hands to her side, she looked back up at him.

"Okay, it was close to my ass. But he didn't touch it. Plus, I told them both that I wasn't interested. Happy?" She shot back, glaring at him.

Bear bit the inside of his cheek to keep himself from grinning. Damn, she was a spitfire when she got worked up.

"How did you exactly handle it?" He pressed, wanting to know exactly what she told them.

"I just did," she replied, giving him a sideways glance. Bear knew there was more to the story, and he was more than curious about what else she told them, considering both men appeared scared shitless as they tucked their tails and ran.

Using his fingers, he lifted her chin, tilting her face towards his. As soon as their eyes met, he spoke in a low deep voice. "What exactly did you tell them?"

Her tongue darted out and took a swipe at her plump pink lips. "I…I told them I was, uhm…shit…" she mumbled, stumbling over her words. She rubbed her forehead, clearly showing signs of her frustration.

Bear wasn't going to waste an opportunity when he saw one. He slid his free arm around her waist, letting his hand graze the top of her ass. That was his ass to touch, nobody else's. Pulling her snug against him, she gasped as she stared into his eyes. His lips were so close to hers that he just had to lean in a few more inches, and he could taste her. And, by God, the urge was there. But that wasn't what he was after at the moment.

"You told them that you…what?" He probed, lightly tapping his fingers against her backside.

"I…I told them that I was married—to you," she whispered in defeat before dropping her forehead against his shoulder.

He wrapped both arms around her, hugging her. He couldn't help the huge smile that spread across his face.

"Are you mad?" She asked. His shirt muffled her voice, and he chuckled.

"Mad? Hell, no. I'm not mad." He eased back a bit so he could look at her. Once he saw her face, he could see clearly that she was embarrassed. Yet she had nothing to be ashamed of. She stated a fact. They were technically married. Her admission gave him confidence that she could be leaning toward them working things out, especially now, with her pliant in his arms, and she hadn't tried to scramble away.

"Joce, look at me," he ordered, though he spoke in a calm, quieter tone.

His smile grew wider when she raised her face and looked up at him.

"Why would you think I'd be mad?"

She shrugged her shoulders and took a deep breath. "I guess because of our situation. I honestly don't know why I told them that. I'm so confused right now," she said.

Bear had an inkling that he knew why she told the twins what she did, but he kept his mouth shut as he didn't want to push. Instead, he offered her comfort, rubbing his hand up and down her back.

"I'm so sorry," she told him. Her apologetic eyes confirmed her sincerity.

Ignoring her apology, he leaned in and pressed his lips against her forehead. "There's nothing to be sorry about. You did what was needed to get your point across to them." He smiled at her, drawing a slight grin on her lips. "Are you all finished for the day?" He asked, hoping her answer would be yes, and they could go somewhere and finally talk.

"Yeah. But I told Kurt and Wayne that I'd stay and help them get the remaining plants in the ground so they have a chance to survive."

Bear made an odd, displeasing sound with his mouth. He sure as hell wouldn't let her stay without him. Then he came up with a solution.

"Could you use some extra manpower to get it done quicker?"

"I'd never turn help. Why? What did you have in mind?"

Bear grinned before turning around and waving over Jay Bird, Joker, Duke, and Aussie.

"What are you doing?" She asked as the four guys approached.

Ignoring her question, Bear looked at his teammates and explained the situation about the plants. "Do you guys feel like getting your hands dirty?"

A resounding *yes* echoed around the group.

Jocelyn scrunched her eyebrows together. "You guys really want to help?"

"Why not. We're just standing around right now," Duke replied, then started walking toward one of the piles needing to be planted.

Jocelyn turned toward Bear and reached for his hand. She gave it a gentle squeeze. "Thank you."

Ignoring his desire to kiss her, he brushed a few loose strands of hair off her face. He was beaming at the headway made between the two of them.

"Sooner or later, you're going to see that I'd do anything for you," he told her.

"I think I'm already beginning to see that," she stated before stepping back and heading toward the others who were already moving plants.

For the next minute or two, Bear stood back and watched Jocelyn interact with his team as they worked together to beat the falling sun. She had no idea that his team had already accepted her into their tight little community. His job now was to make sure she stayed there.

ಹ

Jocelyn rolled from her side onto her back, dropping one arm over her eyes as she lay on her cot, deep in thought. The sun had disappeared for the day, but it was too early to fall asleep. Though, even if she wanted to sleep, she couldn't. Not with the way her mind was racing. She needed this time alone to decompress after the day she had. The day had gone off without a hitch, which was great. Everything went according to what she planned with no problems or concerns until the *Double Mint Twins* decided to make a move on her. Luckily for the two men, she handled the situation before Bear got involved. But she couldn't say the same for herself. She feared all she did was complicate matters.

She wasn't lying when she admitted to Bear that she felt confused. Laying here now, she even felt a little angry. Angry with herself for giving in to him so easily. But she couldn't help it. Even when she tried putting a little distance between them, it never failed that she found herself gravitating toward him when he was near. His every touch made her lose focus on what was at stake—her heart. He had that much power over her. He was her soulmate—her one true love.

It made her wonder if that was why she never pursued another serious relationship. Because in the back of her mind, she was constantly comparing any other man to Bear. Was that her heart's way of telling her that, eventually, their relationship would come full circle?

She let out a low growl as her frustrations came to a boil, and she buried her face in her pillow to muffle the sound.

The sound of a rain shower hitting the roof of the building had her looking up at the ceiling, and a sudden feeling of calmness washed over her.

During her months of recovery, both physically and mentally from the disease that inflicted great sorrow on her, the sound of the pitter-patter of rain was soothing, helping her to push through that scary and painful time in her life.

The sudden sound of a chair scraping against the concrete drew her eyes toward the door. She knew the guys were outside, sitting by the fire pits. Occasionally, she would hear them talking and laughing. It had become a staple in the evenings to gather and talk, and it warmed her heart that they all had welcomed her.

A small smile tugged at her lips as she thought about the men on the team. They were a delight to be around. She enjoyed spending time with them and getting to know each one more personally. In the short time she'd known them, she realized that they weren't just a bunch of macho, hot-headed SEALs who thought they were better than others. Each of them also had a gentle, soft side that told you who they were on the inside. She figured it was a side they didn't show everyone. She was gracious to be given that opportunity.

She placed her hand over her stomach as it rumbled. She had yet to eat dinner, and the fruit cup she had consumed earlier wasn't enough to satisfy her hunger. After the group finished up at the site, everyone returned to the building and took their turn getting cleaned up.

A smile played on her lips, thinking how her *she shower* had become quite popular with the team. When she asked the guys what they did for bathing when deployed and had no access to facilities, Playboy told her that it all depended on the mission and what was at their disposal. Sometimes they'd use unscented baby wipes, or maybe there was a body of water they would use. Many overlook those little things service members endured while risking their lives protecting our country, citizens, and allied nations.

In her opinion, every honorable military member should be commended for their service regardless of their job field. Because, at the end of the day, the military couldn't succeed without the hard work of every service member.

Before her mind could drift off to a different subject, a sudden knock at the door had her sitting up and wondering who it could be. Earlier, when she had walked out of the shower and found Bear sitting by her door, she had told him that she was likely to pass on dinner and that she was going to lie down. Before she could shout to the person to either come in or go away, the door cracked open, revealing Bear's handsome face, though his expression bore some guilt.

"Sorry to bother you, but Flora is here."

She scrunched her eyebrows together, wondering what the Chief's wife wanted. Jocelyn could only think that Flora would venture out in the dark if something were wrong.

Jocelyn stood up and walked towards the door. Before she could get out the door, Bear pulled himself entirely inside the room, blocking her from leaving. He leveled his intense gaze on her, making her retreat slightly to avoid bumping into him.

"Are you okay?" He asked, studying her carefully.

She searched his face, looking for a clue as to why he had asked her that. Judging from his concern, she wondered if she looked like she had felt on the inside—beat up and in turmoil. Feeling self-conscious, she reached for her face when Bear gently clutched her wrist in his extra-large hand, causing her to look deep into his eyes. She swore the longer she stared, the darker his eyes became, slowly drawing her in.

She soon jolted out of her trance and squared her shoulders. "I'm fine. Why do you ask?" She asked, sounding agitated and regretting her actions when the words left her mouth as Bear squinted his eyes and frowned.

She was lying through her teeth. She wasn't okay, and she wanted to tell him so. But then that would lead to them having a conversation that she really couldn't deal with at the moment. Not how her mind and heart felt, especially with him touching her.

With the frown still showing, he shook his head slightly and released her wrist before stepping back, putting some distance between them. He tried to mask it, but she could see the hurt in his eyes.

"Sorry. It just looked like something had upset you."

Damn! Now she felt bad for making him feel like shit. What was wrong with her? As she stood still, staring at him, she realized she wouldn't settle down until they talked about their situation.

She closed her eyes and took a deep breath, trying to draw some serenity. "Bear, I think—" But before she could speak the words she wanted, Bear cut her off.

"Flora's outside waiting. We shouldn't keep her waiting," he said flatly before opening the door and walking out, leaving her standing there wondering if anything else could go wrong. But before she could mull over the situation any longer, Flora appeared with a smile.

"Hi, Ms. Jocelyn. I hope I didn't disturb you," she stated, and Jocelyn sensed that the woman felt bad for having Bear disturb her.

Jocelyn smiled back, wanting to ease her concern, while she pushed her issue with Bear to the side. "Oh no. I was just resting for a bit."

Flora quirked her eyebrow. "Rough day?"

Jocelyn wondered if Flora knew what had happened earlier with the twins and Bear. But she quickly realized Flora knew nothing about her and Bear's situation.

"No. It was actually a good day. Very productive. Did you get a chance to stop by the site?"

"No. But we did hear about it. We planned to stop by tomorrow and look at the progress."

"We?" Jocelyn asked, her head cocked to the side.

Flora smiled. "Kosso and I."

"Oh! Has the Chief returned?"

"Yes. He returned mid-day today. In fact, he's the reason we're here."

Jocelyn's eyes widened in surprise. "Here? Chief Kosso is here with you?" She asked, hoping that wasn't the case because she wasn't prepared for the Chief's arrival.

As Flora pointed toward the fire pits, Jocelyn stuck her head out of the doorway and saw the back of a tall man with a slim build speaking with the guys. She then looked down at her dark gray cotton spandex shorts and cringed. She needed to change if she would be introduced to the Chief.

As if reading her thoughts, Flora placed her hand on Jocelyn's arm before she could turn around and gave her a warm smile.

"You look fine, dear."

Jocelyn scrunched her forehead up before giving herself a second look. She still wasn't convinced that her attire was fit for her first meeting with the Chief of the village.

"Here in Massendai, we don't judge people by appearance or dress. We primarily focus on what's here," Flora stated as she took Jocelyn's hand and placed it over Jocelyn's heart.

"Thank you, Flora."

"No thanks needed. Come. Let me introduce you to my husband."

Flora never let go of Jocelyn's hand as they headed toward the men who appeared to be having an amusing conversation. As she neared the tall man, she found herself trying to pull down the hem of her t-shirt to cover a large portion of her butt. No matter what Flora said, she still felt self-conscious wearing what she had on.

When Jocelyn and Flora approached the group, the man in question slowly turned around and smiled. Flora let go of Jocelyn's hand and stood beside her husband.

"Kosso, I'd like you to meet our savior, Ms. Jocelyn Thompson."

Jocelyn felt the blush creep into her cheeks at Flora's introduction. However, she pushed it aside and extended her hand to the gentleman.

"It's a pleasure to meet you, Chief Kosso."

Shaking her hand, Kosso grinned. "The pleasure is all mine, Ms. Jocelyn. And please, call me Kosso. There are no formalities here."

Jocelyn nodded, acknowledging the Chief's request. He wrapped his arm around Flora's shoulders, pulling her close to his side.

"We won't keep you long. I just wanted to come and introduce myself and meet the woman my dear wife couldn't stop talking about. All good things, that is." Again, Jocelyn felt her cheeks warm. "Flora and I plan to visit the site tomorrow and look around."

"That's wonderful. I also have a surprise for both of you." Jocelyn hadn't told them yet, but Ralph had informed her today that, for unknown reasons, an entire pallet of supplies was added to their shipment. With those extra materials, the crew planned to build a storage shed for the village to store buckets and other items for the well.

"A surprise?" Kosso asked, looking curious. However, Jocelyn didn't miss the excitement in his eye.

"Yes. It is a surprise."

Kosso smiled and looked down at his wife, who was smiling back at him, before turning his attention to Jocelyn.

"Well then, we can't wait to see it. Other than that, how is everything else been going? Nobody has caused any issues, have they?"

The question caused the hair on the back of Jocelyn's neck to stand up. She also noticed the heightened awareness from the guys as all eyes were now focused on the Chief.

"No. Everything has been moving along just fine, and everyone has been nice and gracious that we're here."

"That's good to hear," Kosso responded, but there was a change in his tone. Almost as if he sounded relieved.

Bear got up from his seat and stood beside her.

"Is there something or someone that we need to be watchful for?" He asked.

"No." Jocelyn sensed a "but" coming, and she wasn't wrong. "It's just that many powerful people have become drawn to our land. Some have made offers, while others have tried to use force. Once the project commenced, I thought it might have caused some inquiring minds to see if your business here is legit. But if you say everything has been operating smoothly, I have no concerns." Kosso offered a closed-lip smile to reassure them that things were fine, but it hadn't settled Jocelyn's nerves.

≈

When Jocelyn stepped out of the building and began talking to Kosso, Bear had watched her like a hawk—studying her body language and listening to her voice. He noticed when they had finished up at the drill site that her demeanor had shifted, and ever since they returned to the building, she had kept to herself and holed up in her room, even declining to have dinner with them.

His first thought was maybe she was just tired. After all, the temperatures had been scorching, and she had done a lot of manual labor. But after talking to her when he went to let her know that Flora and Kosso had come to see her, he sensed some agitation radiating from her that was directed toward him. Her brush-off had taken him back, but it only took him about a minute to realize why she had responded the way she had, and he honestly felt guilty about what had transpired back at the drill site.

While it made his lonely heart swell hearing the word husband roll off her lips, he recalled the pain and sadness he saw in her eyes as she admitted what she had told the cowboy twins. But then he couldn't help but wonder what she would've said to them if he hadn't been there. Had she only told them that because she had seen him and knew that he was jealous of them hitting on her?

He then felt another pang of guilt hit him as he remembered what he had told Jocelyn on the plane when he had given her the news about their situation. He had agreed to provide her with all the time and space she needed to decide. And honestly, he hadn't kept his word by following her like a lost puppy. Now he wondered if his overbearing caveman antics earlier had caused her to step back.

Pushing aside those thoughts, he returned to the conversation between Jocelyn and Kosso.

"How has everything else been going? Nobody has caused any issues, have they?" Kosso asked her, and the question struck a nerve with Bear. So many questions came to mind. Had there been a threat made in the past? If so, who? Was Jocelyn in danger?

He stood up and moved closer to Jocelyn.

"No. Everything has been moving along just fine, and everyone has been nice and gracious that we're here," Jocelyn told Kosso.

"That's good to hear," Kosso replied.

"Have threats been made against you or the village?" Bear asked.

"No. We haven't had any direct threats. It's just that over the years, we've had many powerful people come in and try to flex their money to overtake our land. Once the project commenced, I thought it might have caused some inquiring minds to see if your business here is legit. But if you say everything has been operating smoothly, I have no concerns."

Bear understood where Kosso's concern was. Living in a place where laws are not enforced to protect its citizens, he could see how one could be afraid to lose their land because of corruption and power. He had seen it many times during his career—money talks. Knowing there had been past inquiries about the land, Bear wondered if those same people would resurface now with a well being drilled. Clean water was a hot commodity—enough to bring threats.

"If we see or hear anything, we'll be sure to let you know," Bear stated firmly, holding Kosso's gaze. He wanted to ensure the Chief knew he and his team would take this information seriously.

Kosso nodded. "That would be much appreciated. However, I hope it doesn't come to that." Kosso then looked down at his wife and smiled—a smile that reached his eyes. "Well, I guess we will leave you all." He then looked at Jocelyn. "I'll be by the site tomorrow morning."

Jocelyn nodded. "I look forward to it. Have a nice evening."

With a final wave in the direction of the guys, Kosso guided Flora off the patio area and onto the path leading them back to the village's residential area.

Bear watched Kosso open an umbrella, shielding Flora from the rain. The love and care Kosso showed his wife was a stark reminder of how his idiotic decision ten years ago had made him miss those types of small moments with Jocelyn.

Sensing eyes on him, he turned his head and was met by Jocelyn's pinched eyebrows and a look of concern in her dark brown eyes.

"What are you thinking about?" He asked.

After a slight hesitation, she spoke, looking directly into his eyes. "I can't say why, but Kosso's question bothered me. It felt like he was putting us on notice that something or someone could become a problem." She paused a moment, then gave her head a slight shake. "Or maybe it's just my nerves. We are all aware of the dangers this area could bring to our doorstep at any given time."

Bear's expression softened. He understood and couldn't fault her for thinking that. And she was right. The locale was filled with dangerous possibilities, and none of them present, including him and his team, who were trained for situations as such, could afford to lower their guard.

Even though Kosso gave no names, Bear had a hunch that there was a particular person that Kosso was worried about. He'd ask his team about it later as he didn't want to bring it up in front of Jocelyn and have her worry any more than she already was. At least not until he had some answers. He'd ensure that he and his team were more vigilant and that Jocelyn was protected twenty-four-seven.

"You're right. We're in a very dangerous environment. But you still have a job to do. And you can't do that if you're constantly looking over your shoulder, waiting for something to happen. You've got us here with you. Let us do our job, which is to protect you. I'm not saying you shouldn't be cautious because that would just be idiotic. You certainly need to keep your guard up. Tell one of us if you see or feel something is off. We don't want you to put all your focus on worrying. Trust us to know that we've got your back.

"I do trust you—all of you. I just don't want to become a burden for you guys. You know me, Bear. I'm not a damsel in distress, and I won't start to act like one."

Bear shook his head, a slight smirk playing on his lips. "You're never a burden. And you definitely don't strike me as a damsel in distress. All I ask is that no matter where you go, you make sure that at least one of us is with you, though I'd prefer at least two."

He didn't want to scare her. He just wanted to call her attention to the importance of being smart. He hated the extra weight this probably added to her shoulders, knowing how much pressure she was under with a big project being watched worldwide.

"I understand that you guys have a job to do. You don't have to worry about me being uncooperative. I've been in some pretty bad places, though maybe not as unsafe as here. But believe me when I say that I know the risks at stake, and I'd never do anything stupid to jeopardize our lives. I may not be a SEAL or a part of your team, but the moment we boarded that plane a few days ago, I considered *us* a team—all eight of you and me. And I never let my teammates down."

Bear couldn't have been any prouder as he listened to Jocelyn address the team. He glanced around, looking at the guys as they listened, and it could be seen in their eyes how much respect she had gained from each one of them with her little speech. But the moment that nearly choked him up was when she said she considered him and the team a part of her team.

She didn't know how much truth was in her statement because the guys already deemed her a part of their team whether she realized it or not. But that wasn't all. She was more than just a teammate. She was part of their family.

Once she was finished speaking, Jocelyn took a deep breath before she looked at him and raised her eyebrows as if asking if what she'd said was okay. She looked so fucking adorable that he just wanted to wrap her up in his arms. Hell, he wanted to get this assignment over with, so he could take her home and shield her from all this negative shit.

Joker cleared his throat, getting their attention. And thank God he did it before Bear did something stupid.

"Joce, I say this on behalf of every guy sitting here. You are amazing. You are strong, confident, courageous, professional, mature, obedient, and so much more. Just because you don't have a background as we do doesn't make you any less than us. You, Jocelyn Thompson, carry all the qualities of what it means to be a SEAL, and I'd be proud to serve with you because I would never have to worry if you had my back or not."

Several others called out, "Ditto." When Bear looked at Jocelyn, he could see her eyes glistening. He stepped toward her, and he was happy when she didn't try to put any distance between them. She looked up at him, and he smiled, taking a strand of her hair and tucking it behind her ear.

"Joker's right, Joce. You are a part of this team." However, she had no idea how important she was to everyone here. But she'd learn soon enough once they all got home. He was probably getting ahead of the game, but that was okay. He was thinking positively. Jocelyn would be his again.

"Thanks," she whispered, blinking a few times to clear the tears from her brown eyes.

"I'm sorry if I upset you earlier. It just pissed me off seeing those guys touching you. I know that I should've handled myself differently."

The left side of her lips tugged upward. Was that a smile he was beginning to see?

"Apology accepted," she said, throwing him for a loop as he stared back at her, bewildered by the sudden change in her demeanor.

"Really?"

"Really," she repeated, her smile growing. "I think I owe you an apology as well. You caught me at a bad time when I had a lot on my mind. I shouldn't have gotten snappy with you." She paused to take a breath. "So, I'm sorry as well. Truce?" She asked, smiling as if she knew his answer—and she wasn't wrong. Of course, he'd forgive her. They wouldn't even be in this situation if it wasn't for his stupidity.

"Who's hungry?" Playboy called out, interrupting the moment between Bear and Jocelyn, and Bear could've given his teammate a swift kick in the ass for the intrusion. However, it was probably for the best, or it was possible that Bear may have just said fuck it and kissed her.

"Jocelyn, how about you? Duke is going to make some skillet pasta and cheese. It's one of those boxed meals. Do you want some?"

She tore her eyes away from Bear to answer Playboy, and Bear felt their connection disappear. But he wasn't too worried.

"No, thank you. I had some peanut butter crackers and a fruit cup a little while ago. Plus, I have some paperwork I need to take care of. I'll probably turn in early tonight."

"Okay. Well, if you change your mind, just let us know."

"I will. Thank you again," she replied, giving Playboy a small smile.

Before she left, she placed her hand on Bear's forearm. It was the first time that she had initiated physical contact with him. "My brain can't handle it tonight, but maybe sometime in the next couple of days, you and I can find time to talk."

He swallowed, trying to dislodge that imaginary lump sitting in his throat. "I'd like that," his voice coming out hard and raspy.

"Goodnight," she told him before telling the others she'd see them in the morning.

Bear watched her walk back to her room. Once she closed the door behind her, he walked over and retook his seat by the fire pit. He ran his fingers through his hair. The night had definitely been full of surprises.

"She okay?" Joker asked, seeming concerned.

He glanced at her closed door. "I think so. Though I almost fucked things up today." Jay Bird, Joker, and Duke had seen him lose his cool when he saw Kurt and Wayne touch her, but even they didn't know the whole story. So, he started explaining.

"Damn!" Snow stated out loud after Bear finished. "I can see how that could mess with her mind a bit. Even if she did panic, it should give you a good feeling that she thought of you."

"It does, and she just told me that she wants to find some time so that she and I can talk. But I don't want to cause any more stress for her by pushing her until she's ready. I'll give her the next couple of days to focus on her work without me hovering. I trust you guys to keep her safe."

Joker smirked. "That's fine, and you know we'll keep a watchful eye on her. But are you sure that you'll be okay with this arrangement?"

"I have to be if I want any shot of getting her back."

It would kill him not to be around her much, but he'd push through it if it meant spending the rest of his life with her by his side.

"I hope you realize what a gem you've got in her," Jay Bird told him, and Bear nodded.

"I'm well aware."

"Good. Then don't fuck it up again."

"You act like she has already decided and agreed to give me another chance."

"She will," Aussie said, sounding convinced that Bear had nothing to worry about. But Bear wasn't counting his chickens before they hatched.

"And down the road, if you find yourself in a dark place again like you were back then, just remember we're all here for you," Duke said.

"Thank you," Bear responded, trying the fight the lump in his throat. Times like this were one of the many examples of why he considered these guys his brothers in arms and his family. They had each other's backs all the time. It didn't matter if they were on the battlefield or off.

While the guys settled in and started talking about things back home, Bear relaxed in his chair and started thinking about what home would feel like with Jocelyn. They never got to experience the full effect of marriage since they had been living apart. However, during the few times they could see each other, they discussed a lot about their future, like buying a house, living together, raising a family, creating traditions, and so much more. He couldn't wait to see her expression when she saw their home for the first time. *Who is acting confident now?* He laughed to himself. He had to stay positive because he didn't think he would ever feel whole again without Jocelyn back in his life.

CHAPTER TWELVE

"*Good gracious. It's hotter than a horny housewife reading 50 Shades of Grey at the Magic Mike premiere,*" Jocelyn mumbled as she removed the light blue cooling towel from around her neck. She dunked it into the clean bucket of water before wiping her face with it. It was so hot out that the towel wasn't providing much relief. She'd kill for a blast of Arctic air right now, along with a change of clothes, considering hers were drenched from sweating and were sticking to her.

She spotted Ralph walking towards her. Standing beside her, he removed his ballcap and wiped the sweat from his forehead with a rag before readjusting the hat back on his head.

"I think we are ready to rock-n-roll tomorrow."

Jocelyn grinned. "I think so too. It's pretty exciting." She couldn't wait to start the actual drilling. They were one step closer to giving the village clean water.

"It sure is. I have to give it to ya, young lady. You run one hell of a project. The whole crew agrees too. Having been rained out yesterday, I was afraid we'd lose a whole day of work. But with the plan you brought today, we made up for it, and we're still on schedule. Not to mention, some of the guys started building out the bonus shed, which they should finish up tomorrow."

"Thanks, Ralph. I appreciate that." She turned around to get a better look at the shed the crew had started to build, and she was shocked at not only how much they had accomplished in just a day but also how big the structure turned out to be. She thought one of the guys said it was thirty-by-forty. She hadn't paid any attention to it until now since she had been focused on making up for yesterday's lost time and getting the actual site prepped so they could begin drilling.

Yesterday morning, everyone had woken up to a torrential rainstorm. Around noontime, the rain had slowed, and she thought the system had passed. But not even thirty minutes later, a monstrous thunderstorm blew into the area, dumping even more rain and producing dangerous lightning. Though, she had to admit that once the evening sky started to take shape, the bright flashes and streaks of lightning crawling across the sky were fascinating to watch.

Clearing his throat, Ralph lifted his chin in the direction to the left of where they were standing. "Looks like you've got yourself an audience."

Jocelyn followed his gaze, and a smile slowly formed on her lips. Amira, Maxime, and a few other children stood off to the side. They all seemed enthralled with all the equipment moving around. She waved and smiled at the group of onlookers, and they all gestured back, grinning and giggling. Standing behind the children and looking a bit out of place with their serious, tough, and authoritative presences were Duke and Playboy. She knew Nails was nearby, watching things from a different vantage point. Bear seemed to have kept his word when he promised her that she'd be protected, seeing to it that she had not two but three of the guys always assigned to her. In all honesty, it didn't bother her one bit because it was like what Bear had told her, that she'd be able to concentrate on her tasks without having to look over her shoulder every minute. She trusted the guys to have her back.

"They are very excited about getting the well," she told Ralph, and he smiled.

"They should be. It will be very beneficial for them and their families."

Jocelyn nodded in agreement. "That it will." She then glanced at her watch. *Dang! Where had the time gone?* She thought to herself. "I didn't realize it was already after two," she stated.

"Yeah. Time flies when we're busy. If you don't need anything else for today, I'm gonna have my crew start cleaning up for the day."

"Of course. They've done a wonderful job."

Saying goodbye, Ralph headed off in the direction of his men and started issuing orders.

Since she oversaw the project, she was always the last to leave after ensuring the site was in order and ready for the next day. While the crew gathered all their tools and materials, Jocelyn figured that now was as good a time as any to jot down her to-do list for tomorrow. She couldn't function without her lists. A small smile tugged her lips as she remembered how Bear would always tease her, saying that she had a list for her lists.

She grabbed one of the metal folding chairs before the crew put them away and walked toward the tree line. Finding a small shady spot, she planted the chair on the ground and sat down. She closed her eyes and almost groaned as she felt the muscles in her lower back start to loosen.

She placed her clipboard on her lap and wrote down a few tasks that needed to be completed tomorrow. Soon her mind started to wander, and of course, it traveled in the direction of her absent husband. She almost laughed out loud at herself. Apparently, her subconscious had already decided whether to give her relationship with Bear another shot. Of course, her heart still had some reservations about jumping back in with both feet.

With yesterday's bad weather halting work at the site, she hoped to have gotten the chance to speak with Bear. But he had been out of pocket with SEAL stuff for most of the day. At least, that was what Joker had told her when she asked about him. She had expected to see him this morning, but when she opened her door, she was met by Duke handing her a cup of coffee. When she asked where Bear was, Duke told her that he and Jay Bird were helping Flora with something and that he wasn't sure when they would return. A part of her wanted to ask what they were helping Flora with, but after a second thought, she decided not to press the issue. If they wanted her to know, they would've told her.

Even though she and Bear had apologized to each other the other night, she couldn't help but wonder if he was still upset with her for the attitude she gave him. She wouldn't blame him if that were the case because she was out of line. He didn't deserve her snappiness.

Bear didn't know, but she had already taken the first step in putting the past behind them. That same night after she said goodnight to him and the guys, she went to her room, and before she went to sleep, she pulled out the folder with the divorce papers and ripped up the previous documents that she and Bear had signed ten years ago. That didn't mean that she had made a final decision. Before she would give him her final answer, she needed to have a heart-to-heart discussion with him. But to do that, she needed him to make himself available.

Jocelyn hadn't realized she had zoned out until she felt the tiny hand touch her arm. Startled, she turned her head to the left and found Amira smiling at her with that adorable toothy smile.

"Hey, kiddo. What are you up to?" Jocelyn asked, securing the pen to the clipboard.

"Are you done working?"

"I am. We were just about to call it a day. Why? What's up?"

Amira suddenly seemed shy and lowered her eyes as if she was afraid to speak. Jocelyn then noticed something tucked under the girl's arm. Upon further examination, she recognized the board game. *Candyland* was one of Jocelyn's favorite games when she was a child.

"Would you like to play *Candyland*?" Jocelyn asked Amira.

Amira raised her eyes and slowly nodded her head. Jocelyn didn't miss the hopefulness in the little girl's eyes. "Do you want to play with me?" Amira asked, and her small and soft voice nearly melted Jocelyn's heart.

"I'd love to," Jocelyn told her.

Amira's eyes widened, and her smile grew bigger. "Really? You'll play with me?"

Jocelyn chuckled. "Are you kidding? I love *Candyland*."

Jocelyn stood up, took Amira's hand, and walked them over to the new storage facility, where a large piece of plywood was lying on the ground that they could sit on and use the building to shield them from the hot sun.

Duke and Playboy followed and took up positions next to the building. She felt a little guilty for not asking them if they had any objections hanging around for a little bit while she spent some time with Amira. Just as she was getting ready to ask Duke, Nails appeared from around the side of the building and stopped right next to where Jocelyn and Amira were sitting.

"*Candyland*!" He shouted. His excitement drew a giggle from Amira. Jocelyn couldn't help but join Amira in laughing at the big goofball.

Amira leaned over and whispered in Jocelyn's ear. "I forget. What is his name?"

Jocelyn whispered back. "Nails." She wondered why the little girl had asked. But then Amira tilted her head way back as she looked up at the SEAL, who looked like a giant towering over them.

"Mr. Nails, would you like to play *Candyland* with us?"

Jocelyn tried to contain her laughter, hearing Amira call him Mr. Nails. Nails must've also found it amusing, seeing the one corner of his lips twitch upward.

Shocking her, Nails fell to his knees, joining them on the ground.

"I'd love to play," he replied, and Jocelyn appreciated his kindness toward Amira.

"Yay!" Amira squealed in excitement. She glanced at Duke and Playboy. "Do your friends want to play too?" She asked Nails.

Jocelyn saw the mischievous gleam in Nails' eyes before he looked up over his shoulder at Duke and Playboy. "You guys want in on some *Candyland*?"

Grinning, both SEALs politely declined. Playboy then turned his attention to Nails. "We know how much you love the game, Nails. We wouldn't want to upset you when we beat you," his voice was laced with amusement. Playboy then bent down and whispered to Amira, even though they all could hear. "Duke and I will keep an eye on Nails and make sure he doesn't cheat."

Amira nodded and seemed to take Playboy's words to heart as she turned back toward Nails and shot daggers at him. "Cheating is bad, Mr. Nails."

Jocelyn covered her mouth to suppress her laugh as she watched Nails' face turn red as a tomato as Amira chastised him. She couldn't contain the small bubble of laughter that spilled over when Nails reached behind his back so Amira couldn't see and flipped Playboy the middle finger.

"I promise I don't cheat, Amira. Playboy is just envious because he's not the *Candyland* champ."

Playboy snorted while Duke coughed to cover his laugh. Jocelyn couldn't hold her laughter in anymore and fully laughed out loud. Nails threw her a playful wink before taking the lid off the box and helping Amira set up the game. A few minutes later, the three of them were plunged into a battle of who owned the title of *Candyland* champ.

ஒ

Jocelyn leaned back, stretching her back. She'd been in the same position for the last hour and a half while they played *Candyland*. Nails hadn't been lying. He really was the *Candyland* champ. He won all six games they had played. Maxime had joined them for the last two games after his two friends had left to return home. Jocelyn knew that Maxime only played because of Amira. She could see that Maxime loved and cared greatly for this little sister. Otherwise, he wouldn't have stuck around to walk her back to the village. She noticed that many kids, including the ones younger than Amira, roamed freely around the village without parental supervision. Even though she understood the different cultures, it just wasn't something that she agreed with.

Jocelyn had to admit that she enjoyed the time with the kids. It brought her great joy to hear them laugh and see them smile. Nails had made it entertaining with his charming and playful antics. It was apparent that he was very competitive, even playing *Candyland*. Whenever he picked up a card that made him move backward on the board, he'd pout, making the kids laugh. Even Duke and Playboy had made fun of him.

As much fun as they were having, it was getting late as the sun was starting to dip in the sky, and Jocelyn knew that the kids probably needed to get home. She still planned to ask Flora more about their parents, even though Bear told her she should let it go. She couldn't help it, though. She was a big softy when it came to children, and something told her there was much more to their story than what they let on. It would continue to bother her if she didn't ask, so she might as well ask.

Jocelyn glanced at Amira and saw her yawning. *I'm right there with you, girl.* Jocelyn thought to herself as she decided to start packing up. She thought the kids would argue that they wanted to play, but Nails had surprised her and spoke up, promising Amira she could bring over a game to their place the following evening, and they would all play *Candyland*. Duke made the kids' day when he told them they could also make smores again.

Nails was talking to Maxime about astronauts and space stuff while helping Amira put all the game pieces back in the box when he suddenly got quiet and began to stare off into the distance. It was strange because when she followed his line of sight, all she saw was the tree line. It made her wonder what had gotten his attention. When he finally came out of the trance he seemed to be in, he quickly got to his feet and walked over to Duke and Playboy, who also seemed affected by whatever had happened, as their hardened expressions matched Nails'. They were speaking in hushed tones, so she couldn't hear what they were saying, but the sudden change in their demeanor didn't sit well with her.

"What's going on?" Maxime asked, drawing Jocelyn's attention from the SEALs to the boy beside her.

Her gut told her that whatever they were discussing wasn't good. But she wasn't going to share her opinion with the kids. There was no need to make them worry, especially if it wasn't the case.

"I'm not sure," she answered before changing the subject. "If you guys can give me a few minutes to check on a few things, I'll walk you back to your place." Even though daylight was left, she felt better knowing the kids were safely home. Plus, she didn't mind spending additional time with them.

"Okay," Maxime responded, returning to helping Amira box up the game pieces.

She started doing her daily routine of checking to ensure the crew had left nothing behind. The other day she had come across a tool belt that one of the guys had accidentally left.

As she walked toward a pile of debris, she also kept her eye on the three SEALs. Their behavior was still troubling her. As if knowing she was looking at them, all three turned in her direction and walked over to her.

"Everything okay? You guys seem a little...occupied." She asked, wondering if that was the right word to use.

"Oh. Yeah. Just work stuff."

In a nice way, those words meant the discussion was off-limits and for her to mind her own business.

"Oh, okay. I need to finish taking a walk through the site to ensure everything is good and ready for tomorrow. I hope you guys don't mind, but I told the kids that I would walk them back to their place after I finished."

Nails grinned. "Not at all. Duke, Playboy, and I need to conduct a sweep of the site perimeter before we leave. It should take us about ten to fifteen minutes."

Jocelyn quirked her eyebrow. That was something new. She wondered if that was part of their "work stuff" discussion. Of course, she couldn't leave it alone.

"Why do you guys need to do that? There's security in place when we aren't here."

"Bear suggested it. After Kosso's visit the other night, Bear thought taking a few extra precautions would be best. I promise we won't be far, and one of us will always have our eyes on you."

"I think I can handle things alone for that time," she said with a slight grin, and Nails smiled.

"I have no doubt that you can't. We'll meet you and the kids by the entrance to the site."

As Nails jogged toward the tree line to meet Duke and Playboy, Jocelyn continued around the site. Her lip curled up in disgust, hating how grimy she felt. She couldn't wait to get under the shower spray and wash away all the sweat and dirt from her body.

While she had a little time to herself, her thoughts went to Bear. She wondered what he was up to right now. While it had been nice to focus on her job without the distraction of him being near, she had to admit that she missed his presence. She hoped he and Jay Bird were finished with whatever they were helping Flora with so she and he could talk later this evening.

She spotted a large brown rectangular object on the ground as she neared the back left corner of the new utility shed. Upon closer examination, she realized it was one of the metal panels attached to the shed's exterior. She picked it up and placed it inside where the crew would see it tomorrow when they arrived.

Just as she walked back outside, a dark-colored Range Rover entered the drill site, kicking up dirt and creating a huge dust cloud in its wake. Jocelyn's heart began to pound in her chest as the vehicle made a hard right turn and started driving toward her.

It wasn't uncommon for vehicles to drive around the village, but what triggered an alarm was the high-end make of the vehicle.

The windows were heavily tinted, making it impossible to see into the vehicle. She looked around, hoping to spot one of the guys. A wave of uneasiness washed over her when she couldn't locate any of them.

She saw Maxime and Amira running towards her as they watched the vehicle come to a stop next to the building.

"Who is it?" Maxime asked, holding Amira's hand.

"I don't know, buddy. But I'm sure we are going to find out soon enough."

"Are Mr. Nails and his friends coming back?" Amira asked in her small, angelic voice.

"I hope so," she uttered to herself, her eyes scanning the tree line, trying to get a glimpse of the guys.

When she turned her attention back to the Range Rover, three men stepped out of the vehicle.

A sudden gasp from Amira grabbed Jocelyn's attention. When she turned to look at the little girl, Jocelyn became even more alarmed, seeing that Amira's eyes were full of trepidation as she held her brother's hand. Maxime, however, appeared the complete opposite. He was on edge, but his form was tense, and a fire burned in his eyes as he stared at the dark olive-skinned man driving. The man lowered his sunglasses, looking in their direction. Even with the distance separating them, Jocelyn felt the coldness of his stare. But it wasn't intended for her. It was directed at Maxime and Amira.

Jocelyn immediately went into protective mode and stepped in front of the kids, using her body as a shield, making it more difficult for the man to look at them. "Do you kids know that man?" Jocelyn asked them, not taking her eyes off the strangers.

Instead of answering her, Maxime slowly began to back away, pulling Amira with him.

"Maxime!" She called after him, but it was too late as the two kids hurried towards the tree line and disappeared on a path that led back to the village.

Her instinct was to go after them, but now she was curious to know who these men were and what was their relationship with Maxime and Amira.

She slid her phone from the side pocket of her leggings and quickly texted Nails. Even though he told her they would keep an eye on her, she needed confirmation that they knew she had visitors.

She got an immediate response saying they saw and were on their way.

As she slid the phone back into her pocket, the other two men, both Caucasian, started walking towards her.

"Hello there!" The taller of the two called out, offering a friendly wave and sporting a knock your socks off, megawatt smile. His accent reminded her of Flora's and the children's.

If it weren't for Maxime and Amira's knee-jerk reaction to seeing the one guy, she would think these strangers meant no harm. And maybe they didn't. However, she wasn't about to lower her guard.

"Hello," she greeted in return.

The closer they got, the more clearly she could see their features. There was no argument that both men were handsome, but the one who greeted appeared to be the leader, as the man walking with him seemed to follow his lead.

He definitely had a sense of style. Without even searching for the name, she knew his neatly pressed khaki pants and the dark hunter-green dress shirt he wore with the sleeves rolled to his elbows were designer brands. The rays of the late afternoon sun hit the top of his head, making the tips of his short midnight-black hair appear to glow. She couldn't see his eyes because they were hidden behind the designer sunglasses. The man screamed money and power.

When the two men stopped before her, she offered a small smile, hoping it would cover a bit of her nervousness. Plus, she didn't want to come across as being rude, as she didn't know what they wanted.

"Is there something that I can help you guys with?" she asked, hoping neither caught on to her nervousness.

Completely ignoring her question, he turned on the charm, flashing her a gorgeous smile, though she was tempted to shield her eyes from the whiteness of his teeth.

"I'm guessing from your accent that you must be the American everyone has been raving about."

His statement raised her eyebrows. It was obvious from the welcome she received that people were excited about her being there, but that alone didn't make her a celebrity. She also didn't like attention brought to her, especially from strange men who she assumed could have an ulterior motive.

"I'm sorry, but I think you might have me confused for someone else," she quipped with a slight laugh to her tone.

"No. I know you're the one. You're exactly how they described. Only much more beautiful," he declared, making her blush. His sunglasses masked his eyes, but there was no mistaking that he was checking her out, as the subtle up-and-down movement of his head hadn't escaped her, and she felt a sudden chill race up her spine.

He put forth his hand. "Pardon my manners. My name is William Corsica."

She grudgingly shook his hand. "I'm Jocelyn."

"It's a pleasure to meet you, Jocelyn." Will then motioned toward the man standing to his right. "This is my attorney, Tau Kenyetta."

Tau extended his hand, and Jocelyn reached out to shake it. "It's nice to meet you," she offered, then took a step backward. "What exactly brings you, gentlemen, to Massendai?" Jocelyn asked, cutting to the chase.

"Since I'll soon be taking over the ownership of this land, I thought I'd stop by and see the progress of the new well being installed."

The guy's statement threw Jocelyn for a loop. What did he mean by he'd soon be taking over the ownership of the land?

She then recalled Kosso's comment about powerful people wanting to take over Massendai and wondered if this guy was one of the individuals Kosso had been referring to. She didn't want to get in the middle of any land dispute, but she was curious.

"I didn't realize that the Massendai land was for sale."

Will smirked. "It's an off-the-record type of sale."

"Is the government aware of this sale?"

"It's a land sale. There is no need for the government's involvement."

Before Jocelyn responded, she spotted Nails walking around from the side of the building and felt an instant relief wash over her.

"Everything okay, boss," Nails asked, taking up position beside her. He was calm and collected, or so he appeared. So, she fed off his aura to help keep herself grounded and not show the stranger how alarmed she was. Nails had donned a ball cap that he had pulled down low to shield a portion of his face, but she didn't miss his wink and gave him a small smile.

"I was just chatting with our visitors here," she said, gesturing toward Will and Tau.

Crap! How did she introduce Nails to these guys? She knew darn well that the guys would not want her telling these men they were Navy SEALs. She glanced at Nails, who was openly glaring at Mr. Corsica. She had no idea why, but her great-grandmother's dog suddenly popped into her head. Grandma Ruth and the feisty Boston terrier had been dead for over fifteen years.

"This is Petey," she blurted out.

Nails made an odd sound with his mouth, and Jocelyn wanted to dig a hole in the sand and stick her head in it. *Petey? What the heck was she thinking? Nails looked nothing like a Petey. Petey was a dog, for heaven's sake.* She placed her hand on her forehead. *I think this extreme heat has fried my brain.*

Nails didn't appear put off by his new name. In fact, he fell right into the role, stuck his hand out, and smiled.

"Like she said, my name's Petey."

Both men accepted Nails' handshake, though they both seemed intrigued by Nails' sudden appearance.

"Petey is part of our security team," Jocelyn offered the small detail, hoping that was okay to say. She didn't want to venture too far from the truth.

"Security team?" Will questioned.

"The safety of our team is vital. Not to mention that this is a government-funded project, so we are taking all the necessary precautions to ensure the project runs smoothly," Jocelyn answered.

"I see," Will commented as he continued to eye Nails.

"Will is looking to *purchase* land here in Massendai, and he heard about the well, so he stopped by to see the progress," Jocelyn emphasized the word "purchase," hoping Nails would understand the message she was trying to relay.

"Oh! You must be one of the buyers that Kosso mentioned the other night," Nails stated, hoping his comment would bait Will into revealing more information.

"What do you mean buyers?" Will questioned, appearing a bit flustered, which Jocelyn found interesting.

Nails gave his shoulder a slight shrug. "I don't have any names. Kosso just mentioned that there were other offers."

Nails' statement seemed to have struck a nerve with Will, but he tried to laugh off Nails' comment. "I can assure you that nobody can beat my offer."

"You seem very confident. Maybe Kosso could change his mind and decide not to sell." Jocelyn had to fight back her smile, knowing Nails was intentionally trying to rile up the guy.

Will's lips curled into an evil grin. "There are other ways to secure this land without his consent."

"Like what?" Jocelyn questioned. She wasn't liking where this discussion was going.

"You're not in America anymore, sweetheart. Situations are handled differently here." The coldness in his tone froze her in place.

Jocelyn wasn't sure what to think about the situation. Her responsibility in Massendai was to see that a working well was drilled. However, if Will stuck to his word and intended to take over the land using tactics not deemed legal, Jocelyn didn't want herself, the crew, and the team to end up in the middle of a land dispute. Surely, the team who assisted Lana with negotiations for this project would've done their homework and removed Massendai from the list had they known that a potential land war could occur. And, it would indeed be a war, should Will make good on his threats.

She wondered what the draw was to this specific land. Would he even allow the people of Massendai to stay, or would he force them out? God, she hoped not.

"What about this land makes you want it so badly? And if you take ownership, do you intend to let the people stay?"

Will removed his sunglasses, revealing a set of unique eyes, like someone else she knew, except Will's were light blue, as to Bear's grey eyes. Will's eyes could draw someone in with their translucent shade. But Jocelyn wasn't fooled. Her gut knew that behind those vivid orbs lay a hidden darkness full of malice. She began seeing that evilness creep forward the longer he stared at her.

"I'm a businessman, Ms. Thompson. It's a prime piece of land, considering its location and what it's worth. As far as the people here, I can't give you a definitive answer now."

She nodded her head. She was ready to put this impromptu visit to bed, but before she did that, she had one more question.

"You said that the reason for your visit today was to see the progress on the project. However, I'm not convinced that's the real reason. The project is scheduled to wrap up next week, and I'm sure we'll be long gone before your supposed takeover happens. So, tell me, Mr. Corsica. What is the true purpose of your being here?"

"For the record, I was telling the truth. I was curious about the project. And yes, I could've waited and seen the finished project. But by doing that, I wouldn't have been able to meet you, Ms. Thompson."

Jocelyn felt all the blood drain from her face and started feeling lightheaded. If it weren't for Nails sensing her distress and placing his arm around her to steady her, she probably would've keeled over.

"Well, now that you've *met* her and have seen the progress on the project, I assume that we won't see you again," Nails conveyed to Will, making it clear with an authoritative tone that he wasn't wanted around here.

Tau, the silent one, seemed to heed Nails' warning as he retreated to the car. On the other hand, Will held her gaze before his wicked, arrogant smirk reappeared.

She didn't want to appear weak in front of these men, so she wanted to make sure that she issued her own warning.

"Your real estate dealings are not my concern. However, the safety of my crew is. Since this project is backed by the U.S. government and the Chadian government, I hope you understand that I'll have to make some calls that could potentially lead to an investigation into the sale of this land."

She was again met with his stare as he casually slid his sunglasses on, shielding his evil eyes. Before he turned to walk to the car, he left her with some parting words of his own.

"Do what you feel is necessary, Ms. Thompson. Just remember what I said—one way or another, this land will belong to me. And a word of advice to you and your team. Don't test my patience." Then without another word, he ducked into the vehicle and shut the door.

"Well, I think we now know who Kosso might have been hinting about," Nails stated as they watched the Ranger Rover speed away. "That man has got to be the most arrogant asshole I've ever met. I should've just pummeled his ass."

Jocelyn nodded in agreement while still using Nails to lean on. She still felt too weak to stand on her own. She looked up at him.

"Are you okay?" he asked, looking concerned.

"I think so." She gave him a weak smile. "You know, if I weren't in love with Bear, I'd give you a big kiss right now," she confessed, letting Nails support more of her weight.

The low rumble of Nails' laughter pulled her from her semiconscious state, and only then did she realize what she said.

"You didn't hear that," she mumbled. She was too exhausted to worry about it.

"I can pretend I didn't hear you. But I can't say that the others didn't."

She wondered what he meant by that. There was nobody else around. Slowly, she pulled her head back and managed to crack one eye open to get a look at him. The playful gleam in his eyes, paired with his mischievous grin, told her that he was up to something.

"What do you mean by that?"

Chuckling, he pointed to his ear. When she looked, she saw the small black gadget in his left ear. Her mouth formed an "O," realizing he had been communicating with his team.

"My mic was still on," he told her, his expression now a mixture of apologetic and amusement.

"Oh…"

"And before you ask, everyone was connected."

She could feel her eyes growing bigger by the second. "When you say, everyone—"

"I mean everyone. Including Bear."

She pressed her hand to her forehead. *Oh God! How embarrassing!*

"Where is he?"

"On his way here."

"Here?!" She squeaked out.

"Yep. In fact, there he is now," he said, pointing in the direction behind her.

She spun around, and sure as shit, one of their SUVs was heading right toward them. She wasn't ready for this. Yes, dammit. She still loved Bear. But this was not how she wanted him to find out. Nor did she want to announce it to everyone else at the same time.

Her body broke into a cold sweat, and her mouth and throat suddenly went dry. It was all too overwhelming. She covered her mouth with her hand as she sensed the onset of an anxiety attack. Her heart began to beat faster, and her breathing became shallow. She felt her chest tighten, and she struggled to get oxygen to her airway.

In the distance, she heard doors slamming and someone calling her name. When she looked up, she saw Bear running towards her. His rugged but handsome face was etched with worry. His mouth was moving, but she couldn't hear anything with the constant buzzing sound in her ears. She tried to take a step toward him, but she faltered, and everything around her started to spin. It was like she was being swept up in a vortex until everything in her world went black.

☙

When Bear saw Jocelyn lose all the coloring in her face and her eyes started to roll back in her head, he was compelled to make it to her in time before her body crashed into the ground.

Just as he moved around Nails, her legs buckled, and he was able to sweep her into his arms. He pulled her close, holding her limp body against his chest. Her skin felt hot, and she was sweating profusely.

"Joce!" Bear shouted as he gently shook her, trying to wake her.

"What the hell happened?" Duke asked, running over and seeing Jocelyn unconscious in his arms.

"I think she had an anxiety or panic attack," Nails offered, looking worried like the rest of them were.

Duke felt her forehead. "Maybe. But she's also really hot. "Let's get her to the SUV and inside the air conditioning." He turned to Nails. "Grab the cooler."

Bear rushed toward the vehicle. Snow opened the back passenger door, and Bear slid inside with Jocelyn still in his arms. Duke climbed in on the other side, and Nails set the cooler down just outside.

"I need a towel or something," Duke called out. Jay Bird pulled his t-shirt off and handed it to Duke. Duke then dunked the t-shirt in the cooler filled with half-melted ice, then brought it to Jocelyn's face, gently pressing the cold cloth against her heated skin.

Bear looked down at her and whispered, "Come on, sweetheart. Please open your eyes." He brushed back a few strands of hair from her face that came loose from her ponytail.

He felt so helpless not being able to do anything for her. His heart was divided into two. One side was breaking because she was hurt, while the other was bursting, knowing she still loved him.

He was glad that Nails had forgotten to turn off his mic because hearing Jocelyn's voice brought him a little calmness in the wake of what went down with those men. But the true joy was hearing her confess her love for him.

He lifted her head a little and kissed her forehead. Seconds later, he felt her stir, and he pulled back.

"She's coming to," Duke said. They all watched as her eyes slowly began to open.

Bear released a huge sigh the second Jocelyn's dark brown eyes locked with his. He smiled softly.

"Hey, gorgeous."

She started to sit up, but he held her tight while Duke spoke to her.

"Don't move too much, honey. You passed out, probably from the heat and being stressed with everything that happened."

Bear helped her sit up a little more, and Duke handed her a cold water bottle. "Take small sips," he instructed as he held her wrist, checking her pulse. After a minute, he smiled. "Your pulse is good. How are you feeling otherwise?"

Jocelyn scrunched up her nose. "Other than feeling embarrassed, I think I'm okay."

Bear laughed along with the others. However, in the back of his mind, he wondered if she was embarrassed because she passed out or because of what she admitted. In his opinion, neither one was anything to be embarrassed about.

She went to move off his lap, but he tightened his arms around her. She looked up at him, and her cheeks started turning pink.

Get used to it, sweetheart, because I'm never letting you go.

☙

What the ever-loving fuck! Jocelyn thought to herself as she found herself sitting on Bear's lap, wrapped up in arms.

Her head was throbbing, she felt a little nauseous, and she couldn't stop shaking. Her hand went to her stomach.

"Do you feel sick?" Duke asked, looking at her.

"I feel a little nauseous, but I don't think I'll be sick."

Duke seemed to be okay with her response as he nodded his head.

"Keep sipping on the water, and when we get back to our quarters, I want you to rest."

While she took a sip of water, she stole a glance at Bear, and he smiled as he held her on his lap.

"Are you sure that you're okay?" He asked; his voice was low and rough. But boy, did the sound do things to her insides.

"I think so." She inhaled deeply, lowering her eyes, as she was afraid of what else she might do or say if she kept looking into his grey eyes. They were so captivating.

She took another sip of water and then another. Soon she started to feel better as the dizziness subsided, and her body started to cool down. She tried to move off his lap again, and this time he let her, and she slid into the middle seat next to him. The guys started piling into the vehicle.

Duke sat on her other side while Nails took the front passenger seat. Playboy and Snow got in the back cargo area.

The ride back to their quarters only took about a minute, but it felt like an hour for Jocelyn. Everyone was quiet—almost too quiet for her.

"What's for dinner?" Snow asked, breaking the silence.

"I don't know. Ask *Petey*. It's his turn to cook," Jay Bird answered, pointing to Nails and trying not to laugh. But it didn't do any good as everyone in the car started laughing, including Jocelyn.

"I'm so sorry, Nails. I had to introduce you, and I didn't want to tell those guys your real name or what you were." She explained, but Nails waved her off with a smile.

"It's all good. But I do have to ask. Out of all the names, where did you get Petey from?"

Jocelyn chuckled. "Petey was my grandmother's Boston Terrier."

The guys started carrying on about Nails being a dog, and Jocelyn felt bad, but Nails assured her that he was fine and that his feelings weren't hurt even though he pretended to pout. Amidst the laughter, Bear lightly nudged her shoulder, and she looked up at him.

"In all seriousness, you did good out there," he told her, and she shook her head.

"I passed out. How is that good?"

"I'm not talking about that part. I'm talking about how you handled yourself with those men and thought quickly regarding Nails' presence."

She knew that Corsica's visit contributed to her mental exhaustion. However, that incident isn't what triggered her panic attack. It was her and Bear's situation and what had slipped out of her mouth while talking to Nails, not knowing that his mic was on for all to hear.

Looking at Bear, she wondered what thoughts were going through his mind. And what had been his reaction when he heard her words? Whatever it was, she knew she was going to have to address the elephant in the room.

She licked her lips and was prepared to say something on the subject when Bear leaned down, his lips against her ear, and whispered, "We'll talk later. Just you and me." Then he kissed the side of her head.

She stayed still, staring at him. How on earth did he know what she was going to say?

He grinned and winked before opening the door and sliding out. He held his hand out for her to take. Taking a deep breath, she placed her hand in his, slid across the seat, and exited the vehicle.

Joker was standing there with a concerned look as he eyed her over.

"You okay, Joce?"

She smiled. "Yeah. I'm good. Thanks for asking."

"Good to hear. Clover would have our asses if something happened to you," he said, grinning.

"Clover isn't the only one. I can only imagine how my mother would react," Bear added.

"Well, it's a good thing that I'm okay, and they don't have to know about my little incident," Jocelyn piped in, looking between both men. However, neither one looked satisfied with her comment.

"Did you forget that my mom eventually finds out about everything?" Bear commented with his eyebrow raised. He did have a point. Jenelle had a special ability to find things out. It was amazing she hadn't discovered her and Bear's secret.

"Well, we can all pretend that this is a classified mission, and because it is, then nothing can be spoken about it outside of the team," she explained, giving them both a cheeky smile.

Both Joker and Bear barked a laugh.

"She's got a point, Bear," Joker said, agreeing.

Bear looked at her, still smiling. "Yeah. She does."

Joker then became serious, looking at Bear. "I spoke with Derek and updated him on the situation, and he is looking into it and should have something back for us later this evening."

Jocelyn knew the situation he referred to was about their visitors. She was curious about what their commander could come back with.

"What all is he looking at," Jocelyn asked.

"Anything that can tell us who he is. Right now, we've got nothing."

She looked at Bear. "We also need to talk to Kosso and find out if this guy is one of the individuals that has been trying to throw his power around."

"We will. But we have to wait until tomorrow morning," Joker stated.

"Why is that?"

"According to Flora, after he met you at the site this morning, he got a call from one of his brothers who runs another village near the lake. Something about an issue with a boat or something. So, he had to go over there."

That was a bummer. She was hoping to get some answers today. But if he wasn't available, there was nothing they could do about it. It did impress her with how fast they had done things.

"Do you think they'll come back? Will and his buddies?" She asked.

"It's hard to say. He's an arrogant guy. He seems like one of those types who won't stop until they get what they want," Bear told her.

Jocelyn's shoulders slumped. "That's what I thought." But coming face-to-face with Will again wasn't the only thing she was worried about. Her focus turned to Maxime and Amira. Their reaction to seeing that one man didn't sit right with her. She wanted to see them and ask them some questions.

"I need to check on Maxime and Amira," she told them and started walking down the path leading to their property. But then Bear wrapped his arm around her waist and pulled her back. She looked up at him and quirked an eyebrow at him.

"The kids are fine."

"How do you know?"

"Nails, Duke, and Playboy were watching the whole time, and they saw the kids' reaction when they ran off, so they called Joker, and he sent Aussie to follow them home."

"And they're fine? Nobody followed them?"

"They went straight home, and Aussie waited around to make sure. You can ask him yourself when he gets back."

Hearing they were safe settled her nerves a bit, but she was still worried.

"I believe you." She sighed. "If Will was telling the truth, and he takes ownership of this land, my main worry is that these people will lose their homesteads." Just the thought of that happening made her sick to her stomach. If Will evicted everyone, then everything they were doing here would be for nothing.

Bear placed his hands on her shoulders and gave them a gentle squeeze.

"We'll have to wait until we talk to Kosso to know this guy's intentions."

"I know. I just worry."

Joker excused himself, saying he was helping Nails, aka Petey, with dinner.

Jocelyn rubbed her arm and felt the sweat and grime against her skin. She felt gross. And she was tired. She didn't tell Bear or any of the others, but she also still felt a little woozy.

She turned toward Bear. "I think I'm going to shower and then try to call Lana and let her know what happened."

"Derek called Rick, so I'm sure Lana already knows." He stepped closer and rubbed his hands up and down her arms. "Are you sure that you're feeling okay?"

"If you're referring to me passing out…I won't lie. I still feel a little off-kilter. But if you're asking if I'm okay about the other thing…then no." She saw Bear's small smile slip, and she was quick to elaborate. "But not because of the reason you're thinking."

"What do you think that I'm thinking?"

"That what I said wasn't true."

"Was it true? What you said to Nails."

He was backing her into a corner. She stared at him. Finally, she caved. "Yes."

"And you panicked because you said it out loud?"

"Yes, and because everyone heard."

"Well, I'm glad that everyone heard you."

Her head jerked up, meeting his eyes. He removed his hands from her shoulders, and she immediately felt the loss of his touch. But she didn't need to worry because his strong arms slid around her waist a second later, and he pulled her flush against him. The feel of his embrace and the scent of his intoxicating cologne consumed all her senses. He then lowered his head and gently kissed her just below her ear, against her neck. He knew his touch there would send tingles throughout her body, which it did, making her want things she couldn't have. At least not yet.

"Bear..." she breathed out, closing her eyes as she tried to regain her composure.

"Do you know why I'm glad that everyone heard you?" His warm breath felt like a feather caressing her ear.

She couldn't speak, so she shook her head and held her breath, awaiting his answer.

"Because now they all know that you're mine," his voice came out breathy and raspy. And it did a number to her insides, sending her libido into overdrive. She felt herself getting hot and knew she needed to pump the brakes before they got carried away. They still had much to discuss because they could even think about jumping each other's bones.

She pulled away first, and he released her, but seeing the cocky smirk on his face told her that he knew exactly what he had done to her.

"I'm gonna go get that shower now. A very cold shower," she said more to herself as she walked toward her room. But Bear's laughter behind her told her that he heard what she said.

God help me!

☙

Jocelyn threw the light sheet off her legs and sat up. She'd been tossing and turning for the last hour and a half. Even though her body craved some rest, her mind was restless, making it difficult to find that inner peace to drift off to sleep.

Several topics were occupying her brain.

Thank goodness Bear controlled himself during dinner, and nobody spoke about her expressing her love for Bear over their open comms system. But even though it wasn't discussed, it didn't mean it wasn't on her mind.

But the more important issue at hand was figuring out what this Will character was up to. They still didn't have much information on the guy. Derek, the team's commander, had called while they were eating dinner. He told them that several federal agencies had been notified and were looking into the situation and hopefully would have more for them in a day or two.

After dinner, Bear got his laptop out and googled Will Corsica. The search pulled up different articles and photos. The photos were mainly of him with different women. Reading how he was considered a ladies man wasn't surprising, seeing how he tried to use his charm on her when they had met. She assumed he was wealthy, but she hadn't expected to read that his estimated worth was eight hundred million dollars. That fact had even surprised a few of the guys. But what caught her attention was learning that most of his fortune was made in the mining and real estate industries. The bit of information had the wheels in her head turning. She knew that Africa as a whole was a beacon for mineral mining. It had the largest reserves of diamonds, cobalt, platinum, and uranium. It also had forty percent of the world's gold. But the question that sat in the back of her mind was, what made the land in Massendai so special that Corsica and possibly others would go to extreme lengths to get their hands on it?

She massaged her temples. She needed to quit thinking so much. *Yeah, like that would happen.*

She lifted her hand and sighed as she looked at her watch. It was only a little after two in the morning.

She lay there in the dark staring at the ceiling. The only sound was a low hum coming from her small solar-powered fan.

She slid out of bed and slipped on her flip-flops. She wondered which one of the guys was standing watch. When she stepped out of her room, she saw Duke sitting in one of the chairs, a small fire burning in front of him. She spotted the cup in his hand and wondered if it was coffee. Even though she shouldn't, a cup of coffee sounded good.

As she approached, Duke met her gaze. His eyebrows were furrowed.

"Everything okay?" He asked in that deep southern drawl of his.

"Yeah. I just woke up and couldn't go back to sleep."

"I'm sure you've got a lot on your mind. Wanna sit?" he asked, gesturing to the empty chair beside him.

"Sure."

He reached down and lifted a thermos. "Coffee?"

She smiled. "I'd love some, but I know I shouldn't. Though, I don't see myself getting any sleep tonight."

Duke eyed her curiously as he poured the coffee into a paper cup and handed it to her.

"Are you worried about your meeting with Kosso tomorrow?"

She wrapped her hands around the cup and took a sip.

"That's one reason. There's just something about this Corsica guy that has me worried. This may sound weird, but when he took his sunglasses off and glared at me. I felt like I was staring into the eyes of the devil himself. His eyes gave off a strong vibe that he has no good intentions."

Duke nodded. "You can learn a lot about a person just from their body language."

"Is that something you guys practice?"

"It is. Knowing what to look for can sometimes save a life."

"That's cool. I mean, not the saving a life part. I wouldn't want any of you to be in that kind of position. Though, I'm sure you have—numerous times. And oh, my God. Listen to me. I am just babbling now."

Duke laughed. However, Jocelyn felt mortified. Maybe she should go back to bed.

"I get what you mean. And yeah. It's kinda cool. It's like a secret weapon."

"Anyway, getting back to Kosso. I know there really isn't anything we can do because it isn't our land. But it just doesn't make any sense why our government would enter a project with the Chadian government knowing there was a possibility that the village could be wiped away."

"That's true."

They were both silent while they sipped their coffees.

"What else is going on in that mind of yours?"

She snapped her head up. "What?"

He grinned. "When I asked you earlier about your meeting, you said that was one of your thoughts. What else are you thinking too hard about?"

She nibbled her bottom lip nervously and looked around. She wondered who else was up.

"If you're looking for Bear, he's asleep. They all are except for Aussie and me, of course."

When she looked at Duke, he was smiling over the rim of his coffee cup.

"What made you think I was looking for him?" She asked, trying to play it off that she wasn't.

Duke quirked his eyebrow. "Honey, I may be from the south, but I ain't stupid," his southern accent was thick.

She stared quietly out into the dark distance before looking back at him.

"Have you ever been in love, Duke?"

"I have."

She glanced at his ring finger, noticing that it was bare, and she wondered if he was married and just didn't wear his ring when he deployed.

"Are you with her now?"

Duke shook his head. "Nope. She broke my heart."

"What happened? That is, if you don't mind me asking."

"She was unfaithful."

Jocelyn felt terrible for Duke. He seemed like a really sweet guy.

"That's awful. I'm so sorry."

He shook his head and gave her a small smile. "It's okay. It's been almost two years. I'm mostly over it."

"Mostly?" She questioned.

"She and I were high school sweethearts. The worst part about it was that I never saw it coming. There were no warning signs. I'm just glad I never proposed." He snorted a sarcastic laugh. "Maybe the sign was there. Several times I had planned to propose to her, but something always interfered before I could. As much as I loved her, it was obvious that she didn't feel the same love for me. She said she loved me but wasn't in love with me if she felt she needed to share another man's bed."

"Well then, that means your soulmate is still out there waiting to be found."

He smirked. "Maybe so."

They both sat there for a few minutes, listening to the fire crackle. Suddenly, a question that had been lingering in the back of her mind the last day or two came to the forefront.

"Has Bear been in any serious relationships?"

"Have you?" He answered with a question. One of his eyebrows was raised.

"I'm sorry. That was wrong of me to ask that, especially to ask you."

She felt embarrassed now. She started to stand when Duke placed his hand on her arm.

"Wait," he said, and she sat back down.

He took a deep breath. "Look, I'm not going to get between you and Bear. However, Bear is my teammate and friend. I'm not condoning what he did, but I do believe that people make mistakes. You need to let him explain things to you. Then, if you don't like what he has to say, you move on. But at least give him an opportunity. What he has to tell you may surprise you."

"I'll always listen to what he has to say. I just wish there was more time in the day so we could talk soon. I think the waiting is what is driving me crazy."

Duke chuckled. "Love does make you crazy—in many ways."

She downed the rest of the coffee and then stood up.

"Thank you, Duke. And I hope you find your one and only soon. You're too good of a man not to have a strong, loving woman by your side."

He smiled. "Thanks, Joce. Goodnight."

"Night."

She started to walk back to her room when Duke called her name.

"Hey, Joce?"

She looked over her shoulder. "Yeah?"

"The answer is no."

She scrunched her forehead up.

"The answer to the question you asked. It's no."

She nodded and smiled. "My answer is also no."

CHAPTER THIRTEEN

"Has Moussa checked in yet?" Will asked, looking at Tau as the duo each sat at the bar inside a tavern in Johannesburg. It was a little after midnight local time, and Will was spent from his long day. He probably should've gone home and tried to get some needed sleep, but with his mind racing, he knew sleep wouldn't come easily. So, after getting off the plane, he decided a strong drink or two at the small tavern near his home would help alleviate the restlessness that was seizing him.

Since leaving Massendai hours ago, a heavy feeling of anxiousness consumed him, which wasn't typical for his character. It was out of the norm for him to get this worked up. Previously, when he would run into issues, he handled them efficiently, using any means necessary. However, the matter plaguing him didn't allow much time for drafting and executing a plan. Not to mention, there was a huge obstacle in the way.

Even though Will was a household name for many in the mining and real estate industry, that didn't mean he had an abundance of friends. Most were considered acquaintances, as he was selective with who he allowed into his private life. Being a multimillionaire and one of Johannesburg's most sought-after bachelors made him a magnet for opportunists.

The select few who knew the real Will Corsica would chalk up his current frame of mind to the fear of him knowing he might lose out on a deal that would've had him set for life financially. Of course, money was important, especially the hundreds of millions that were on the line. But that wasn't the case. The anxious feeling overwhelming him was all because of the feisty yet stunning little firecracker Jocelyn Thompson.

His instincts hadn't proved wrong with the decision to make the trip north to Massendai, using his potential land deal as a pretext. The moment he stepped out of the car, laid eyes on the tall, voluptuous woman, and felt the front of his pants tighten, he knew he wanted to bed her. She was stunning in how she presented herself—a little timid, yet he could see her confidence grow as she spoke. But that feistiness and determination radiating from her captured his full attention. Whenever she opened her mouth and spoke, it was like listening to his favorite melody. Her voice was mellifluous—smooth, sweet, and musical. He could only imagine what she would sound like calling his name as he fucked her, though he didn't see that happening. She seemed to come with a lot of baggage. But who knew, maybe their paths would cross in the future.

Hearing Tau speak pulled Will back into the conversation and away from his sexual desires. Man, he needed to get laid.

"He left a voice mail. Nandi wasn't home. There was an emergency at a neighboring village, and they asked for her assistance. Moussa said she should be back sometime in the morning. He'll call after he speaks with her."

Giving his head a nod, Will sank his hand into the peanut bowl in front of him. Throwing a handful of the salty snack into his mouth, he couldn't stop thinking about *her*.

After leaving Massendai, Will and Tau flew back to Johannesburg while Moussa stayed behind to conduct a little reconnaissance. He was skeptical of Jocelyn and her little security team.

Moussa had connections inside the village, including Nandi, his wife. Nandi had a way of seeking out information they needed. He also needed to ensure that Moussa's kids wouldn't be a problem. Even though Moussa assured him that the kids weren't privy to what was happening, Will wasn't convinced. He wasn't so much concerned about the girl. It was the boy that Will believed could soon be a problem, and he voiced his concern with Moussa. The last thing he needed was to have two nosey kids ruin his plans.

"What will ya have?" Barron, the owner of the tavern, asked.

"Two witblits shots, please. On second thought, make it four," Will ordered, drawing an amused look from Tau.

"Someone's thirsty," Tau uttered, one of his eyebrows cocked, knowing for a fact that three of the four drinks would be consumed by Will.

Will shook his head, a grin spanning his face. He gave his shoulder a slight shrug as Barron set four shot glasses down on the bar and filled them with the clear, potent liquid. Will's mouth watered as he anticipated the slow burn the drink would bring to his insides. After all, there was a reason the locals nicknamed it firewater. But on the upside, because of the high alcohol content the drink contained, it was perfect for numbing his mind.

"I figured I'd save Barron the hassle of making another trip. Plus, I feel like I'm going to need it."

Barron smirked, hearing Will's comment as he handed over the drinks.

"Enjoy, my friends."

"Thanks," Will replied, handing over his credit card.

With a shot in his hands, Will raised it in the air before throwing it back. It didn't take long for the warmth to begin seeping through his system.

Will felt Tau's eyes on him as Tau took a tiny sip from his shot glass. *Pussy!* Will knew Tau wouldn't drink too much, knowing he needed to be the sober one to drive them home. Will couldn't ask for a better friend than the man beside him. Tau always looked out for him, especially when he was in a vulnerable state.

"Okay. Your odd behavior is confusing me," Tau finally admitted, setting his drink down. Will raised a questioning eyebrow as if asking his friend to elaborate, causing Tau to release a deep sigh. "You've been unusually quiet ever since we left Massendai, and instead of going home to get some rest, you drag us here, and you are indulging yourself with shots of witblits." He paused for a moment as if thinking about his next words. "Look, I know you make your own decisions, especially business dealings. But I have to ask. You're so close to forcing Kosso's hand. Why rock the boat? Just put the brakes on the pressure for at least a bit until they get that well done. Then once they're gone, you don't have to worry about anybody else getting involved. Because you know that if you stir up trouble while the Americans are here, the government could intervene just to keep the peace. But once they're gone, the Chadian government won't care what happens to that land." The disappointment in Tau's tone was clearly heard.

Nonetheless, just because Tau served as his attorney didn't mean he was always privy to why Will made the decisions he did. There was no doubt in his mind that he knew his friend was concerned because Will would never walk away from a deal such as the one sitting in Massendai.

Will eyed Tau with one eyebrow cocked. "Trust me. I know what I'm doing. I don't plan to do anything drastic while the Americans are there. But I also don't plan on sitting on the sideline either."

"You told Moussa to tell Nandi to lay low."

"No. I told him to tell her to tone it down for a little while."

"Oh! I apologize. I misheard you."

Will smiled. "It's okay, man. But there is another reason besides the Americans being there for why I want Nandi to tone it down."

Tau stared at Will with a questionable gaze.

"What's that?"

"I've noticed Nandi's been getting a little sloppy in her work. I've also heard she isn't well-liked by many and causes riffs with people. Rumor says she's also been disappearing often. I think she may become a liability sooner or later."

Raising his eyebrows, Tau leaned in and spoke in a low, whispered voice. "You want her gone?"

"Her and Moussa."

"Both of them?"

With a slight nod, Will returned to the drinks before him.

"I was going to tell you at our meeting later this week. I discovered that Moussa has been skimming money off the top of some of our deals."

"He wouldn't dare," Tau gasped.

"He would. And he did. Not once, but four times that I know of."

"Holy shit!"

"My thoughts exactly. I'll keep them on a little longer, as I still need someone on the inside to help facilitate my next move. But after this deal is done, I'll have no use for any of them, and they can all be eliminated, including the third player in their little party."

"Just tell me when, and I'll see that it's done."

Will reached for another shot while keeping an eye on the red-haired bombshell sitting directly across from him.

She met his gaze and smiled. He returned the gesture and winked, ignoring whatever Tau was carrying on about. He watched her as she waved down Barron and asked him something. Barron then disappeared to the other end of the bar but returned moments later, handing her a pen and a piece of paper. She wrote something down before folding the paper and handing it back to him. She leaned forward and whispered something into his ear. He nodded his head. She then stood from her stool and walked toward the back rooms used for poker games and other provocative activities. As she disappeared down the dimly lit hallway, Barron appeared before him and slid a piece of paper across the bar to him, a knowing smirk pulling on his lips. Will raised his eyebrows.

"From Ms. Pinkerton, Sir."

Will picked up the paper and unfolded it. He smirked as he read the elegant cursive penmanship. The note told him to meet her in the *Blue* room when he finished.

He grinned, feeling encouraged that his night would include a little action. She'd take care of his needs. She was pretty, but he'd imagine Ms. Thompson's gorgeous face as he had his way with her.

He downed the shot and glanced toward the hallway where his company waited for the next few hours.

"If you'll excuse me, I've got some private matters to handle."

As he stood, he threw a wad of cash on the bar and gave Barron a wave. As he made his way toward the hallway, he started thinking. He wouldn't have to succumb to high-priced prostitutes for a roll in the hay if he could have someone like Jocelyn. Why would he want that when he could have a beautiful, submissive wife waiting for him at home? Even with her feistiness, he did not doubt he could make her an obedient wife.

Again, maybe their paths would cross, he thought as he pushed the door to the *Blue* room open.

CHAPTER FOURTEEN

"What do you mean you saw the kids yesterday? Did they see you?" Nandi asked Moussa as the pair stood just outside the family home in Massendai. Nandi kept an eye out, ensuring no prying eyes were watching them.

"They were with that American woman when Will, Tau, and I showed up. And yes, they saw me. As soon as they realized it was me, they ran."

"I told them to stay away from her." Just from her one interaction with Ms. Thompson, Nandi knew the woman could become a problem, especially the way she cooed over Maxime and Amira. She also saw the way the kids took to the woman as well.

"Well, they didn't listen, which is no surprise because they never listen to you," he hissed. And his overbearing attitude was pissing her off. He acted like everything was always her fault.

"Well, we're kind of stuck with them for the time being." Though, she hoped not for much longer. Having to pretend to be their mother was repulsive. If her identical twin sister hadn't been such a greedy and evil bitch she never would've found herself alone on that dark road when her car mysteriously veered off the road, went up an embankment, and flipped before coming to a rest against a tree. She was killed on impact. All it took was switching their purses that held their identification, and on that wet and blistery night, Zuri became her sister Nandi, and nobody blinked an eye.

They had no family, and her sister wasn't a social person. The father of her children was a deadbeat dad who up and left and was never heard from again. Maxime had just turned three, and Amira was just months old, so the kids never realized that their biological mother had been replaced by her evil twin sister.

When their parents died, their estate was left to the real Nandi. They had deemed her the responsible one. Zuri had a wild and rebellious streak which her parents disapproved of. She wasn't close to her small family, and it was during that time she met Moussa. He wined and dined her until she was pliant under his command. Eventually, they married, and that was when she met the "real" Moussa. He was a swindler, a fraud that rubbed off on her in time.

When he learned about Nandi holding their parents' inheritance hostage, Moussa concocted a plan to eliminate Nandi so Zuri could take over Nandi's identity. And it worked. Nobody ever suspected a thing, but she began resenting the children over time and wanted them gone.

As more time passed, Nandi saw a change in Moussa. He started having affairs with other women when he would go off on his so-called business trips. She became accustomed to his infidelity, and she, too, began to keep her bed warm with other men while Moussa was away. But when she discovered he was hiding money from her, she devised her own plan, and very soon, he would see just how capable she was without him.

Moussa gripped the back of his neck and began to rub it. Nandi sensed there was something he wasn't telling her.

"What is going on, Moussa? I can tell that you're hiding something from me."

"Will wants you to tone down the tactics while the Americans are here."

Nandi's eyes widened. "What?! Why? Visitors to the village never stopped him before."

"He wants to wait until the Americans leave and let things settle for a bit."

Nandi found that hard to believe. Will was a hardcore businessman. He'd do whatever it took to get what he wanted—including murder.

Using her skills as a traditional healer, Nandi played a role in the schemes to help Will secure deals. But she was getting impatient with the current one. It had been nothing but delay after delay, and she was itching to get her hands on the prize—two hundred fifty thousand dollars.

"I don't understand?"

"None of us understand Will's thinking sometimes. But we have to accept it. That woman today practically threatened to have Will investigated."

"And he stood for that?"

Moussa smirked. "She's beautiful. You know how Will gets around beautiful women."

The comment didn't sit well with her. "Well, that's just great. While he goes whoring around, we're the ones left to suffer. This deal should've been done months ago. Now he's saying it's going to be even longer?" She was seething inside. She wanted out of this village so badly. She felt like she was suffocating. She wanted to get the promised money, then find someone to take those bratty-ass kids off her hands.

"I don't know why you're so upset about this. I mean, we'll all get our money eventually."

"You're asking why I'm upset? You do realize that the longer this façade goes on, the more at risk we are of being discovered!" Her voice was raised, showing her anger toward the situation.

Moussa was too fast and smacked her across the face.

"Don't you fucking raise your voice with me. Do you need to be reminded of your place?"

She dropped her glare, lowering her eyes. She held her stinging cheek. She hated the man standing in front of her. She couldn't wait until this deal was done because she planned to leave his ass.

"I'm sorry," she gritted out through her clenched teeth.

"What are you going to do about the kids?"

"I'll take care of them."

"See that you do."

"Well, if that is all you came here to tell me, you can leave. I have things I need to do."

She went to turn away, but Moussa grabbed her arm firmly, stopping her. She glared at him.

"Don't fuck this deal up."

Nandi had no intentions to fuck anything up. Knowing that Will wanted to push back the Massendai deal again, it was time to enact Plan B.

Nandi had her own agenda, which didn't include her husband or Will. When she started having doubts that the Massendai deal would fizzle out, she sought another investor who had been interested in the land before. He was a rival of Will's. Once she explained what she had been doing for Will and told him she could do the same for him, the man was interested. The only difference was that the new investor agreed to triple her pay cut once he secured the land. She ensured all her tracks had been covered so nobody would suspect her betrayal.

She pulled her phone out and hit the contact name. On the third ring, he answered.

"Nandi."

"Hello, Samuel."

"Since you called me, I assume you're ready to do business."

"Yes." A sinister grin appeared on her lips. "Yes, I am."

CHAPTER FIFTEEN

Jocelyn, Bear, Joker, Duke, and Jay Bird piled into one of the SUVs to head over to Chief's home to discuss the land situation.

They had been eating breakfast when Derek called with an update. At first, they were disappointed to learn that none of the U.S. government agencies had much on Will. It was noted that he uses bullying tactics to secure deals, which wasn't surprising considering his actions the other day. His name had popped up during a few foreign real estate transactions monitored by a couple of federal agencies. But he never broke any laws. So, they hit a dead end. What it comes down to is he is just a bully.

The shocking news of the morning came from a friend of Derek's who works at the U.S. Geological Survey. It made sense why Will was hell-bent on getting Massendai's land. According to Derek's friend, Massendai's ground holds a large amount of uranium. Uranium is one of the world's most important energy minerals. They also said there were gold deposits along the western edge of the village.

Kosso and Flora were waiting out front. Bear parked the vehicle, and they all got out.

"Good morning," Kosso greeted the group.

"Morning," Bear replied.

"Please come in," Kosso told them as he and Flora ushered the team inside the home.

Kosso owned the largest parcel of land and had built an actual concrete block home. It reminded Jocelyn of the building she and the team were staying in.

Everyone took a seat in the chairs that were in the front room. Flora offered everyone coffee or tea.

Kosso cleared his throat. "Flora tells me you had the pleasure of meeting Mr. Corsica."

Bear pointed to Jocelyn. "Unfortunately, it was Jocelyn who got that opportunity."

Kosso grimaced. "I'm sorry you were subjected to his presence."

"Me too. But it is what it is. He isn't a nice man."

Kosso chuckled. "No. He definitely is not a nice man."

"How long has he been after your land?" Bear asked.

"About two years, I'd say."

Wow! Jocelyn thought. Two years of defending your land against a guy like Corsica had to be exhaustive.

"We had our boss back home do some digging. Unfortunately, they didn't find much on Corsica. But one of our contacts did discover something interesting," Bear said. Jocelyn let him take the lead in the conversation.

"What's that?" Kosso asked, looking unsure.

"Did you know that your land is sitting on uranium and gold?"

A small smile formed on Kosso's lips. "We know what is in our ground."

"You do?"

Kosso nodded and laughed lowly. "That is why we refuse to sell. Plus, this land is sacred. There are burial grounds on the outskirts of the village that shouldn't be disturbed. My ancestors lived and farmed this land. I will go down fighting for this land. I intend to have this well because it will bring people to Massendai. I want to grow this land and populate it with more families and farming."

"Now and then, we'll get a visit from an investor who wants to make us an offer, and every time I politely decline and explain to them why. Most understand and walk away, and we never hear from them again. But then you have a few like Mr. Corsica who are persistent and won't take no for an answer." Kosso rubbed his forehead. "I'm afraid he won't stop until he pushes us out."

"Have you talked with others who live in the village? See what they think about the situation?"

Kosso sighed. "I get mixed reviews. Though I'd say, the majority of the people here want to stay. Like me, their land has been in their family for generations."

"And what about the others?"

"They want to leave, and some do."

"Why? Did they give you a reason?"

"Some believe the land is cursed."

"Cursed?"

Kosso nodded. "We've had some strange occurrences in the village. Out of nowhere, animals started dying, crops weren't growing, and people were getting sick. We had some that even died.

"When did all that start happening?" Bear asked.

Kosso looked at Flora. "Maybe seven or eight months ago."

"Hmmm."

Bear glanced at Jocelyn. Listening to Kosso, she had chewed her nails down to the skin.

"Has there been any suspicious activity or people?"

"Not that I can think of."

"What about any newcomers to the village?"

"We're always getting new families. But I haven't met anyone who has given me any bad vibes. Sometimes neighbors have small arguments, but those just blow over."

Jocelyn had a question she wanted to ask.

"Kosso. Will told me that no matter what that this land would eventually be his. I consider that a threat. Do you think it's possible he could be behind the strange things happening?"

Kosso shrugged. "I guess anything is possible. He definitely has the motive. But we can't prove it."

"We know he lives in Johannesburg. Does he come here a lot?" Bear asked.

"No. Maybe every other month or every two months. It isn't often."

Bear looked around at the team, and Jocelyn knew they all thought the same thing.

"If that's true, then that means you have someone here in the village doing his dirty work."

Jocelyn saw the defeat on Kosso's face.

"I'm afraid you are correct, my friend. And I've asked myself that question many times. But I think I've been in denial. I just didn't want to accept the fact that someone—a neighbor could be that deceitful."

Flora rubbed Kosso's back and kissed the top of his head.

"It's not your fault, sweetheart."

"But it is. This is my village. I'm supposed to protect the people here."

Jocelyn reached out and covered Kosso's hands.

"The First Lady is aware of what is going on. She has pledged that our government will do whatever it can to ensure that nobody takes your land from you."

Kosso gave her a warm smile. "Thank you. I'm just sorry you all must get dragged into this mess."

Bear shrugged his shoulder and grinned. "We deal with messes all the time. We're happy to assist where we can."

~

While Bear and the team finished talking with Kosso, Flora pulled Jocelyn.

"Jocelyn, I just want to thank you again for everything. As Kosso said, we hate to involve you guys in our diplomatic problems."

Placing her hand softly on Flora's arm, Jocelyn smiled. "Flora, like Bear said. We don't mind helping out. I mean, we're here, so accept the help."

Flora smiled. "You are a good person."

Jocelyn felt her cheeks warm at Flora's compliment.

"Oh! Your friends mentioned you had a little spell yesterday."

Oh, God! How did Flora know about that? Hopefully, she didn't know why.

"I did. The guys think it was heat-related and the stress of everything happening."

Flora nodded. "That will do it. Around here, you need to drink plenty of water."

"I will going forward."

"I have some herbal tea that helps relieve stress and helps you sleep. Let me get you some, so you'll have it."

Flora disappeared into the kitchen, returned with a couple of tea sachets, and handed them to her.

"It's best to drink a cup before bed. I can guarantee you'll sleep like a baby," she winked.

Jocelyn thanked her. She could smell that one of the bags had lavender mixed in it. She'd definitely could them.

"Do you have to go to the drill site today?" Flora asked.

"I'm planning to go later this afternoon just to check-in. Today, the crew started breaking ground, and they don't need me there."

"Would you like to walk around the village with me? You could even do a little shopping as many villagers will have products for sale."

That would be cool to buy some authentic Massendai products she could take back home.

Jocelyn smiled. "Yeah. That sounds nice. Let me just let Bear know."

Flora nodded. "I'll meet you out front."

༄

Jocelyn was enjoying Flora's company as they strolled through the village. She hadn't realized how large Massendai was. And she only saw a few streets as she and Flora walked up and down, looking at all the beautiful handmade items. She even bought a few necklaces and bracelets.

While they walked, Jocelyn decided to ask Flora about Maxime and Amira.

"Flora, can I ask you something?"

"Sure, dear."

"I don't want to overstep my boundaries, but what is the story with Maxime and Amira?"

Flora gave Jocelyn a knowing smile. "You are smitten with them."

"Who couldn't be? They're adorable and so full of life. But I do worry about them."

"Let me guess. You're worried because of the lack of supervision."

"Was I that obvious?"

Flora laughed. "No. But we get that often around here."

"I'm sorry. I know it isn't my place to judge or say anything. Bear told me the other day that I should let it go."

"He did?"

"Yeah. He reminded me that there are numerous cultures in the world."

"He's not wrong. I can see that both children are very attached to you and your friends. They talk about you guys to everyone around her."

"They are lovely kids. What is not to like?"

Flora frowned. "Their mother is a different story. She keeps to herself mostly. They say she is married. Yet, I've not seen him. When I initially inquired about him, she told me he works various jobs and sends money for her and the kids. I think now, and then she travels to see him."

Jocelyn was debating on telling Flora about what Maxime said that night the kids came over for Smores. But then, a table full of colorful clay pots snagged her attention.

"Oh! These are beautiful," Jocelyn cooed, pointing toward the table. They were arranged by size. Each pot had a unique color and was adorned with symbols and designs. But the pot sitting to the far right caught her eye. She picked it up and slowly rotated it in her hands. The color was fascinating. She loved how the top of the pot was a dark grey but then faded to a lighter shade the further down it went. What really intrigued her was the symbol painted in black in the center. Jocelyn knew that many tribal families use symbols to tell stories, among other things.

Flora followed. "Yes. That is Afia's work. She's well known for her decorative pots." Flora smiled and pointed to the pot in Jocelyn's hand. "The one you're holding represents love."

Jocelyn held up the pot and studied it. "Love," said aloud. It was perfect. What other souvenir could she possibly find that would harbor such a meaning when she and Bear found love again here in this village?

After paying for the pot, she and Flora spoke with Afia and her husband for a few minutes before they started walking again.

"Afia's husband seems nice," Jocelyn said.

"He is." Flora cleared her throat. "Speaking of significant others. I hear that you've snagged yourself one of those handsome bodyguards."

It was good that Jocelyn had stopped walking, or she probably would've tripped over her own two feet. When she looked at Flora, she was surprised to see a coy smile playing on Flora's lips.

"H-how..." Jocelyn uncharacteristically stammered. How on earth did she know? The only time she and Bear showed any kind of PDA was during the twins' debacle the other day. Then it hit her—the kids. That one night, when the kids visited with them, was the same night Amira held her interrogation, and Jocelyn admitted that she and Bear were married. "You must have been talking with Amira and Maxime."

Flora laughed softly and nodded her head. "Why do you keep your relationship with Bear a secret?"

Heaving a deep sigh, Jocelyn looked out into the distance. "It's not so much of a secret now. It's just very complicated at the moment."

"Every relationship has its complications."

Oh, if this woman only knew how complicated her and Bear's status was.

"You and Kosso seem very smitten and in love with each other." Jocelyn tried to steer the discussion away from her.

"He's the love of my life. He came into my life at a time when I needed some stabilization."

Jocelyn cocked her head, eyeing Flora.

"You? Stabilization? I find that hard to believe. You seem so put together and calm all the time."

Flora smiled softly.

"I wasn't always like this. I mean, I was most of my adult life. I met my previous husband when I was seventeen."

"So you were married before you met Kosso."

Flora nodded. "For almost thirty years. His name was Ade. We met at the university."

Jocelyn was shocked but also perplexed, as it sounded like Flora came from a well-off family, making her wonder how she ended up in Massendai.

"If you don't mind me asking. What happened? It sounds like the two of you had a beautiful relationship."

"It was. But it all came crashing down one day. Ade had woken up one morning with a severe migraine and blurred vision. Thinking it would subside, he took it easy for the next few days." Flora stared off into the distance. The pain was etched on her face as she recalled her final days with her husband. "His symptoms never improved. Instead, they worsened. The morning he was supposed to see his doctor, his pain became so bad he couldn't function. His doctor told me to take him directly to the hospital. Even though I was so afraid, I drove him, but I stayed calm for his sake. He would've worried about me. As I pulled in, doctors were waiting for us at the entrance. They got him out and onto a gurney. I needed to park the car."

Flora wiped a tear from her eye. Jocelyn was even feeling Flora's emotions.

"That was the last time I saw him alive."

"Oh, Flora! I'm so sorry."

"Thank you. The doctors told me he went into cardiac arrest as they were triaging him. For months I blamed myself for not making him call his doctor sooner. Or not forcing him to go to the hospital."

Jocelyn covered Flora's hands. "Flora, you can't blame yourself."

"I know that now. I was so distraught that I pushed all my friends away."

"What about your family? Did you and Ade have any children?"

"No. Ade and I decided early on that we didn't want children. Not that we didn't like kids. In fact, we both adored children. But we were so in love that we didn't want to share that love."

"After Ade's death, I fell into a deep depression. I was left with a huge void, both in my life as a whole and my heart. I started spiraling out of control. We didn't have much, but I knew Ade would want his money to go to the children. So, I sold everything he and I had and donated all the money."

"How did you survive?"

"I took on odd jobs in towns that I passed through. I'd move to the next interesting town when I got tired of what I was doing. I had been down to my last few dollars when I ran into Kosso. My mind was set at the time that I didn't want to live anymore. I wanted to go and be at peace with Ade. The day I had planned to take my own life, I had a fateful run-in with Kosso. He knew right away that something was wrong. I don't know what it was that drew me to him. Maybe his compassion. His smile sent a stream of warmth through my body. It instantly calmed me. I always tell myself that it was a sign from Ade.

She shrugged her shoulder. "Maybe it was his way of telling me it was okay to move on. As hard as it was, I know deep down that is what he would've wanted for me—to be happy and live my life to the fullest."

"It sounds like you have the honor of having two wonderful and meaningful men in your life. I'm so glad you found happiness again."

Flora's eyes suddenly came to life as she eyed something behind Jocelyn. "Speaking of doing the right thing, here comes you're bodyguard now."

Jocelyn spun around and saw Bear walking towards her. A sexy grin graced his handsome face.

"Hey!"

Bear stopped next to Jocelyn and looked between the two women. "What are the two of you up to?"

Flora gave him a warm smile and winked at Jocelyn. "Just having a little girl talk."

"Girl talk, huh?" Bear smirked.

"Yep. And shopping," Jocelyn told him, holding up the bags she had clutched in her hand.

"I was on my way back and stopped to see if you wanted some company walking back."

"I always have company," Jocelyn joked, even though she was being serious. There was always one of the guys within striking distance.

Bear chuckled. "True. But how about my company?"

Smiling, Jocelyn glanced at Flora, who was grinning.

"I'll let you two have some time alone. Jocelyn, dear. Don't forget to drink some of that tea."

Jocelyn hugged Flora. "I won't. And thank you for the walk. I needed this."

After saying bye to Flora, Jocelyn and Bear started walking. They were both quiet at first until Bear spoke.

"So, what did you buy?" He asked, pointing to the bags.

"She showed him the bracelets and necklaces that she bought. Then she pulled out the clay pot, and Bear took it from her hand and held it up to look at it.

"This is interesting. Does the symbol mean something?"

Jocelyn smiled. "Love. The symbol means love. I thought it was fitting since the two of us—"

"Joce," Bear interrupted her as he stepped closer to her. Bear placed his hand against her cheek. It was warm, and she closed her eyes as she leaned into his touch, absorbing his show of affection. His fingers gently caressed her skin, and she slowly opened her eyes. She stared right into his grey eyes.

"Joce," he spoke her name again. His voice had a little more rasp to it. The sound made her belly quiver.

"Yeah?" She whispered back.

"I—" he started to say but then shook his head slightly. "Not here. I don't want us to talk here."

She smiled. "Okay."

He reached for one of her hands and raised it to his lips, kissing the back of it.

"Come on. Let's keep walking."

She smiled, feeling giddy as she followed him. Shit, she'd follow him to the moon and back.

They were almost to the last house before the turnoff to their building when Jocelyn spotted another table with accessories and clothing.

"Oh! This must be the woman that Flora mentioned. The one who makes a lot of the clothes."

Jocelyn spotted a familiar person standing in front of the table as they approached it.

"Amira?"

The little girl turned around, and the moment she saw Jocelyn and Bear, her cute little face broke out into a big smile.

"Ms. Jocelyn! Mr. Bear!"

She met them and practically leaped into Jocelyn's arms. Luckily Bear had grabbed the other bags out of her hand. Jocelyn lifted her.

"What are you doing, munchkin?"

Amira eyed the area of the table where a few colorful scarves lay. Jocelyn saw the little girl's smile fall.

"What's wrong, sweetie?"

"Mummy isn't happy today."

"She's not?"

"Uh-uh."

"Well, maybe she just has a lot on her mind."

"Maxime told me that she was upset with him and me."

"Did he say why she was upset with you and him?"

Amira shook her head. "No."

Jocelyn looked at Bear. He seemed curious.

"Where's your brother?" Bear asked.

"He left this morning with Mr. Emmanuel."

"Who is that?"

"He lives next door to us. Maxime sometimes helps Mr. Emmanuel with his crops on the village's far side." She turned her head so she was looking directly at Jocelyn. "I think he went with Mr. Emmanuel to avoid mummy and the bad man."

Jocelyn felt her body still. She looked at Bear, and his face was twisted up.

"Amira, sweetheart. What bad man?"

She looked at Bear. "Mummy says he is our daddy. But Maxime says he's a bad man."

Suddenly, Jocelyn realized who Amira could be talking about.

"Amira, is the bad man who scared you and Maxime yesterday?"

She nodded and wrapped her tiny arms around Jocelyn's neck, hugging her.

"He's mean to mummy. He was yelling at mummy this morning."

Bear and Jocelyn looked at each other.

"Is he still here?"

"No. He left. He doesn't come here a lot—only when he comes to yell at mummy."

"So, you heard him yelling at your mommy today?"

"Yes. That's why I came over here to Ms. Mariam. Mummy likes her scarves. It makes her happy when she gets a scarf. I don't like it when mummy is sad."

Jocelyn eyed the scarves on the table, and an idea came to her. She glanced at Bear, and he nodded, knowing what she was asking. Jocelyn unwound Amira's arms from her neck and set the little girl back down on her feet.

"Amira, do you want to get your mommy something special? Something that would cheer her up."

"Like what?"

"You said that she likes scarves. We can get her a scarf." Jocelyn walked Amira back to the table and pointed to an orange and blue scarf. "What about this beautiful one here."

As quickly as her big brown eyes lit up, that light faded.

"What's the matter? You don't think she would like it?"

"No. She would love it. But…"

"But, what?"

"I don't have any money."

Before Jocelyn could reach into her own pocket to get some money she had stashed in there, Bear handed the woman some money.

Mouthing a thank you to him, Jocelyn turned and squatted in front of Amira. She handed her the scarf.

"Here. Give this present to your mommy. Maybe it will make her smile."

Amira hugged Jocelyn. "Thank you!" she shouted. "I'm going to go give it to mummy now," she said, skipping down the road.

Jocelyn was reluctant to go after her. Amira made some accusations that Jocelyn couldn't ignore. If those kids were in danger, Jocelyn wanted to protect them.

She turned toward Bear. He appeared to be biting the inside of his cheek

"Well, that was interesting," she stated, and Bear nodded.

"I don't like it. If we can get some additional information on the dad, I can have Derek look into him."

"Do you think we should check on them later?"

Bear smiled. "Yeah. Of course, we can check on them later."

"Thanks." She looked at her watch. "Do you want to come with me to the site? I just need to stop in and see how the drilling went for today."

"Sure." He touched her lower back and guided her toward the site.

❧

Later in the evening, Bear was sitting around the fire talking with the guys when he felt a nudge on his arm, followed by Aussie's whispered voice.

"Incoming."

Looking to his left, he smiled as he saw Jocelyn walking towards them. Bear looked her over, noting she had changed into a pair of leggings and a long-sleeved t-shirt. Her hair was wet, fresh from the shower, and hanging loose around her shoulders.

She also looked a little tired, which was understandable. She had a lot going on, plus the added stress of worrying about Amira and Maxime. About two hours ago, they had checked in on the kids. At first, they became worried when they couldn't find either Amira or Maxime. But then Amira came out of the house next door with an older lady, who they learned was Mr. Emmanuel's wife. After talking with them, it appeared that Nandi had left the village, claiming she was picking up herbal supplies. She would be gone the entire weekend, so the kids were staying with Emmanuel and his wife. He knew if Jocelyn had her way, she would've wanted the kids to stay with her.

Bear had been hoping to talk to Maxime to ask him a few questions about their dad. However, he was still out with Emmanuel on their crop farm.

It had been a busy day around the village. The drilling crew began boring into the ground. When Bear and Jocelyn showed up at the site, they both were surprised to see how many villagers had come out to watch the production. It warmed him to see their smiles, knowing that by next week they'd have clean, fresh drinking water at their fingertips. There would be no more paying to bring water into the village or walking hours to get water.

As Jocelyn approached, Bear smiled.

"Hey. Everything good?" He asked.

"Yeah. I just took a break from the computer to get cleaned up."

"You're more than welcome to sit with us," Joker told her.

"I'd like that," she replied, taking the open seat beside Bear. Sitting down, she pulled a hair tie off her wrist and tied her wet strands up in a messy bun or whatever women called those things. The sweet floral scent of her shampoo flooded his nostrils.

Once she was settled in, Bear cleared his throat.

"You had a productive day."

Her smile was infectious, and Bear could see the happiness in what she and the team had accomplished.

"It was. In a day or two, we'll shift to wet drilling."

"What does that consist of?" Playboy asked.

"It's where water is pumped through the drill stem. As the drill hits the rock and penetrates further, it will flush out sand, dirt, and other debris through the drill stem. If we hit the water, which we should. The crew will drill a larger hole and flush it. We then take a four-inch plastic well casing pipe and cut slots near the bottom to allow water to flow inside. It is then placed in the hole before packing gravel around the casing at the bottom to keep the pipe in place. Then we'll backfill the hole with the dirt displaced from drilling."

"What happens if you don't hit the water?" Aussie asked.

"Well, hopefully, that doesn't happen. But if it does, the casing will be cemented to the rock, and the crew will use another type of drill with an air compressor. That drill lowers through the casing and will punch through the rock. It is pretty slow-moving as the drill usually works through ten feet per hour until it hits the water. As I said, hopefully, that doesn't occur because depending on how far down we have to drill, it could add hours or even days of additional drilling. But in all, it's pretty exciting."

Bear could hear the excitement in her voice, and he could tell it was something she was passionate about.

They discussed the rest of the process before Joker asked her another question.

"What do you do when you aren't working?"

"Hmmm...that's a tough one. I don't have much of an interesting life outside my work. But if I had to pick something, I'd say getting lost in my photography hobby."

"Photography?" Bear asked.

She smiled. "Yeah. Years ago, earlier in my career, there were a few months when I wasn't traveling, and a friend introduced me to it. Since I had some time on my hands, I took a class. I figured when I could travel again that I'd be able to take some good pictures."

"Photography is a great hobby," Duke said.

"Do you shoot?" Jocelyn asked him, and Duke nodded.

"When I have the time."

"I didn't know you liked photography," Aussie commented, and Duke offered a wry grin, then playfully winked at Jocelyn.

"I have my secrets."

"I have a question for you guys. What is one of your most memorable moments of being a SEAL without divulging classified information?"

Nails immediately threw his hand up in the air like he was a student waiting to be called on by the teacher.

"Oh! I got a really good one!"

"Oh, goodness. I can't wait to hear this one," she said nervously, and everyone laughed.

"This was before I was recruited for BUD/S. I was still at Recruit Training. Anyway, one very cold morning, my company was once again familiarizing ourselves with the pavement doing mountain climbers. I was just having a really bad day, and I was fucking tired. So, I just stopped and snapped to attention. My Recruit Division Commander was in my face in a flash. He was always waiting for me to screw up. Anyway, he was screaming, 'What the hell are you doing.' Not much gets me riled up, so my calm response to him was, 'I've reached the top.' He looked at me like I had grown two heads. He then asked, 'You've reached the top of what, Recruit?' I replied, 'the top of the mountain.' I mean, we were doing mountain climbers."

"What did he say to that? Or did he just let you stand there?" She asked, with her hand over her mouth, trying to stifle her laugh.

"Fuck no!" Nails grinned. "After he quit laughing, he told me to turn around and climb my ass down the other side. I think I did more mountain climbers that morning than I did in all recruit training. By the time noon hit and it was chow time, I don't think I could feel my legs."

Still trying to control her laughter, she looked at Nails. "What were you thinking?"

"That's the problem. He wasn't," Joker said, laughing.

"As much as I hate mountain climbers myself, I don't think I would have had the courage to do what you did. You've certainly got some balls."

"Christ, don't tell him that," Duke chimed in.

Nails gave her a flirty smirk. "Oh, I've got some balls."

"Here we go," Bear mumbled, running a hand down his face.

Hearing Nails go back and forth with the guys about his balls made Jocelyn laugh so hard that her stomach hurt. She had to finally beg them to stop because she couldn't take the pain any longer. She now knew more about Nails' balls than she wanted to.

"See what you started," Bear whispered in her ear. His warm breath tickled her skin.

Turning her head in his direction, she gave him a playful grin.

"I guess I know not to mention anything about his balls in the future."

Bear chuckled, and soon everyone began to have side conversations about all kinds of stuff, leaving Bear and Jocelyn to themselves.

Bear leaned closer. "Tell me something that I don't know about you."

"What?"

"We've been out of each others' lives for many years. Tell me anything about you that could be new to me."

She had to think hard. Bear had known everything about her. But then she remembered something.

"I'm claustrophobic."

"What? When did that happen?"

"A few years ago. I was assisting with another well project. It was a big undertaking. It was in Cuba after they got hit with that category five hurricane."

"You were in Cuba?" Bear questioned. He wasn't sure if he wanted to know the other places she had been to.

"I was. The drill kept getting caught on rocks in the earth, and we thought it was stuck at one point. Unfortunately, I was the only one small enough to fit inside the hole."

"You had to go down the well hole?" He asked as his eyes widened in surprise.

She nodded. "I did. However, when they were hoisting me up, the wench broke, and I dropped my flashlight, leaving me dangling in the dark, about twenty feet below."

"Holy shit! How long were you in there?"

"They told me it was two and a half hours, but I swear it was longer. I think I may have even blacked out for a short time. Since then, I'm not fond of tight, enclosed spaces."

"Damn. That had to have been scary."

"A little, but probably not as scary as some things you've done or encountered."

He smirked. "Possibly." He'd been in tight spaces that made him uncomfortable, but it didn't bother him. Even if it had, he would have dealt with it to ensure the mission was accomplished.

He thought about a story that his friend Ace, the team leader for Alpha team had told him when they had been sent to Afghanistan with Ace's now-wife Alex. Alex, at the time, had been an Intel Analyst and was assisting Ace and his team with tracking a terrorist. One night when they were conducting an operation, Alex became separated from the team and was forced to hide in a cramped hole until the team found her. She, too, was borderline claustrophobic. However, she did what was needed to survive. Alex was an amazing woman and a staple within the special forces community.

Bear looked at Jocelyn, who was staring back at him.

"What were you thinking about?" She asked him, and he shook his head.

"A good friend, and how much you remind me of her."

The smile on her face disappeared, and Bear quickly realized what Jocelyn probably thought.

"Hey, Alex is just a friend. In fact, she's married to Ace. Remember him from the plane ride?"

"Oh! Yeah. He was very nice, and so were his teammates."

Bear laughed, and she squinted her eyes at him. "What's so funny?"

"Just thinking how you also remind me of Tenley and going all mama bear with Maxime and Amira."

"Who's Tenley?"

"She's Alex's best friend and married to Potter. You also met him on the plane.

"Oh yeah. The tall, wide, brooding guy who doesn't smile."

Bear snickered. "That would be him. But don't take it personally. He's like that with everyone. Tenley is a nurse, and two years ago, she assisted a humanitarian group in Ecuador when they had a bad earthquake.

She befriended a little girl named Alejandra. She was cute as a button. She lost her mom and dad in the earthquake. It was a miracle that they even found her beneath the rubble of what was once their home. Luckily, she escaped with only a few cuts and bruises. But she and Tenley formed a special strong bond over the weeks."

"What happened to her?"

Bear grinned. "Potter and Tenley adopted her."

"Wow! What a heart-wrenching but happy ending for the little girl."

"Well, they had their work cut out for them, but thankfully they knew people in high places who pulled some strings and were able to speed up the process of getting her to the States."

"That must be nice."

"What must be nice?"

"To have friends and a community who support one another."

"They're a great bunch, including their families. All the women are great. You'd like them."

"Maybe one day I'll get the opportunity to meet them," she replied shyly, looking away.

"I think we can make that happen," he said, winking at her.

He decided that now was as a good time as any to talk with her.

"Jocelyn?"

"Yes?" She answered, whipping her head around and looking hopeful.

"I—" The squawking of the radio beside him cut off his words. Seconds later, Snow's voice came over it.

Seriously?

"Hey assholes, is someone planning to come to relieve Jay Bird and me? We're fucking starving."

"Shit," Bear mumbled, but hearing Jocelyn's light laugh brought a small smile to his lips.

"I'll let you get back to work," she told him.

"I'm sorry."

"It's okay."

"Do you have plans tomorrow after you finish at the site?"

She gave an airy laugh. "I'll have to check my jammed packed schedule. But I think besides having dinner with you guys, I'm pretty open. Why? What do you have in mind?"

"I want to take you somewhere. Just me and you."

"Okay. I'd like that."

"A date then?"

She grinned. "A date."

Bear stood up with her. She said goodnight to the guys. He decided to walk her over to her door, even though it was only a few feet away.

He couldn't stop himself when she stopped and turned to face him. Leaning in, he kissed her cheek, letting his lips linger against her soft skin.

When he pulled away, he didn't know what to say. He remained holding her hand, staring into her chocolate pools. With her lips slightly parted and pink staining her cheeks, she appeared to have been shocked just as much as he was.

She cleared her throat. "Night Bear."

"Night," he said, letting her hand go and watching her walk into her room and close the door behind her.

Baby steps, he kept telling himself.

CHAPTER SIXTEEN

Jocelyn was trying to concentrate on some reading material she received from Lana regarding future projects. However, the persistent headache plaguing her all day was annoying.

She had woken up with a slight ache, but it amplified when she arrived at the drill site and was delivered some disturbing news.

According to one of the crew's security guards, he caught someone snooping around the site last night. He tried following the person, but they slipped away. He did say there were fresh footprints where he had seen the person walking.

The guard couldn't see the person's face but estimated that the individual was approximately five foot five or six, with a medium build. He said they had been wearing a ballcap.

Of course, everyone's suspicions were directed at Will Corsica. But without any proof, there was nothing they could do about it. The security company said they would put an extra man on the overnight shift, bringing them to three guards.

She reached up and rubbed her temples, trying to massage away the dull headache that had been plaguing her all day.

Her eyes shifted to the stack of paperwork she needed to sort through before she began the tedious task of filling it out. Several were grant applications that, if received, could help cover the expenses of future wells.

A soft knock drew her attention to the open doorway. She smiled when she saw Bear standing there, leaning his shoulder against the doorway with his hands in the front pockets of his jeans. He looked good. His hair was wet from his shower.

She felt her cheeks warm, thinking about the view she had earlier of him when he exited the shower and walked by her door. She had been struck by the glorious sight of him shirtless. The sight of his defined chest, and abs, made her mouth water.

The clearing of his throat pulled her from the naughty thoughts she was having.

"Hey," she greeted. Her voice sounded tired.

He pushed off the doorway and walked in.

"You doing okay?" He asked, looking concerned.

"Yeah. I just have a little headache, and reading over all this paperwork isn't helping."

"If you're not feeling well, we can postpone our date."

"No!" she shot out, and he smiled. "No. I still want to hangout. Plus, I need a break from all of this."

She got up, walked over to her duffel, and found the bottle of ibuprofen she kept on hand. She grabbed a bottle of water from the case sitting on the floor, twisted off the top, popped the two pills in her mouth, and washed them down.

Bear pressed his hand against her lower back, and her belly did a little somersault. She looked up at him.

"Are you sure that you're okay?"

"Yeah. I promise. The medicine should help."

"Are you still getting the headaches often?" he asked, and his concern touched her.

"They aren't as bad as when I first got out of the hospital. But yeah. I still have some lingering effects, especially when reading or doing something that strains my eyes."

He ran his knuckle down her cheek, and she found herself leaning into him.

"Are you ready to go now?" He asked.

"Sure. Where are we going?"

He gave her a mischievous grin. God, he looked so sexy.

"It's a surprise." He gave her a playful smirk. "I promise you're gonna love it."

"Alright," she said, and he flashed her that smile of his that she adored.

When they got outside, Jocelyn was surprised when she found out they were taking one of the Jeeps the drilling crew had been using. It reminded her of a safari Jeep with no top. When she questioned the means of transportation, Bear told her it was part of the adventure. Without asking anything else, she hopped in, and they drove off toward the setting sun.

She'd admit a nice drive in the open air was exactly what she needed. She fell back against the seat as she relaxed and enjoyed the scenery. Even though Chad was an underdeveloped country, its land was beautiful and full of hidden gems.

She could never understand why countries like Chad weren't run better—and why those governments didn't care about the people they served. Watching how innocent citizens suffered because of greed and power was heartbreaking.

"You look like you're doing some pretty heavy thinking over there," Bear said, breaking the silence between them.

She looked so youthful as she grinned and turned in her seat so that she was facing more toward him.

"I was thinking about how much I needed this."

"Is that all?"

"And how beautiful it is here, and how sad it is that those in charge of this country don't seem to care. I just don't get it."

"Get what?"

"Why those in charge of leading can just ignore their people and not be proud of their land. I know we aren't perfect and have some issues back home but look around. Most people here don't even have access to clean drinking water, and children are forced into labor at five years old when they should be getting an education and enjoying their childhood."

"Your job means a lot to you, doesn't it?"

"It does."

"You've always had a big heart."

She sure did, and look where it had gotten her. Thirty-five years old, a workaholic, and alone.

"Hey. I didn't say that to upset you."

She gave him a small smile before looking straight ahead. "It's all good."

They drove silently for a few more miles until the landscape began changing before her eyes. It was fascinating to watch. She was about to ask where they were when it dawned on her.

A few minutes later, Bear pulled the Jeep off the road and turned the ignition off. She turned toward him but kept her eyes on the sight before her.

"Is that the Sahara Desert?" She asked, not wanting to take her eyes off the magnificent sight.

"It is."

He unbuckled his seatbelt. "Come on," he said, sliding his magnificent body out of the Jeep.

She followed and met him near the front. She still was in awe of the landscape. It was more than she imagined it would be. She wondered if she should pinch herself to ensure this wasn't just a dream.

"Beautiful," she whispered.

"Yes, you are," he voiced in a tone she had only ever heard him use with her. It was low, raspy, and so, so sexy. She moved her eyes to his face. He was in a dead stare with her.

৵

This was it. The moment of truth and juncture that will most likely decide whether he goes home a happily married man or a dejected divorcee. Sure, he had snuck in a few touches here and there, but nothing was final until she told him her decision.

He stood there, taking in every bit of his beautiful wife. The frisson sensation surging through him could only be described as that thrilling shiver one could experience on a roller coaster or something extreme like it. He hadn't been this anxious since the day he told Jocelyn that his feelings towards her had gone deeper than friendship.

"Beautiful," he heard her say about the vast desert she was gazing at. He couldn't disagree with her, except he wasn't staring at the desert. He was focused only on the beauty of her.

When her gaze met him, he knew she could sense his feelings. Her cheeks turned that cute shade of pink. Then she cleared her throat.

"I wish I had my camera," she said aloud.

He held his finger up, telling her to hang on, then walked toward the back of the Jeep and pulled out her camera bag.

As he handed the bag to her, their fingers brushed against each other, and they locked eyes simultaneously. Not only did he feel the spark, but he saw it in her brown eyes, which seemed to darken.

"If I didn't know any better, I'd say you had this all planned out."

His lips twitched, and she smiled. She had a beautiful smile, especially when it reached her eyes like now.

"Thank you, Bear."

"You're welcome." He curled his finger. "Come here," he said, shocked at how shaky his voice sounded. Only Jocelyn could do that to him.

She stepped closer, and his hands moved to her curvy waist, causing a soft gasp to escape Jocelyn's lips, which made his cock harden beneath his jeans. The subtle yet sexy sound reminded him of the soft purrs she rendered when he made love to her. He closed his eyes as a montage of visions from their private, intimate moments from their past occupied his mind.

"Bear?"

He gave his head a bit of a shake. "Hmmm?"

"I asked if everything was okay. You zonked out on me for a few seconds."

"Just thinking," he told her, but he knew she wouldn't let it go. But he wasn't ready to spill all his feelings just yet. "Hang on," he said, lifting her and settling her on the hood. She felt so good in his arms. It had been a long time since he felt that warm sensation hit that spot in his stomach.

Standing between her splayed thighs and looking deep into her eyes, he wanted nothing more than to lean in and taste her plump, soft lips.

"I'm sorry," he whispered.

Her forehead wrinkled. "Sorry for what?"

"For ruining what we had all those years ago. For destroying our future."

"Bear..."

"No. I need to get this off my chest. You deserve to know why I did what I did, even though I know now it was impulsive and stupid. But at the time, I was young and thought I knew everything. Hell, I obviously thought I had been doing the right thing by ending our relationship, even though it killed me."

She reached for his hands and laced her delicate fingers with his. The warmth of her touch brought him comfort and calmness. He had always told her that she was the calm to his storm. How had he let her go?

"Something happened on that deployment, didn't it?" She asked.

He nodded before looking away as flashbacks from that mission in Iraq flooded his memory.

The local time was nearing midnight. Their team had just received word that they target they'd been seeking for the past eight days was nearing the building they had been watching for days.

Once it was confirmed their target had arrived through an underground tunnel, which wasn't uncommon, Hawk and Terp advanced ahead of the rest of the team to clear the ground path while the remainder of the team covered from their positions above.

Everything was going according to plan, exactly what they practiced. But before he could blink, a car that Hawk and Terp were using for cover exploded. They never stood a chance and were killed instantly. But the battle didn't stop there. The terrorist group knew they were there, and bullets started raining down on them.

They had to retreat because they were outnumbered. But they couldn't leave their teammates behind. They all knew that if they didn't get their teammates' bodies out of there right then, they never would. The Taliban would ensure that.

It had taken hours of fighting until they could reach the spot where Hawk and Terp lay lifeless. And it didn't come without costs either, as several of his teammates suffered injuries during the recovery.

Even though he survived that battle, the experience changed him mentally. It made him question many things, ultimately leading him to do what he had done to Jocelyn. It was a decision he still regretted.

He made eye contact with her. "It was awful, Joce," he croaked out, trying desperately to keep his emotions in check. "I came back from that deployment a changed man. I lost two of my teammates. But the hardest part was witnessing their families grieve as they buried their loved ones."

He watched her brown eyes fill with tears. *Dammit!* He felt awful for making her cry. Her tears were one of his weaknesses. It was why he refused to take any of her calls when he initially filed for divorce because he knew if he heard her crying, he wouldn't have been able to go through with it. But it was too late now. She needed to know the truth. She needed to know that he didn't divorce her because he didn't love her.

"I literally stood across from one of the widows, holding onto her two-month-old baby girl, as she watched her husband's casket being lowered into the ground."

He wasn't ashamed to admit that he had cried for days following the funerals. Even now, it killed him to think about it. He felt the onslaught of tears rushing to the surface. It had been years since he'd cried. But there was nothing he could do to stop them now. He released her hands and quickly turned his back to her so she couldn't see it. He closed his eyes, hoping that would act as a dam to prevent the coming flood.

Behind him, Jocelyn was quiet, and he wondered what was going through her mind. Would she think he was a fool? Maybe a coward? If that were the case, he couldn't blame her. His actions were inexcusable. He chose the easy way instead of fighting for what he really wanted. And, dammit, all he ever wanted was her. He wanted his sweet, beautiful Jocelyn. She was the only one who made him feel whole. She was the light of his life and his true love.

Just as he was about to turn around to accept his fate, Jocelyn took him by surprise, wrapping her arms around his torso from behind, and gently guided him backward until his back was flush against her chest. She pressed her cheek against his upper back, hugging him from behind.

He kept quiet, knowing that she would speak when she was ready. He covered her hands that were fisted in his shirt as if she was afraid to let go.

They stayed silent in that position for a good five minutes or so until Bear couldn't take it anymore. He needed to see her face and to know what she was feeling.

Slowly, he unwrapped himself from her arms and turned to face her. He had been unsure of what was waiting for him. But when their eyes met, he was nearly brought to his knees.

The tears staining Jocelyn's cheeks left him speechless. Hearing her little sniffles broke his heart.

"Joce…" he whispered, using his thumbs to wipe away her tears.

"You pictured me, didn't you?" she blurted out in-between her small hiccups.

"What?" He asked because he didn't understand.

She hiccupped again as another tear slipped from her eye. "You pictured me when you were standing across from your teammate's grieving widow, didn't you?"

He couldn't lie. He nodded before gently pressing his forehead against hers.

"I did. And it scared the life out of me. My head was all fucked up. At the time, I thought I was doing the right thing. But it was too late when I realized it was the worst decision I've ever made."

He held her cheeks between his hands and looked into her glistening eyes. He wanted her to feel the honesty of his next words. "I never stopped loving you." He lightly pressed his lips against her forehead.

At first, she didn't say anything. He thought she was going to shut him down. Finally, he couldn't take the deafening silence.

"Please talk to me," he begged her.

Shaking her head and wiping her face, she said, "All these years, I thought I had done something wrong."

Fuck!

He pulled her close and hugged her. "No, baby. I swear. You did nothing wrong. It was all me and my fucked-up head."

"It still feels awful."

He lifted her chin so she'd look at him.

"Why would you feel awful? I was the idiot."

"Because you were hurting, and I wasn't there to help you."

Bear was moved to silence. Here, he was the one who had fucked up, and she felt awful. That wasn't fair. He was the only one who should feel terrible, and he did. But to hear her admit that proved once again how big of a heart she had. He needed her like he needed his next breath.

They continued staring into each other's eyes until she broke the silence with the words he'd longed to hear.

"Just so you know. I never stopped loving you."

She was eating him up with her eyes, and he wanted to do nothing more than take her into his arms and show her just how sorry he was.

"Bear?" She questioned.

He said nothing as he moved closer, wedging himself between her legs. Clutching her chin, he bent his head, and his lips touched her cheek. His lips stretched into a smile when he heard her breath hitch. From there, he couldn't stop. She was too enticing. He made his way along her jawline, leaving a trail of wet kisses before hovering over her lips, begging to be kissed.

There was no way he could pull away. Not when he could feel her warm puffs of breath against his lips.

He kept his movement slow, wanting to give her time to rethink though he prayed she wouldn't push him away. He took a deep breath. He'd give her one last chance to stop him.

"Tell me right now if you don't want me to kiss you."

When she didn't respond but instead fisted her hands in his shirt, he considered that a greenlight.

He leaned forward and covered her mouth with his. He tried to go slow, but when she pulled him closer, he deepened the kiss and slipped his tongue into her mouth. As their tongues tangled, her soft moans intensified his desire. He was running out of air and needed to breathe, but he couldn't get enough of her as he continued to explore her mouth until he was forced to pull away before he passed out.

Her eyes were still closed, but he could hear her heavy breathing as her chest rose and fell with every breath she took. He placed his forehead against hers as he let his racing heart settle.

"I've missed you so much, baby," he told her before pecking her lips again.

She placed her hand against his cheek. "I've missed you, too."

"I always envisioned us spending our lives together. I still want that, Joce."

"I do too."

"You do?"

"Yeah, Bear. I do. I understand why you did what you did. But you need to understand that I knew what I was getting myself into when I accepted to be your wife. I knew the risks of being married to you. I get that you won't be home every night holding me in your arms as we lay in bed. I get you can't talk about your job and that I can't ask you questions."

"But if there is ever a time where you begin to feel like you did before, I want you to promise me that you'll come to talk to me. I don't have to know any top-secret details. I just want my husband to be honest with me about his feelings. And I want to be that wife who is there for her husband to lean on."

"We've already wasted ten years. I don't want to waste another minute. Let's start over," he told her, and she shook her head.

"I don't want to start over," she told him, grinning when she saw the confused look on his handsome face. "We have shared too many wonderful and significant memories to start over. Starting over would feel like we're abandoning a huge part of our lives." She laid her hand against his chest and looked deep into his stormy eyes that held hers. "Let's merge the lives that we live now. We'll call the last ten years a part of our journey together. It's as if we were traveling. There's always going to be bumps in the road. But in the end, we'll always make it home.

"Sweetheart, you and our marriage come first."

Squeezing his hands, she looked deep into his eyes. "I appreciate that, and I love you. But you need to know that I will never keep you from your job. I'm proud of who you are and what you represent. All I ask is for honesty. If you're having a bad day or returning from a mission that didn't go well, just tell me. I don't mean you have to spill classified secrets, but just a heads up would help me know to handle you differently."

He brushed his nose against hers before giving her a peck on the lips and hugging her.

"I love you. I always have, and I always will," he whispered.

She pulled away and wiped her eyes again. She smiled at him.

"Before we do anything else, there is one last order of business we need to take care of."

Bear looked at her oddly. He had no clue what she had planned.

He watched as she unzipped her large camera bag and pulled out a folder. It was then he realized what folder it was—the divorce papers.

She looked up at him. "I think we should make it official." Before he could ask what she had in mind, she tore the folder and its contents down the middle. She then handed him one-half. "When we get back, we can each throw half of our past into the fire pit."

A huge smile broke out, and he pulled close and kissed her hard. Once he had his fill, he pulled away.

"You've made me the happiest man. I love you."

Grinning, she pecked him on the lips. "I love you, too."

~

A few hours later, they arrived back at their building. They were both on cloud nine. He walked her to her door and pulled her close.

"Are you going to invite me in?" He asked, and she grinned.

"As much as I'd love to, the answer is no."

"Why?" He asked with a slight pout.

"Because if I invite you in, I'm not sure if I can keep my hands to myself, which would then lead me probably waking up tomorrow morning and having to face the guys who clearly heard what I was doing the night before."

A slow, mischievous grin spread across Bear's face. "You mean they would know *who* you were doing."

"You're awful," she said, laughing.

"But you love me."

"Yeah. I do."

"Well then, I guess this is goodnight."

She leaned in and pecked his lips. "Goodnight."

Once she was secured in her room, she set her camera bag on the table before taking a seat on her cot.

She couldn't believe it. She and Bear had officially reconciled. She was filled with so much joy that she felt like she would explode. God, she had so much to do.

She eyed the tea sachets that Flora had given her yesterday. Maybe a little bit of calming tea would be good for her before bed.

CHAPTER SEVENTEEN

The banging on the door had Jocelyn lifting her throbbing head off the pillow. She woke up in the middle of the night with a splitting headache. She had taken some over-the-counter medicine, but it barely eased the pain.

The pain in her head was so intense that she felt nauseous. Before she could see who was at the door, a wave of nausea hit her, and she quickly rolled onto her side and ended up throwing up all over the floor.

Despite the warm temperature inside the room, she was freezing. Her body began to tremble so badly that her teeth were even chattering. Her eyes felt heavy, and she let them close, but not before she heard the door to her room open, and someone called out her name.

Jocelyn felt her stomach tighten again and gagged as the dry heave continued. She gasped for air as her gag reflex choked her.

Suddenly, she felt a hand on the back of her neck.

"Joce, baby, what's wrong?" Bear asked, gently rubbing his fingers up and down her neck. She couldn't speak as another wave of nausea overtook her, and began dry heaving again.

She knew the others were also there because she could hear different voices but wasn't paying attention to what they were saying.

*

Bear was concerned when Aussie informed him that Jocelyn hadn't left her room yet. She was normally up when they were.

As Bear entered the room and saw Jocelyn's shaking body curled under a blanket, he knew immediately that something was wrong. He quickly got to her when she didn't respond to him calling her name. That was when he saw the vomit on the floor next to the cot.

He put his hand on her cheek and swore when he felt how hot she was.

"What's wrong with her?" Joker asked, looking worried as soon as he saw the vomit on the floor.

"I don't know but go find Duke!"

"Come on, sweetie. Keep your eyes open for me," he begged her.

"Don't feel good. Head hurts bad," she mumbled.

Seconds later, Duke raced into the room, looking concerned but still holding a calm presence. He had his medic bag in his hand. He put his hand on her forehead.

"Shit! She's burning up!" He then saw the vomit on the floor. "Was this already here when you found her, or did she just get sick?"

"It was already there when I got here."

Duke examined the bile on the floor. "Looks recent."

"Yes," Jocelyn whispered. Bear was happy to hear her voice again and that she was coherent enough to respond to a direct question.

"Jocelyn, are you saying that you just got sick?" Duke asked, wanting to confirm what she said.

"Yes. Woke up in the middle night. Head hurt. Took medicine and fell back asleep. Puked when I woke up again."

She was talking in incomplete sentences, but at least she was talking.

Bear kept a hand on her neck, gently running his thumb up and down it while Duke asked her more questions.

"What type of medicine did you take for your headache?"

"Ibuprofen."

"What other symptoms are you having?"

"Headache...bad. Stomach pain. Dizzy."

Bear looked at Duke, hoping he had an explanation for Jocelyn's sickness.

"My first assumption is food poisoning. Hold her still so I can get a line in her. She needs fluids." Duke glanced at Snow. "Run next door and get some electrolyte packets."

Bear continued gently running his hand up and down Jocelyn's back, trying to soothe her. Her body was trembling so badly. He thought back to what she ate yesterday. But unless she snacked on something in her room, she had eaten what they had, and none of them were sick.

Joker and Playboy had taken the initiative to clean up the mess on the floor, and Aussie had found an empty bucket and set it next to the bed in case she got sick again.

"Help me sit her up a little so we can give her some Tylenol," Duke instructed Bear, and between the two, they were able to rouse her enough to get the two pills down her throat.

Bear gently laid her back down. She had a few strands of hair that had slipped out of the bands securing her ponytail. Lightly, he pushed them away from her flushed face.

"I assume you're going to stay with her," Duke stated with a knowing smirk, and Bear nodded. "Alright. Let's see how she responds to the Tylenol and fluids. I'll check back in about thirty minutes. If her symptoms get any worse, come and get me."

"Thanks, man," Bear said, expressing his gratitude to his teammates.

"No thanks, needed. I'm just glad I was here and could help."

As Duke left, Playboy and Aussie returned, carrying another cot and a light blanket.

"We thought she could use a clean cot and bedding," Playboy said as the two set up the cot and placed the pillow and blanket on it.

Bear thanked them both before they left. He went to lift her into his arms to move her to the other cot when he spotted some vomit on her clothes. He rummaged through her suitcase, picking out a clean T-shirt and a pair of mesh shorts. He spotted a pack of wipes and used those to clean her face, hands, and arms.

Getting her into clean clothes proved to be challenging for several reasons. He had to be extra careful maneuvering the t-shirt around the IV. He moved her to the other cot and covered her with the thin blanket. He moved her fan closer, positioning it to hit most of her body. Her soft snores indicated she was out cold. She never even stirred when he placed the two ice packs wrapped in small towels between her legs.

Once he had her situated, he pulled up a chair and stood watch over her in case she woke up and needed anything.

Jocelyn awoke to a blanket of heat wrapped around her. Feeling Surprisingly, she wasn't hot. She tried to snuggle closer to the warmth. She raised her head and found Bear looking back at her.

"Hi," he said, looking a little worried.

She smiled. "Hi," she replied. She then wondered how they got into this position. How was he sleeping beside her when she could barely fit on the cot herself?

"How are you feeling?" He asked.

"Exhausted."

"Well, you should be. You were really sick when I found you."

"I don't even remember," she admitted.

"How are you lying here next to me?"

He smiled. "The guys brought in another cot so I could lay with you."

"Oh, now I get it. This was your way of getting into my room since I wouldn't invite you in last night," she teased, and Bear laughed.

"Considering that you are cracking jokes, the good news is that you seem to be feeling better." He touched her forehead and her cheeks. "You don't feel warm. How is your head and stomach?"

"I have a little bit of a headache, but my stomach feels fine."

"Duke left some Tylenol if you want to take that for your headache."

"Okay. What time is it?"

"Eleven hundred."

"Wow! I must've been sick for me to sleep for a few extra hours."

"A few hours?" Bear quipped. "Try a whole day and then some."

Her eyes widened. "What?! I've been asleep for an entire day?" Her voice cracked.

Bear grinned and looked at his watch. "Actually, you were asleep for a day and five hours."

"Holy shit," she whispered, drawing a chuckle from Bear. She must've been really sick.

Smiling, he leaned in and kissed her forehead.

"What happened? Does Duke know what made me sick?" She asked, looking at him.

"We don't know, but Duke thinks you might have gotten food poisoning. He also took a blood sample to have it checked."

She was about to nod her head in understanding even though she wasn't processing much in her brain because it hurt to think, but Bear's comment about a blood sample had her backtracking and wondering who was checking her blood.

"You look puzzled. Whatcha thinking about?" Bear prodded, gently stroking her forehead with his thumb as if trying to iron out the worried wrinkles.

"Uhm…I'm a little confused about the whole blood sample thing. I don't remember ever seeing a lab set-up in your room. Unless Duke pulled it out of your team's Mary Poppins bag."

Bear chuckled, and Jocelyn could tell he was trying really hard not to laugh loudly.

"What is a Mary Poppins bag?" He asked, still looking amused.

She forced a small smile.

"Remember in the movie Mary Poppins, how she had that bag that seemed to produce anything she wanted from it?"

Bear tried to stifle his laughter, but he couldn't contain it and barked a loud laugh that made Jocelyn snicker. Once he got himself under control, he explained.

"While we strive to be prepared for anything, unfortunately, a mobile blood lab is a little too far complexed for us to carry around." He paused for a moment and grinned. "But to answer your question, we have many options should we need something we can't access on-site. In your case, our commander made a couple of phone calls after Duke took the samples. Duke, Jay Bird, and Aussie drove to N'Djamena. There is an FBI field office there. They are going to handle it.

"Why would they do that over a simple case of food poisoning?"

"Well, one, because we care about you," he gave her that cute grin of his that melted her insides. "And two, after going over everything you ate or drank yesterday, we think that the only thing different you consumed was that tea Flora gave you."

"You guys think it was the tea that made me sick?"

"We don't know for sure. But it was the only thing we could think of that you had that we didn't. We just want to make sure that you don't have any type of infection or anything."

She hoped it was just a simple case of food poisoning and not something significant.

"Was I really that bad?"

"Yeah, babe. You were. We had plans to have you medevaced out to the nearest military base for treatment."

"Seriously?"

"I wasn't going to lose you."

"I'm sorry for worrying you."

"Don't apologize. It wasn't your fault. You need to take it easy today and rest. I'm going to go next door and change. Then I'll be back. Maybe you'll feel up for a light meal or a snack."

He slid out of the bed and stood up, giving her a direct view of his body. His shorts sat dangerously low on his hips, giving her eyes access to that sexy V-line on his lower abdomen. She licked her lips.

"Uh-uh!" Bear shouted, shaking his finger at her.

"What?"

"Don't look at me like that."

"Like what?" She asked, playing innocent.

"Like I'm your snack."

Well, she certainly wouldn't mind taking a nibble of him. She eyed him again.

"Joce!"

"What?"

"You're doing it again."

"Sorry. I can't help it," she admitted, grinning.

He shook his head at her, but he was smiling. "If you want to shower, Playboy set it up for you."

"Okay. Thank you."

Bear stepped over to the cot and bent down. He kissed her forehead, and she closed her eyes. She loved it when he kissed her there.

"You don't ever have to thank me for caring for you," he told her before heading out.

She lay there for a little bit. She couldn't believe she was as sick as he said she was. She did feel sleepy still, even though she had slept that long. After a while of laying around, she thought a shower would make her feel a little better. Then she'd see about a little snack and then lay back down and do what Bear suggested and just rest.

CHAPTER EIGHTEEN

Two days had passed since Jocelyn had woken up sick as a dog. After taking Bear's advice and taking that extra day to rest, she had woken up this morning feeling like she was her old self again.

As she walked over to where Ralph was standing with his crew, she couldn't help the thrill and excitement pouring off her.

Today was a monumental day for Massendai and one of the most anticipated moments of the project. As long as all the calculations and data were correct, the drill would hit the water line in a matter of minutes.

Many from the village came to watch. And they all appeared just as excited as she was.

Ralph smiled. "There she is! The woman of the hour," he teased her, knowing she would get embarrassed.

"Hey, Ralph."

"Are you ready for this?" He asked her. She saw the excitement radiating off him.

"You bet I am," she replied as a large smile swept across her face.

"Then lets the show on the road."

Jocelyn walked with Ralph over to the drill rig, where Steven was checking over different things on the rig.

Because they would use the moment as a photo opportunity, Ralph explained how the process would go.

"We are going to drill down about three feet. If our measurement is accurate, that will put the placement of the drill two feet from the water line. When we hit that mark, I'll wave to you, signaling for you and the kids to go and stand near the drill."

After talking with Lana and even the guys on the team, they all decided that it would be really cool to have some of the kids from the village in the picture with Jocelyn.

Jocelyn couldn't wait to see the expressions on everyone's faces when that drill hit the mark, and the water gushed up through the drill as it pumped sediments out. It was a moment she definitely wanted to be documented. Duke had volunteered to take the photos since he had some experience with photography and cameras. He would know the best angles and how to navigate the lighting.

After going over the plan with Ralph, she searched the crowd for Bear. She wanted to laugh when she found him and Jay Bird surrounded by fifteen to twenty kids.

As she was walking toward Bear, he looked up and met her gaze. A big smile pulled at his lips. He excused himself from the kids and met her halfway.

As soon as she was in front of him, he gently pulled her in for a hug and kissed her cheek.

"Hey, babe."

"Hey, yourself." She nodded in the direction of the kids. "Looks like you've got yourself a little fan club over there."

He grinned. "No. They are here for you. Jay Bird and I were just occupying their time until the show started."

The closer it got to the time to start, the more nervous she got. Bear must've picked up on it because he hugged her again. She looped her arms around his neck and nuzzled her nose on the spot just below his ear. She smiled when she felt him shiver.

"You're playing with fire right now," he told her.

She giggled. "Sorry."

"No, you aren't," he said, laughing with her.

"Okay. I'm not," she laughed a little harder when he started tickling her.

He then pulled her flush against him. "You're nervous."

"I am. This is a huge moment."

He pulled back just a smidge so he could look into her eyes.

"I'm so proud of you, Joce."

She pressed her hand against his cheek. "Thank you."

He looked at something over her shoulder.

"I think they are ready for you," he said.

When she looked, Ralph and the crew were waving to her.

Looking back at Bear, she leaned in and softly kissed him.

"I love you."

"I love you, too."

☙

Jocelyn nervously stood to the side with the group of kids who would be taking the picture with her. She looked around at everyone in attendance. When she met Kosso's gaze, he gave her a thumbs up.

As Steven started up the rig, a vibration spread through the ground, adding to the anticipation. Maxime and Amira were holding her hands. Thank goodness their vile mother hadn't come to watch if she was even back from her trip. They still hadn't had a chance to talk to Maxime, but Bear had planned to speak with him soon.

Amira squeezed her hand, pulling her from her thoughts. When she looked down at the little girl, Amira was smiling.

"Look, Ms. Jocelyn! That swirling thing is moving."

Jocelyn chuckled. "That's part of the drill."

"It's so cool!" She heard Maxime say next to her.

She looked at him. "It's going to be even cooler when that water shoots out."

As the minutes passed, Jocelyn held her breath. Then after what seemed like an hour though it was only like fifteen minutes, Ralph waved for her and the kids to take their place.

She looked down at their smiling faces.

"Are you guys ready?"

They both laughed and nodded their heads.

As she and the group of kids made their way toward the well site, she stole a glance at Bear. He smiled and winked, making her smile. God, she loved him.

Once they got to the spot Ralph had marked, Jocelyn squatted between Maxime and Amira while the other kids formed a semi-circle around them.

Jocelyn's heart was pounding in her chest. Knowing they had hit the water was the most important part of the process for her. All the data in the world could say there was water below, but she wouldn't celebrate until she saw it with her own two eyes.

It was also an emotional moment because it was a huge milestone for her and because she had given people hope and a new way of living. And seeing their smiles was all that she needed.

Suddenly, the water mixed with sediments began to sputter up around the drill shaft. The kids started shouting excitedly, and the crowd was clapping and shouting in their own excitement. Jocelyn could only stare at the scene unfolding in front of her. Seeing the joy on all the faces around her brought tears to her eyes. Maxime and Amira were hugging her.

Just as Jocelyn started to stand up, she heard a grinding noise, followed by a high-pitched squeal. She looked up toward the rig's top just in time to see one of the steel cables holding a fitting snap. The large steel fitting that was being held by the cable came crashing down on a pile of pipes that were sitting right behind where she and the children were standing. Fearing for their safety, Jocelyn yelled to the kids to move.

She was just about to move away when she heard Bear shouting at her to run. Looking over her shoulder, she saw the stack of pipes starting to shift. Fearing she could be crushed, she started to run when the pile collapsed, sending some of the pipes crashing toward her location. She wouldn't be able to outrun it, and panic set in. She looked around her for a place that could shield her. Seeing her only option, she dove under the large truck the rig connected to. She landed hard on the ground, feeling a sharp pain hit her side, and she screamed out.

Once the dust settled, she saw two pipes lying where she had just stood. They were blocking her exit. She could hear people screaming. She tried to move but was again hit with a pain in her side that made her freeze.

She felt around the area, and when her fingers landed on something wet, she knew without looking that she was bleeding. How bad? That she didn't know. But when she finally could look shift to her other side, she could look down, and all she saw was blood on her yellow shirt.

Suddenly, she heard Bear. "Jocelyn!"

"Bear!" she called out.

Seconds later, she saw his face appear under the truck.

"Are you okay?" he asked. His voice was shaking.

"I don't know. I landed on something, and my side is bleeding. It hurts when I move."

She heard him curse. Then moments later, she saw the pipes blocking the way start to move, creating enough space for Bear to crawl under. The moment she saw him, she thought he was going to cry. It was obvious he was struggling with his emotions.

He crawled over to her, went straight to her shirt, and lifted it up. "Fuck!" He roared, making her jump, which made it hurt worse. Realizing what he had done, he kissed her forehead. "I'm sorry, sweetheart."

She tried comforting him with a smile and letting him know it was okay, but the pain was increasing.

"It hurts, Bear. How bad is it?"

"I'm not gonna lie. It's a pretty good gash."

"What did you hit?"

"I don't know. It was something on the ground. I felt it cut me as soon as I landed."

"Duke's on his way, and we'll have him look at it. Can you move so we can get you out from under here?"

She would bear the pain if she had to because, being stuck under the truck; her claustrophobia was starting to creep in. And that was the last thing she needed.

"Yeah. I can move, but you're going to have to help."

"We'll get you out."

A few of the guys appeared and helped. After a few minutes of inching her way out, she was finally free.

Duke knelt next to her and lifted her shirt. "Damn…" he mumbled as he reached into his bags. He pulled out a bottle of something and a bunch of gauze pads.

"On a scale of one to ten, how bad does it hurt?" He asked her.

"About a six or seven," she admitted.

Duke looked at Bear like he was asking permission for something. Before she could ask, Duke handed her a lollipop.

"Suck on this," he told her as he returned to gathering more things from his bag.

She couldn't help it. Maybe she was getting delirious, but she looked at Duke. "I thought you get a lollipop after you get treated."

Duke started laughing, but when she looked at Bear, he didn't seem to find her comment amusing.

"Put the lollipop in your mouth, Joce," Bear ordered.

"Why?"

He rolled his eyes, grabbed the candy from her hand, unwrapped it, and shoved it in her mouth.

"Because it is for your own good."

She lay there wide-eyed, staring at Bear. He did not just do that. She thought to herself. But after about a minute or two, she started to feel different. The pain in her side started to subside, and she felt lighter. What in the hell? Did they give her some type of psychedelic drug? Whatever it was, it was good shit. Before she knew it, she felt like she was flying in the clouds. Then gradually, she felt her eyes beginning to close until all she saw was darkness.

ಞ

Bear held Jocelyn's head in his lap while Duke cleaned her wound with alcohol and an antibiotic. They all wanted to take as many precautions as possible to ensure the wound didn't get infected.

"She's going to need stitches," Duke told him as he put aside the gauze pads he had used to clean the cut.

Bear bit the inside of his cheek. He hated this. He kept having flashbacks of those pipes coming straight at her. She would've been crushed if she hadn't thought quickly on her feet.

He looked down at her. She was out cold.

"Okay. Do what you have to do."

He leaned down and kissed her forehead. "I'm so sorry."

Joker and Aussie walked up. Bear noticed Joker had something in his hand.

"What's that?"

Joker held up a long, sharp piece of metal. "We think this is what she fell on. It's all we could find."

Bear took a deep breath, still trying to calm himself down.

"Is she okay?"

"I think so. Duke said she needs stitches."

"Damn," Aussie mumbled.

"Let's move her back to our building before I start on the stitches. It's a little more sanitary there."

Bear agreed and lifted Jocelyn in his arms. As the started to walk, Bear heard Ralph call his name.

"Bear! Hold up a minute."

Bear looked over his shoulder and saw the Army Vet jogging up the path toward him.

"What's up, Ralph?" He was in a hurry to get Jocelyn back.

Ralph pulled an orange and blue piece of material out of his pocket and handed it to Bear.

"I didn't want to give this to you in front of everyone, but one of my guys found this near the rig. It was tucked under one of the fittings."

Bear took a closer look at the material. It looked familiar.

"You said you guy found it by the rig?"

"Yeah. At first, I didn't think anything of it. But it didn't make sense after pondering on it a little more. This is a woman's scarf. And I've never seen Jocelyn wear one, so I don't think it is hers. It made me wonder if the person who messed with those cables caused one to snap."

"You think this accident was deliberate?" Bear asked, feeling the anger inside him begin to grow.

"Looking at the frayed ends of the cable where it broke, I can tell you it wasn't an accident. Someone cut that cable."

Bear felt the hair on his neck stand up. He looked around. Many people were still there watching. He couldn't help but think every person was a suspect.

"Do me a favor and keep this under wraps. If it does belong to the person responsible and they're from around here, I don't want them knowing we have this."

"Yes, sir. I'll let my guys know."

ॐ

Jocelyn blinked her eyes open. Her vision was a little blurry, but Bear's warm smile met her once she could focus, though she could see the worry in his grey eyes.

He ran is knuckles lightly down her cheek. "How ya feeling, sweetheart?"

She closed her eyes, recalling the accident. She tried to sit up and winced, feeling the burn in her side. She looked down and saw the bandage stuck to her skin.

"Sore," she admitted and tried again to sit up. This time she accomplished the feat with Bear's assistance. Her head also hurt, but that could be from stress and her prior injury a few months ago.

"What time is it?" She asked, noticing her watch had been removed from her wrist.

"Nineteen hundred," he replied, then got up, walked over to the small table, and retrieved a bag.

She bumped her brows together, trying to figure out what nineteen hundred was. She knew it was military time, but her brain wasn't functioning, and she didn't want to have to try and think. Bear must've seen her frustration because he grinned as he sat beside her on her cot.

"It's a little after seven."

"Thank you. My brain can't function." She ran a hand down her face. "How long have I been asleep?"

"About six hours."

"Damn. What in the world did Duke give me? It felt like I wasn't asleep for that long."

Bear's smile grew. "You didn't like your lollipop?"

"I didn't have much time to enjoy it. All I remember is someone shoving the candy into my mouth. Moments later, I was in la-la-land. I expected a needle to be jabbed into my arm or leg, not a lollipop shoved into my mouth."

Bear chuckled. "The lollipop has taken the place of the morphine syrette. The drug in the lollipop is absorbed faster in the mouth than from a needle being stuck into a muscle. That way, it eases the pain faster."

"Huh. I guess you learn something new every day."

Bear squinted his eyes at her. "You shouldn't have had to be given a lollipop."

Her stomach growled, and she rubbed it with her hand.

"Guess I'm hungry."

"Sounds like it. I think the guys were trying to decide what to eat. Do you feel up to going out there?"

She didn't want to, but she didn't want to lay there either.

"Sure."

With Bear's help, she managed to get to her feet. She hissed when a bit of pain hit her side.

"How bad is it?" She asked.

"Duke had to put in fifteen stitches. We think you landed on a strip of metal. At least, that was all we could find."

"Hmm…"

"Did Ralph say what he thinks may have happened? Why that cable snapped."

Bear looked away, and she could see that he was struggling with something. She put her hand on his arm. When he looked back at her, the look in his eyes frightened her. He was angry. But she knew it wasn't directed at her.

"Bear…" she pressed.

"Ralph thinks the cable was cut deliberately."

Jocelyn sucked in a breath.

"But who?"

Bear walked over to the table and picked up something. When he returned, Jocelyn recognized the scarf right away.

"That's the scarf that Amira gave her mom." She looked at Bear. "Are you saying that Nandi cut that cable?"

"We don't know for sure, but the evidence points to her. Ralph found this tucked under one of the fittings by the rig."

Jocelyn couldn't believe it. She knew the woman wasn't nice. But to tamper with the rig. Then she realized what she hadn't asked.

"The kids! Did any of the kids get hurt?" She would have been devastated if one of the kids had been injured.

"No. Just you."

"Thank God," she whispered.

Bear took her in his arms. He was gentle, but Jocelyn could still feel the anger radiating from him. She hugged him.

"I don't like seeing you hurt."

"I know. But I'm here—with you. And I'm okay."

"You're not okay. You've got fucking stitches and bruises all over."

She pulled back just enough to look him in the eyes.

"But I'm alive."

"Fuck!" He stated before crashing his lips down on hers. She let him take what he needed. Before things got out of hand, he released her lips and hugged her.

"Let's go get you some food."

She smiled. "Lead the way."

୶

They were all sitting around, still deciding what to have for dinner.

"God, I could go for an original Philly cheesesteak, packed with onions, peppers, and mushrooms with a bit of seasoning to top it off," Nails stated, rubbing his stomach.

"I'll take the onions, peppers, and mushrooms on a deep-dish pizza," Playboy said with a small smile.

"I'll go the Italian route too," Snow said, but it wasn't a surprise since he was Italian. "Spaghetti with my mom's homemade meat sauce and meatballs covered in parmesan cheese."

Duke laughed and pointed at Snow. "I'm with you, although instead of Italian, I'm going to go with my mom's southern fried chicken seasoned perfectly with creamy mashed potatoes and her zucchini squash medley."

"I'm skipping the meal and going straight to dessert," Joker said, looking at Bear. "You know as well as I do that your sister can't cook worth shit, but damn, put her in front of an oven, and that woman can bake the most amazing and delicious treats known to man. I'd take anything baked by her right now."

Jay Bird shook his head. "If it weren't for all the training and exercising we do, every one of you would be obese with that shit you eat."

Jocelyn knew he was teasing. She had heard that Jay Bird was a health nut, and when he could help it, he was very conscientious about what he put in his body. "I will elect for a tasty salad with fresh tomatoes, onion, cucumbers, green bell pepper slices, olives, some feta cheese, and a dash of salt. Dress it up with some Greek oregano and olive oil, and you've got one badass Greek salad."

"Man, y'all don't know what good food is," Aussie stated. "There isn't anything better than a medley seafood platter filled with steamed shrimp, a nice piece of baked garlic buttered cod, some clams, and throw in a crab cake topped with lemon, parsley, and Old Bay seasoning."

Everyone looked at Bear. He was the only one who hadn't said anything. He reached for Jocelyn's hand before looking into her eyes.

"Cinnamon French toast, smothered with a sweet cream cheese frosting and sausage links on the side."

Jocelyn tuned out the comments from the guys as she looked at Bear. He was still staring at her with that sexy lopsided grin plastered on his face. He was so handsome.

"I can't believe you remembered," she said to him.

"How could I ever forget our signature breakfast." He winked, and she immediately felt the heat hit her cheeks. How could either one of them forget, considering it was their go-to staple food after tangling in the sheets together? Damn, now she was craving her famous cinnamon French toast with an extra-large dollop of frosting on the side that would be used for an edible yet pleasurable experience.

Bear cleared his throat to get her attention. When she looked, he was grinning like a fool and had a gleam in his eyes.

"You're thinking about extra frosting, aren't ya?"

Her eyes shot wide open, and her mouth opened to protest, but she closed it quickly, knowing she had busted. He knew exactly what she'd been daydreaming about. Thank goodness the others were engrossed in their own conversations and not paying attention to her and Bear.

Even though her face was probably the color of a ripe tomato, she couldn't stop smiling. The fact that he remembered those blissful, intimate moments touched her deeply.

Bear chuckled at her reaction, then brought his hand up and placed it against her cheek. He moved closer, resting his forehead against hers. She closed her eyes and breathed in his heavenly scent of evergreen and mint.

"Do you know how bad I'm craving your French toast right now?" He whispered against her lips.

Feeling a little brazen herself and ignoring the slight pain in her side, she slipped her hand around the nape of his neck, giving her something to hold onto as she moved in to make her move.

"I actually have an appetite for frosting," she confessed before playfully nipping his bottom lip. "That sweet, creamy frosting that I can lick—"

Before she could finish, she was interrupted by a low growl and found herself at the mercy of Bear's lips.

She could hear the snickers of the guys. Then someone commented on her wanting Bear's lips for dinner. Yes, she was embarrassed, but she was in heaven.

When they finally separated, she looked around, and they were all staring at her and Bear. They all had some sort of grin on their face.

"Well, unless you have enough of those kisses to satisfy our hunger, how about we see what our options are." Nails commented as he pulled out a box of MREs. He was ignoring Bear's growls.

"Have you ever had an MRE?" Duke asked her, and she shook her head.

She knew what they were, but she'd never had one. She did hear that they weren't very good. However, she was curious. Even though she was picky, she always at least tried something once. Well, most of the time.

Before passing them out, Nails let her choose first. She chose the cheese tortellini. When she opened the package, she was surprised by the amount of stuff inside. Besides the tortellini in tomato sauce, there was a package of crackers, mango peach applesauce, a packet of orange electrolyte powder to mix with water, an apple cinnamon energy bar, and even a packet of peanut butter and a pack of M&Ms.

She found it very interesting as Bear showed her how to make it. She took the heater bag, tore it open, and placed the tortellini pouch inside it. Bear handed her a water bottle, and she poured water into the heater bag until it reached the fill line. He showed her how to roll down the top of the heater bag and tilt it to ensure the water fully activated the heat pack. She set it down on the ground and used a tree log to prop up the bag at a slight angle so the water wouldn't run out and the heat could rise through the pouch. She waited about ten minutes before removing the pouch from the heater bag, then stirred the contents. She added a little salt and pepper, then took a bite.

Expecting a very bland taste, she was surprised it wasn't that bad.

"Good?" Aussie asked, and she nodded as she swallowed the bite she had in her mouth.

She used a paper towel to wipe her mouth. "It's not too bad."

"Not all of them are tasty," Jay Bird quipped.

"Some taste like shit," Playboy added.

As Jocelyn sat quietly and ate her meal, she looked over the rest of the contents, deciding which item she would try next. She reached for the crackers but noticed two white bubble gum-type tablets in a small package. She grabbed it and held it up.

"What are these? Gum?"

The snickers from amongst the group should've told her they weren't what she thought they were. Bear leaned over and whispered.

"They're laxatives."

Her eyes went wide, and her mouth formed an "O."

"Well, I won't be needing those," she admitted, and everyone laughed.

As she sat back and enjoyed the team's camaraderie, she realized just how close these guys were to one another. They weren't just teammates. They were family—a family that she hoped to belong to.

CHAPTER NINETEEN

Will picked up a crystal vase and threw it across the room. It shattered into hundreds of pieces.

"What part of tone it down didn't she understand?" Will shouted at Moussa over the phone. It was good that Moussa wasn't here, or else Will might have just killed him. He couldn't believe the bind that Moussa's bitch had gotten him into. The last thing he needed was the government on his ass.

"I don't know, Will. She's been acting funny over the last couple of months."

"And you didn't think to let me know about these suspicions? It doesn't do me much good now," he spat.

"I was going to. But I was first trying to find out what she was doing."

"Where is Nandi?" he asked Moussa. *The fucker better not lie to me.*

He was silent for a moment before he spoke. He was hesitating, which wasn't a good sign.

"I honestly don't know. But I heard they found her scarf near the well rig that was tampered with."

"So they think it was her?"

"They don't want to assume until they speak to her. But she hasn't returned from her trip yet."

A sinister smile spread across Will's lips. "What trip was that?" Will asked, already knowing what Nandi was up to. The bitch was double-crossing him.

"She said she was picking up supplies for her herbal medicines."

Will wanted to laugh in Moussa's face. Did he take him for a fool? Or did Moussa really not know what Nandi had been up to? He did say that he noticed a change in her.

"You said you suspected something about Nandi. What do you suspect exactly?"

Again, Will was quiet before he said anything.

"I think she's seeing someone else."

Oh, she was seeing someone else, alright. It just isn't the relationship you think it is.

"What if I told you that Nandi has gone rogue?"

"No!" Moussa spat. "Nandi knows what the consequences of doing that would be. Plus, she's weak."

Not as weak as you think.

"Well, I would suggest that you track down that wife of yours and find out exactly what the fuck she's been up to. Because you don't want me to," he threatened.

"Yes, Sir."

"I expect some information within the next two days."

"Yes, Sir."

Will disconnected the call and threw the phone on his desk. Tau was sitting across from him, listening in.

What was Nandi's aim? Then it hit him. She wasn't out to screw him over. She was out to destroy him. She was the only one of the three who complained about the delays.

He looked at Tau.

"Get me a flight to N'Djamena tomorrow morning."

"Why? I thought you were going to let Moussa handle Nandi?"

"Obviously, he can't. He doesn't even know that she's plotting to destroy every single one of us, including him."

"What are you going to do? You need to tread carefully with this and not bring more attention to yourself."

Will grinned. "Don't worry. By the time I finish, all that attention will no longer be on me because It'll be on the real culprits who've been murdering innocent people to take their land. There won't be a shred of evidence pointing to me."

"They have no power. If the government finds out what's been going on, they'll squeal their first chance. You'll be screwed either way."

"They can't squeal if they're dead."

CHAPTER TWENTY

Jocelyn sighed as she closed up her laptop. Because of the recent incidents, the Secret Service was not allowing Lana to attend the ribbon cutting for the well. It was understandable, but Jocelyn was sad at the same time because she had been looking forward to seeing Lana.

It had been two days since the incident at the well site. Luckily, Ralph and the crew were able to fix the cables on the rig and complete the final processes of the installation. All that was left was to cement the well base, which they are scheduled to complete tomorrow. Then the day after, the well should be ready for use.

Flora was organizing a big celebration to recognize the milestone. Jocelyn and the guys were getting antsy and were ready to go home. They still weren't any closer to finding out who was behind the cut cables on the rig. Their only evidence was Nandi's scarf; nobody could question her because she hadn't returned from her trip. According to the kids and Mr. Emmanuel, they had expected her back a day ago.

The other upsetting news they got yesterday was her blood test results from when she had fallen ill. According to the FBI's lab, her blood had traces of toxins from Nerium oleander. Oleander is a flowering tree that can be deadly should its leaves be ingested. She never consumed oleander leaves or even saw an oleander tree around the village. So, the only logical explanation for the toxins in her blood was the tea she had drank.

They had spoken to Flora about it, and she had become distraught when she learned that the tea she had given Jocelyn had made her sick. She admitted that she purchased her tea from various vendors, so pinpointing where those tea bags originated was fruitless. The good news was at least the tea hadn't contained enough toxins to kill her.

She and Bear had FaceTimed with his parents, and they were over the moon when they announced that she and Bear had reconciled. Jenelle already wanted to plan a vow renewal ceremony and reception. She really was an awesome mother-in-law. And Ray was tickled pink that he had gained another daughter.

She heard laughter coming from outside and decided to see what all the fun was about. On the way out the door, she grabbed the pack of M&Ms that came with her MRE.

When she walked outside, she found the guys engaged in a kickball game with a group of kids.

She stayed back and watched Bear as he interacted with the children, patting them on the back or giving them a high five. It didn't take long for her emotions to hit her hard. Since that night in the desert, she and Bear found time every night to talk. Mostly they talked about what they've been up to over the last ten years and about the future. She already knew she'd leave her D.C. apartment and move to be with him. He had made her cry when he told her about the house he bought and that he purchased it because of her. It was her dream home.

The one topic she had been avoiding until now was important. Especially now, seeing how Bear interacting with the kids.

Knowing she could never give him kids of their own, she became teary-eyed and couldn't bear to watch anymore.

Slowly, as she walked back to her room, she looked up and watched the half-moon as it started to ascend into the sky above – another one of the beautiful aspects of life.

She thought about her future as she stood there gazing out at Mother Nature's creations. She had been given a rare but amazing opportunity. Second chances like her and Bear's don't come along often. She loved him so much, and after the last couple of days of getting to know each other again, she wasn't sure if her heart could take it if he decided he couldn't be with her once she told him she couldn't bear his children.

A tear slipped out of her eye, followed by another one. Soon she was a blubbering mess and couldn't see because of the tears in her eyes.

Suddenly, the sound of that voice she found solace in spoke from behind her.

"Joce?"

She was afraid to turn around and face him. But she didn't have a choice because as soon as Bear's strong arms wrapped around her waist, pulling her back against his chest, her mind was already accepting his comfort, and she turned in his arms. She couldn't stop her tears and buried her face in the crook of his neck.

中

Bear wasn't sure what had happened. One minute he saw Jocelyn standing off to the side, smiling and laughing as he and the guys played kickball with the kids. But the next minute, her beautiful smile had disappeared, and her expression filled with anguish.

He followed the rocky path leading back to their building. His worries were put to rest in less than a minute as he saw her standing outside. But he knew something was wrong. She buried her face in her hands with her back to him, and he could tell she was crying.

"Joce?"

When she didn't turn around or acknowledge him, he pressed up against her back and slid his arms around her waist. He hugged her close. He could hear her sniffles and feel her body shake.

She turned suddenly, wrapping her arms around his waist, and buried her face in the crook of his neck. He could feel her hot, wet tears against his skin. He held her close, letting her cry, though she was starting to scare him.

Finally, he pulled back slightly when she seemed to be calming down, but she still wouldn't look up at him. Using his fingers, he gently lifted her chin, tilting her face up toward his.

The moment he locked onto her tear-ridden eyes, he saw the pain and anguish.

"Sweetheart, you are scaring the shit out of me right now."

She opened her mouth to speak but then closed it before trying to look away.

"Joce, baby, you gotta talk to me? What's going on?"

She looked directly into his eyes. "Would you still love me if we don't have children?"

The question came out of left field, and he wondered what in the hell triggered it.

"Where is this coming from, Joce?"

"Just, please answer the question," she pleaded, tears rolling down her cheeks. Her voice sounded pained.

He took her face between the palms of his hands and looked her dead in the eye as he spoke from his heart.

"When I say that I love you, I mean that—kids or no kids. If you don't want kids, that is fine. We can have dogs or cats instead if you want them. Hell, I'll give you a farm if that's what it takes. I just don't want to lose you. Not when fate gave us a second chance. It's always been you." He paused and took a deep breath. "So, my answer is one hundred percent yes. I would still love you, kids or no kids."

She blew out a big breath. "It's not that I don't want kids. If I could, I'd have any many as I can. Or as many as you would want."

"Joce, we can still make that happen. Though I don't know how many considering our ages," he joked, trying to lighten up the mood.

She covered his hands with hers. "I have always wanted to be a mom someday." She took an unsteady breath. "But I know it will never happen."

"Come on. I know having sex doesn't automatically make a baby. But we can keep trying until we do. That's the fun part," he said, slightly wiggling his eyebrows.

"You're not understanding."

"Then tell me, so I will understand."

"I can't have babies," she blurted out, and Bear gave her a sideways look.

"What?"

She took a deep breath. "I have no reproductive organs. I was diagnosed with stage four endometriosis. All of my baby-making organs were removed."

Bear felt like he'd been knocked backward. How did he not know about that? He ran his hand over his mouth in disbelief. He couldn't believe this.

"What? When?"

"It was about three months after we separated."

He thought back to that time, and it hit him.

"That was when you stopped calling."

She nodded. "Nothing I said would have made you change your mind. Plus, I knew I was going to be facing an uphill battle and needed to put all my strength and energy into my treatment and recovery and figure out how to pay for all the medical bills."

Bear felt all the blood drain from his face. He remembered in the divorce papers that Jocelyn had opted out of his medical insurance.

As if sensing his upset, she hugged him.

"I didn't tell you this to make you feel bad. I needed you to know before you expected me to get pregnant."

"Jocelyn. I don't know what to say. I'm so sorry. I should have been there for you."

She managed a small smile, and she gazed into his eyes.

"I'm alive, and that's all that matters. I was given a second chance at life. Yeah, it is a life where I endured some tough challenges, but also a life that led me back to you."

Bear pulled her close. This woman—*his* woman, was a survivor—a warrior in more ways than she knew. Not only did she have the guts to stand up to him, but she endured a disease and kicked its ass.

There was no way in hell he was letting her go. Not now, not ever. He lowered his head and whispered in her ear, "We were both given a second chance, and I'm not about to fuck it up. I will make up to you all the time we've missed."

She grinned. "I love you, Tripp Walker."

It had been ten long years since he'd heard those exact words roll off her tongue, and he thought his heart would burst.

"I love you too, Mrs. Walker," he said and winked before taking her lips in a deep kiss until neither could breathe.

CHAPTER TWENTY-ONE

Jocelyn and Bear were lying on the cot in her room. After explaining her entire ordeal with endometriosis, she felt exhausted.

What made her happy now was being with Bear. She felt a lot better knowing that he was content not having kids of their own, and that he was supportive of adopting if they both wanted.

Thinking about adoption made her think of Maxime and Amira. She wanted to take those kids away from the life they have now. They deserve parents who will truly act as their parents—parents who would shower them with love and care.

A knock sounded on the door.

"Yeah?" Bear called out. Jocelyn could tell he was tired.

Joker poked his head in. He looked serious, and Bear must've noticed because he sat up a little more.

"Hey. Maxime just showed up. He was looking for you."

Jocelyn looked at Bear. She knew that Bear was planning on seeking him out to talk to him. But it looked like Maxime was doing the seeking.

She gave Bear a nudge. "Let's go talk to him."

They both got up and walked outside. Maxime was sitting by the firepit alone. He had his hands clasped in his lap with his head down.

Jocelyn let Bear take the lead.

"Hey, buddy," Bear greeted Maxime, then sat beside him. Jocelyn took the seat on the other side of Maxime. She wanted him to feel protected and that she supported him.

Maxime's head lifted, and he offered a forced smile.

"Hello, Bear and Ms. Jocelyn."

"Is everything okay?" Bear asked.

The boy was extremely nervous. Even without training, she could see how the kid's hands trembled.

Maxime was quiet. Then he looked between the two adults.

"Amira told me she talked to you two."

Bear nodded. "She did. And I have to say, both Jocelyn and I are a little worried."

"It all started when I heard my mum talking to the man one night. I had gotten thirsty and was getting something to drink from the kitchen when I heard them in the living room. They were trying to whisper, but Moussa never knew how to be quiet."

Both Jocelyn and Bear met each other's questionable gaze.

"The man. Are you talking about your dad?" Bear asked, and the boy shook his head.

"I thought he was my dad. But I found out that night he wasn't. Everything changed after that night."

"How so?" Jocelyn asked.

"We moved shortly after. That's when mummy started getting angrier. She'd take it out on Amira and me."

"You said that you moved? Where were you living?"

"Near Cape Town. Mummy told us we were going on a trip to stay with family."

Jocelyn again looked at Bear.

"Didn't you guys move here so your mom could help care for her aunt?" Bear questioned.

"That's what she told us. But I didn't believe her. Not after hearing her and that man talk that night."

"You said the man's name is Moussa?"

Maxime nodded his head. Then he looked at Bear.

"He's a bad man, Bear. He works with that investor guy, Corsica. Somehow I think my mum is involved too."

Jocelyn took a deep breath.

"Besides the other day, how often have you seen Moussa with Corsica?"

"When we lived in Cape Town, I saw him a few times."

"They both don't like Amira and me," Maxime said, looking defeated, and Jocelyn wanted nothing more than to pull that little boy in a hug.

"You kids deserve so much better. Is there anyone else who you guys could stay with? To get you away from that mess?" Jocelyn asked.

Maxime shook his head. "No. It has always been the four of us. Until the night that I heard Moussa admit he wasn't our dad. That our dad was a nobody who just knocked up mummy. He talked about how he hated us and wished mummy never had us. That Amira and I were nothing but thorns in his side."

Jocelyn was pissed. How dare those assholes! Bear didn't look like he was fairing any better.

Maxime had a haunted look on his face and looked down at his hands, where his fingers were all twisted together.

"One time, I heard mummy and him arguing on the phone. She had him on speakerphone. That's what woke me up. Moussa was really mad about something. He told mummy that if she didn't finish the job, he was going to finish her."

He then looked at Bear. "After that night, I tried to shield myself and Amira from him."

Bear clasped the boy on the shoulder. "You're very brave, Maxime. And I'm sorry you and your sister have had to go through this. You both deserve so much more.

"Do you think you and your friends can help us?"

Jocelyn met Bear's eyes, and she could see he was struggling.

"I'll do whatever I can. Let me make a few phone calls."

"Thank you."

"You don't have to thank us, Maxime. I'm just glad you came and spoke with us. That isn't a good homelife for you and Amira."

"I worry about Amria. She just wants attention, and I know that gets on mummy's nerves."

"As I said, let me make a few phone calls and see if there is any way we can help you and your sister. Maybe you guys can stay close to Mr. Emmanuel and his wife for now. They seem like really nice people."

Maxime then shocked both Bear and Jocelyn when he threw himself into Bear's lap. The sight nearly brought Jocelyn to tears.

CHAPTER TWENTY-TWO

All the excitement was creating a buzz in the air. That day had finally come. In just a few minutes, the village of Massendai would officially have a functioning water well.

Jocelyn hadn't seen this many people since she and the team had arrived two weeks ago. Many brought their buckets to fill. A few of the ladies, mostly friends of Flora's, cooked food. Popular sai music was playing. The kids were running around and laughing. As Jocelyn looked around, she didn't see anyone who wasn't smiling. It truly was a great day.

Bear draped his arm over her shoulder and pulled her into his side. He kissed her temple.

"Look at all these happy people," he observed and was smiling himself.

"They should be happy. This is huge for them."

Bear turned her so she was facing him. He pulled her close; his hands snug on her waist.

"You did that to them. You put that smile on their face."

She lowered her eyes, feeling a bit bashful, but Bear touched her chin, lifting it so she was looking at him.

"Don't sell yourself short, Joce. I know there are others who contributed, but it was your leadership that saw this through to the end. You confronted obstacles, and you dealt with them. I'm so proud of you and who you represent."

She felt tears prick her eyes, and she tried to keep them at bay.

"Thank you. I appreciate your words."

He leaned in and kissed her forehead.

Kosso and Flora then appeared.

"Ms. Jocelyn. I think it's time," Kosso said, smiling. "Are you ready?"

She smiled. "Yes. I'm more than ready."

She turned back to Bear and gave him a small peck on his lips. "I love you," she told him.

Grinning, he winked. "I love you, too. Now go."

☙

Jocelyn couldn't stop smiling as person after person stepped up to the well with their bucket.

The ribbon-cutting ceremony went off without a hitch. Now everyone was partying.

Tomorrow morning, she and the team would be leaving. Even though she was excited to get back to the States and begin her new life with Bear, she was sad to leave. She had met so many amazing people, including Maxime and Amira.

After talking with Maxime, she and Bear visited Mr. Emmanuel and his wife. The older couple assured Bear and Jocelyn they would be keeping an eye on the kids.

As for Nandi. She still had returned from her trip, leading many to think she wasn't coming back. Her absence has only made her appear more guilty of the rig tampering.

Bear had spoken with Derek about Amira and Maxime's accusations regarding their mom and Moussa. Derek had seemed more interested in Moussa. He said that he would forward the information to some contacts of his at several federal agencies and have a look into his background.

She saw Ralph standing with a few of his crew members, and she walked over. She wanted to thank him again for all his help. Of all the crews she had worked with in the past, Ralph's team had to be the best, including the *Double Mint Twins.* They quickly accepted that she and Bear had no intentions of ending their relationship. However, they liked to test their limits and would still flirt with her. They reminded her of Nails.

"Hey, Joce!" Ralph said.

"Hey, Ralph!"

They both stood there for a moment taking in the scene.

"You did good, Joce. The crew and I agreed that we would happily work with you on any given day."

"Thanks, Ralph. I appreciate that. And the same goes for me. You and the crew have been amazing to work with. You guys stepped up when needed."

"So, where are you off to next?" He asked her. Lana had given her a few choices on where she wanted to go next. Her choices included countries in South America and Africa. However, her focus was on one particular project for the next few weeks.

She smiled. "I'm headed to Virginia Beach."

Ralph furrowed his eyebrows. But then a smile slowly tugged the corners of his mouth.

"You're moving in with Bear?"

She nodded. "I am."

"I'm happy for you both."

"Thank you. But after I get settled, I think I'm leaning toward a South American trip—maybe Guatemala or Honduras."

Ralph smiled. "Well, when you know, let me know. I'd love to work with you again."

"I definitely will. And I gave Lana your information and recommended you and your crew for all of our future projects.

"Thank you."

"You're welcome."

"There was something else I wanted to talk to you about."

"What's that?"

"Some of the guys and I were talking and were a little concerned about the casing. It hasn't cured yet. Before we leave, we want to make sure that it's stable. So, we were wondering if it's possible that you could stay an extra day or two.

This was new for her. Normally, her job was finished once the well was fully functioning with no issues.

She nibbled her bottom lip as she looked toward where Bear was talking on the phone. She didn't want to decide without talking to him since she was scheduled to ride home with them.

"Ummm...I'm unsure since I'm supposed to fly home with the guys. So, I'm kinda on their schedule. Can you give me a few minutes, and I'll let you know."

"Sure."

Seeing Bear slip his phone back into his pocket, Jocelyn walked over. "Hey, everything okay?"

He shook his head. "That was our commander. We have a change in plans."

The slight frown on his face told her he wasn't pleased with the new plans he had just received.

"I'm guessing these plans involve you heading out to save the world from bad men."

Chuckling, he snagged her around the waist and pulled her close. Dropping his head, he placed his lips on her neck. He felt tense as he breathed deeply.

"Want to tell me what else is bothering you?" She ran her hands up and down his back, loving how his muscles jumped under her fingertips.

Pulling back, he looked her in the eye. "The team and I have to leave tonight."

"Wait! Tonight?"

"Unfortunately."

"Well, this could actually be a good thing—sort of."

"How is that good? We need to get you home. Derek said that Lana's office was looking into it. He said they would call when they had something."

"I was just talking to Ralph." She explained to him about casing. "If Lana's office can't find me a flight until late tomorrow or early the following morning, I'd be here to help Ralph if anything did happen."

She could already tell that Bear wasn't fond of the idea. Honestly, she wasn't either. But what choice did she have?

"Let's talk while we walk," she told him, and they headed toward their building.

"Shit, Joce. I don't like leaving you, even if it is just for the night."

"I understand. But think about it. What choice do we have? Either way, I'm stuck here at least through late tomorrow. And you guys are leaving tonight. Plus, Ralph wouldn't have asked if it wasn't important."

He seemed to be thinking about it.

"I promise that I'll be fine. It'll only be two days max. The crew will still be here, so their security will still be around."

"I just don't like you being here alone without one of us."

"Bear...You know, this is something we would have to talk about eventually."

"What's that?"

"My work. You guys can't be everywhere that I am."

He closed his eyes and sighed. "I know."

She looped her arms around his neck and hugged him. He hugged her back, giving her a big squeeze. When she pulled back, he was smiling. But she could see the worry deep in his eyes. That was the last thing she needed. His focus should be on his new mission, not her.

She reached for his hands and pulled him close to her. She smiled when he dropped her hands and wrapped his arms around her waist.

"I want to hug you for as long as I can," he told her, and she chuckled. She rubbed his back. "You don't need to worry about me. I'll be fine."

"I'll always worry about you."

"I get it. I feel the same way, but I know and understand that you have a job to do. A critical job, I might add. We can't stop living our lives because we're worried about each other. More so you. An entire team is counting on you to be at your best. If you're not, you'll endanger yourself and your team.

His silence told her that he knew she was right.

"Bear, I love you."

His stormy grey eyes softened, and a small smile played on his lips.

"I love you, too. That's why I worry."

"I know, babe. But trust me. Everything will work out just fine. Plus, just think. Maybe I'll be all moved in by the time you get home."

Bear's smile grew larger.

"That would be the best welcome home gift."

"Oh, you have no idea what kind of welcome home you'll get."

"Tease," Bear mumbled against her lips right before he kissed her.

CHAPTER TWENTY-THREE

Jocelyn threw the last of her clothes into her suitcase and zipped it. *Done!* Now she just had to wait for Ralph to get there. Lana's office had secured a ticket on a flight around the same time Ralph and his crew were leaving. So, Ralph offered her a ride to the airport.

Thankfully, the casing was cured with no issues. She was so happy to be leaving. Although, her departure was bittersweet. She had planned to spend the morning with Maxime and Amira, but when she got to Mr. Emmanuel's home, he told her that Nandi had returned and had taken the kids somewhere. She had hoped they would be back before she left so she could say goodbye.

"Jocelyn? Are you there?" Clover's voice said through the phone.

"Sorry. I'm here. I got distracted. My flight is supposed to land at Andrews around eleven," Jocelyn told her.

"That's late. Do you have a ride?"

"My car is there. So, I'm good."

"Ok, then."

"You haven't heard from Joker, have you?"

Clover's light laugh echoed through the phone. "You miss my brother already?"

"Guilty."

"Hey. I feel the same. As soon as Joker walks out that door, I feel like a lost puppy. But to answer your question. No. Sometimes I hear from him, and sometimes I don't. It all depends on the mission."

Jocelyn knew that, but hearing it from someone else feeling the same way she did helped her.

She went to ask Clover another question, but there was a knock at the door.

That must be Ralph.

"I think my ride is here."

"No worries. I'll let you go. Just do me a favor and call me when you land so I know you got in. Oh! And you might want to call my mom too. She's been nagging me about when you're getting home."

Jocelyn smiled. "I will. I'll talk to you soon."

She grabbed her backpack and two larger bags. When she swung the door open, she was shocked to see Nandi standing there.

"Nandi...what are you doing here?"

The woman shifted nervously on her feet.

"I'm sorry for just showing up. The kids told me that you were leaving." She took a deep breath. "They wanted to say bye to you. They are in the car."

Jocelyn peeked around Nandi's petite frame and could see the heads of the kids in the backseat. When Jocelyn met the woman's eyes again, she sensed nervousness.

"I also want to apologize for my behavior. I've been under a lot of stress. I've recently found out that my husband has been having an affair. Then toppled with my aunt's declining health, I'm sure you can understand the impact that could have on someone."

Jocelyn did understand, but that didn't mean that was believing every word this woman was saying. There was something about her that told Jocelyn to keep her distance.

"If you could just come and say goodbye to the kids, I promise you won't ever see me again."

Jocelyn didn't doubt that. She had no intention of ever setting an eye on her ever again.

"Okay. But I'm only doing this, Maxime and Amira."

Jocelyn slowly walked toward the tan sedan that was idling. The windows were covered in a heavy tint. She tried the back door, but it was locked.

"Oh! Sorry. I left the child safety locks on."

Jocelyn wanted to roll her eyes. This woman hasn't given a shit about her kids, and suddenly, she's all conscientious about child car safety.

Give me a break. Someone grab this woman an Oscar.

Getting a little irritated, Jocelyn grabbed the handle of the front passenger door and pulled. She ducked her head in, putting her knees on the seat so she could see into the back.

When she laid eyes on the kids' sleeping bodies, Jocelyn felt the warning tingles all over her body.

Out of the corner of her eye, she saw Nandi sneaking up behind her. Jocelyn quickly pulled herself out of the car. She started to run in the opposite direction, but she was immediately met with a forearm to her throat. The force of the hit knocked her to the ground. She grabbed her throat and coughed as she had trouble breathing. Before she could pick herself up off the ground, she felt the pinch to her neck. A warming sensation began to flow through her system, and within seconds her extremities started going numb.

When she looked up, she saw Nandi standing there with a syringe in her hand. She was leering at her. Her smile was evil and malicious.

Suddenly, a gunshot rang out, and Jocelyn watched as Nandi's lifeless body crumpled to the ground.

Oh my God! Being paralyzed by whatever Nandi injected her with, Jocelyn couldn't move to see who the shooter was. But then, a familiar figure came into view, and Jocelyn felt relieved.

Flora!

Flora walked over and stood above Jocelyn, looking down at her. Jocelyn could only follow her movements with her eyes.

"I'm sorry you were caught in the middle of this fiasco," Flora began. "You weren't even supposed to be here. This village shouldn't even be here."

What in the heck was this woman talking about? Jocelyn thought as she lay there, helplessly on the ground.

"But then my stupid ass daughter-in-law just couldn't be patient. She had to have the prize right away."

Daughter-in-law? Flora had told Jocelyn that she didn't have any kids.

"I thought the tea and then the little mishap at the well would convince you to leave. But, of course, you wouldn't dare leave. You're the village's savior." She then looked at Nandi's body, and lip curled up in disgust. "Her medicines caused people to believe that the land here was cursed. She'd sicken people and animals. We felt we had almost back my stubborn husband in a corner, but then your government had to stick its nose in our business, causing to delay our push to overtake the land. But then Nandi decided she had waited long enough and decided to take matters into her own hands. She was going to double-cross all of us, including Will Corsica."

Was Flora working with Corsica?

Suddenly, another car pulled up, and Moussa exited the driver's seat.

"Mom!" he called out and rushed to Flora's side.

Mom?

Flora hugged the man and assured him that she was okay. Then she turned back to Jocelyn, and she sighed.

"I guess you can see that Moussa is my son."

Jocelyn just lay there. What else was she supposed to do?

"Mom. We have to go," Moussa told her.

"What about her?" Flora asked, pointing to Jocelyn.

"We don't need her. Plus, she knows too much."

Even though she couldn't move, her heart rate increased as Flora raised the gun in her hand and aimed at Jocelyn.

Out of nowhere, a familiar voice spoke.

"I wouldn't do that if I were you."

Will Corsica stepped into Jocelyn's view. He looked down at her and gave her a sympathetic look.

"Will!" Flora exclaimed. "Nandi was here to hurt Jocelyn. Plus, we discovered she was trying to double-cross all of us."

Will sneered at the older woman.

"So you killed Nandi because she hurt Jocelyn, but just now, you were going to kill Jocelyn."

The woman faltered. "Well, she knows too much."

"And whose fault is that?"

"If she and her friends would've just kept noses where they belonged. And—"

Will cut her off. "Don't lie to me, Flora."

Her mouth gaped open. "B-but. I'm not lying."

"Really? So, you didn't just stand her and confess everything to Jocelyn."

"I...I..." she stuttered, and Will raised his eyebrow as if taunting her.

"I heard everything you said."

"Will, maybe we should just all take a breath and talk this through," Moussa interjected. Jocelyn could tell he was nervous.

"I think we've all done enough talking."

"What does that mean?" Moussa asked, taking a step toward Flora.

Will shrugged his shoulders. "It means I'm done talking."

Before Moussa or Flora could move an inch, Will pulled a gun from his waistband and fired a shot, hitting Flora in the forehead.

"What the fuck!" Moussa shouted and lunged at Will. However, Will had been anticipating Moussa's move and lowered his shoulder into Moussa's moving body and flipped him onto the ground. Before Moussa could recover, Will fired two shots into Moussa's chest.

Jocelyn watched in shock as Will walked out of view and returned, carrying a large duffle bag he threw on the ground next to Nandi. Unzipping the bag, he pulled a few items out and placed them strategically around the three dead bodies. Once he was finished, he walked over to Jocelyn.

"Just for the record, I never intended you to get mixed up in this. But since you know the truth, I can't let you go. But I also don't want to kill you. So, it's time for us to head out," he told her, lifting her body off the ground and flinging her over his shoulder like a sack of potatoes. A car was sitting on the other side of Nandi's, and he tossed her into the trunk, slamming the lid down and plunging her into darkness.

She heard him open the back door and throw something into the back seat before slamming the door.

She couldn't feel the tears leaking from her eyes, but she knew she was crying because her eyes had become blurry.

As the car started to move, all she could think about was what was next for her. And the kids! Oh, God. *I'm so sorry, Maxime and Amira.*

CHAPTER TWENTY-FOUR

Bear was in the middle of the best fucking dream involving him and Jocelyn when Duke woke him up.

"What?" He grumbled. He wanted to see the end of the dream that involved Jocelyn giving him his welcome home present.

"One of the pilots wanted to talk to you," Duke gestured toward the cockpit.

Bear saw the guy and got up, trying not to be noticeable when he had to rearrange himself *down there*.

"Lt. Commander," the pilot said.

"First Lt.," Bear greeted the Air Force pilot.

"We just received word from our command that we are diverting to Johannesburg, South Africa. This order came up through your command."

Bear furrowed his eyebrows. "Did they say anything else?"

"All that was relayed was that a situation requires you and your teams' presence. We should touch down in approximately three hours."

"Okay. Thank you."

Bear returned to tell the team they wouldn't be heading home just yet. But the longer he sat there, the more uneasy he felt.

ॐ

Three agonizing hours later, Bear and the team touched down at Johannesburg International Airport. They gathered their gear and exited the plane when Aussie spotted someone.

"Is that the Commander?" Aussie asked as the team gathered on the tarmac.

Turning in the direction of where Aussie was looking, Bear was shocked to see Derek walking toward them.

"Commander," Bear greeted, not saluting since they weren't in uniform.

"Lt. Commander," Derek replied before glancing at the rest of the team. "Welcome back, team."

"Not that we don't appreciate the warm welcome, though it's a little unexpected, but what are you doing here? Or I should ask, why are we here?"

Derek took a deep breath, and for some reason, Bear braced himself.

"We've got ourselves a situation."

"Situation, Sir?"

"It's Jocelyn, Bear. She's missing."

"What? What do you mean by she's missing?"

"When Ralph showed up to take her to the airport, she wasn't there. But, three dead bodies were."

Bear took a step back as he felt his head spin. Thankfully Joker was there to support him. Jocelyn was missing?

He looked at Derek. "I don't understand. Do they have anything?"

"We believe she was lured out of her room and abducted. All her bags were packed and still in her room. Clover spoke with her that morning. So we can at least narrow down a time frame of when she was taken."

"Who is we? Who is involved? Are there any leads?" His voice started rising, and he didn't mean any disrespect by it. *But...fuck!*

Derek held his hand up. "I know this is not what you expected, and I know how you're feeling. But you need to calm down."

"Calm down? How the fuck do you expect me to keep calm when you're telling me that my wife is missing?"

"I get it, Bear. I really do. But getting worked up isn't going to help bring Jocelyn home. You need to have a clear head. The South African government is assisting us. We've been given a few conference rooms in the airport that our agencies and the South African agencies are operating from. So, let's go inside, and we can update you on everything we know."

They started to walk, but then Derek stopped him. He looked torn on what he wanted to say. But when he bit his lip, Bear knew there was something else. Like another bomb about ready to be dropped.

"There is one more thing you need to be aware of before you go in there."

"What's that?"

"Maxime and Amira. The two kids that I hear have become your shadows."

No, no, no! Not the kids! "What about them?" Bear choked out, fearing Derek was going to tell him the worst. He did say there were three bodies found.

Even the team was on alert.

"They're missing as well. We don't know, but we hope they are with Jocelyn."

Bear closed his eyes. This wasn't fair. What the fuck did he do to deserve this? And the kids! What evil bastard would take those kids? Once he found out who was behind all of this, he would show them that they had messed with the wrong family.

❧

When Bear walked into the conference room, the Feds were using; he was shocked when his mom and dad pulled him into a hug. They were both visibly upset with the situation. His dad told him that when Derek called him, he and his mom said they wanted to be there. Even Clover was there, as well as the President and First Lady. They pulled in every Federal agency that could provide information about her disappearance.

Derek sat in the seat next to Bear.

"How are you holding up?"

Bear shook his head. "Confused. Sad. Pissed off."

Bear couldn't believe she had been missing for three days. With Corsica's money and connections, Bear feared they could be anywhere in the world.

Derek nodded as if understanding. "They're doing everything they can to locate her. The FBI has Corsica's attorney in custody. From what I hear, he is talking."

That was something Bear supposed.

"There are a few other things I want to let you in on." Derek shook his head like he was in disbelief. "This shit is so fucked up. Since Jocelyn is a U.S. Citizen, the FBI was called in to investigate. When they were at the crime scene, they were able to obtain a blood sample from each victim."

"Have they gotten any of the results?"

"They have. And this is the fucked up part. Nandi isn't who she claimed to be."

Bear squinted his eyes. "Who is she then?"

"Her real name is Zuri. Nandi, was her identical twin sister."

Bear was confused at first. But then the words became clearer.

"You mean that Zuri took her sister Nandi's identity?"

Derek nodded. "Exactly."

"How?"

"The real Nandi was killed in a car accident about seven years ago. They believe that Zuri was behind it. Once Zuri got Nandi out of the way she was in control of her family's inheritance."

"So, Zuri killed Nandi, then switched their identities to make it look like Zuri was the one killed?"

"Yes. And it worked. I saw pictures of them, and they are identical. And being they had no family, and Nandi wasn't very social, nobody realized what was happening under their noses."

Bear then looked at Derek. "What about Amira and Maxime? We know that Moussa isn't their father. But if Zuri killed the real Nandi, then that means—"

Derek took a deep breath. "It means that Amira and Nandi are legally orphans. Zuri only kept them because of the money. Nandi had arranged it that if anything happened to her, he inheritance would go to Amira and Maxime."

Bear understood. Zuri would have complete control of the money. He closed his eyes and pinched the bridge of his nose. Those poor kids. They already thought their lives were fucked up. Now when they hear about this, it'll be ten times worse.

"I still can't believe that Flora was a part of the plan. Kosso has to be devastated."

"One of the agents on the scene said he was beside himself. He was having a hard time believing it."

"Once we get a lead on their location. Who are you sending in?" Bear asked Derek. He already knew Derek wouldn't Bravo team. They were too close to the situation.

"I've got Ace and his team on standby."

Bear felt good knowing Alpha team would be taking the lead. It actually made him laugh.

Derek cocked his side to the side. "What's so funny?"

"I just find it ironic that Bravo team technically were the ones who went in for Alex. And now Alpha team is going in for Jocelyn."

Derek grinned. "I never thought about that." He slapped Bear on the back. "We're gonna find her, Bear."

God, he hoped so.

☙

Bear was talking with his mom and dad when a call came in on the main line the agents were using. Everyone in the room quieted down as the Agent In Charge answered.

Whoever the agent was talking to was doing most of the talking, so Bear couldn't really make out what the conversation held. But the tension in the room started thickening again. The agent was jotting something down on the pad of paper in front of him. After about five or six minutes, the agent hung up the phone, and everyone waited on pins and needles for him to speak.

"The attorney finally broke. We've got a location. And it was confirmed that the two missing children are with them."

"Where?"

"Maseru, Lesotho. About a four to five-hour drive from here."

Derek picked up a headset, and Bear knew he was contacting Ace.

The entire room erupted in cheers. People were giving high fives and slapping each other on the back. It was great news, but Bear wasn't going to celebrate. Not yet. He wouldn't celebrate until Jocelyn and the kids were back and safe in his arms.

CHAPTER TWENTY-FIVE

Jocelyn shivered as she sat on the dirty floor of an old abandoned block house. She wasn't a hundred percent sure where they were, but she thought she overheard Will on the phone with someone telling them they were in Maseru, Lesotho. All she knew was that she was tired, cold, and hungry. Her hands and feet were tied.

They'd been there for three days after two days of traveling all over South Africa trying to cover their tracks. They only traveled at night, making it easier for them to move under the cover of darkness and harder for her to escape.

The only thing keeping her grounded was knowing that Bear would tear the world apart until he found her. For now, she just needed to keep herself and the kids alive until he came to rescue them.

She looked over at the sofa where Maxime and Amira were sleeping. She had been shocked to see them when Will carried them into the house. She had asked him why he took them instead of leaving them, but he never answered. The only thing she hated more was that he was drugging them to keep them asleep. She had begged him to stop, but he wouldn't listen. But maybe it was best for them. At least they were out of his crosshairs.

Will had admitted everything to her, how he used Flora, Moussa, and Nandi to try and force the land deal in Massendai. All that evilness for nothing. None of them got anything. Well, Will ended up with her. That was scary because she had no idea what he had planned.

She couldn't believe how twisted people were. It was the type of situation that would show up on the news, and they'd think, "Oh, that's terrible, but it will never happen to me." Except it was happening, and she was living in the nightmare of it and had no idea how to get out of it.

She curled into a ball as a few tears slipped down her cheeks. She tried not to cry because crying wasn't going to solve her problem. But she was human and had emotions. She's not even sad anymore. She was angry and felt hatred and rage bubbling up inside her.

The front door flew open, allowing a few rays of sunlight to enter before he slammed it shut. At least she knew it was daytime.

He set a brown grocery bag down on the counter with too much force, making the loose countertop rattle.

Slinking back, she didn't want to be in his wrath.

She watched him closely. He pulled a phone from his pocket, dialed, and put it to his ear. He looked paranoid. She assumed he was to call his attorney, Tau. Tau had been in contact with him as they traveled, but he had yet to check-in, and it had been over twenty-four hours since he was scheduled.

She heard him curse before slamming the phone down on the countertop. He stood in the kitchen that was just big enough for a mini stove and a mid-size refrigerator. He started making a lot of racket, banging pots around, and slamming drawers. She wondered what he was doing.

Several minutes later, he appeared in front of her with a bowl.

"Drink," he commanded as he lifted a spoon to her mouth, but she turned her nose up at it. The aroma of the liquid in the bowl was pungent. Plus, she'd rather starve than consume something he made, knowing he could've put something in it to harm her.

The backhand came fast and hard, nearly knocking her over, causing her head to snap to the side. Before she could recover from the blow, he grabbed the back of her neck and yanked her upright so she had to look at him. He no longer looked like the calm, arrogant businessman she was introduced to last week. The guy standing before her looked deranged and volatile. His jaw was clenched, and his nostrils flared in anger.

"Disobeying me isn't going to work in your favor. You should know that by now." He growled, his face right up against hers. "I said to drink it."

She stared into his cold eyes because there was nowhere else to look with his large hand holding her in place. She shook from the fear running rampant through her. However, she refused to cower to this lunatic.

She didn't know what came over her, but she was determined she wouldn't let him control her. If he didn't like it, he could kill right now. Squaring her shoulders as best she could with his bruising grip on her neck, she looked him right in the eyes.

"Fuck you!" She spat at him and threw her body into him, causing the bowl to spill all over him.

Will squealed like a little girl as the hot soup was dumped on his hands. He released her, and she fell back to the floor. While he was still hopping around like hot grease in a skillet and with limited mobility, Jocelyn made her move.

She got to her feet and rammed her shoulder into Will's stomach, causing him to fall backward. But as he was falling, he grabbed onto her shirt and pulled her down with him. With her on top of him, she started swinging her hands. Since they were tied together was using them like a hammer, hitting his face, his chest, and any part of his body that she could.

Suddenly, he let out this roar and threw her off of him. She landed on the awkward on her arm and swore she had broken it.

When she looked up, she saw his bloody face contorted with undeniable rage as he slowly stalked toward her. She couldn't help the slightly giddy feeling deep inside her, knowing she had done that to him.

With her back up against the wall, she had no way out. She was trapped, and the death daggers Will was sending her way told her that there was no chance in hell he was going to let her walk out of the house alive.

She knew that her future and the future of the kids rested squarely on her shoulders. If they were going to make it out of this alive, she was going to have to go down fighting.

Will lunged at her. She dodged him, but before she could get her feet set, he jumped on her back and started beating any part of her that he could reach. She screamed out in agony as he continued to strike her.

"I can kill you right now. Is that what you want?"

"What are you waiting for? I rather die than spend another minute with your sorry ass," she screamed back at him.

He was cursing up a storm as he scrambled to his feet and pulled her up by her hair. He pulled a pistol from the back of his waistband and pressed it against her head. She slammed her eyes shut, waiting for the death shot, when suddenly, the tiny home was plunged into darkness.

"What the fuck?" Will mumbled and stilled his movements, giving Jocelyn a reprieve.

Nobody uttered a word as they sat in the dark, a heavy silence filling the room as if waiting for something to happen. Jocelyn could only hope it was a sign that her nightmare was coming to an end. As the seconds passed, she could tell Will was getting more anxious. But Jocelyn knew it was a sign. She knew that she and the kids' freedom were just on the other side of that door.

"What's the matter, Will? Are you afraid?"

"Shut up!" He spat, squeezing her tighter. She whimpered. Christ, it felt like he was going to break her ribs.

He pulled the gun away from her head and aimed it toward the front door.

Suddenly, the door exploded, sending splinters of wood flying everywhere. Then before she could see what caused it, a blinding flash of light appeared, followed by a thunderous bang that left her ears ringing.

The next thing she knew, she was being shoved to the ground. Will was on top of her, striking her repeatedly in the back of her head.

Two gunshots rang out, and Will's body fell off of hers. She heard several men shouting, "All clear."

She lay there on her belly, crying and in extreme pain. Someone knelt beside her and pushed her hair from her face. She turned her head and found a few men dressed all in black, wearing skull masks that looked like Halloween costumes. Or maybe it was just one person, and she was seeing double or triple.

"Who are you?" she slurred, feeling as if all the energy inside her was being sucked out. She was crashing hard, and seconds before she succumbed to the darkness that was reaching for her, the men lifted their masks, revealing a few familiar faces. *Alpha Team.* Knowing she and her kids were in safe hands and would be reunited with her friends and family, she allowed her body to go into sleep mode.

꙳

The video cut out, and the lights in the room were turned on. Bear was holding his head in his hands. He felt like he was going to be sick. Because of the snake camera used to see into the house, he and everyone else had seen Jocelyn fighting for her life prior to Alpha team breaching the home. Never in his career had he felt so helpless as he watched that scene play out. But the important part was that Jocelyn and the kids were safe. The next stage would be all of their healing. Both mentally and physically.

"You okay?" Derek asked, clasping his shoulder.

All Bear could do was nod. He looked around the room. Everyone important to him was there. His team, his mom and dad, and even Clover. They, too, had witnessed Jocelyn fighting for her life.

"Be thankful you have a strong woman. She fought to survive. Just like a few others I know," Derek said, looking across the room at Clover, and Bear knew he was also referring to the woman from Alpha team.

So many things were running through his mind that he knew he would have to deal with. But two stood out on top and would be his priority. He wanted Maxime and Amira. Jocelyn took on that mama bear role as if her cubs were in danger, telling Bear all he needed to know. Those kids were going to be his and Jocelyn's. He knew there was something special about them when he first met them, and now he knew why. They were meant to be a family. Unfortunately, some bad shit had to happen for that to occur, but in the end, the kids were safe, and they had two adults who would love and care for them.

Now, he just needed to figure out how to make that happen. Glancing across the room toward a group of people, the person he was looking for met his gaze.

As if knowing he was seeking him out, Rick stood up and walked over.

"You okay, man?"

"Yes, sir."

"Cut the formality shit, Bear. I'm not asking as your commander-in-chief. I'm asking as your friend. That was tough for me to watch. So, I can only imagine how you felt."

"I know. I'll be better once I can see her in person. But, there is something else I need—maybe guidance, or you could maybe call it a favor.

"I'll assist you with whatever I can."

"It pertains to my family."

Evans appeared confused. "Has something happened with one of your brothers?"

"No. I'm talking about Maxime and Amira. I want them. Jocelyn and I want them. We want them to come live with us. We want to adopt them."

Rick's expression softened, and a look of understanding crossed his face.

Let me make a few calls and see what I can do.

CHAPTER TWENTY-SIX

Jocelyn watched through the private plane's window as the city of Johannesburg grew larger and more visible as they descended.

After the team had rescued her in the middle of the night, they whisked her and the kids away to an airstrip, where a private jet was ready and waiting for them.

Once they were all on board and the plane was in the air, Stitch, Alpha team's designated corpsman, cleaned up her cuts and mobilized her arm in a split. He told her what she already knew, that her arm was indeed broken. She didn't even need X-rays to make that assumption.

One of the other team members, Skittles, had offered her a clean t-shirt and a pair of shorts, while others offered some hygiene supplies so she could clean up in the plane's bathroom.

A few of the other guys were sitting with Amira and Maxime. Amira was sound asleep on Frost's lap, and Maxime was talking to Dino and Diego.

It was interesting to see how alike Alpha team operated compared to Bravo team. They worked as a team under the direction of their team leader, Ace, whom she found out held the same rank of Lt. Commander as Bear. She could see so many similarities between the two leaders in how they watched over their team and those they were assisting.

Stitch gave her some strong over-the-counter pain medication to help alleviate some of her discomforts. They offered her the soft leather couch near the back of the plane and even found a pillow and a blanket in a storage cabinet to make her as comfortable as possible.

She appreciated everything they had done for her and promised that when all the dust settled and everyone's schedules permitted, she wanted to have them and their families over at her and Bear's home for dinner. Of course, they jumped on that idea.

Once she was settled in and closed her eyes. It wasn't long before one of the guys told her they would be landing soon.

Knowing that Bear would be waiting for her had her stomach in knots. He was the only person she wanted right now. She yearned to feel his muscles fold around her, making her feel protected. However, on the flip side, she knew he would ream her a new ass for risking her life with what she did. But in the end, there would be a lot of loving and forgiving.

She was worried about Maxime and Amira. Having them safe made her happy, but her heart hurt, thinking they could've been left behind with nobody to care for them. It made her think of the story Bear had told her about Potter and Tenley and the little girl they adopted from Ecuador. Maybe there was a chance she and Bear could find a way to free Max and Amira from a life alone. She planned to discuss it with Bear as soon as they were alone.

When the tires hit the runway, and the pilot applied the brakes, Jocelyn wiped the lone tear from her eye. She was very emotional. When she lifted her head, she was surprised to see Potter standing there.

"You okay?" He asked.

She could only nod because she was afraid that if she told him what was going through her head that she would lose it. And that the effect of the painkillers that Stitch gave her was starting to wear off, and her arm and head were throbbing terribly.

A small grin appeared on the big guy's face, which shocked her because it was the first time, she'd seen him show any emotion. He squatted in front of her, putting them more at the same eye level.

"I understand what you're going through. But I know you'll overcome this situation and become an even stronger person."

She managed a teary-eyed smile. "Thank you," she whispered and gave his extra large hand a gentle squeeze with her good hand.

He winked before reaching for her and lifting her into his arms.

Shocked by his action, she looked at him. "What do you think you're doing?"

"Carrying you."

"Uh, not you're not. It's my arm that's broken, not my feet or legs. I can walk perfectly fine."

Irish, the team's sniper, appeared next to them. He was grinning like a fool and gave Potter an amused look.

"Jesus. She's just like the rest of them. Isn't she?"

"Rest of who?" She asked, looking between Potter and Irish.

Irish shook his head and grinned. "You'll see soon enough."

Potter thankfully took her words seriously and gently set her down on her feet. As she went to take the first step, she bit her lip, feeling the aches and pains all over her body. But she was determined not to say a word.

Slowly, she made her way to the cabin door, and Ace was there to help her down the stairs.

"You've got quite the homecoming," he said to her with a smile.

She didn't understand at first, but then she looked up and saw the group of people walking toward the plane. Bear was right up front with President Evans and Lana. She could see Bear's teammates, Clover and even Ray and Jenelle. Everyone who meant the world to her was there.

Bear's eyes locked onto her as if she were his target. He started towards her at a quickened pace, his long legs eating up the space between them until he reached her.

Before she even reached the bottom step, Bear was there, pulling her into his arms. She let her body lean into his. She ignored all the pain and let the comfort and protection of his embrace sweep over her.

She had no idea how long they stood there holding each other. She didn't want to let go of him—not ever.

"I've never been so scared in my life," Bear told her, his voice filled with so much emotion and his eyes filling with unshed tears.

"I know how you feel."

"You and I will have a discussion when we get home."

"We are? About what?"

"A little thing called obeying orders."

Jocelyn felt her cheeks warm.

She gave him a pain-filled smile. Bear took her hand and linked their fingers.

"Come on, sweetheart. Let's go home."

They had only taken two steps when Jocelyn remembered the kids.

"Wait!"

"What's wrong?"

"The kids!"

"What about them?"

"I can't just leave them here. They have no one."

Grinning, he cupped her face. "That's not true."

Rick stepped up with Lana.

"I've already called the Immigration department regarding Maxime and Amira. They'll be permitted into the United States under your and Bear's care. Once we get some paperwork ironed out, you can start the adoption process."

"Adoption process?" Jocelyn asked, looking between Rick and Bear.

Bear took her hand into his. "I know how much these kids mean to you. Over the last two weeks, I saw how you bonded with them, and I watched that connection grow stronger as the days went on. They are wonderful kids who were put into a shitty situation they had no control over." His sexy grin appeared. "I've come to adore them, and I don't want them to be placed with anyone other than us. They belong with us in a loving home, surrounded by people who will also love and provide for them. They have us. Maxime and Amira are coming home with us."

"Seriously?"

"Yeah, babe. They're coming with us. And my parents said they would come and stay for a bit if you don't mind and help with their transition and us. They've just met them and already have fallen in love with the kids."

She looked over where Ray and Jenelle stood, with Maxime and Amira between them. Amira held Ray's hand, and Maxime held Jenelle's hand.

"Did you hear that, kids? You're coming home with us!"

The kids ran toward her, happy with the news they just heard. Both Bear and her squatted down, inviting the kids into their open arms—arms that would provide love and protection.

As they hugged, everyone surrounded them.

Jocelyn wrapped her arm around Bear.

"I love you."

"I love you, too. What do you say we get these kiddos home and start our future together as a family?"

They all walked hand-in-hand toward what promised an exciting and bright future for everyone.

CHAPTER TWENTY-SEVEN

Jocelyn slowly awakened by her phone vibrating on the nightstand beside her. Blindly reaching over, she felt the phone and grabbed it. She looked at the screen, and a smile began to spread across her face. Her crazy sister-in-law, Clover, seemed just as excited about today as she was.

Clover: Rise and shine my dearest sister-in-law.

Clover: Today is your special day!

Clover: I can't wait! Neither can Mom!

Clover: Jocelyn?

Clover: Jocelynnnnnn?

Clover: Jocelyn, are you there? Ugh! Bear told me I had to wait until ten to call or text you. I waited until five after ten. Where are you?

Clover: Did my brother leave you in a sex-induced coma last night? WAIT! DO NOT ANSWER THAT! On second thought, I don't want to know about your bedroom details.

Jocelyn was trying to contain her laughter. Clover was too funny.

Yes, she and Bear were technically married, but today was extra special since they'd be renewing their vows with their family and friends being their witnesses. They had rented the private party room at Bayside to hold their event, though they would be holding the ceremony on the beach.

She typed a quick response back to Clover, telling her that yes, she was up, and she was excited about today, and that she'd see her in a few hours when they met up to get ready for the ceremony.

She looked around the room that was bathed in a warm glow from the side lamp seated on Bear's nightstand. Normally the room sat in almost complete darkness thanks to the blackout curtains hanging over the windows. Bear bought and installed them when they returned home to help keep the sunlight out because of her migraines. The last few days, the pain hadn't been so bad, mainly just a dull headache that some over-the-counter pain relievers helped.

She pushed back the covers, threw her legs over the side of the bed, and gave them a good stretch before standing up and walking to the bathroom.

After taking care of her full bladder, she brushed her teeth and threw her chocolate locks into a messy bun. Seeing her and Bear's toiletries intermingled on the vanity made her smile. There were still some days that she had to pinch herself to ensure she wasn't dreaming and the joy and happiness she had been basking in wouldn't be ripped from her.

As she made her way down the curved staircase, she could hear the murmured voices coming from the kitchen. When her feet hit the bottom step, she paused to take in the sight before her. Her heart felt full as she watched Bear standing at the stove cooking breakfast while Amria and Maxime sat at the island. All three were engaged in a conversation.

"What's going on here?" She said, walking over to them

Both kids spun around on the stool. Their faces lit up with excitement.

"We're making you breakfast," Amira told her, sporting her infectious grin that Jocelyn just ate up.

"You are?"

"Yep. Bear is making your favorite—French toast and sausage.

"How do you know that is my favorite?"

"He told us."

"He did, did he?" She smiled, giving Bear a side glance and wink. Apparently, he was not surprised by her presence. But that wasn't anything new. After living together for the past month, she had concluded that nothing got passed the man.

Amira nodded her head. "Yep!"

"Well, he is right. That is my favorite."

As if sensing the intensity of her stare, his grey eyes peered over his shoulder, and he flashed her that sexy grin, making her insides melt. She kissed Max and Amira on the side of their head before going over to the stove.

She wrapped her arms around Bear's and kissed his cheek.

"I love you."

"I love you, too." He kissed her temple.

"Are you guys ready for today?" Jocelyn asked, turning back to the kids.

Both of them nodded. "Yes! I can't wait to wear my new pretty yellow dress that you got me."

Jocelyn glanced at Max. "How about you, buddy?"

"I've very excited. Not only for you and Bear, but Bear also told me about some of the other kids Amira and I will get to meet today."

Jocelyn beamed. Right after the ceremony, she and Bear had a special announcement that would affect the kids.

Walking back to the island, she slid on the stool between the kids while Bear plated the food.

Shortly after they had gotten home, Bear had gotten called up and was gone for a short time. Well, he considered two weeks short. But she thought two weeks was horrible.

Before he left, they sat the kids down and explained the specifics of Bear's job. Maxime understood it more than Amira did.

Jocelyn couldn't wait to tell the kids they were now officially part of their family, especially after hearing Max and Amira talking the other night. She and Bear had been heading to their room when they heard Amira ask Max if Jocelyn and Bear would ever consider adopting them. Of course, Jocelyn wanted to barge in the room and shout yes. But Bear's firm grip around her waist prevented her from doing so. With that sexy smile, he just reminded her how much more special it would be for them to share their good news on their special day. It would be a special day for all of them. Not just because of their anniversary, it would also represent the day the four of them became a family.

CHAPTER TWENTY-EIGHT

Jocelyn stood at the railing overlooking the beach where everyone had gathered for the bonfire. She smiled, watching all the kids preparing their sticks to make smores. What warmed her heart the most was seeing her two brave, bright, and beautiful children right smack dab in the middle of the action, laughing and just being kids.

She was in her happy place, and nobody could take that from her. She was surrounded by family and friends who watched out for one another. As she eyed everyone, a tiny part of her was hurt that her parents chose not to be involved in their lives. It was their choice, though, and she could do nothing about it. She was disappointed, but she didn't hate them. After all, they gave her life. And what she has gained in life was enough to make her happy for the rest of her life.

She felt Bear's hand on her shoulders as he stood behind her, silently watching everyone.

"Are you happy?" He asked, moving his arms so they were tight around her waist. His warmth enveloped her like a blanket.

"Of course I am. How could I not be?" She asked him, looking over her shoulder and meeting his stormy eyes.

He turned her around, keeping her secured in his hold.

"Good, because I want you always to be happy." He was silent momentarily as he looked past her, staring out toward the calm ocean illuminated by the bright light of the half-moon overhead. When his eyes moved back to her, she was shocked to see his eyes were glistening with tears. "Thank you, Joce," he said, his voice cracking.

"What are you thanking me for?" She whispered.

"For giving me—for giving us a second chance. For believing we're right for each other. For loving me for who I am, faults and all."

A tear leaked from his eye, and she brushed it away with her thumb.

"I love you, Bear. I always have. We were always meant to be together. Life happens for a reason." She pointed toward Max and Amira, who were surrounded by their new extended family. "If things hadn't happened like they had, we wouldn't have them. The heavens work in strange ways. But who are we to question their actions? Let's just cherish what we have now and not look back."

"I love you, too, Joce. I always will."

Duke and Hannah's story coming this summer!

BOOK LIST

The Trident Series
ACE
POTTER
FROST
IRISH
STITCH
DINO
SKITTLES
DIEGO
A Trident Wedding

The Trident Series II - BRAVO Team
JOKER
BEAR
DUKE *(2023)*
PLAYBOY *(2023)*
AUSSIE *(2023)*
SNOW *(TBD)*
NAILS *(TBD)*
JAY BIRD *(TBD)*

ABOUT THE AUTHOR

Jaime Lewis entered the indie author world in June 2020, with ACE, the first book in the Trident Series.

Coming from a military family she describes as very patriotic, it's no surprise that her books are known for their accurate portrayal of life in the service.

Passionate in her support of the military, veterans and first responders, Jaime volunteers with the Daytona Division of the US Naval Sea Cadet Corps, a non-profit youth leadership development program sponsored by the U.S. Navy. Together with her son, she also manages a charity organization that supports military personnel and their families, along with veterans and first responders.

Born and raised in Edgewater, Maryland, Jaime now resides in Ormond Beach, Florida with her husband and two very active boys.

Between her writing, and her two boys, she doesn't have a heap of spare time, but if she does, you'll find her somewhere in the outdoors. Jaime is also an avid sports fan.

Follow Jaime:

Facebook Author Page:https://www.facebook.com/jaime.lewis.58152
Jaime's Convoy: https://www.facebook.com/groups/349178512953776
Bookbub: https://www.bookbub.com/profile/jaime-lewis
Goodreads: https://www.goodreads.com/author/show/17048191.Jaime_Lewis

Made in the USA
Monee, IL
21 June 2023